When a cloud falls to earth, Calla sets out to find what lies beyond the sky. Father says there's nothing, but Calla knows better. Something killed that cloud; someone brought it down.

Raised on legends of fabled skymen, Calla never expected them to be real, much less save one from drowning—and lose her heart to him. Who are the men who walk on water? And how can such strange creatures be so beautiful?

Infatuated and intrigued, Calla rises out of her world in pursuit of a skyman who doesn't even speak her language. Above the waves lies more than princes and politics. Above the sky awaits the discovery of who Calla was always meant to be. But what if it also means never going home again?

A NineStar Press Publication

Published by NineStar Press
P.O. Box 91792,
Albuquerque, New Mexico, 871099 USA.
www.ninestarpress.com

Walking on Water

ISBN: 978-1-947904-25-5

Printed in the USA
First Edition
November, 2017

Also available in eBook: ISBN 978-1-947904-24-8

Warning: This book contains sexually explicit content, which may only be suitable for mature readers.

Glossary of German Words at the end

Walking on Water

Matthew J. Metzger

Für Maria, weil ich dich liebe.

And for my readers, whose response to my asking for a transgender Little Mermaid was to tell me to write it myself. Thanks...I think.

Chapter One

WHEN THE SAND settled, only silence remained.

The explosion had gone on for what felt like forever—a great boom that shuddered through the water, a shadow that had borne down on the nest like the end of the world had come, and then nothing but panicked escape from the crushing water, the darkness, and the suffocating whirlwind of sand and stones. In the terror, it had seemed like it would never end.

But it did end, eventually. When it did, Calla lay hidden in the gardens, deafened and dazed. She was shivering, though it wasn't cold. An attack. They had been attacked. By what? Orcas and rival clans could hardly end the world. And what would wish to attack them so?

She took a breath. And another. Her attempts to calm herself felt pathetic and weak, like the desperate attempts of a mewling child. Where was Father? Her sisters? Where even the crabs that chattered and scuttled amongst the bushes? She was alone in the silent gardens, and Calla had never been alone before.

Slowly, she reached out. Slipped through the towering trunks, to the very edge of the gardens, to where the noise had come from. Drew aside a fern and—

Ducked down, clapping a hand over her mouth to prevent the gasp.

A giant beast lay in the courtyard.

Still. Oh, great seas, be still. She held her breath and closed her eyes. It had to be an orca, a beast so huge, and it would see her if she moved.

Yet even in her fear, Calla knew that wasn't quite right.

Orcas didn't come this far south—did they? Father had said they would be undisturbed here. Father had *said*.

She peeked again. Daring. The beast didn't move.

Nor was it an orca. It was impossible, too huge even for that. Oh, she'd not seen an orca since she'd been a merling, but they'd never been *that* big. It had squashed the courtyard flat under its great belly, its tail and head—though she couldn't tell one from the other—spilling out over the rocks and nests that had been homes, once. It would have crushed their occupants, surely. What beast killed by crushing?

Hesitantly, she drifted out of the garden. Her tail brushed the ferns, and she wrapped her fins around them, childishly seeking comfort.

The beast didn't move.

In fact, it didn't breathe. Its enormous ribcage, dark and broken, was punctured by a great hole, a huge gaping blackness longer than Calla's entire body, and wider by far.

It had been slain.

Bloodless. It was quite dead. How could it be dead, how could its heart have been torn out so, without spilling blood into the water? Where was the column of red that marked its descent? Where was—

Oh.

"A *cloud!*"

It was no beast.

Calla fled the safety of the gardens in a flurry of excitement. No, that great oval shape was familiar. How many had scudded gently across the sky in her lifetime? How many times had she watched their passage from her window? Beautiful, dark, silent wonders. Oh, a cloud!

She rushed closer to look. How could a cloud have fallen to earth? Father had said they were simply things that happened in the sky, and no concern of theirs. But this one had fallen, lay here and near and so very touchable—and now Calla wanted to touch the sky.

It was—

She held her breath—and touched it.

Oh.

Rough. Sharp. Its body was dark against her pale hand. And hard, so very hard. She had imagined clouds to be soft and fluid, to walk on water as they did, but it wasn't. Huge and heavy, it was a miracle that it walked at all.

And a home: tiny molluscs clung to it. As she walked her webbed fingers up the roughness and came over the crest of its enormous belly, she mourned its death. This must have killed it. Such a deep, round belly—clouds were obviously like rocks and stone, but this one had been cut in half. Exposed to the sea was a sheer, flat expanse of paleness, with great cracks in the surface. A column stuck out from the middle, and two smaller ones at head and tail. It had been impaled by something, the poor thing.

"Calla!"

The hiss reached her from far away, but Calla ignored it. The poor cloud was dead. It had been slain, and whatever had dragged it from the sky must have been immense, to wield spears like those jutting from its body. And it wasn't here.

Clouds were harmless. Dead clouds, even more so.

"Calla, what are you doing?"

"Meri, come and see!" she called back to her sister and ducked to swim along its flattened insides. Great ropes of seaweed, twisted into impossible coils, trailed from its bones. Vast stains, dark and pink, smeared its ragged edges. When Calla peered up into the sky, at the stream of bubbles still softly rising from its innards, she could see the gentle descent of debris. It had been torn apart.

Orcas? But an orca pack would have followed it down. Sharks? Calla had never seen a shark, but Father had, long ago when he was a merling, and he'd said they were great and terrible hunters. Were sharks big enough to do it?

"Calla!"

That was not Meri's voice. Deep and commanding, it vibrated through the water like a blow. Calla found herself swimming up the side to answer automatically, and came clear of the cloud's gut barely in time to prevent the second shout.

Father did not like to call a second time.

"Here. Now."

She went. At once. The immense joy at her discovery was diminished in a moment by his stern face and sterner voice, and Calla loathed it. She felt like a merling under Father's frown and struggled to keep her face blank instead of echoing his displeased expression.

"You should stay away from such things. The guards will deal with it."

"But Father—"

He gave her a look. She ducked her chin and drifted across to join her sisters at the window. The window. Pah. What good was the window, was seeing, when she had *touched* it?

"What is it?" Balta whispered, twirling her hair around her fingers.

"A *cloud*," Calla said in her most impressive voice and then pushed between Meri and Balta to peer out. The guard were swarming over the cloud's belly, poking more holes in the poor thing's body. "Something killed it."

Meri snorted. "Talk sense, Calla."

"Something did!"

"You sound like a seal, grunting nonsense."

"I do *not*!"

"Girls!"

They subsided under Father's booming reprimand—although Calla snuck in a quick pinch before stopping—and returned to watching.

"Clouds don't fall out of the sky," Meri whispered. "It must be a shark. There's nothing so big as a shark. Father said so."

"Father also said sharks don't come this far north," Balta chirped uncertainly, still twirling her hair.

"That's a cloud," Calla said and peered upwards to the sky, her eyes following the great trail of bubbles, "and I bet something even bigger killed it."

Chapter Two

ALARIK'S FIST HIT the table with a meaty thud. A plate jumped from the wood, landed a little too far over, teetered, and fell.

The shattering of ceramic on the stone floor was met with uneasy silence.

"Leave us."

Nothing.

"Leave us!"

The advisors jumped, before scrambling to gather their reports. The king was not unlike his late father—amiable when in the mood but quick to turn. And judging by the clenched, shaking fist on the table, the king had indeed turned. Janez, more than used to such moods, simply waited.

Only when the door closed behind the last stuttered, "Your Majesty," did Alarik unclench his fist.

"This," he said gravely, "is what happens when interest and bootlicking is permitted over merit. What business did Reiswitz have commanding a ship in the first place? The man was incapable of finding his backside with both hands if given instructions!"

Prince Janez shrugged. He was one of perhaps four people in the kingdom utterly unshaken by the king's temper.

"A ship sunk, another captured, three hundred men lost to me. The guns won't be replaced quickly or easily, and the men even less so. We're pressing them as it is!"

Still, Janez said nothing.

"We're running out of money, out of food, and out of men. There are rumours of mutiny as it is. I can only thank God that—so far—we're evenly matched. But one alliance, Janez, *one* alliance—!"

Silence fell. The king breathed heavily, his palm flat on the wood.

The prince, very slowly, lifted his boots to rest on the seat of another chair and sat back.

The king's eyes flicked up.

For a split second, rage thundered in that icy blue gaze—and then it died. It drifted away like a storm before a warm southerly breeze. Brushed away, and dissipated. Janez watched it fade as plain as any real storm out over the waves.

"Father would have known what to do," Alarik said quietly and sank into his chair.

"Father isn't here."

Janez's low assertion seemed to echo in the room, and both king and prince fell silent. Years had passed, and the wound still bled.

"Mother sends her love," Janez continued. "She begs us both to be safe and sends music for Ingrid's lessons. I gave her letters to Sofia on my arrival. They'll be waiting for you when you retire."

"I cannot. I have to—"

"The admiral will be dealing with the loss of the *Held*. The enemy were badly grazed, as well, and winter is coming. Likely this was the last action before the ice sets in. If it's a savage one, they'll be blocked in—and even if it isn't, they'll concentrate on feeding their own and not freezing to death in stranded ships on the sea. They always have. This is a demoralising blow. An action to startle, not to truly wound. A show of force."

"A show that worked!"

"For now. They suffer winter worse than we do. While they shiver, we can strategise In the meantime, focus on rebuilding—both ships and safe harbours. Our answer lies in alliances—and you cannot forge an alliance tonight."

"I can—"

"Tonight, you can do nothing. Rest. Kiss your children goodnight, and go to your wife. Make more children."

A faint smile flickered on the king's face.

"Tomorrow, wage war again. But a war cannot be won by a shattered king."

Alarik finally leaned back from the great maps on the table, a dark mark in fresh ink picking out the spot where the *Held* had gone down. She'd been no great ship, little more than a sloop, and built in foreign harbours some forty years ago, but she'd been a stout sloop, a great weatherer of ice and enemy action. Janez had sailed in her, once or twice. He remembered her faults and fancies well.

Until Captain Reiswitz had set his incompetent boots on her boards, and she'd been set alight and sunk, with all hands aboard.

"I only thank God you were not with them," Alarik said.

Janez said nothing.

Alarik fell quiet for a long moment, staring almost blindly at that inky stain—and then started as if woken from a dream.

"This is maudlin. And useless. A drink, brother?"

"Too kind."

"Cut the formalities, Janez. We're alone."

"So I am speaking to my brother and not my king?" Janez asked, voice full of amusement as Alarik filled two cups with dark, sweet wine.

"Always, when we're amongst none but family."

"Then go to your family."

"After a drink with one of them."

Quite suddenly, Janez pulled a face, and then both men were laughing. The weight of a kingdom lay at the harbour below. The weight of a war snuffled at the closed door. But for a brief time, in the sputtering candlelight, they were merely brothers, children again, with little more worries than a common distaste for their music tutor.

"I've missed you," Alarik said with undisguised fondness and slid a brimming cup across the table as he sank back into his chair.

"And I you," Janez said, raising the cup. "To family."

"To family," Alarik said and lifted his own a little higher. "To brothers."

"You are maudlin."

"And you could have been on that ship—you were supposed to be."

"I was?"

"Yes. When you returned from the Winter Palace, I had instructed the admiral to have you posted as first lieutenant, to attempt to curtail some of Reiswitz's stupidity."

"Well, then we ought to be grateful that Reiswitz's stupidity is faster than two hundred miles by horse."

"You rode?"

"Of course."

"Alone?"

"I'm going to say no," Janez said, "as I'm enjoying a drink with my brother and don't wish my king to make one of his enraged appearances."

Alarik shot him a foul look but subsided with a grumble, making his feelings well known on the matter.

"You're a fool, Janez."

"But a living one, and fully intending to eke out a few more years. In any case, it would have been a poor choice on your part."

"Why?"

"You don't remember the last time Captain Reiswitz and I were in the same room?"

Alarik's face eased from its scowling countenance, and he laughed. "He thought you had propositioned his sister, and challenged you to a duel—"

"—so his sister dutifully took my pistol and shot him in the arm," Janez finished with a crowing laugh, and rank and privilege were both forgotten as the men hooted like sailors in a tavern at the memory.

"And the look of horror on your face!"

"Any man who propositioned her most likely wound up dead— I wanted to ask if he thought me suicidal!"

"I've quite forgotten her name."

"Catherine," Janez supplied. "I saw her at the Winter Palace. Still as formidable as ever—and as forthright. Damned be the uniform and my standing, she hit me and then hugged me."

"What did you do to deserve that?"

"Oh, breathed, I imagine. She did insist on drinking to the health of every man, woman, and child in the kingdom—and individually, too. After such a greeting, I couldn't begrudge her a moment of it."

"I do sympathise," Alarik said, reaching over to top up Janez's cup. "I find the urge to hit you quite strong, sometimes. Perhaps I ought to change the laws and have the lady knighted."

"You never hug me."

"Would you let me?"

Janez laughed. "That would depend, dear brother. Often, if you're kind to me, you have some plan in mind."

"Now, you know that isn't true..."

"No, of course not—which reminds me, what price the wine?"

Alarik chuckled, called his younger brother suspicious, and sat back. His shoulders were easing, Janez noted with a smile. The king had slipped away, and the exasperated brother, so easy to aggravate, had returned full-force.

"Your silence?"

"I think not," Janez said, raising his cup with a smirk.

"I take it that now you are back, I won't be able to keep you from the ships any longer?"

Ah. Perhaps the king was indeed still in the room.

"People will talk if you try."

"People will talk regardless."

"I should go. You need a presence on those ships. The men can't fight your war for you, without—"

"Without the knowledge that I, too, may lose something."

"Yes."

Alarik pursed his lips but didn't argue the point.

"Fine," he said eventually, "but no damned heroics, Janez. You're right—an alliance is our best hope for a swift resolution. They would not wage war with a united coast."

"You'll never get—"

"Let me worry about who I can and cannot sway to our side. You forget," Alarik said, levelling a look much like Father's stern eye at Janez, "that you are still considered something of an eligible—"

Janez hesitated, biting back the curse. Alarik knew very well the reasons why Janez was considered an eligible bachelor. And he ought to know better than to wield them.

But he wished to speak with his brother, and not with maudlin kings, so Janez wrenched a smile into place and crudely said,

"One bastard child, and the world suddenly thinks you have the dimensions of a dockyard donkey."

Alarik laughed.

"The truth need not be known until *after* such an alliance."

"Very cruel. The poor lady, to be saddled with me."

"The poor *kingdom*, to have you for a potential ruler."

Janez objected, and Alarik insisted, and they cackled together like children a little longer, before Janez broke off to yawn heavily. Too heavily. He eyed the cup suspiciously, and set it down.

"Alarik."

"You looked tired. I'm surprised Sofia didn't try the same."

"If I could damn you both without being taken for a traitor—"

"Please," Alarik said evenly, leaning back with a fond smile. "You damn us both half a dozen times a day, and nobody's thrown you in the dungeons yet."

"There's still time," Janez grumbled, yawning widely again. "Last time I drink alone with you, *brother*."

"You're a wicked liar," Alarik said, "and none too good at threats. Come. You'll sleep in the royal chambers tonight."

Janez staggered when he rose, and the slide of the king's arm under his felt oddly reminiscent of their younger days when Father had permitted them to discover wine and women. Janez had never been much for the women, not since Greta, but the wine—ah, the *wine...*

"The next toast I shall utter—" he said determinedly as they passed from the room. A sentry caught at his other arm to lift him. By the man's unperturbed amusement, he was plainly sly to the king's plot.

"The next toast, Janez, can be whatever you wish," Alarik said in that maddening, benevolent tone. "But for once, you can do as you're told."

"By whom?"

"Well, if you must know, it was Sofia's idea."

"Ah, well, for *Sofia—*"

"I wouldn't finish that sentence if I were you."

The royal chambers were not far, but Janez was a heavy man, a veritable pile of muscle and bone. They struggled with him to the cushioned seats under the great window of the sitting room. The sentry was dismissed, and Janez heard the familiar sounds of a father—albeit one with a crown about his temples—checking on his children.

Then a blanket settled over Janez's exhausted form, and the low light of the candles was snuffed out.

Janez sighed and took his own advice, sagging into the dark, warm hold of sleep.

The ships, the sea, the war and world, would wait a while longer.

Chapter Three

ONCE THE PALACE had settled, and the only sounds were snoring and the gentle scuttle of the night-crabs on the sea floor, Calla fell straight out of the window and swam clear across the open courtyard to the corpse of the cloud.

Father's guards had explored every inch of it and declared it to be nothing more than a rock. Calla knew them to be wrong. Rocks didn't feel like the cloud did. Rocks weren't shaped like the cloud was. It was a cloud. And it had been slain. Under her palms, it felt so utterly beautiful.

There was something ethereal about its surface. Something otherworldly. That was fitting, wasn't it? Because it *was* from another world. It had fallen from the sky, and it could walk on water. It was obviously magical. Calla was touching *magic*.

Father hated magic. Calla ought to—the only magical thing in the sea was the Witch of the Whalelands, who had driven them out of their previous nest. But there was something alluring, exciting, about magic. As if it could make anything possible.

And now it was *here*.

Calla pressed her body to the magic and sighed.

Meri would be disgusted by it. Balta would lose interest in moments. All they cared for were singing, shells, and staring after witless mermen. Calla had never felt so distanced from her sisters since they'd outgrown their first set of scales and become mermaids rather than little merlings. She'd never felt quite right since, as though somewhere between her youth and her beauty she'd lost some of herself.

But with her palms against the cloud and nothing but silence surrounding her, Calla could simply *be*.

She'd always wanted to touch a cloud. It was impossible, of course, as the water was too hot and thin so high, and merfolk would never be able to breathe so close to the sky. It had always been an impossible little dream of hers, like running away or becoming a dolphin. Just silly, childish fantasy. She'd never once imagined that clouds could *sink*.

It was like a cave inside—perhaps when Meri finally spoke to that insufferable bore she liked, they could nest in here and give Calla an excuse to visit her little nieces and nephews in the cloud. Calla flitted in and out of jagged holes, touching their edges and wondering what teeth had ripped them there. She found strange contraptions made of some thick seaweed or skin and took them to wear like smocks. She tugged a little rope free to tie in her hair. It was rough, unlike any weed she'd felt before, and although it floated amongst her hair, it was heavy and alien.

There was a spear, thick and grey with a strange point, caught in the weeds by one of the holes, and Calla worked it free before wielding it like a guard in Father's command. She laughingly challenged a wandering cod to a duel. It eyed her with dumb distaste and swam away.

"Fine," she said. "Be like Meri."

She would only have tonight. By morning, the nest's sons would crowd their new plaything, and the king's daughters would not be allowed. This great slaughtered beauty was not for shells and singing. It was for spears and shields. The guards would likely make a training arena of it until the sea claimed it and it rotted away to a mere hulk.

Calla pressed her webs and fingers against the dark surface until they turned grey, and—for a split second—hated being herself. If she were a merman, even a royal one, she could have played here. Could wear clothes like commoners and explore this grand new thing. Not have to swim bare all the time, and practise nothing but singing and combing seashells into her hair.

"You're lucky," she told the cloud. "You can walk on water, and do whatever you please. I imagine clouds can be anything."

The cloud didn't answer.

Her bright mood diminished, Calla shed the makeshift shirt and ripped the rope from her hair. She swam high above the cloud to stare at its crippled body from above, and then dropped in a slow, drifting spiral to its head, running her hand over the huge, jutting beak.

And—stopped.

Below the broken beak was rock. A great grey stone, protruding from the dark, alien surface like a giant barnacle. Only, rather than a smooth cloud-shape, or a rough bubbled bottom of a barnacle, Calla found herself staring at a mermaid.

A *mermaid*.

It was like a stone reflection. A slim figurine, rising out of the cloud like a prophecy. The telltale lip around the top of her tail was buried and hidden within the beast. She had the flat belly and bare breasts of a princess, with her arms streaming out behind her as though she was about to burst free from a great current.

And her face. A blank, beautiful face, crowned by shell-adorned hair. Calla touched her fingers to the cold face, and a shiver ran up her arm.

A sign.

Oh, it was a sign.

MERI WAS NOT convinced.

"Clouds," she said over breakfast, breaking off from combing her coral-bright hair only long enough to throw Calla a contemptuous look, "are like rocks. They have different shapes all the time. It's just happenstance."

"It's not. It's a mermaid. I'll show you!"

"You won't," Meri said. "We have singing lessons. And—"

Calla pulled a face that made Balta giggle.

"I don't want to have singing lessons. There's a *cloud* in the courtyard, Meri! A cloud with a mermaid on it!"

"A cloud with a chance shape on it. The belly looks like a whale, that doesn't mean the whales are anything to do with clouds."

"They look a bit like clouds," Balta said, "when they swim over us."

Meri threw her a withering glance. "Balta, eat your breakfast and don't encourage her."

Calla opened her mouth, insulted, but Meri shot her a sharp look.

"Just don't, Calla. It's a cloud. Nothing more. Father's guards will break it up and remove it, and—"

"And it's a cloud that fell to earth with a mermaid on it! These things don't just *happen*, Meri! They don't—"

"Father!"

Meri's raised voice coincided with the opening of the dining hall door, and Calla subsided as her father's imposing form shadowed the entrance before gliding serenely to the table. He was long and sleek; his deep green tail faded into pale green fins and patterning on his back, where scales and skin mingled in an intricate tattoo and ended in green hair so fair it was nearly white. That hair was long but, in the male tradition, coiled up onto his head in an intricate weave. Calla had always thought mermen wore their hair better than the loose flow of the mermaids, but that was yet another thing Meri would say 'just don't' to.

"Father, do clouds fall from the sky often?" Meri asked loudly, and Calla frowned at her.

"Not often, but it is known. Calla, don't scowl at your sister."

His voice was a rattle in the water. Calla smoothed out her expression automatically.

"There's a mermaid on it!" Balta said, and Father eyed her.

"And how do you know that?"

"Calla said so."

"And how do *you* know that?" he asked, his great stern face turning towards her.

"I saw."

"You went, you mean."

"I—well—"

"A king's daughter should not be playing in clouds."

Something inside flinched at such a remark. "Nobody saw me. And I didn't mean a live mermaid, I mean—"

"Someone has died there? You should have informed the—"

"No! A stone one!"

Father paused.

"Oh, Calla, *stop it*," Meri whined, but Calla ploughed on.

"Under its beak, there's a stone mermaid."

"Whatever do you mean?"

"There's a stone that looks just like a mermaid. A carving!" She seized on the idea hungrily and stared up at the great columns around them. The palace had been carved into the greatest rock on the seabed, and suddenly it was obvious. Meri was right: a stone mermaid wasn't by *chance*. "Someone carved a mermaid onto that cloud!"

"Oh, now you're being ridiculous," Meri said.

"Calla," Father said. "You're not a merling anymore. Silly stories of stone carvings on clouds are—"

"It's not a silly story!"

Father thumped the table abruptly. "Don't answer back to me!"

Calla fell mutinously silent.

"Clouds are natural things that walk on water," Father said sternly.

"There is nothing that could have carved anything onto it, because nothing exists above the sky. It is chance. Nothing more."

"Skymen could."

There was a sharp pause.

Then Balta started giggling. *"Skymen?"* she trilled and clapped. "Skymen made the clouds! I like that!"

"Oh, *Calla*."

Father's face was dark. "Ridiculous," he said flatly.

"It's possible! Mother used to say—"

"Your mother used to tell you eel-stories to make you sleep," Father boomed. "They were make-believe. There is no such thing as skymen."

"Then who carved that mermaid?"

The next fist thump made the plates jump. All three sisters cringed back from the table. Father's knuckles were grey.

"Nobody," he grated, "carved anything."

Calla opened her mouth.

"Not a word! You are no merling, Calla! You must stop with these silly stories and start applying yourself. You haven't sung a note in months, and now these silly fantasies of skymen and carvings in clouds—it is an embarrassment!"

A lump swelled in Calla's throat and cut off her voice. An—an embarrassment?

"You will not go to that cloud again," Father said. "And I will check that you have been to your singing lessons this evening. It is time—beyond time—to start acting like the mermaid that you are."

Like the mermaid she was? Like Meri and Balta? To sit around playing the pipe and singing until some boring clot of a merman from a neighbouring nest was picked for her? So she could—what? Go and swim naked in some other waters and bear a shoal of merlings and do nothing else?

Like Meri and Balta.

Only she wasn't like them. She didn't know how, but she *wasn't*.

There was a mermaid on the face of that cloud. Someone had put it there. And stories—stories came from somewhere, didn't they? How could Mother have invented skymen? Mermen with *legs*, who could walk on water but couldn't breathe under it like everything else—that sort of thing was so strange that it couldn't be made up!

There had to be a grain of truth in it, and that grain wore a mermaid's face and was jutting from the beak of a fallen cloud.

Calla curled her fingers into fists on the table and lowered her face.

"Yes, Father," she said.

She lied.

Father had also once said that nobody could touch the clouds. That the merfolk couldn't breathe all the way up there.

But Calla had touched a cloud last night.

So tonight, she was going to try to touch the sky.

Chapter Four

THERE WAS SOMETHING about the sea.

The smell, the sound, the sway of a ship under one's shoes—it was a maddening and addictive drug, and until he stood on the deck of the *Vogel*, Janez didn't realise just how much he had missed it. Mountains were all fine and good. The Winter Palace and Mother's time were wonderful things...but God, how he'd missed the sea!

She was rough this morning. A fog had risen off her in the night, and the watchmen had seen the flash of guns and shadow of a foreign sail. And to hell with Alarik's orders to the sentries—Janez was a commissioned officer. He would answer those horns even if he had to—as he indeed had—leap from a window to do so. The *Vogel* and the *Ente* had launched, and now sulked in the open water, watching and waiting for their phantom enemies.

Privately, Janez rather thought a ship called Duck was appropriate in such conditions.

"See anything, Lieutenant?"

He lowered his eyeglass and shook his head at the captain's question. The fog was lifting—foam-tipped waves licked their sides and crashed back into the water, visible now to fifty feet—but there was a sense, perhaps. Some intuition.

"Something's out here," he murmured, "but I cannot say where."

The captain hummed. He was a great fat man, gnarled and weather-beaten into some grotesque figure, but he was a good one. A true seaman. He knew as well as Janez that something lurked beyond the rising mists.

"Keep looking, Lieutenant. We must see her before she sees us."

Janez nodded and lifted the glass again.

This world was simple. He was no more a prince here than the ship's cat. He was an officer, on watch, and his duty was simple. No politics. No pretences. No gauging what he was, or whom he was speaking to, before answering as demanded.

He had to spy a sail. Nothing—
There.
"Captain."
He came at once. They were close. Whisper.
"There."
The glass passed between them. A nod. And Janez slipped away to give the order. Quietly now, quietly. Bring her about. Men to the guns—quickly, quickly!

The men were a hardened crew, used to doing such manoeuvres in far stranger conditions than quiet. As the sun began to poke through the mists at last, and their time ran low, Janez raised his sword, the glimmer bright in the early morning.

A horn rang out over the water.

They were seen.

"Fire!"

The guns roared. Smoke rose in thick, dark clouds as they jumped and bellowed. The roll of them being drawn back to reload was like a thousand-chambered heart, pounding on the boards. Janez squinted against the sun, and it burst through the last entrails of fog to reveal a frigate, turning in a slow arc to show her broadside.

Alone, and this close to shore?

Oh, yes. They had been emboldened by the *Held* all right.

In fact—Janez raked her with his eyes—this monstrous whale had likely brought her down. Her sails had been double-patched and were unnaturally tight. Her railings were a rainbow of different woods. Two of the gun ports had no hatch.

No hatch.

"She's taking water!" he bellowed. "Sink her! *Sink her!*"

The captain took up the roar, ordering the soldiers into the netting and up the masts. They swarmed like brightly coloured bees, and musket fire began to pepper the enemy deck. And their own. A shot whipped past Janez's ear, taking a lock of hair with it. He ignored it. Stood firm and fast at the railing. The men would not see their officers yield.

"Blast her at the waterline! She's lame, and means to sink us like the *Held*!"

The name spurred them. Several hundred hands lost, many that these men would have sailed with, fought with—and would have, *would* have, died with.

"For the *Held*!" the captain roared, and the cry went up even as the guns roared again, and splinters flew from her hull as the great broadside drew up, and the hatches—those that remained—flew up in a wave.

The boom was deafening. A railing was torn away. Smoke belched over the deck. The mast shuddered under the impact of two eighteen-pounders, but held. The sails shivered, and then filled gluttonously with the breeze. They raked her stern and came about, tighter than their larger prey, and the men flocked to the starboard side to load the guns again.

They circled for perhaps an hour. The frigate was better armed and better manned, but the *Vogel's* size allowed them to weave around her and tire her men, and her battered hull worked to their advantage. She began to visibly tilt when they brought her rudder clean away, yet she would not hoist her colours. She would not yield.

"This is a suicide," Janez breathed, and the midshipman at his side nodded, eyes wide and streaming against the smoke. "They mean to sink us, or be sunk."

Why so determined? What ship would risk all hands for an insignificant prize like theirs? They were a sloop, not a merchant ship. An enemy, certainly, but were they no longer in the practice of taking prisoners?

"Sink her, or she sinks us!" the captain roared as he gestured wildly at the soldiers clinging to the netting and firing blindly into the darkness. "Her gunners! Remove her gunners!"

Janez shook his head, staring. They had to make contact. They had to board her. The *Ente* had joined them, but her crew was a boarding crew, unskilled at gunnery and captained by a man more attuned to close warfare. They would be better boarding.

"Here." He thrust the eyeglass at a midshipman before launching from the quarterdeck. His boots slipped on the boards—blood—and he near-skidded into his captain. "Board her!"

"What?"

"Board her! Signal the *Ente* round to her port side, and we can clutch her between us!"

"Are you mad? A frigate! She's a frigate!"

"She will not yield!"

The captain stared wide-eyed at him. Shot whistled past them. A ball careened into the deck, a splinter flying up and neatly severing a man's fingers.

"Board her," Janez said. "She will sink us if we do not board her."

There was doubt there.

And then the captain seemed to shake himself. The men were watching. He squared his shoulders—and the order came.

"Hooks! Bring us alongside. Mr Dietrich, signal the *Ente* to assail her starboard, and board her if they can!"

In the smoke and sunlight, both ricocheting off each other in a blinding darkness, heaving the battered *Vogel* around the enemy's bow and up her pockmarked port side was a dangerous game. They collided once, the guns bouncing inwards. A boy fell, screaming, into the void between the two ships, and the sound cut off with a sharp crunch as the wooden hulls kissed once more. Janez slid towards the broken railings and caught at the ropes to steady himself.

And braced.

The almighty crash as they collided once more coincided with a terrible howl from the enemy guns. Two simply exploded, the gunpowder and ball caught between wood and metal, and the smell of burning flesh, the cry of death, rose over the chaos like a reminder. Janez flinched, even in his newfound deafness, like a newly launched loblolly boy without the faintest idea of sailing.

Focus!

"Now!"

His sword swept down; the hooks flung outwards and clattered into the torn deck and shattered railings, some catching and some not. The heave of ship to ship was immense—in his bones and under his feet, Janez could feel an answering pull. The *Ente* had seized her from the other side. The rush of men to cut the ropes was confused.

They had her. They could have her.

"Board!"

The soldiers swarmed. Musket fire answered, and Janez leapt the gap with a roar that came from some primal place deep inside, fuelled not by king and country, but by brotherhood. His sword crashed with that of some faceless, nameless man fuelled likely by the urge to protect his own family, yet Janez fiercely did not care. They meant to sink him. And he would not be sunk!

But even with the *Ente* and her men, this was no sure thing. The guns boomed and rocked below them, the enemy frigate determined to sink her captors while their men ravaged her decks, and Janez ploughed amongst the guns, slashing at their masters.

Something caught.

One of the *Ente's* guns roared, and a ball ploughed through the railing past him. Janez howled as a splinter—two inches thick and seven long—was driven into his thigh. He wrenched it free with a gasp, and bitterly ground down the urge to fall. That meant death. They would cut him down, and Alarik would never forgive him.

The caught thing was around his boot.

And too late, he realised.

As the great gun slipped, strangely silent, through the ragged maw gouged into the ship's side, its rope coiled around Janez's ankle and dragged him with it.

For a moment, he simply hung.

Hung in the smoke between two great walls.

He could hear—very faintly, through a distant memory, and very long ago—a woman's humming. It sounded like Mother's, yet he knew it to be Sofia. Sofia, humming to his newborn nephew.

The only heir left to Alarik's throne.

Janez sent up a brief prayer, a brief apology, some desperate hope that his childhood priests and tutors had been right, and he had some soul that could ascend and wait to meet his family again, for some reunion, for some forgiveness.

He had not even kissed little Ingrid goodbye.

Then the water clapped shut over his head, and—

Chapter Five

CALLA DID NOT mean to sleep, but she had done so, drifting off waiting for her sisters to do the same. But she woke early, while the night-crabs still explored the gardens below her window, and so without second thought, she slipped away.

Swimming alone was one of Calla's greatest pleasures. Alone, she could dispose of decorum, and wear clothes if she wished. Alone, she could control her hair and coil it up without a scolding. Alone, she could pretend she was perfect, without a single thing amiss, and that Father's frown and Meri's mutterings were nothing but a dream.

Alone, she could simply *be*.

Calla had never been like her sisters. As she'd shed her baby-blue fragments and grown her darker adult scales, and her skin had deepened to the subtle aquatic green of maturity, she'd felt more different than ever. She was exposed, not only because of her nakedness, but also her bare back. Sometimes, faintly, she wondered if the fin that rose from her father's waist to the base of his skull did not make him stronger and bolder, did not ground the mermen in a way absent from the mermaids. Why did they have it, and not she? Why could she not obtain that? Why must she swim bare breasted, and they don seaweed shirts over their spinal frills?

"You don't want one for yourself. You want your husband to have one," Meri had said, the one and only time Calla had given rise to such thoughts. But that was not quite right, either. The frill itself was ugly and rough. She liked the smooth bareness of a mermaid's back, although that, too, undoubtedly would horrify Meri. So why would she want it, and hate it, at the same time?

She'd only once said such things, but Calla knew others thought her to be an odd one. Even little Balta, only just turned green herself, had begun to treat her with suspicion. Father kept closer watch on her than the others. And the mermen that came to flirt and court and try their hand at obtaining a king's daughter, and perhaps siring the future clan leader, always avoided Calla, as though they sensed her not to be a real mermaid at all.

Somehow, she was evidently strange.

But if evidently strange could get her to the sky and touching clouds, then she would show Meri. If she could break off a piece of cloud and bring it back, then she'd have her proof. Father would apologise, and Meri would stop commenting all the time as if she knew better than Calla.

But first, she had to get there.

Straight up was the obvious choice—the shortest distance, and no chance of getting lost—but as the darkness eased to a pale grey, Calla became disoriented anyway. So high from the ground she had lost sight of her landmarks, and all around was the same uniform, uninterrupted grey. She swam until her tail ached—yet there was still no end. Perhaps the sky never came? The sea was hostile and rough so high; she could feel a push at her very being that she had never felt before, like a great hand wished to drag her—somewhere. Anywhere. Then she saw it.

A great blot on the sky, still so very far away.

It was so very much larger than she had ever seen before. A cloud. A great cloud, immense and black above the paling grey.

She could—oh, she *could, couldn't* she?

Arms outstretched, she struck out for it even though it was yet leagues away. With a new goal, a landmark at last, the weariness abated. She could breathe. She could see the cloud, and it was just like the one in the courtyard. It had a ribbed, bubbling surface. Little marks. Barnacles—again? Were barnacles magical, that they could touch clouds?

Closer, closer.

And—

Oh. Calla drew up under the cloud until it was so vast it blotted out the sky itself, and she took a great gulping breath. Her heart beat bloody music against her chest. All she had to do—was touch.

She reached.

And breathed out in ecstatic joy as her fingers brushed the rough surface of the cloud.

Oh, it was beautiful.

Rough and alien, just like the one in the courtyard. And yes, there were barnacles. It *lived*, too. She could feel it shuddering under her webs. She could hear, from very far away, the booms of its heart. They lived! It let her touch it, like a gentle great whale.

She was the only mermaid to have ever done this.

Wouldn't Meri be silenced! Wouldn't Balta be jealous! Nobody had ever done this before. Perhaps—just perhaps—Father might stop this insistence on singing lessons that she loathed, on forcing her to screech in her high, painful voice. For who cared for singing when she was the first, the *only*, to have touched the sky.

Ah, but no. She'd touched a cloud.

A wide beam of mad joy on her face, Calla pressed both hands to the cloud in a fervent kiss and ducked down to swim along its great belly. If she could touch the cloud, then she could touch the sky. She could. She *would*.

Something boomed.

In a moment, Calla froze. She tensed up small, tail to chest. Ready. To—what? Flee? She was exposed out here. No weeds, no gardens, no rocks. Nothing. The sheer stupidity of her actions came to her all at once, in a seizure of terror, and she prayed fervently to the seas that it was nothing. That clouds were simply loud.

The boom came again, and then the darkness above her swayed open, and light broke in. Not one cloud, but two. A storm? Was this what storms looked like, so far above—

The water shivered, and something fell out of the sky.

A—

Calla's eyes widened as the little creature drifted downwards. An arm was flung out, streaming a dark trail of blood. Hair, gold and gleaming, fanned out around its face. But it was no merling. It was—

She uncoiled. Followed daringly as the tiny broken creature spiralled gently down like an abandoned kelp dolly.

A skyman.

Oh, but it was!

It had the upper body—broken, so very visibly broken—of a merling, tiny and delicate, with hair as pale as sand. But there was no tail. Instead, two more strange little arms dangled loose, with club-like hands wrapped in strange fabrics. Calla reached out in morbid curiosity—and then recoiled, and the little body drifted away into the dark.

A skyman. No, a skyling. They were—they were—

"Real," she breathed, turning stunned eyes to the sky. They *were* up there. And the great boom and shudder of the clouds…were *they* what had killed the cloud? How could something so tiny kill something so—

The water broke with a terrible sound, and a great pointed rock fell from the sky, seaweed streaming from its nose.

And caught in the weeds, a skyman.

A real one, and—*alive*! It thrashed and wriggled like a fish on a spear, those four arms all writhing and—and—slowing, and—

Hadn't Mother said that skymen could walk on water, but not breathe it?

He—he was caught in the weeds. That was why he couldn't just walk up to the top again. He was going to suffocate.

Calla threw caution to the currents and shot after the rock. It was crashing down with a terrible purpose like some ugly great orca, intent on eating this strange creature; Calla was sure of it. She bashed at it with her hands, but it only kept swimming down, so she caught at the rough seaweed and tore, trying to rip it from the skyman's—limb. It wasn't an arm, this close. It was so much thicker and longer. Harder. The strange fabrics clothed no hand, as Calla could not bend the wrist to slip it free like a hand would.

But the weed was not tied, only twisted, and she wrenched it open. The rock-whale didn't notice, plunging downwards, and the skyman drifted beside her.

"Walk!" Calla urged and pushed him upwards a little, encouraging. "Go on. Walk!" How did they walk? What even *was* walking? Mother had said it was like crabs, but crabs scuttled. How could a four-armed skyman scuttle? Unless…

She eyed the strange hands and pushed them up, too. The arms bent in the middle, but the wrong way. The elbows were on wrong. Like—

Like crabs. Legs. These were his legs.

"Walk," she insisted, pushing them both. He rose a little in the water, and then she saw it. Dazed blue eyes, staring upwards. The feeble twitch of unwebbed fingers.

He couldn't breathe.

Calla looked up desperately. Perhaps—perhaps—

Oh, hadn't she been about to touch it anyway?

Decision made, she seized the creature under his arms and struggled for the surface. He was heavy and awkward, limp like dragging a seal carcass. Was he dead? He couldn't be dead. She hadn't meant to—

Bright light.

She took a deep breath, expecting impact—

And—

Cold.

The—

There was—

Calla tried to breathe, and her gills screeched and clawed for water. Terrified, she ducked under and gulped in air. The sky *ended*! It just ended!

Was *that* what skymen breathed?

Tentatively, she heaved another great gasp and then pushed through again. Water slapped at her face in waves. Something stank, sharp and awful. Her face was icy cold, and two huge, hulking clouds swarmed around them. Deafening crashes and screams echoed from them. Fire spat from their bellies, like volcanoes in the deep.

The clouds were—

Swarming. There was movement all along them, like fish on whalebones. Skymen. So many, many skymen. The clouds spat fire again, and another fell with a screech into the water.

Calla's mouth opened soundlessly.

The clouds were attacking each other. And the men—the men were—

The cloud on the courtyard was no whale. It was an *orca*. A terrible, murderous beast! And these skymen—so many tiny skymen all over the clouds' great, white faces—were trying to kill the pod.

She ducked back under for another breath, and then back up. The skyman in her arms coughed and raked in a great gasp. He could breathe here. This was *his* water.

What to do with him? She shook him, wanting him to get up and walk, but he simply drifted there with her. He was hurt. And if she gave him to the cloud, the cloud would spit fire at him and kill him.

So—what to do?

She turned this way and that in the water, looking for somewhere else, and spied a dark mass far away over the churning sky, low and long like a bank. Perhaps that was where the skymen came from? They had to have nests and homes, too, didn't they, to be so like merfolk? Perhaps if she took him there—

He stirred feebly in her arms, and Calla struggled to keep them both above the sky. She could never swim so far with him. She looked around and caught for a drifting scrap of cloud. It did not want to go beneath the sky, but she forced it, pressing it under the man until he floated on it, head and torso clear of the waves.

And there he lay, bathed in bright light, and gasped.

Calla grasped both hands about the cloud-cutting and began to swim.

It was hard work. Skymen were heavy, and she kept having to duck below the sky to breathe. His legs drifted beside her head, one bleeding sluggishly, and he nearly slid back below the sky once before she righted him.

But every time she looked up, the bank grew closer.

In time, it formed into a green and yellow cluster, like bright coral. As she drew yet nearer, she could see tiny shapes moving on the edges and great windows in pale stone. They were nests carved into the bank. They lived as merfolk did. They *lived*.

The sky punctured into their nest in a circle, and Calla dared not enter it. Instead, she pushed her charge onto a spray of dark rocks beyond the yellow stone. She could hear people shouting, though she didn't understand the words. They would come for him. They would find him here.

She turned to slip below the waves and escape the dangerous rocks— and fingers wrapped around her arm.

Warm.

Calla froze and found herself staring into blue, blue eyes. The skyman was awake. And—oh, so—so very—

"*Geh nicht,*" he said, all ajumble and alien.

"I—I don't understand," she breathed, and that beautiful face frowned.

Mother had never said they were so beautiful. So—so much like merfolk. His skin on her arm was warm, like a southerly current, but so lacking in water that it felt strange and rasping, rough yet smooth all at once. His face was pale and marked in tiny dark spots over a straight nose. Bright hair streamed from his head, heavy and hanging down. Like—like her own. It didn't float up here, above the sky, and it was a brilliant, reddish-gold she'd never seen before.

She reached and touched it. It was clumped, soft, and slipped through her fingers.

And he kissed her.

Her arm jolted as if he'd struck her instead. But his fingers touched hers. Unwebbed and waterless. So alien, so strange, yet such a gentle, tender kiss she'd never felt before. She wavered. How was she supposed to breathe below the sky, now, when she knew skymen were walking above it, looking like this? *Feeling* like this?

"Geh nicht," he breathed again, and the kiss tightened. Their fingers rubbed. *"Bitte—"*

"Hier drüben!"

Calla jerked. Skymen. Swarming over the rocks. They were coming.

"Hilfe!"

She wrenched her arm free—and it *hurt,* how it hurt, the cold water washing that wondrous kiss away as she plunged below the surface and struck out, diving blindly into the depths until there was no sound but the thunder of her heart in her chest.

Then—only then, with the sky impossibly high above her once more—did she stop.

Drifted in the deep.

And clutched the hand he'd kissed to her chest, as though she could preserve the feeling forever. He'd been so beautiful. He'd spoken to her. They were—courageous and wonderful, so very beautiful. Mother had only told the half of it.

Calla knew, with a fierce certainty, that she had to know the rest.

Chapter Six

"DRINK."

Janez accepted the steaming cup. It was filth, but it was hot. He drank it down, hacked, and coughed up another mouthful of dirty seawater.

"In the bucket, if you please. Sawdust hardly grows on trees."

"Oh, but it does, Doktor," Janez croaked and smiled benignly at the foul look cast his way.

"If you prefer the butchery of the harbour hacksaws, then by all means, seek your medicine with them," Doktor Hauser said. "Open."

Janez permitted the stick that shoved his tongue down, and the affronted hum. Sometimes, Janez suspected, Hauser was more put out by those who dared to be healthy than those who dared to be sick.

"I am quite fine, Doktor. Just cold."

"You are lucky to have survived. Your greatcoat and boots saved you."

"A sailor saved me," Janez said, and the doctor harrumphed.

"Yes, the great swimming saviour, I was told."

"I must thank him."

"If you can find him. The hands that brought you up said he swam off the moment they had you."

"To save more unfortunate souls, no doubt," Janez creaked. He hacked again, but obediently coughed the salt up into the bucket, this time. "He must have seen me go over the edge."

"If he went back for another, he'll have frozen to death by now," Hauser said and then sighed in an extremely put-upon manner when a fist hammered on the door. "Those blasted sentries! My orders mean nothing—*don't you dare!*" he added in a thunderous growl when Janez cast the coverlet back.

The door cracked open. "Doktor?"

"Away!" Hauser snarled, his rasping voice—usually so quiet and whispery, so understated and almost sulky—raised in a great cawing shout, like an affronted raven. "Away, lest I kill this maddening idiot prince for his own safety!"

Luckily for Hauser, the royal family fondly tolerated his temper. He had served them for most of his life, so the queen entered with little more than a benign smile and kind eyes for her brother-in-law.

"Dear Janez," she said. "Do let Doktor work."

"Doktor is fussing," Janez protested and yowled when a sharp prod was delivered to his bandaged thigh.

"*Doktor* can flush you with fouler tinctures than a warming brew," came the waspish warning.

Queen Sofia simply smiled, her skirts rustling as she seated herself in the chair by the bed. She was the picture of composure—the very definition of beauty. Yet under the divinity ran a streak of something a little more bloodthirsty, something that echoed from the depths of a more brutal, warlike past, of their forebears pillaging the seas, man and woman alike, and terrorising the known world.

And she showed it in her soft voice saying, "The enemy are burning."

"It was sunk? The *Vogel*? The *Ente*?"

"Both safe. They have not yet returned to shore, but they can be seen."

Janez threw back the coverlet again. "I must—"

He was felled not by Doktor Hauser, but by Sofia, who calmly plucked a pin from her perfectly coiled hair, and jammed it down onto the dressing around his thigh.

"My lady, I have rarely had the pleasure of a woman so level-headed and sensible in the art of medicine," Hauser said—and followed it up by roughly thrusting Janez back into the pillows and handing him a cup full of dark liquid that fizzed ominously. "Drink."

"What will it do to me?"

"If I had my way, kill you, and rid me of this impertinent child of a patient."

"But what will it do?" Janez persisted.

"Dull the pain."

Janez set it aside. "The pain is not so—"

"If the pain is not sufficient, I will increase it until it is," Hauser said, and Janez picked up the cup again.

"The guards said you were brought ashore by a sailor?" the queen asked as Janez drank, and when he'd drained the vessel, he nodded. "He must be thanked. What was his name?"

"I've no idea," Janez confessed. "I was half out of my mind."

Hauser's eyes narrowed. "Did you drown?"

"I don't know. One moment, I was staring at the belly of the beast—and remind me, Doktor, *Vogel* needs her bottom scraped again—"

"I cannot think of anything more urgent," came the dry reply.

"—and the next, I was on a bit of driftwood and being shoved up onto the rocks at the point."

"Well, you must have recognised him, if he was from the *Vogel*."

"He wasn't. Perhaps the *Ente*. I fell from that side, you know, from the enemy ship. We'd boarded. And the *Ente* is packed with those western hands—he was a foreigner, anyway. Didn't understand when I told him to stay, muttered some gibberish, and then he was gone."

"Could have been from the enemy frigate," Hauser said as he applied a foul-smelling paste to the savage graze above Janez's ear, where a musket ball had missed his brains by mere skin.

"No," the queen said. "They would have left him to drown. Well, I hope he is safe, whoever he is. And should you see him again, or recall his face, then we must have him to the palace to be thanked personally."

"I would rather pay for his next evening in the taverns," Janez said and managed—just—to duck the slap his sister-in-law aimed for the back of his head.

"I think I will leave you to Doktor. Perhaps he can dull your cheek before Alarik comes this evening," she scolded, and Janez grinned up at her, unrepentant.

"Come, Sophie. If I weren't abrasive, Alarik would think something deathly wrong."

"If he comes before sunset, you'll be asleep, and he can satisfy his curiosity without you attempting to undo my hard work," Hauser said, winding a bandage around Janez's hair and over the vile paste.

"Sleep?"

"Certainly. It is that peaceful thing often done at night, which you neglect so often."

"You said the potion was for pain," Janez said accusingly. Sofia laughed. Hauser grumbled, but a flicker of good humour glowed through the severe countenance.

"Sleep is an excellent remedy for pain. And I am not a fool. The windows have been locked."

Janez protested until there was only one candle left lit, and the great door to his room had been closed with finality behind the doctor. And then he was alone. In the distance—beyond the undeniably awful pounding in his head and the sharp agony in his thigh—he could hear the sounds of a busy harbour drifting up from the sea, and a brewing storm.

He dozed—though didn't truly sleep—and the drift in and out of vague consciousness was punctured by strange waking dreams and visitations. Doktor Hauser came and went, his hands and voice soft for once, and great pale eyes under sleek hair so fair it was nearly white peered at him from the end of the bed, a phantom of a memory. He only imagined the fingers to have been webbed like a duck's feet when he had clutched them. How could—no, no, a dream. He had been shot at, stabbed, and sunk. The hand had been cold and wet and that was all, that was all—

"Don't go," he murmured to the phantom, once or twice, but the hand that squeezed his arm in reply was warm, and Doktor Hauser's quiet assurance of safety and instruction to sleep so real that it had to be a memory. Such wide eyes, such very wide, wide—

Outside, the light died.

When Janez blinked, his mind cloudy with the undeniable fur of a drugged sleep, the curtains had been drawn, and the lanterns lit, their flicker soft in the quiet room. The murmur of voices nearby was low and soothing, and he turned his head towards them to find his brother seated in the chair and looking through one of the doctor's books. Hauser himself was bent low over the bandaging on Janez's thigh, and Janez frowned muzzily. Had that much time passed? Or—ah, of course. The blackness.

"Must you remove it here? The blood will stain the bed."

They both jumped at his voice, and then Alarik laughed. It was a welcome sound, and Janez closed his eyes in relaxed contentment at the hand that roughly brushed his hair back from his face and neck.

"Idiot brother," came the affectionate reply. "You've had worse scrapes falling from trees as a child. It bled. You simply need to be sewn shut."

"Oh," Janez said. He felt a dull tug on his skin and reached out a hand. "Hold it?"

"How much of the stuff did you give him, Doktor?" The complaint was sour, but the smooth grasp of the king's fingers slid into his own regardless, and Janez clutched hard.

The other hand had been—it *had been.*

"Webbed."

"What?" Alarik asked idly. "Oh, come now, Doktor, you can't expect me to believe *that* is what a man's innards look like?"

"They were webbed."

"It is a perfectly accurate diagram, Your Majesty. I can attest to that myself."

"They were *webbed*, Alarik."

"Your Majesty? I beg pardon, Doktor, if I am distracting you..."

"Who has webbed hands?"

"You are not. The constant bleating from that mindless lout, however—"

"Alarik!"

"*What*, Janez? They're only stit—"

"The sailor. The sailor had webbed hands."

Alarik rolled his eyes and shook the hand in his own. "You were semi-conscious and freezing. I'm surprised you could feel any hands at all."

"He did," Janez murmured and heard Alarik sigh. When Janez closed his eyes, the lip of a cup was pressed to his mouth. He pulled back.

"Drink it, Janez. You're exhausted. It will help."

"The ship—"

"We took the victory."

"My leg."

"Your leg will be quite fine in a day or two. It's your brains I'm a little more concerned about. *Drink*."

"Brains? What brains?"

Janez opened his mouth to protest Hauser's remark, but then gasped at the sharp tug of thread in flesh. Sweet wine filled his mouth, and he drank.

The shadows grew.

A hand—warm, familiar, and definitely not webbed—soothed the lines from his forehead.

"Don't go," Janez breathed and felt the fingers tap his scalp in reprimand.

"Not before Doktor is done. Sleep."

Janez let go.

And fell into the dark, cold water, to be caught by wide pale eyes, and webbed hands.

The last thought that spiralled away below his feet into the fathoms, following the gun that had dragged him into the depths, was so inane that Janez barely grasped it before it slid away again and dissolved into nothingness.

Who could swim without so much as a splash?

Chapter Seven

SHE LAY IN the dark for the longest time.

It seemed so cold below now that she had touched him. The soft rasp of his fingers, so alien and so alluring...

Was this what Meri spoke of when she lauded the joy of kisses? Was this what Balta wanted from her suitors? No. How could it be? Mermen did not—could not—have a touch like that.

Even when Calla stopped floating and began to dive down, away from the shimmering sky and roaring clouds, she could feel his kiss. In her skin, in her veins, in her very blood. It hummed hot and crept around her heart, tight and warm. She had an energy she'd never felt before—she wanted to dive, to twist, to burst through the sky again, but also sink to the deepest, darkest parts of the ocean to cool the heat in her head. Did he have a name? What had been that emotion in his eyes? Did skymen even feel, want, love, the way merfolk did? Oh, but she didn't even care. Just to lie in the shallows with him, to feel that warm rasp against her face, her hand, her hair...

She could hardly breathe yet was full of water. She drifted, yet was caught. And the only thing that made sense, the only thing she could think, was that she had to return.

But the clouds were dangerous, and she couldn't breathe above the sky. And he had nearly suffocated when the grey creature had dragged him down.

The knowledge was crushing, and Calla hugged herself tightly, curling up against the cold. She sank, slow and listless, as the thought chased itself around in her head. When he'd kissed her, she'd felt something that would have explained everything. All those feelings of being out of place; all those little thoughts that perhaps there was something wrong with her. When he'd kissed her, when the cold sky had touched her skin and her hair had been heavy about her head, straight like the skyman's had lain, it had all been right.

She was meant to be one of them.

It all fitted into place, tight and secure. Every moment of feeling like some strange traitor, some outsider in her own clan, had been swept away above the sky. She had saved him when she ought to have let him drown. She had kissed him when she ought to have been afraid and repulsed. And she felt *right*, like that alien touch was familiar, like those blue eyes were home.

She was meant to be up there.

With him.

A bolt of determination struck her, and she untwisted herself and dived straight down. She had proven skymen to be true. The clouds were dangerous beasts that spat fire, and the skymen were gods to bring them down. And she had kissed one. She had *kissed* one.

It did not occur to her until the dark seabed rose up, and the waving weeds of the palace gardens brushed her belly, that she would be in trouble. And by then, it was too late. The guards had spied her and called her name, and then Balta was flying out of a window to catch at her in a hard embrace.

"Where did you *go*?"

"I must see Father!" Calla insisted, trying to wriggle free of her sister's grasp.

"He's furious! Everyone's been out looking for you! You've—"

"Balta!"

Calla seized her sister's arms and shook her. Her skin felt smooth and cool, nothing like the skyman's.

"They're *real*, Balta!"

"What are?"

"Skymen!"

Balta's elegant face was wreathed in confused uncertainty, and Calla squeezed her tight before letting go, spreading her arms and whirling in pure, unadulterated delight.

"They're real!" she repeated. "And we can touch the sky. I've been there. I've seen them!"

"That's—that's *silly*, Meri says that's—"

"What does Meri know?"

"She's oldest," Balta recited, and Calla scoffed at her.

"Well, she's wrong. I saw them!" she repeated. "And Mother was right, they can walk on the water but they can't breathe here—one of them fell in—you should have *seen* him, Balta, he was so beautiful..."

The confusion turned to disgust.

"How could a creature with crab-legs be beautiful?"

"They weren't like crabs at all, they were like—like—oh, I can't describe them—like arms, but with odd little hands at the bottom, to walk on, and—"

Balta's face screwed up in distaste, and Calla abandoned the attempt.

"Come with me," she urged. "Come with me, next time."

"Next time? Wherever you went—"

"The sky."

"—Father's furious with you, Calla. There won't be a next time. And stop telling *stories*."

"It's not a story!"

"It must be. Father says it's impossible for merfolk to touch the sky."

"Well, *I* did."

Balta shook her head—and then a cry went up from the courtyard, and Meri was a blur of pale colour as she shot from column to Calla, catching her in an embrace for the first time in years.

"Where have you *been*?" she cried, and shook Calla like a naughty merling. "Father is worried sick! *I* was worried sick! It's been nearly a day! Where did you *go*—have you been with someone? You've been with someone. Who was it?"

"It was a—"

"Don't!" Balta pleaded.

"—skyman," Calla finished stubbornly, and Meri stared.

"What?"

"I touched the sky, Meri!"

"If you don't want to tell us," Meri said, "then that's your concern, Calla, but don't make up silly lies about the sky. Father will punish you if you tell such stories."

"But I can prove it! Come with me—I can show you the clouds, and the shore, and *skymen*. Meri, there was a skyman, and he was so beautiful and I saved him so he kissed me and—"

"You're mad," Meri said in horror. "You must be mad. That's—none of that's *real*. They're just bedtime stories."

"They are real. I saw them. I—"

"Calla!"

The boom was a shock, after the shrill voices of her sisters.

And it was displeased.

She turned. Father hovered at the edge of the courtyard, arms folded across his chest. Sternly scowling. Meri was the first to move, drifting back across to him and whispering, and his expression darkened further.

"Is this true?"

"I—"

"Have you been telling stories about the sky?"

"They're not stories, Father," Calla said. Her sisters could be brainless, but Father would listen, if only she could prove it. "I was curious. After the cloud that landed here. So I swam up to the surface."

"That's dangerous and foolish. A king's daughter should not be—"

The remark rankled. Calla's mind jumped to the heavy weight of her hair on her head, above the sky, and how powerful it had felt. How her neck had had to work at keeping her head up. How—masculine. Not the floating, flowing tresses of a mermaid, but the firm coils of a merman—and heavy, above the sky, like her hair had become muscle. How dare he speak to her like that? Who cared what a king's daughter might do? If she were his son, she would have been granted a complement of guards and sent to find the edge of the world.

"It doesn't matter if I *should*," she retorted. "I *did*. That's what matters. And they're there. I can show you. Come with me. I can show you, and—"

"I am disappointed," Father said with a sorrowful look. Her heart twisted in regret, even as her mind went blank before demanding to know how he could think her a liar. "If you have a suitor, then I expect to be told, Calla. Not be fed silly little lies and—"

"I'm not lying! There's no suitor!" If only because he would drown if he attempted it, but he *had* kissed her, and her skin *did* still tingle from his alien touch. "They're up there, Father. I saw—I saw clouds spitting fire, and the skymen trying to—"

Balta started to giggle, and a raw heat brewed in Calla's face.

"It's true!" she shouted, but dully, as she realised how ridiculous it all sounded. How could she possibly convince them of it—convince *any* of them of it—unless they saw it for themselves? "Come with me. I'll show you. I'll—"

"Don't be ridiculous; swimming to the surface is forbidden—*and* impossible. You'd have died," Meri said at Father's side.

"I did it, though."

"You can't have done. You're lying."

The heat was getting worse. Calla balled her hands into fists.

"I *did*. Father," she implored, turning her gaze to him. "I did. They're real. You believe me, don't you?"

He frowned. His arms remained across his chest, folded and firm.

"No, Calla, I don't. I know they're not real. Now tell the truth. Where have you been."

It wasn't a question. It was a command. And usually, the very idea of disobeying one of Father's commands was unthinkable.

But the heat in her face made something shift. Coiled up on her head, the phantom weight of her hair gave her strength. The tingle of her entire arm, numb and wounded from the skyman's touch, was a reminder. She hadn't imagined it. She hadn't made it up. It had been real, every moment of it, and she would have to prove it. Could she find the creature that had tried to eat the man? Was there someone else who—

Who knew.

Of course.

"I'll prove it," she whispered. And before Balta could grasp her arm—before Father or the guards could start forward—she turned tail and fled.

"Calla! After her! Calla!"

She swam with all her might, until her tail ached, until her hips burned, until her back cried for mercy. She swam until the seabed blurred below her, and fish darted around her with snarls and whistles of anger and aggression.

She swam until the water cooled, home fell away, and she crossed the patrolled border to the north.

Because north lay Ahtola. North lay ice and orcas, where the clan had once lived until the threat from the Witch had grown too great, and Father had moved the nest south.

Because the Witch—half truth and half legend—knew everything. She could tame orcas and talk to dolphins. She could turn fish into foam, and foam into fish, and the legends said she had once been married.

They also said that long before Calla had even been born, the Witch's husband had gone above the sky. And never returned.

So the Witch of the Whalelands would know all about skymen.

Chapter Eight

HE DREAMED OF wide eyes and webbed hands, and—even as he became aware of the warmth of the coverlet over his chest, and the soft purrs that said one of the kitchen cats had managed to sneak her way into the room without anyone's noticing—Janez fought to hold on to the dream. He fought to hold on to the feeling of soft fingers sliding away from his own, and the puzzled frown that had met his command.

"Geh nicht," he murmured again to the dream, and then the strange man was gone, and in his place came the deep, mumbled voice of a sentry outside the door.

And, above it, a shrill cry of argument.

Janez shook himself from the dream and pushed himself up on his elbows. "Let them come!" he bellowed, and the voices fell silent. A moment later, the door was cracked open, and a blur of yellow and blue flew across the carpet.

"Uncle Janez, Uncle Janez!"

He caught his little niece up in his arms, crowing a war cry in her ear to make her laugh. The cat shot off the bed, affronted, and he laughed in childish delight at the warm awakening.

"I am quite decent, my lady, you may look," he called to Ingrid's governess. A proper young woman by the name of Ekaterina, she'd come from the east a year ago to begin schooling Ingrid in the art of being a lady and in her general education. She spoke six languages, played a handful of instruments with virtuosic grace, and—although not at all beautiful—had a way of carrying herself in supreme confidence that appealed. She was the kind of woman Janez would have rather liked to catch him in a state of complete undress, but alas, Ekaterina appeared to have little interest in men. She offered a smile, and a little joke about his decency and his appearance being separate things, but seated herself in a chair by the windows, and remained at a distance.

"*Uncle!*" Ingrid cried, offended by his distraction and far too young to understand it. "Papi said you fell from the ship! Why did you do that, Uncle?"

"Why, my foot became caught in a gun rope and I was dragged. I didn't jump overboard on purpose, my little bee."

He had long called her a bee, as her first entire sentence had been nothing royal, but rather a demand for one of the servants to kill a poor and unfortunate bumblebee that had found its way into her nursery.

And as always, she turned up her nose and called him her silly uncle.

"Well, silly uncles tickle," he said and attacked her until she shrieked, kicked her way free, and jumped down from the bed to seek protection from Ekaterina.

"Silly uncle!" she shouted again from there, and Janez laughed as he turned back the coverlet and eased himself from the bed.

"Is that wise, Your Highness? Surely, the doctor would prefer you to remain in bed a while longer," Ekaterina murmured.

"Since when have I obeyed Doktor?"

"You ought. He only mixes the viler venoms for you as punishment for your disobedience, you know."

"Uncle is *never* disobedient!" Ingrid insisted with childish loyalty, and Janez laughed once more as he belted a heavy robe around himself to ward off the chill.

"Now, that is simply not true, little bee, and you know it. Come," he added, crouching and holding out his arms. "We will breakfast together, you and I, and hide in the nursery from Papi and the mean old doctor, yes?"

"Is Papi being mean?"

"Papi laughed when the doctor sewed me up, so Papi is *very* mean," Janez confirmed, and Ingrid leapt at him for the offered hug and lift with immediate faith. Ah, to be the favourite. As the baby was now the crown prince, no longer Janez, he would be sheltered from any and all undue influences that might overshadow the gravity and importance of his stature. But for Janez, now, and Ingrid always, there was a little time to be silly and accuse their king of meanness.

"How did you get out of the water, Uncle?" Ingrid asked as he carried her back to the nursery. Janez felt tired, and his legs in particular ached, but his steps were steady and his mood pleasant. He didn't even begrudge the guard that followed them, knowing he likely had orders to ensure the wayward prince didn't escape via another window.

"Somebody rescued me," he replied.

"Papi?"

"No, Papi was here at home. One of the sailors. I don't know his name. He had webbed fingers, though—do you think I ought to call him Frog?"

He was berated by a four-year-old for his stupidity and crassness, commanded to apologise to the stranger—however that was supposed to come about—and then, on entering the nursery, promptly abandoned in favour of breakfast, which was being laid out by the maids. There was no indication of either king or queen intending to join them, so Janez joked with Ekaterina as though friends, rather than royalty and servant, and encouraged Ingrid's little games.

They were not disturbed until after their meal. When Doktor Hauser arrived, seeking his escaped patient, it was to find the prince teaching a future queen—albeit of some foreign land, one day far from now—a lively jig found more commonly on privateers than in palaces.

"I take it that your leg is feeling better, Your Highness?"

Ingrid shrieked and hid behind Ekaterina's skirts, terrified of the doctor, with his cold, reptilian gaze and endless supply of leeches.

"Oh, much," Janez said, not nearly so perturbed. "It was hardly a scratch, Doktor."

"It was a scratch that required five stitches, and you to hold your brother's hand."

"You held Papi's hand?" Ingrid chirped and then shrank back again with a squeal when the doctor fixed a beady eye on her.

"I did indeed, little bee, and Papi was very mean to me about it, too," Janez said, feigning a wounded look. "Doktor, where is the king? I would have expected him to be flitting about my rooms like a worried mother."

"He has called the war council," Hauser said and took Janez's arm. "Come. I must have that dressing off and a look at the wound for pus. And bees are not well-suited to such sights."

"I *am*!" Ingrid hollered after them in indignation and then gave chase to catch at Janez's knees at the door. "Kiss!"

Janez stooped to offer a kiss on a sticky cheek and had his neck choked for his efforts. And then, to his surprise, he received his own mashed kiss in return.

"Give that to the mermaid that saved you," Ingrid ordered, before rushing back to Ekaterina.

"Mermaid?" Doktor Hauser echoed in bemusement as Janez closed the door behind them. "How fanciful of her."

Janez laughed—although a part of him, the child that had been fed the same fairy tales as Ingrid heard now, wondered if that didn't explain webbed fingers and a soundless swimmer—and then pushed the fanciful notion aside.

"The men would never sail again if they thought mermaids were in these waters."

"Superstitious nonsense."

"Sailors *are* superstitious, Doktor. It is a wonder to me that they don't still worship sea gods and make blood sacrifices to fish," Janez commented as they paced to the sickroom in easy steps. The leg twinged, and little more. It'd been damned unfortunate luck to be struck, but a lifetime of good luck that the sailor had seen him go overboard. He'd have to ask the captain if he wouldn't allow Janez sight of the *Ente's* log. He'd have remembered those great eyes from the *Vogel*. And at the very least, a foreign lad at the ropes would likely have little income or patronage. He ought to be promoted for his courage or at least given a substantial sum. He likely had a sweetheart on some foreign shore, maybe a gaggle of hungry mouths to feed.

The doctor's examination was cursory and painless. The wound was clean and crusted neatly, the torment minimal, and there was no trace of swelling or feverish heat. Although he insisted on listening to Janez's lungs with that infernal cold device, it was over shortly, and once left, Janez dressed for company. In times of war, sickness and injury within the royal family were seen as weakness. And Janez would not be—would never be—the crack in his brother's armour.

Once dressed—hair tied back, shirt sleeves shaken out, shoes buckled—he strode out powerfully, ignoring the twinge. What was a ducking in the sea, after all? Hadn't they all played in the water as boys, with Ingrid's stories of mermaids coming to drown them in the weeds? He greeted the guards warmly, and in the great hall, ran into one of the foreign ambassadors, who he hailed with a few clumsy words in the man's own tongue.

"A pleasure to see you well, Your 'Ighness," came the warm reply. And as the ships and churches alike beyond the palace walls began to chime the hour and a great rumble in the war room beyond spoke of the end of the council, Janez strode for the doors and threw them open.

"Brother," he said, leaning against the wood and beaming at Alarik's grouchy expression. "I trust you have everything well in hand?"

"As well as can be, after surprise attacks and thirty-eight dead men."

"Better than thirty-nine," Janez quipped. The admiral smirked before slipping past him and away from any potential royal wrath, and Janez stepped further into the gloomy room. "And a captured frigate is no small benefit."

Alarik looked very tired and far older than his years. He didn't rise to the optimism, instead standing from the table and stretching.

"I have to find a solution," he said, "and none offers itself. Our allies are wary of engaging an enemy on our behalf. I do not have enough to offer them."

"No trade or treaty?"

"We've exhausted our trades and treaties. King Harald will have nothing short of a union of our kingdoms—and as he has no daughters, that would mean my daughter to his son, and his line carrying supremacy."

"You have a son. He will inherit the throne, not Ingrid."

"I have an infant son and a brother in a war," Alarik said, and they knew the truth of it. Infants died often. Soldiers and sailors more often. Ingrid still had great potential to become the heir to her father's crown, and if she should, any marriage to a prince of his own kingdom would render their lineage—their people, their lands—the subordinate. And what did they fight for, if not their freedom and independence?

"What of Sigurd and Olaf? Or the Prince Regent, Magnus?"

"Magnus's father has fits of sanity. *I* will not risk an alliance there. One moment of sanity and he could undo everything. And Olaf has never been friend to us."

"So Sigurd remains," Janez said and licked his lips. Mother had spoken of it. Oh, she'd meant a southern match, to extend the kingdom south and away from the ice and cold, and the terrible sea that beat upon their shores. "He has daughters, does he not?"

It wasn't really a question. Sigurd was an old king, nearing seventy, but had married a commoner from some southern kingdom and sired three girls by her, all of them with northern temperaments and southern beauty. They were considered only half-royal, typically poor matches, but Sigurd's kingdom was also valuable.

And Janez had never been much for pedigree.

"Three. All grown. By the time the boy comes of age, they'll be beyond alliance."

"You have two children, brother, but three tools."

Janez spoke carefully. And Alarik's gaze came up, equally carefully.

"Sigurd's succession is undecided," Janez said. "If the boy were to have a male cousin as heir to Sigurd's throne, then the alliance would outlast any war."

"You mean to seal a blood alliance with Sigurd."

"It would be the wisest option."

"You've always avoided such…options."

"We've never been in such need before."

Alarik paused, thinning his lips.

"If I wed the eldest daughter, and she birthed my son, there'd be no fear of union, but a long-lasting alliance," Janez pressed.

"And if you were to do so, you'd be a powdered prince in Sigurd's kingdom, too valuable for war and too important for—" Alarik glanced at the closed door and lowered his voice "—your entertainments."

Janez frowned. "My entertainments, brother?"

"You'd be the father of a king, Janez. A certain…decorum is required. One servant girl is all it would take, especially in a foreign land."

One servant girl was all it *had* taken, Janez thought bitterly. He'd learned his place from Greta. Learned his destiny. This had always been…inevitable.

"I am perfectly capable of discretion, Alarik."

"Are you?" came the doubtful reply, and Janez cracked a thin smile, brittle as his brother's.

"Of course," he said. "Can you name the last entertainment, or when it was taken?"

Alarik waved a hand. "Some maid at the Winter Palace, no doubt."

"Doubt, dear brother," Janez said before turning for the door. "Send a messenger to Sigurd. Perhaps some meeting at the Winter Palace to welcome the snows would be fitting? I've heard his daughters are quite fond of the mountains, and I of southern roses."

Chapter Nine

NIGHT HAD FALLEN before Calla reached the Whalelands.

They were so named as though a nested territory, but no merfolk lived here. It wasn't the bitter cold that had driven them away, nor the orca packs that kept them shy. No, it was the Witch.

She was a real being, shrouded in legend. Father had said she was just a mermaid clever with trickery, and hungry for revenge after being abandoned by her husband. Mother had said she was not a mermaid, but an ancient water spirit, last of a race of powerful creatures who could manipulate their surroundings with a dark magic that had all but gone from the world.

And that, once, she'd been a wife.

And that, once, her husband had gone to walk upon the shore and never returned.

Calla didn't know whether she really believed the story, but her flesh itched with the fading memory of the skyman's touch, and she had to know. If there was even a chance the Witch could gift her with some way of touching him once more, of kissing his strange hands and wonderful skin, then Calla would take it. Even an hour in his arms would be worth it.

But when the seabed dropped and formed a deep hollow of darkness, through which white stone glowed, Calla found reason to pause.

And that reason was fear.

Had she not grown up hearing the stories of the Witch's terrible power? She could summon storms and command orcas. She'd driven the whole nest before her, when Father would wage war against any clan who dared to challenge them, and would win without fail. But he hadn't beaten back the Witch of the Whalelands from their territory.

Father had simply moved the territory itself.

So Calla hesitated at the lip of the great bowl, before slowly—oh so slowly—swimming forward. She held her breath as the vague white glow grew brighter, and as she came closer, the shadows peeled away in soft layers from the ruined palace.

And, oh, it had once been such a grand palace.

It jutted up from the floor of the bowl like a great spear, seven great columns of white in varying heights forming a circle. The tips were sharply pointed, and an old nest—walls, floor, and ceiling—occupied the space inside the circle from a third of the way up to the top of the shortest column. It was not unlike Father's palace, but for the startling colour and the lack of cell-caves lining its base. Underneath it, a white courtyard glowed through the gloom, surrounded outside the pillars by gardens.

But the gardens had consumed it.

The courtyard was barely visible and would be inaccessible to an orca. It resembled a poor nest; the gardens had eaten up the base of the columns and were growing on the outside of the nest in great slimy patches. Inside, Calla imagined, all sorts of creatures might live.

Or perhaps not.

Because this sea was abandoned. There was loneliness in the air, the sense that she was the only thing breathing for miles. The water hugged her, still and undisturbed, and rubbed through her hair as though it wished to taste her. The terrifying emptiness overwhelmed her as she pushed through the weeds into the courtyard, an elaborate mosaic barely visible through the carpet of spotty leaves.

"Hello?"

Her voice shivered around the abandoned palace and disappeared. Seaweed waved disapprovingly back. And silence rolled in like a thunderous cloud. Of course it did. Why would the Witch help her? Why would the Witch help any mermaid?

But she was here, so Calla spoke out again, her voice shaking in the dark quiet.

"I—I'm here to see—"

"I know who you are here to see."

Calla gasped. The voice whispered out of nowhere, high and dangerous. It was like a breath: delicate and soft, and so impossibly loud. And it came from everywhere, all at once, as though it were in her very *head*.

"I—I have...questions..."

"Which are?"

Unsure of where to look, Calla stared straight ahead. In the middle of the pillared courtyard was a circle of white stone from which rose a flat plinth, and she watched it without really knowing why as she asked for the voice's name.

"You know who I am."

"Then—then you can help me?"

"I could. Whether I should...that is something else."

Calla twitched nervously. Her heart was beating in her throat.

"Please come out," she whispered.

"Why?"

"You—you—"

"Do I *frighten* you?"

The word was breathed in her ear; a wash of warm water brushed her hair, and Calla spun with a shriek, lashing out at—bubbles, put there by her own frantic turn.

"You are a jumpy little thing, aren't you?"

Calla spun again—and there she was. Atop the white monument lay a mermaid, draped over it like a cloth. An immensely long mermaid, at least forty hands, and terrifyingly handsome. Her face was carved from raw beauty itself, perfect in every way, and framed by a rush of thick, dark hair that rippled and danced around her like a living shawl. She was not bare, like a royal mermaid, but wore a long dress of kelp and sea foam—however was that possible?

"You—you are the sea witch?"

The mermaid hummed. Propped her chin, atop a long neck, on her upturned hand.

"Far greater than any *witch*, my dear."

"I'm—I'm sorry—"

"You are the king's daughter."

"Yes. Calla."

"I know." The high voice was bored, and the mermaid examined her nails. "And why has the king's daughter come this far north to talk to witches? I cannot imagine her great father would look kindly on it."

Calla's mouth thinned.

"Her great father," she said, "has lied to her about skymen. They exist! I saw one. I touched one."

"Of course they exist," the Witch said, as though they were discussing dolphins or cod. "If that is all you require help with—"

"No!"

A sharp look. Calla wilted.

"I'm sorry," she said, "but no. There's—I think there's something wrong with me."

The look turned quizzical.

"I touched the *sky*," Calla whispered.

The other brow rose, and a smirk adorned the mermaid's face.

"I assure you, you did not."

"I did! I touched a cloud! And a skyman!"

"A human."

"A—what?"

"Human. They live above the sea. The sky—the true sky—is above them. And their clouds. Tell me, do the men run amok over them, and do they sport great white faces?"

"Yes," Calla breathed. "You've seen them."

"Ships. Not clouds. Ships."

"Ships?"

"The men make them, to sail across the water."

To walk on water. They walked on water with ships.

"I rescued one," Calla whispered. "He fell into the water, and I rescued him, and he—he kissed me."

The Witch eyed her but said nothing.

"It was like nothing I've ever felt before," Calla breathed, curled her fingers around each other into fists. "It felt—it felt like magic. Real magic. And Father says I must stop telling silly lies, but they're not lies. They're *real*. I know they're real. And him—he was so beautiful. So *beautiful*..."

The mermaid looked faintly disgusted at that.

"I want to see him again."

"Then drown him, and keep the corpse."

"No!"

"There are plenty of mermen in the sea. Content yourself with one of those."

"They aren't like him. He felt different. His skin, his warmth—he was entirely waterless, when he touched me, and—"

"That is their world. They cannot breathe underwater for a reason. And you cannot breathe above it for the same."

"I want to be in their world," Calla whispered.

It leaked out, like a secret she'd never known she had. But there it was. She wanted *their* world. In her own, she was out of place. She didn't fit. There was something that wouldn't let her be happy in her proper place.

And when those warm fingers had kissed her own, she'd felt it all become so—so insignificant.

"I should have been born human," she whispered.

"Really." The word was an idle roll as the mermaid twisted over her back and stretched. "A fanciful dream."

"But the story is that you can do anything!"

"Stories are stories. Not real."

"The skymen were stories, and they're real."

"If I could make you sprout legs and lungs, then I would, if only to remove this chirping from my home. Begone. I have no need for silly stories of love on the shore."

"Please," Calla begged. "The stories are that your husband used to walk above the sky. You must know how he did it. You must know some way of helping me!"

The Witch had gone very still.

Then, slowly, she rolled back onto her front.

Stared.

Then, in a swooping dive, she nearly fell from the pedestal, and towered at once over Calla, black eyes searching her face, two cold fingers pinching her jaw to examine her. The dress fell so long that her tail was entirely hidden.

And then she smiled.

Her beauty was suddenly a terrible ugliness, and something cold and terrifying hardened in Calla's stomach.

"Yes," the Witch murmured, as if to herself. "He would miss you."

"I—I'm sorry?"

The fingers let go.

"There is a price."

"For—for what?"

"I have a potion. One that my husband used. It will turn you human, and allow you to breathe in their air, but only for three days. At sunset on the third day, your body will change back, and you must return to the water."

"Three days?"

Three days above the sky? She yearned for it, yet she recoiled from it, too. Would the Witch just give it to her? What would she have to exchange for three days? And what if she wanted more?

"I fell in love," she whispered. "I want—I *want* him. What if three days isn't enough?"

"Then you will return and beg me for more time," the Witch said. "More likely, I think, you will fall very out of love with their world, and return gratefully to your own skin."

Their world, perhaps. But him? That intoxicating touch, that infecting stare? The very blue of his eyes was burned into the back of her mind, and she was shaking her head before the Witch had even finished speaking.

"I love him."

"You are infatuated with something exotic and exciting, nothing more. It will fade," the Witch said, drifting lazily back. The dress lifted a little in the water. There was no tail, and Calla caught her breath.

"What are you?"

"A water spirit. Have you heard of me?"

"Mother—Mother said the water spirits can control the world."

"Oh, no, nothing that exciting," the Witch murmured, and that terrible smile emerged again. "I have magic, but—it's been years. I haven't brewed potions since Aht was taken from me."

"Aht?"

"My husband."

"He—Father said he le—"

The gardens shivered. The water chilled, and Calla clutched her arms about herself.

"Aht was forced to leave," the Witch said. "He died alone and in agony, where it was ensured I could not follow. And now you—"

She stopped.

"Me?" Calla whispered.

"Three days," came the abrupt reply. "Take it or leave it."

She turned, and the water rushed around them as her enormous form swam back up to the plinth.

"Wait!"

She settled herself there, almost eel-like, and propped herself up on her elbows again. The smile was a smirk. The posture that of a gleeful merling.

Calla's fingers trembled as she reached up imploringly.

"Please," she said. "I need this."

"No, you don't. But you want it, very much."

"Yes."

"You will become human. The transformation will hurt a great deal, and you will be unable to breathe or swim. I suggest you get yourself to shore before you drink, unless you wish to drown. And believe me—" A hand waved as she turned over onto her back again, like a dozing seal "—it is no concern of mine if you do."

"What—what price?"

"Hmm?"

"What do I have to pay for this potion?"

The Witch turned back over. Her eyes were black hollows in her head, and nothing more. Awful, yet Calla could not look away.

"After you change back," she said, "you will come straight here. You will not go home. You will come straight to me. That is the price. If you do not—if you steal that potion from me—"

She curled her fingers into a fist. Something crackled in the water, and a great whiteness began to form over the slime and seaweed. Ice. Calla's stomach turned as the cold crept up the great pillars and froze the very gardens beyond the courtyard in their places.

"—then I will come for your entire nest and eradicate every last scaled creature there."

Calla's voice shook. "I—I won't steal it. I promise."

And then—

There it was. Just like that, the ice vanished. The gardens waved, fluid and free once more. And a gourd sank from the great white roof, purple and stoppered with sponge like any drink from home. Calla cupped it carefully in both hands and felt the gentle slosh of liquid inside.

"Drink at dawn, and see your first day. And at sunset on the third, you will be turn back." The Witch turned back over, her hair streaming down the pillar as though tied to a great weight. "I would wish you well and hope the pain does not drive you out of your mind, but—if you claim to love a man who held your hand just once, there is clearly not a mind to drive you from in the first place."

Calla frowned. Was—that an insult? She peered down at the little bottle.

"Do I drink all of it, or—"

She looked up. The plinth was empty. The Witch had gone. And the gardens were waving, just waving, in the shadows beyond the pillars.

She had to leave.

Driven out by the stony silence and still waters, Calla clutched the bottle tight to her breast long after the Whalelands had faded away behind her, and long after the light of the sky was warming her back as she swam just shy of the surface. She searched for sounds, and just as the light above was growing brighter, found the bellies of great clouds to the south. Beyond them, when she held her breath and peeked above the sky, lay those dark, sharp rocks upon which the skyman had kissed her.

Soon, she would learn his name.

But the rocks would be dangerous. She circled them, staying low in the shallows, until around the side of the steep, sheer rock that bracketed the bay, she found a little sandy bank upon which the sky breached and great foam fingers ran up the yellow surface. Sand. When she dared to reach out of the water and touch it—thick and powdery beyond the sky's reach—it clung to her skin, heavy and rough.

Land. Land-sand.

Here, in the shallow waters where she could just about breathe, but quickly drag herself to air once a skymaid, she uncorked the potion. Stared at the dark liquid, like squid-ink and poison, which lay still inside.

Her fingers tingled from the kiss of a myth.

She drank.

And it *burned*.

Chapter Ten

THAT EVENING, JANEZ dined alone.

The Winter Palace was more relaxed, with fewer guards and giving less of an impression of a fanciful gaol. Here, his every move was watched. Yet here, too, lay a little more freedom than was immediately visible to the naked eye. For the castle was old, and its history came with benefits that boys discovered one generation after the next, and forgot as age and duty slowly consumed their bodies.

But age had only just begun to dampen Janez's enthusiasm for life into a sense of duty, and duty itself had been temporarily released upon the birth of his nephew.

So he ate alone in his rooms, and when the sun sank below the lip of the horizon, calmly walked from them and down the passage to the nursery, as though to kiss little Ingrid goodnight. Instead, in the crook of the passageway where neither his own sentries nor those at the nursery door could quite see, he ducked aside, into the tiny passage concealed behind the tapestry, and down the stone steps beyond. Halfway down, he pressed against the ledge, and opened the hidden door—and was away.

The palace was a great labyrinth of such passages, and Janez held no illusions that he'd ever found them all. But he'd found enough, and enough served his purpose. He had no desire to run from his life for long, merely long enough to clear his head, exercise his body, and then return.

He'd made the offer in seriousness. With three daughters, one was bound to make a tolerable wife. Janez found it easy to get along with most people, commoner and crown alike, and surely, at least one of the eligible princesses would make a fine companion. Love need not be part of the equation.

But...

He had always hoped not to need to. He'd resigned himself to the duty as crown prince, even steeled himself to its inevitably when the much-anticipated first child had been a girl, but with the birth of his nephew, a certain hope had flowered. Despite his station, despite his duty, Janez rather wanted love. He'd loved before. He would likely do so again. And he'd hoped, when the mantle of crown prince had passed from him to his nephew, that he might be permitted to find love, and marry that, rather than marry and hope love arrived on the scene somewhere in the rest of his days and somewhat focused upon the woman on his arm.

Alarik would scoff and call him a romantic, and Doktor Hauser would likely prescribe something foul for the notion, but there it was. Janez had hoped to marry the one he loved, rather than the one with the best birthing hips and a decent claim to a foreign throne.

Still, Sigurd was hardly a viciously ugly man, and his queen was famed for beauty. His daughters would likely all be pretty, and certainly would be well educated. If she could play a little music with Janez from time to time, or liked to dance, then perhaps they could at least brew a friendship, a companionship, and be happy with one another.

But the sense of a dashed dreamed dogged him, and he drew up his cloak to cover his head as he emerged from the passage into the base of the western guard tower, and passed from the great oak door to cross the grass. There was a sharp breeze, west-north-west in origin, and the sounds of the high tide licking at the harbour walls rose gently off the bay. He marched, giving the impression of a soldier to anyone who might have seen him, and was soon swallowed by the shadows of the gatehouse. He stepped out without being challenged—but who cared who left? Only those who approached were of importance. And then he disappeared into the town.

It was quiet and late, the ships on guard out in the water. The little red door, found halfway down the tiny alley that ran two streets back and parallel to the harbour wall, was closed but yielded to his hand. It was dim inside, and he left his hood up against the idly curious looks cast his way. A pub, to the unsuspecting. Not, to those who picked it out on purpose. He didn't wait downstairs, instead paying a coin to the woman at the bar, and going straight up creaky stairs to the next floor. The second door on the left was closed. He opened it anyway, and a young lady at a dressing table jumped violently, and then beamed.

"Karl, my darling! Where you be!"

The assumed name brought a smile to his face as he locked the door and hung his cloak on the hook. In a moment, the dove was on him, plucking the ribbon from his hair and taking it for herself, before working the buttons on his shirt. She loved him—if only for his money—but she did, in her own sweet way. She would embrace him later, and croon in her own tongue, and...well, she was generous for Janez, and there had been many a free turn in this little room. He often paid her double, and had asked time and again to allow him to secure her a position in the palace, with only one customer. She had only laughed though, called it a boring time, and said if he were to provide some other job, she would simply continue in her little room for free.

"Too long," she murmured in her thick accent. "Too long, too long. Your ship, she has been away?"

"Yes," Janez said, "and I find myself in need of distraction. Distract me, dear Rosa?"

She—her warm body, her gentle laugh, the sweet sounds she made as he found those familiar places under her blouse and skirts and kissed them into life—provided plenty of distraction.

For the messenger would fly tomorrow, and then he would have but a month or two left for the Rosas of the world, for pleasure and purposelessness.

A lifetime ahead for duty.

Alarik felt uneasy.

He couldn't quite explain it. His wife slumbered in their bed, peaceful and sated. His children slept, little porcelain dolls in their cribs, in the neighbouring room. The guards were at watch, and the bay peaceful. The weather was calm.

There was nothing wrong, yet his mind wouldn't rest.

Janez's offer had taken him quite by surprise. Alarik's father—also a Janez—had been a second son himself. He'd borne a great scar all along his face for Alarik's whole life, a memory of an attempt on his life by Alarik's uncle, his father's younger brother. The third son of King Erik had coveted that throne and had attempted to slaughter both brothers that stood in his way. The eldest had succumbed to his wounds. The second had fought him off and killed him.

Alarik had been gripped by fear, even as a tiny child, upon staring at his baby brother in the crib on his naming day. The babe had survived the first year, which meant he earned a name and title, and became not a baby, but a threat. Surely, this child would come to loathe Alarik the way his uncle had loathed his father?

It had never come to pass.

Alarik had been groomed for the throne, and Janez had encouraged him. He had no interest in his duties as a prince, much less any duties whatsoever as a king. Oh, he *was* dutiful—he'd joined the navy in the royal tradition for younger sons. He'd been an image of perfection at every diplomatic function and developed an easy affinity and charm for the fairer sex that he unleashed with great success at balls. Alarik knew perfectly well his brother was a target for many kings with daughters that sought royal blood, healthy money, and trade opportunities.

But it had always been surface.

It was done from duty, not pleasure. Janez was pleasant and polite during such things, but it was not until the doors were closed and the perfumes and powders washed away that he came alive again. The man who crawled laughing upon the floor with Ingrid, or bellowed at the guns of a man-of-war, was the true face of the second son of Janez III.

To offer to be the tool, the gift, to another kingdom in order to secure an alliance...

It was duty.

Part of Alarik was proud, and determined to use the opportunity. Janez was a valuable asset, and Sigurd would certainly agree to such a match. It could end the war if Sigurd joined their effort.

And part of him—the part that was not a king, but a brother—wanted to find another way. Janez was...a spark. He was bright and effusive, but prone also to great dark swells, as if a tide had washed over him. He was the image of their grandfather in that respect: emotional under a layer of stoic cheer as thin as spring ice. If the match were not well made, if there were no love in it, then...he would be miserable. Truly miserable. There were men—and Alarik counted himself amongst them—who could be married to a pretty woman and never mind love. Alarik had been lucky enough to love a sensible match, completely and utterly.

Janez would suffer, with a merely sensible match. He needed life for life. He would need someone who could at least burn bright with him, someone to enrapture him and keep him stretched both in body and in mind. He needed some reason to dedicate himself to her, as husband and father of her sons, over and above duty.

Neither Alarik nor Janez had ever met Sigurd's daughters. They were rarely invited to functions, shunned for their low-born mother by most royal families. He knew nothing of the wisdom of seeking one of them for Janez's wife.

And Alarik did not like not knowing things.

He stared out over the dark sea, turning the matter over in his mind, knowing full well Janez would be somewhere making another bastard child in quiet attempts to be at peace with his decision. Alarik did not know where or with whom, but he knew it would be happening.

He could only hope Sigurd had at least one daughter prone to laughter, fond of dancing, and with a wit about her.

If not, he was about to make his brother quite miserable for the sake of the kingdom. While Alarik would make no other decision—could not, *would* not, sacrifice ten thousand lives and more for the sake of one man's happiness—bitter regret sat heavy in his stomach like turned milk, and he scowled at the sea.

Would that the gods of ancient times had been real, and could spit him up a storm to drown his enemies in their hammocks.

Then, perhaps, he would sleep soundly.

Chapter Eleven

THE POTION BURNED, lancing hot agony from her lips right down into her stomach. It turned; she choked and then swallowed back the vomit. Dropped to the sand, the bottle dissolved into a pool of black ink. And as the last traces of darkness disappeared into the sea, claws seized her tail, her belly, her chest and neck, and *dragged*.

It was like orca teeth, ripping off her skin. She writhed and opened her mouth to scream, but her throat was blocked. Her gills hissed and shrivelled. She scrabbled at them, trying to wedge her fingers into the slits and hold them open, only for them to close. Her ribs heaved. Water. *Water!*

And then her chest opened. Space ballooned inside, and the rush of salt water down her throat was not cool comfort, but fiery fury. She coughed. Choked. It burst out of her in a rush of sickness and scoured her nose, her eyes, her lips—

Air. *Air*, she needed air, *please*, air—

Her hands scrabbled in yellow powder, and she dragged herself from sea to shore. Her entire body screamed with the effort. A crushing pain had seized her spine, and she opened her mouth to scream again. Air rushed in. Cold, delicious air. It filled her chest, and she gulped it desperately. Heaving. She shuddered with the effort. They turned to great sobs as her scales were scoured away. The skin rolled back, and blood gleamed smoky and red in the waves that washed up under her belly and crippled chest. There was water on her face again, but from leaking eyes. Salt burned at exposed muscle. She tried to crawl, but her tail spasmed, unable to move, and then—

Oh, and then.

The split. It split in two, from fins upwards, until she thought her very hips would be torn in two. Great hands of pain forced the splits apart. Her bones broke with terrible snaps inside—the blood, the *blood*—and then the agony of a thousand spiny barbs buried themselves in her flesh and danced, danced like crabs, until she begged the Witch to kill her, until she called for death itself, until she wished the skymen had been stories and Father had beaten her for her stupidity. She would die here; she would die here.

Her fins grew thick. They prickled. The crackle of bone forming from dead scales was obscene. She sobbed brokenly as her frill was plucked loose by the sea. It washed by her arm, and she threw up a stream of thin bile as part of her body, part of *herself*, drifted away into the water without her. When she reached for it, the webbing between her fingers frayed and cracked, breaking off in brittle flakes, and when she cried and tried to stop it, it only dissolved faster.

And then a red-hot spear, like lava from a crack in the seabed itself, lanced into her hips and belly. She yowled, impaled upon it, and felt it dragging almost backwards, as though something was being torn out of her. The heat and pain balled under her body, and she curled around it almost protectively, bringing—

Bringing—

She gasped, drunk with terror and pain, and fumbled. Her hands met—skin.

Skin.

Not scales. The bend was—was no tail. She had—bone. Skin. There was—*hair*, soft and fine and fair. On her l—

The pain ebbed. Slowly. Leaking away with every wash of an uncaring tide. And she lay in the light, shaking so hard she might break. Her chest felt bruised and tight. Her throat burned. Her hips shattered. And everything below—

Everything below. Oh. A great gap between her—

A split between her—

She gulped and stared valiantly at the great expanse of blue above her. Slowly, she brought a shaking hand to her neck. Nothing. No gills. She—she had no gills. She was breathing air.

She was *cold*.

Of course. She'd been bare. Royalty did not wear clothes. And now she was cold. Shivering on the sand. With painful, stiff movements, she dared to put her broken hands to the sand and pushed herself up.

With her eyes closed.

She had been mutilated, surely. The shift of her chest was all wrong. Had the sand scoured her very breasts away? Did skymaids look nothing like mermaids? Was she terribly bloodied? Oh, perhaps that had been the Witch's plan all along. Turn her into a hideous skymaid, so the beautiful man would never kiss her, and Calla would be driven back to the sea with a broken heart and in debt to an all-powerful water spirit. How *stupid* had she been? How utterly foolish—and now she was like this, broken and horribly mutilated on the shore.

She took a breath.

Another.

And opened her eyes.

Two white limbs floated in the water in front of her. The sea was pink. And when she bent her tail—or thought she did—they rose.

Oh.

Oh.

Like—like elbows, they bent in the middle. Strange, clubbed hands below them.

Legs.

She had legs.

A delirious laugh burst from her chest, and she hugged the strange elbows to herself. Legs! She was human! She was—

Flat-chested.

And—

Endowed.

With a reeling gasp, Calla dragged herself from the water, and—although it looked quite different—knew very well what had formed beneath her now. She had seen indiscreet couples intertwined before. She knew what this was.

She was—*he.*

This was—

She clutched at her empty chest. Flat. Hard. Her shoulders were wider. Her hips had been crushed together. And this—this—

He.

Shouts rose up from somewhere far away, as Calla drew her—his—her—his?—feet in. Attempted to stand.

He would walk on water. He *would.* He w—

Was seized in iron and rough, burning hands, and dragged to stand on clumsy leg-hands. Buckled. Fell. Dragged up again, with a cry of pain, by the hair. Cried out her—his?—name, and asked for help, asked for that man s—h—she?—had saved.

And a torrent of angry sounds, jagged noise and nonsense, was returned.

And the terrible truth dawned.

The Witch had turned a mermaid into a human—but the tongue remained the same.

Chapter Twelve

"CAPTAIN KÜHE TO see you, Your Majesty."

Alarik gave the guard a sour look.

"I believe I said that I was not to be disturbed."

"I—yes, Your Majesty, but he—ah—says—"

"A captain's word is greater than a king's now, is it?"

The guard coloured. The king was in a waspish mood, and Janez, tiring of the sport, swung his booted feet to the floor and rose from his chair.

"I will speak with the captain, if it please Your Majesty?"

Alarik grunted, already consumed once more in his letters—one of which, no doubt, was bound for King Sigurd—and Janez took his leave.

Captain Kühe waited just beyond the door: a vast man, both tall and fat, and made larger by his insistence on wearing his full uniform, breastplate and all, irrespective of need. In a predominantly naval city, this army captain was obvious and unpleasantly so. Janez rather disliked him—paranoid, sycophantic, and with delusions of adequacy, never mind grandeur. But for what the captain lacked in any other arena of his existence, he made up for in perspective. If he was moved to disturb the king, then there was good reason for it.

"Your Highness," he said, clicking his heels. "A spy has been captured."

Janez raised his eyebrows. Or perhaps not. "A spy? Well then, interrogate him. You know your duties."

"That's the problem, Your Highness. The guard won't have it, Your Highness. Says he don't speak the right foreign, Your Highness."

"Then find an interpreter."

"Not the guard, Your Highness. The spy."

"The spy doesn't speak the right language?"

"No, Your Highness. The guard says he's never heard anything like it, Your Highness. And he speaks just about six foreigns, Your Highness."

"Foreign *languages*, Captain," Janez corrected. "And you don't have to address me by title with every breath."

"Yes, Your Highness. Like I said, Your Highness, six foreigns."

Janez sighed and shrugged. "All right. Let's see this spy of yours. Where was he found?"

"On the beach, Your Highness."

"On the *beach*?" Janez echoed. What kind of a spy came in from the beach? It was far too close to the castle. No wonder he'd been caught.

"Yes, Your Highness. Stark naked and like he'd swum in off a boat, Your Highness. Babbled complete nonsense at us, Your Highness, and this shock of great long hair like a woman, right down to his a—ah, well. Ahem. Looks mighty foreign to me, Your Highness."

As they passed from the great hall and out of the palace, Janez frowned and said, "Indeed, Captain, but there are many different kingdoms, and I'm sure some of them have long-haired men."

The harbour cells had, of course, no access to the palace. Far too dangerous. But in this case...what kind of spy turned up naked on a beach within a half mile of the harbour walls? It seemed far more likely someone washed up from a sea battle. But the last one had been his own, two days past now. Was it possible to survive two days, swimming naked in this sea? The cold could kill in a matter of hours—minutes, even, with winter so close.

And winter *was* close. A fine mist hung over the city, and beads of water formed bright on Janez's hair and coat. If not for Captain Kühe's grating voice, and the puzzling task at hand, it would have been pleasant to enjoy the bracing air and that chill right before the bite of true cold set in. It was certainly preferable to stuffy rooms, stuffier letters, and Doktor Hauser hounding him about rest.

The cells were little more than the cellar rooms below the old harbourmaster's house, which now served essentially as offices. They stank of damp and decay, and the alarmed look of the guard on duty said it all: what madness had possessed the captain to bring a member of the royal family into this dank, reeking hole?

"I ain't touched 'im yet, sah." The guard fumbled and was clouted by the captain with a roar to use the appropriate title.

Janez drew back from the flash of temper and muttered an assurance, letting his cold disapproval stop the captain's tirade more effectively than an argument would have done.

"Sorry, Your Hahness," the guard mumbled. "Sorry, sorry. It's jus', with them no clothes and being in the water, s—Your Hahness, I thought 'e might be one of them foreign sailors off our ships, like, not like them foreign sailors off them foreign ships, like."

The heavy cell door groaned open, and a slim form, huddled in the corner, stared up at Janez and the captain with wide, pale eyes.

Those eyes.

"You fool," Janez breathed, staring right back. Those long fingers—not webbed, of course not webbed, they had never been webbed—and that hair so fair it was almost the bright white of sea foam crashing on the shore.

This was no spy, no spider. "Get those chains off him. Now! This is no spy, you absolute fools!"

The guard jumped violently; the captain began to babble.

"But he speaks foreign, Your Highness. Speaks—"

"And how would you know any language not your own from another?" Janez demanded hotly and wrenched the great ring of keys from the guard's limp fingers. "This is the man who dragged me from drowning, and likely a great many others as well. Lord knows how long he's been out there. He requires a doctor, not a dungeon!"

A terrible fury was burning in his chest, and it must have shown. The stranger cringed back as Janez unlocked the chains from around his thin ankles and wrists, and simply sat, still and silent, even when freed.

"Are you hurt?" Janez asked but was only met with a blank, uncomprehending stare. Perhaps he really did speak nothing of their tongue—although Janez suspected were he to tell the sailor to reef a topsail, he would be instantly and competently obeyed. "Come," he said instead, tucking a hand under one slender elbow and tugged. "Up."

The man still didn't move, and Janez removed his overcoat and crouched again to tuck it around the man's naked form. That sparked a flicker of response—if only that a hand clutched the warm fabric and tugged it a little closer.

"Where are his clothes?"

"I said, Your Highness, he didn't have any—"

"And you didn't think to provide them?"

The captain fell silent.

"Are you in the habit of capturing naked spies on beaches, Captain?"

"I—no, Your Highness—"

"If you find more, in future may I suggest a doctor?"

"I—I'll find a physician, Your High—"

"No," Janez said. He cupped both elbows and lifted. The man rose with him this time, on shaking legs. But they gave way, seemingly unable to bear his frame, and he collapsed against Janez's chest, fingers grasping at the shirt. "Captain, go and find Doktor Hauser, and ask him to attend in his sickroom if he is not already there. I will bring your so-called spy."

Lifting the man was not easy. He seemed alarmed by the action, and although thin and light, he was still tall enough to stand perhaps a head shorter and no less than Janez. But he settled after the first few steps and then ignored the bustle of the gawping harbour—princes carrying naked sailors from the cells were not, after all, commonplace sights—in favour of staring quite fixedly at Janez's face. Did the sailor remember him as well, or had he been only one of a number that he'd saved?

A dungeon, indeed. The man was a hero.

The guards eyed him in barely muted surprise. A servant nearly dropped her linen basket at the sight. Janez rolled his eyes, certain he would receive a scolding from the queen about decorum. He'd done worse. Captain Kühe, looking understandably green about the gills, was emerging from the sickroom as Janez approached. He held the door, and Janez entered the realm not of kings and admirals, but of Hauser.

And severed heads, usually.

The sickroom was, in truth, a suite of rooms. The large bedroom was little distinguishable from any other, but it was the adjoining room that disturbed the peaceable image. There, Hauser had created a strange laboratory of sorts, full of foul potions, stinking corpses, and *jars*. Jars of brains, feet, and odd squishy things Janez was sure ought to stay inside one's body, not be floating in jars in a doctor's rooms.

"What was that idiot soldier barking about, and *that*—" Hauser extended a stubby finger towards Janez's load "—can suffice with one of the harbour-side butchers."

"Be nice, Doktor," Janez said, depositing the man carefully on the bed. He curled into the loose overcoat, his gaze roaming the room only briefly before it came back to rest on Janez's face. The stare was becoming unnerving. "This is the man who saved me."

Hauser harrumphed, but set down his instruments and stalked from his room of horrors into the land of the living. The man cringed back from him, and Janez could not blame him for it. Though Hauser was trusted and beloved by the royal family, it wasn't for his kindly demeanour or elegant looks. In fact, he was a short, balding man, with very pale eyes the colour of dirty water. They stared, unblinking, and there was a certain terrifying chill about them. Reptilian, almost. He would fix his gaze upon a patient, and the patient *knew* they were a breathing corpse, nothing more, and that this doctor would gain equal pleasure from saving a life as from boiling the brains out of a still-warm skull.

His fascination with dissection and study had made him a phenomenal doctor and surgeon, and his service was unswervingly loyal, but it came at the price of enduring the coldest stare any living man was capable of giving.

"Hmph," Hauser said, peeling back the man's eyelids, and leaning in to sniff at his breath. He ripped the overcoat open, easily batting off the hands attempting to close it, and then let go to stalk back into his rooms. "Cold. And dehydrated. Get him into some woollens. In the drawers. *Those* drawers, you incompetent fool..."

Janez grinned at the insult, and found the woollens (in a wardrobe, not drawers at all) and offered them to the man. When he stared blankly, Janez had to help him place his arms into a shirt. Fingers tried to clasp his own. He shook them off, but was grateful when he'd done only two buttons before the sailor seemed to catch up and buttoned the rest on his own. He curled his legs back under the overcoat, using it like a blanket, and Janez opted to let him. He could get a servant to come and dress the man properly if need be.

"Is he in shock, Doktor?" he asked as Hauser returned with a steaming cup of...something.

"Probably. What's his name?"

"I don't know. He hasn't spoken."

Hauser handed the sailor the cup; when the man did nothing but stare blankly at it, Hauser said, "Well, drink it, then."

No response.

"Foreign?"

"I think so."

"Drink," Hauser said again, loudly, and moved the man's wrist up until the cup pressed against his lips. "Drink," Hauser repeated, tipping it. The man drank, wrinkling his nose at the taste, and the doctor didn't let go until the cup was empty.

"What was that?"

"A sleeping aid. It will warm him and knock him out. He can remain here for the night, or in the servants' quarters."

"What's your name?" Janez asked, but the sailor apparently didn't even understand that. "Name?"

Nothing.

Janez tapped his chest. "Janez," he said and then pointed to the doctor. "Doktor." He pointed back at the sailor, and—

Nothing.

"He could be simple," Hauser opined.

"He's not," Janez said. "The way he looks at me..."

"Yes, fixatedly and unblinking. Simple," the doctor said. He snapped his fingers, causing those great pale eyes to be turned on him. "You stay here," he said as he gestured at the carpet. "Stay here."

Janez rolled his eyes before turning to the little laboratory. Steadfastly ignoring the jars of disgusting things that should not be outside living bodies, he found parchment and a piece of dirty charcoal. He returned and carefully wrote his name in large block letters before presenting it to the sailor. It was a long shot. Most of the hands were illiterate, but if he was a midshipman or higher, he might have been educated in his home country. He looked young, perhaps twenty. It was possible.

The sailor brightened and took the things in shaky hands. He began to—draw. Rather than write, he drew: A long curved rectangle. The soft shading of planks. And then a semicircle with a flattened edge. Two sharp lines, meeting at a right angle. Another line, on three legs. And two lines, joined at their bellies by a shorter one.

Hauser chuckled.

"*Held*. He's from the *Held*. Good Lord, I thought all hands had been lost."

"He must have been picked up by the *Ente*. She was on patrol that day," Janez said and beamed. "How apt! We can call him *Held* until we can figure out his real name."

Hauser laughed, and Janez grinned up at him.

"It's perfect," he insisted. "A hero named hero! You hear that?" he asked, turned to the bemused-looking sailor. He tapped himself on the chest. "Janez." And then reached out and tapped the thin frame under a borrowed woollen shirt. "Held."

The man smiled.

"Held," he echoed, in a thin, croaking voice. "Held."

Chapter Thirteen

THE SKYMAN WAS called Janez.

No matter how clearly they spoke, the words were a jumble of harsh, clattering sounds. But three things became clear. The beautiful man from the cloud was called Janez. The other man, with the fish-like eyes, was called Doktor. And they called Calla, Held.

Held.

It meant nothing to—to him. But—

It fitted, somehow. It was short and blunt, and it fitted better against this body. And this body was...

It was male. Calla—Held—knew that now. There had been a skymaid who'd dropped her basket when Janez had rescued him. She'd had the flow and form of a female—the breasts, the hips, the soft face and small hands—and this body had none of those things. It had narrow hips and wide shoulders, sharp cheekbones, and a flat, hard chest.

The chest was the strangest thing of all. Calla kept touching it, expecting fingers to touch flesh long before they did, expecting the roll of breathing to be heavier than it was. Instead, she—he—found hard bone and muscle, tiny nipples, and a soft layer of fine hair.

It sank in when another man came with armfuls of clothes. He bowed to Janez, bowed his head alone to Doktor, and set about dressing Cal—was her, *his* name even Calla now, if it didn't fit and if this body was male?—in a sleeveless jacket over the shirt. This was followed by heavy fabric that swarmed each leg and clutched them and the pieces between them. There were long nets that came up his legs to meet the base of the leg-coverings, and some kind of sleeveless undercoat in a dark brown, and it made no sense at all.

But what did make sense was there were no skirts. The skymaid had worn a dress, like the Witch had, like mermaids did. But the man brought no dress and wore the same leg-covers. As did Janez and Doktor. These were men's clothes, and the body was dressed in them, and then Cal—Held?—was stood in front of a looking glass, and a skyman stared back.

He.

He looked just like them.

He looked—not unlike he had, either. The same eyes stared back at him, the same chin and long neck. There was a ghost of the mermaid. It was as though...as though he'd been moulded and reborn, rather than a whole new body formed. As though the differences between mer and sky, between female and male, had been scraped away, and the core remained.

But the mirror showed a man.

A sharp jaw. That flat chest. The sleeveless undercoat made his hips seem even narrower and his shoulders wider. There was a muscular line to his frame that maids did not possess. He'd shrunk—to perhaps thirteen hands, from the twenty-three he'd been before—but he stood as tall as Doktor, almost as tall as Janez.

And the long hair, falling to the floor in a rush of white-gold light, was jarringly out of place, even as the man who had dressed him gathered it up in both hands and looped it round a fist.

Raised, it exposed neck, ears, face. Exposed the man in the looking glass. Exposed—

"Held."

Nobody replied.

"Held," he said again, and it fit around the image. He was—Held. Up here, in the sky, he was Held. And it felt...good. How could it feel good? His body had been ripped apart and remade. His name had been snatched away and replaced by another. How could it feel good? How it could possibly be a good thing?

Yet it *was*. Something burned bright and happy inside his chest, and when the razor flashed and the bundle of hair was felled, leaving only fine strands to fall to his shoulders, he laughed. The sound bubbled up, loose and free and joyous, and he could have sung. For the first time in his life, he wanted to *sing*.

Janez said something, a smile on his face, as the remaining hair was gathered into a dark ribbon. It hung behind his head, loosely tied at the nape of his neck just like Janez's, and Held loved it at once. His neck and ears were naked to the cool air, and he felt lighter. Free. Floating, as though in water. Could one float, in the sky?

Held was in the mirror. And for the first time, Calla felt *comfortable*. In this strange world, where they didn't speak the same tongue.

He was Held, and he felt good.

When Janez said something, the new man bowed again and left. And then Janez said, "Held," again, and a jumble of words that Held couldn't understand, no matter how intently he stared at Janez's lips. Still—the clash of noise, all jagged and harsh with sharp stops and spiky points, should have sounded frightening and ugly. Skymen spoke nothing like merfolk—they chattered and choked. Their throats did not release the smooth sounds of the underwater world. But the way Janez's throat bobbed above his collar, the way his lips twisted and his teeth flashed...

It sounded—seemed—so utterly beautiful that Held was captivated. He couldn't begin to pick apart the words; he could barely pull his new name from the mess, and yet, *and yet*, he would have undergone hours more of that agonising transformation in order to understand every last murmur that dropped from those lips.

Eventually, though, Janez seemed to tire of repeating the same sounds, and caught Held's eyes to firmly say a single one.

"Kommt."

It meant nothing to Held, but the intention was clear when Janez grasped his arm and turned him from the mirror to the door. Held stumbled on shaky legs—they didn't want to obey, nor did he know how to force them to do so—and tottered ahead of Janez's easy lope with utter gracelessness.

The going was, therefore, slow. Held had to stop frequently, feeling dizzy on these unstable legs, but Janez was kind. He would simply stop as well, and the perpetual half smile was warming. Others stared. Another maid with another basket lingered with wide eyes, but at a glance from Janez bowed and bustled away. Were they guards, like Father had? But no—the guards had to be the men standing at every door, perfectly straight and unmoving, with swords at their sides, and bright overcoats and hats. They would bow to Janez and open every door without a word. Janez would nod back as though this was commonplace. He must own the great building, Held decided. But as the passageways stretched out forever in every direction, and the sheer number of people there became apparent to him, he began to wonder if Janez was not a king's son. Or even the king himself. The deference, the quiet way he seemed to assume it would take place...it was like Father and his guards.

The final door let into what was unmistakeably a kitchen. The smells were rich and alien, but the sounds and activity were familiar. Chopped fish lined boards; a squid hung from a hook over a bowl. A lobster was chittering in a cage. Men and maids wearing aprons rushed about, and then one skymaid—short and plump, with a round red face—squealed.

"Prinz Janez!" she cried, and performed some odd bow in which her skirts were lifted out on either side of her like wings. A stream of high chatter followed that had Janez laughing and replying in a low, easy drawl.

"Prince Janez," Held attempted softly, whispering it to himself so he would not be heard and thought foolish.

He was led through the cavernous kitchens, and—outside. A tiny garden, floored in marble and ringed by low rocky wall, jutted from the back of the kitchen. A balcony, he realised, when he looked down at the tops of people's heads in a lush green garden far below.

The back of his shirt was caught, and he was hauled backwards and sat at a little table in the weak, cool light. Janez said something, and Held smiled at the attention, ignorant of the sentiment.

"Sie verstehen kein Wort von dem, was ich sage, oder?"

The lilt said it was a question, but Held had no hope of grasping it. He shook his head and earned himself another pleasant laugh. The light was playing in Janez's hair, turning the faint hint of red into a brilliant copper, and Held wanted to touch it again. Somehow, he sensed that he ought not to—but he wanted to. It wasn't as straight, nor as dark as he'd supposed that morning on the shore when it had been wet. It almost floated in the air, short wisps free around his face and ears. The majority was pulled back loosely into that ribbon, but it curled like plant fronds or relaxed fins, rather than hung straight. They looked as though they'd bounce back into their coils if Held were to pull them taut. And his fingers itched to touch—so he pushed them under his legs on the seat and prevented it.

"Ich verdanke Ihnen mein Leben," Janez murmured, so softly Held was unsure if he was supposed to hear it. But as before, it made no sense, so what did it matter?

The plump maid bustled out and placed a plate in front of Held, and a cup in front of Janez. And Held—stared. The plate was overflowing with food, some of it recognisable, most not. The fish was dark and shrivelled, yet smelled delicious; plants decorated the edges. A great flat rock sat in the middle, yet when he picked up the offered fork and prodded it, it was soft and gleaming. He poked it again, and looked to Janez questioningly.

"*Pilz.*"

"Pills," Held echoed, and Janez chuckled.

"*Pilz,*" he said, slightly more loudly.

"Pilz."

"*Ja.*"

Held blinked, and Janez rolled his eyes but didn't repeat himself. Was *ja* 'yes?' He poked the fish and raised his eyes again.

"*Fisch.*" When Held copied, he received another small smile, and another, "*Ja.*"

So *ja* meant yes. Perhaps their language wasn't so complicated after all. They had a yes. And different names for different foods. He had heard of a nest across the other side of the Narrow Mouth that called all foods simply food, no matter what type or ingredient.

He learned the plate—*Pilz* and *Fisch* and *Speck* and the assorted plants, *Salat,* that tasted foul, like chewing on unripe seaweed. Janez didn't seem to have a name for the plate itself, or he didn't understand the question, but the longer they sat together in the cool light, Held memorising all the sharp little words for simple things from the smiling prince, the more he felt—

At home. In this body and above the sky, with this man's gentle gaze upon him, he was at home. It made no more sense than Janez's tongue, or the strange clothes they had dressed Held in, but—it was as true as both all the same.

And then a guard came crashing through the kitchen, too large and blushing red from the angry shrieks of the skymaids, clumsily raised hand to his forehead, and nearly fell.

"*Prinz Janez.*"

"Prince," Held echoed to himself in another whisper.

The guard fumbled out a torrent of words. Held caught none of them, but Janez did, the easy smile slipped from his face.

"Ah," he said.

That was a sound Held understood perfectly.

Chapter Fourteen

WHEN THEY FINALLY arrived at the throne room, Alarik was practically oozing 'unimpressed.'

He was alone, yet seated on his throne, and Janez sensed that perhaps a little decorum was called for. So he clicked his heels and saluted, keeping both the smile and the irritation from his face and voice.

"Your Majesty. You wished to see me?"

Alarik's gaze slid right past Janez to Held.

"Why have half my councillors reported to me that you removed a spy from the cells, dressed him like one of us, and have shown him round half the palace?"

Janez stiffened.

"Held is no spy."

"Really. He doesn't speak a word of our language, and he could offer no explanation for his presence here."

"Because he can't talk to offer it," Janez said. "And any spy *would* speak our tongue."

"I am not arguing with you about this, Janez. Return him to the cells. Do you know how this looks? We are at war. I cannot afford to have questions over—"

"You question my loyalty?"

Even to his own ears, Janez's voice sounded like ice. And he meant it to. Alarik's eyes narrowed, and his fingers tensed on the arm of the throne.

"You know I do not. But others..."

"Half your council are idiots."

"You speak out of turn."

Janez stiffened, drawing himself up to his full height. "My apologies, Your Majesty. Ought I remove myself and my saviour to the Winter Palace again, for your convenience?"

"Your what?"

Janez almost poked at his brother's sudden apparent deafness, but considered it perhaps unwise, given his mood. "My saviour."

"And what is that supposed to mean?"

"Had you spoken to me before summoning me before the throne like a traitor, I should have told you that Held—"

"Excuse me?"

"Held. He can't seem to tell us his name, but he drew us the ship when we asked."

"So you named him Held?" Alarik asked.

"We did."

"And who is we?"

Janez raised his eyebrows, and Alarik sighed heavily, pinching the bridge of his nose.

"And why," he asked, "could you not have employed the skills of a physician, and not the royal surgeon? Doktor is too skilled for use on spies and sailors."

"But not on the man who saved my life."

Alarik paused again, and Janez pressed the advantage.

"I recognised him at once. And what spy would save an enemy life in the midst of battle?"

"A spy who wanted to secure passage into the palace."

"There are easier ways to do, less risky ways."

"And spies are averse to risk, in your experience?"

Janez tightened his jaw. "A spy would have been better to allow me to drown."

The words were stark. He saw the colour recoil a little from the king's face, some shadow of distress pass behind familiar blue eyes, and then it was gone.

"Unless you are not the target. By securing a place at your side, he secures entrance into our family. He secures access to me. To the children."

"Then I'll remain with him at all times."

"That is not what I—!"

"It's the perfect solution," Janez interrupted. "I can ensure his—lack of spying. And you can rest easy, knowing he's not roaming the palace for secrets."

Alarik groaned. He leaned forward, placing his head in his hands.

"Janez—"

"Am I dismissed, Your Majesty?"

"No, you are not, and stop with that damned majesty nonsense."

"Then you speak as—"

"As your brother."

"My brother has no power to stop me leaving this room," Janez said. "Only my king has that. And neither have the power to question my loyalty."

"I do not. I question your judgement, perhaps, but never your loyalty. But others—"

"If others have concerns regarding my devotion to duty, perhaps they ought to speak to you."

"You are smarter than to pretend this is not dangerous, Janez. I cannot have rumours about my own blood!"

"Then your blood may remove itself."

"Excuse me?"

"I presume you plan to extend an invitation to Sigurd and his daughters to the Winter Palace, being more splendid and liable to result in an agreement. I can always remove myself to it early. I'm sure Mother would appreciate the extended visit, and I can leave you in peace."

"And allow rumour to run rampant that you have been murdered by some spy, or run off with some sailor?" Alarik threw a filthy look at Held. "I think not—"

"It seems to me neither you nor I can win," Janez said, loudly enough that the sentry outside would be able to hear. Alarik flinched, and offered him a powerfully venomous look. "If rumours will abound no matter the course of action, then what does either course matter?"

"Except for the course of action where you return him to the cells, and let the guards deal with him."

"No."

The refusal rang in the room, cold and sharp. Held took a step back towards the door, his shoe clacking loudly on the stone. Alarik narrowed his eyes. Janez fought the urge to hold his breath or avert his gaze. 'No' was not a phrase he uttered often to his brother—and never when said brother was seated on his throne, with the crown adorning his temples. It was a word reserved for the royal chambers, for laughing demands to let Ingrid plait his hair or paint his face. It was a word reserved for too many cups of wine and the dark privacy of the king's study, exchanging stories of younger, freer days when they had given their tutors the slip and run rampant through the palace grounds.

It was not a word for here.

"He saved my life, brother," Janez said, hoping to ease the sudden tension in the room. "He's quite stupid, nothing more than some sailor pressed from a foreign port. He cannot even say mushroom correctly. He's no northerner. If anything, he's southern-born."

Alarik's eyes flicked to Held, still stood by the door.

"He is far too fair for that."

"You and I have both seen fair southerners before."

Alarik sat back at last, eyes still fixed on Held.

"I do not want him in the palace," he said.

"Then I shall remove us to the Winter Palace."

"You misunderstand me. I do not want him in any palace."

Janez shook his head. "He's lost and alone, and he speaks nothing of our language. I wouldn't turn him out to fend for himself."

"I would."

"And what thanks is that, for preventing my death?"

Alarik fell silent. Janez simply waited. Those wide, enchanted eyes across the table on the kitchen balcony had been guileless and gentle. They were oddly adoring when they looked to Janez, and he had the strange urge to reach out and touch that thin face when Held turned his almost lamp-like gaze on him. There was something ethereally beautiful about Held, and Janez would be damned if he'd see him handed back to cell torture for having dared speak some other tongue.

"How many hands have we seen and heard in the harbour, brother, who speak nothing but nautical terms in our tongue, and everything else in theirs?" he whispered.

Alarik frowned.

"He can probably curse us both in seven different languages, but does not understand me when I ask for his name. Let me at least find his family or his shipmates, so he can be returned safely to them."

Alarik's jaw clenched.

"Fine," he ground out, clearly incensed with the idea. "But you are to be armed at all times, Janez. He will sleep in a guarded room where he cannot reach anyone, and he is not to go unattended at any time. I will not hesitate to have him executed for a spy should he bring attention to himself."

"He will not. I swear it," Janez promised, but he promised, nonetheless. If necessary, he would take Held to the Winter Palace with him. Alarik would not come, not in the midst of war, and Mother would be too preoccupied with her painting to pay any mind.

"And one more vicious whisper, Janez, one more—"

"Have you sent word to Sigurd?"

Alarik sighed.

"Stop with this subject dancing—"

"Have you sent word?"

"Yes. I have."

"Then I have things I must attend to. If you please."

Janez snapped his boots together sharply and, without giving Alarik time to argue, turned on his heel. He took Held's shoulder to steer him— still walking like a newborn foal, but somewhat steadier after a full meal than he'd been before—and only when they were clear of the throne room and halfway up the stairs to the east wing did he let go.

And rubbed his chin, thinking.

If Alarik was this suspicious, this soon, then Janez was going to have to take steps to protect Held, or allow Held to protect himself. If he could find his family or his service, then it would be enough. If he could find some mention of his name in a logbook—but how, when the *Held* was at the bottom of the sea, logbook and all? If the *Ente* had picked him up from the water, it would have been mere hours before her engagement with the frigate, and the *Ente* was not known for a captain or crew studious with their papers.

Or perhaps there was another way, Janez reflected, as Held stopped dead and reached out to stroke the curtains of one of the great windows, a look of rapture on his face. What man, of any land, could look like that at the mere touch of a curtain?

Janez snapped his fingers and beamed. Of course. Spies were clever, cunning crows. And yes, there was an intellect behind those pale eyes. There was a wit, in the swift capture of little words, and the quiet understanding of when to follow and when to remain out of sight and shy.

But Alarik need not know that.

"YOU WISH FOR me to declare a plainly intelligent man to be simple-minded?" Hauser asked.

From another doctor, it might have been an incredulous question. But Hauser said it almost absently, intent instead on administering exactly four drops of a foul-looking green liquid to a severed foot.

A foot that had been severed for some time, judging by the smell.

"Yes."

"He isn't."

"You said he was before."

"I was being facetious. He's far too aware of language, and how to dress himself. I've worked in asylums, Janez, this man was not pressed from one."

"Then I wish you to say it again."

"It would be a lie."

"Then I wish," Janez said very deliberately, "for you to lie."

Hauser's gaze finally lifted from the foot.

"Why?"

"Because Alarik suspects him."

"As do I. The man ought to be dead. I may leech him, and see if his blood has some property to withstand the cold..."

Janez grimaced.

"Alarik suspects him to be a spy," he clarified, and Hauser snorted, returning to his foot.

"Rather an idiotic spy, if he is."

"I did raise the point, but he wouldn't listen. But if you were to declare him a simple-minded, harmless fool..."

"Then you think the king would not be so suspicious?"

"Yes."

"And why are you not suspicious?"

"He saved my life, Doktor."

"You are very certain."

"Yes."

"Half-drowned, half-frozen, and quite addled. You do recall, do you not, that you asked the king to hold your hand whilst I stitched that gouge in your leg?"

A dull heat crept up his neck. "That was your mixture."

"It was not. It had not taken effect."

"I have no fondness for your needles."

The doctor said something rude to that idea, and Janez sighed.

"I *am* certain, Doktor. I might have been wounded and weakened, but I wasn't out of my mind. And it wasn't a fleeting glimpse, either. I tried to hang on to him, so they would drag him from the water alongside me, but he slipped away."

Hauser hummed, finally looked up from his fetid foot, and glanced towards the open door. In the next room, Held was clearly visible, seated on the bed and staring back at them—at Janez—avidly.

"He is harmless, Doktor."

"He watches you."

"Well, yes..."

Hauser hummed again and looked back down to his foot.

"Anyone who stares in that manner at you is obviously simple."

Janez frowned. "Wait—"

"I will go to the king shortly. And if you do not leave me to finish my work, I will declare him quite the genius, and tell Alarik he has been rummaging through my papers. Out."

"You are an old cad, Doktor."

"Proudly so. Now out."

"What are you trying to prove?" Janez asked as he made for the door.

"Prove?" Doktor Hauser said and then smiled beatifically over the foot. A maggot wriggled free from a bloated, fleshy toe, and was sharply executed by the downward swing of the doctor's scalpel. "Oh, I am merely interested. It is not at all about proof."

Janez swallowed back the urge to vomit, and left.

Chapter Fifteen

HELD COULD NOT stop touching himself.

Every little movement of this body felt strange to his unused mind. The lack of weight against his chest. The strange, uninhibited roll of his shoulders. The legs—oh, the legs in their entirety—but also the simultaneous strength and weakness in them. They were skittish and ungainly, and he could not imagine they could swim well, yet how could such thin and fragile-looking things carry his weight above the water? Everything was so heavy here—the loss of his hair had felt...

He felt light without it. So—beautiful. He'd never understood, below the sky, why he'd been beautiful when he'd felt ugly. But he saw it now. Framed by the shortened locks, sharpened by the Witch and her craft, his face was pre—

Handsome.

And the word sounded deliciously sweet. He was handsome. Oh, but he'd never been handsome before. Held wanted to keep this face, this body—although perhaps not the legs and lack of gills, they would be quite problematic—after his three days were up.

And when Janez would touch his hand and guide him, speaking slowly in words that were made no clearer for it, Held wanted to never go back.

They stayed in the little room with the cold-eyed man for much of the morning, until Janez finally made a face—wrinkled nose, downturned mouth, and roll of blue eyes so strong Held wondered he didn't do himself an injury—and steered Held into the cool passageway outside. Bright light, white and warm, was streaming through the great windows, and Held touched the curtains with wondering fingers. So like home— but the texture was different. Like his clothes, but heavier and rougher to the touch.

Janez seemed amused by Held's fascination, lingering with a smile rather than towing him onwards. Their progress was thus slow: Held wanted to see and touch everything, feel the waterless rasp of the world above the sky between his now-separated fingers. Between the fingers of the very same hand, even. He slid a rope on a wall between the first and second fingers, and it caught and grated against skin that had never been there before.

These creatures, these skymen, they mustn't be able to swim. What could possibly swim with limbs like these? So how brave they were, how mad, to swarm the clouds when the clouds might submerge and suffocate them beneath the waves.

The passageway came to a grand flight of stairs curving down into a white chamber of stone that was decorated with statues and plants in great white pots. Dark doors led off in every direction, and as they reached the bottom, one opened and a skymaid emerged. Held stared. Their fashions were very different above the sky: the maid had her hair piled in tight coils upon her head, in the male habit, exposing her long neck and the high collar of her coat. In fact, the fashions were reversed—Held touched his fingers self-consciously to the short tail he'd been left by the cutting of his hair. Janez had one too. And the guard who followed the maid, clad in bright clothes and armed with a sharp, sinister sword.

A shriek.

A child, a tiny skyling who came but hip-high to the guard and was a smudge of pink skin and bright blue dress under a mop of frizzy fair hair, followed the man and maid. Upon seeing Janez, she squealed and launched herself across the stone floor towards him.

"Onki!" she cried, and Janez swept her up in his arms with a deep laugh.

"Guten Morgen, Biene," he answered, and she choked him tight in a hug.

Held's stomach clenched with a painful twist. A daughter. Janez had a daughter. They looked much alike, never mind the affectionate greeting. The same crooked nose adorned both faces, and she smiled as he did, spreading from one side to the other and far too large for her face, as though all her humour and good grace could not possibly fit within her tiny body. And if there was a skyling with his blood in her veins, then there was a maid with his love in her heart, too. He loved another. Oh, but of course he did. Held knew nothing of how long a skyman lived, but Janez was full grown, that was for sure, and strikingly handsome. And important! Did Held not know, from his own world, that the handsome and important were married first? Of course, Janez had found love. Of course he had created this little life.

But then, was the maid the mother? Held doubted it. Her gaze was most distant; she made no approach to Janez, nor even spoke to him. When he set the skyling down again, the maid simply said, *"Ingrid,"* and held out her hand. The skyling pressed her mouth to her father's cheek and bounced back with enthusiasm.

Nothing passed between the parents.

So—was she? Could she be? But why, then, would Janez breakfast with Held and not with his wife and daughter? Did skymen have no role in their offspring's upbringing, like fish or eel? Or were they like whales, or—?

The wondering was cut off when Janez turned back to him and led him through a set of double doors opposite the stairs—and onto more stairs.

Far grander stairs.

The stairs swept into an unmistakeable entrance hall. They met another flight in the middle, only for both to turn and form a single spiral, twisting downwards into an enormous cavern of gold and red. Huge paintings of skymen in uniforms and skymaids in enormous dresses adorned the walls. And below, just beyond where the stairs finally met the gleaming floor, an immense pair of doors were held wide open. They were nearly floor to ceiling, obscenely large, and could have fit the longest mermaid in the world if she walked like skymen did.

And beyond, Held could see nothing but light.

Nothing but a blinding, brilliant light. He stopped on the stairs, staring, and Janez laughed at him and tugged his wrist to urge him to move. But Held was reluctant. What lay beyond the light? Why had the skymen not drawn that beauty inwards, and controlled it as they did the clouds?

"Kommt," Janez said and pulled. Held followed, transfixed by the light. It ricocheted off the walls and the floors. It shattered on the guards' helmets and shimmered along their swords.

He stepped through the doors, and—

Oh.

Gardens. Fountains of water sparkling in the light. Paths that swept white and grey amongst the greenery. Bright bursts of colour, like coral and anemones, amongst the deep greens and gentler hues. And the smell! The smell was like nothing Held had ever known. Sweet perfumes crowded his face, a gentle hand upon the senses, and he stood still as stone, simply breathing for the longest moment on the white steps above the gardens.

They were not just plants, growing as they would on the reefs or in the shadows of nests, creeping and cautious. They grew in patterns. Rows. Great green walls lined the paths; a literal wall of pale brown stone was visible beyond a line of enormous plants that stood like dark brown towers. The corals were set by colour and height—one huge arrangement formed white and gold stripes, like a brilliant fish.

Held carefully picked his way down the steps and crouched on the gravel path by the side of the white and gold coral stripes. He glanced up at Janez, who made no move, and then carefully reached out to touch. The colour was thick and soft, smooth and full, under his fingertips. It felt as wonderful as it looked, nothing like the trickery of coral. He brushed the soft yellow fern in its centre, and his nails were coated in a furry smear. He wiped it off on another—

What *were* they? They were not coral. No coral felt like that.

He looked questioningly back at Janez, who seemed to read his expression, and came down the steps. He said something with a questioning lilt, and Held pointed at the corals.

Janez looked blank.

For the first time, a deep frustration welled up in Held's chest. How the very basest of questions escaped him—he didn't even know how to ask *what?* in Janez's tongue. Knew nothing. Barely understood his name, and perhaps he didn't. Perhaps Janez was a title. Perhaps Doktor was a position. He knew nothing.

But he knew how they had asked for his own.

Pointing at Janez—and sensing, without knowing why, that it was an oddly rude gesture—Held said, "Janez," clearly. Then tapped his own chest and said, "Held." Then pointed at the corals and waited.

"Ah," Janez said and smiled. *"Blumen."*

"Blooming."

"Blu-men," came the patient repeat.

"Blooming," Held said uncertainly. What was different between what he said, and what Janez did?

Janez seemed to think it was close enough. He chuckled and stooped down to touch the colour.

Then pulled it right off the plant.

Just—tore it off. Tore it! Held's jaw sagged open at the careless gesture. Coral took years to grow so bright and beautiful. Did these blooms grow faster than that, or were skymen so powerful that it didn't matter to them if the blooms were all torn away and died? Or could only Janez do that, as the ruler of this palace?

"Eine Blume," Janez said.

Held picked apart the two words, thanks to the speed. Janez ripped another off and held them both out.

"Zwei Blumen."

Oh. One bloom, two bloomings. All right. That seemed easy enough. He took one of the offered blooms and pressed his nose into the silken softness.

The perfume. The scent. That gentle sweetness was coming from the blooms. Held inhaled it deeply until he fancied its peaceable beauty was filling his very veins, and when he finally breathed out, it was as though his soul escaped for a moment and hung in the air, stretching out in every direction and absorbing all of this wonderful world.

Janez cleared his throat and then rose to his feet. Held blinked, brought back into himself, and stared up at him. The man's face was flushed faintly pink, and he seemed suddenly uncomfortable, shifting on his feet uneasily.

Held knew that look.

The way his eyes had darted away, when before they'd been trained with such gentle amusement, such kind fascination. The way he'd moved as though too aware of himself. The glance around them as though there could be others watching—and the simple fact that he cared for anyone watching at all.

Held knew this. Oh, not from personal experience—but from Meri's suitors and Balta's innocent little flirtations.

Janez—

Held's heart sped up inside his chest. His palms were damp. He wanted to—to touch. He didn't know how to touch a man, but he wanted to find out. He wanted to kiss him and feel that infectious burn, like salt in a wound, exquisite pain and inescapable sensation. Like that very first time when Janez had kissed him and tried to make him stay.

Held reached, without quite realising he was even moving. Their skin brushed. Grazed.

Held closed his eyes as their hands kissed. As Janez's fingers tightened on his. As a great wash of heat rushed from hand to heart, a wave, a current. As his chest tightened, and his heart burned. As he—*he* always should have been. He—and never she—caught the devastating power of a skyman and held it harmless in his hand. Kissed it, caressed it, like lovers.

He could never go back.

He could *never* go back.

Chapter Sixteen

HE COULDN'T.

The decision had circled in Janez's mind from the moment Held had touched his hand. It hadn't been a friendly touch. Rather, it had carried the heat and intent of a carnal wish, a lustful desire, the want to travel from simple hand to other complexities, and Janez had wished equally to allow it.

But he couldn't.

He'd twitched away with a soft smile and urged Held to come deeper into the gardens to see the willow trees and the buds of the winter roses. But Held had stolen little looks from that moment on, and Janez had wanted, with every fibre of his being, to turn them into the shadows of the trees, uncover the pale form he'd carried from the cells in his own overcoat, and kiss every inch of it. Rouse that bright excitement into something darker and hungrier and allow it to take him.

But. He. Couldn't.

Janez had always been careful with his liaisons, ever since Greta. The brothel in the harbour stood more to lose by loosened tongues than it stood to gain by gossip. They guarded their customers jealously, and Janez was certain, though had nothing set in stone, that he was not the only lord to visit, nor perhaps even the only royal. He'd never yielded even to the most beautiful temptations at royal functions and diplomatic balls—despite the suggestions of one such princess some years ago during the longest and most difficult waltz of Janez's life. He'd never so much as slept with his servants, certain of their predilection for gossip, and led a staunchly chaste life, almost saintly, when at sea.

And to risk a scandal now, when he was to be married off to secure this alliance... Sigurd would jump at the chance to secure a prince for one of his daughters rather than some ambitious lord, but he was not a desperate man. Janez couldn't possibly risk the match by a dalliance with a—

A what, exactly?

After all, despite his assurances to his brother and the doctor, what did Janez know? Held was as foreign as they came. He was clearly from some poverty-stricken family—who else would find such joy and wonder in curtains, of all things—and didn't even have the sensibilities of a servant. It was likely he'd been a ship's boy his whole life, and how long had that been? Held was a man, true, but Janez had known sixteen-year-olds as tall and gruff-voiced, and forty-year-olds as smooth-skinned and wide-eyed. He knew nothing about Held, and so, the risk was far too great.

But he hadn't wanted like this since—

Well. Since the very first one.

The first had been a girl, and Janez but fifteen and quite hopelessly in love. A man now, he knew it to be infatuation, passion, lust, and little more—but at the time, it had been love, his first love, his only. Greta had been the woman he would marry, the mother of his thousand sons, and they would all have those beautiful dark curls that had driven him wild.

She'd been a scullery maid.

She'd also been hypnotic by lamplight, with the sweat on her sweet skin, her little moans like music to his ears, her kisses the very air he breathed. Nothing short of captivating—he'd have sacrificed all for her, every drop of blood, every breath in his lungs. He'd utterly loved her, and she him, and the world had been—in her embrace—completely perfect.

She'd borne him a child—or at least, Janez supposed she had. Father had sent her from the palace, to serve some other lord. Had told Janez, stern and imposing, that one liaison as a barely grown man was excusable, perhaps even beneficial for when the time came to find him a true wife, but it would be the only time.

He'd never seen Greta again, never mind the child she must have birthed that autumn, and now nearly fifteen years on, Janez rarely thought of it. Secrecy was second nature now. He could ruin his family, his very kingdom, by indiscretion and infidelity. And so, as negotiations would surely commence the moment Sigurd received Alarik's messenger, he couldn't possibly take what Held's grasp had offered, however much he wanted to.

Janez had long since learned, fifteen years since, that his life had no room for the things he wanted.

It was about duty. And duty made him pull away, smile, and continue as though he'd never noticed the offer. Duty made him show off the gardens as though to a visiting princess. Duty made him leash his want, leash even the very thoughts that escaped, now and then, about how wonderfully enchanted Held was by the simplest things, how his mouth begged to be kissed, how euphoric he'd look in the grip of pure ecstasy—

Janez clamped down on them all, one by one, but they came regardless.

And they had enough grip that, while he stuck to duty and kept his hands to himself, he shirked the other parts of it. He ought to have been at his king's side, or at the harbour assisting his captain with the restocking of the ship. Instead, he kept following this stranger, showing him gardens and trees and greenhouses, showing him the great ballroom and the portraits of his forefathers in the hall that led towards the south wing and the library.

There, Held took great interest in Janez's portrait—painted just shy of Alarik's coronation, when Janez had become the crown prince for two mercifully short years, and thus depicting that thrice-damned crown and grotesque fur cloak. The damn thing reeked; the stench was so bad Janez swore it was the same as worn by the first-ever king north of the mountains in all of history. But Held seemed to like it, staring in fascination for a long time, and finally gesturing at the crown and mumbling something Janez didn't even recognise as language.

"My crown?" he asked. "I was the heir to the throne. Now I am second in line, so I don't have to wear it."

Held stared blankly, and Janez thought on it. Finally, he pointed to Alarik's portrait—not from the coronation itself, not in this hall, but from Ingrid's first painting. It was a simple family portrait: king, queen, and tiny princess, her golden curls a mess even in this respectful depiction.

"My brother," Janez said clearly, tapping Alarik's oiled face. "Brother."

Nothing. Damn.

"Come with me," Janez said and led Held to the library. It was gloomy and dusty, undisturbed likely for days now that Doktor Hauser was buried in his vile experiments, and Janez shook open a heavy set of curtains before finding some parchment and an ink bottle in a desk. The quill was wilting and feeble in his hand; the nib was crooked, and the ink therefore blotchy, but it serviced well enough that he was able to scratch his stick figures and a brief family tree. The line joining himself to his brother went above; the line between Alarik and Sofia went below, and from it sprouted Ingrid. The baby, yet too young to be named, would not appear in the history of the world for nearly a year yet, in case it drew fate's foul attentions and he was damned to die in his crib as so many babies did.

"Me," Janez said, gesturing to his little depiction. When Held stared blankly, Janez sighed and tapped it again, saying his name instead.

A spark of recognition. Aha.

"Alarik," he continued, tapping his brother. "King Alarik."

Slowly, Held reached out and took the quill. It shifted clumsily in his fingers, the ink staining them at once. He examined it as if it were some strange new invention, and then pressed nib to parchment—too hard, but no matter—and scratched, very carefully, a crown above Alarik's round head.

Janez beamed. "Yes!"

Held smiled, a white flash of brilliance that had the breath catching in Janez's chest for a split second before he forced his gaze away.

Hand's finger tapped the tiny Ingrid, then, with her inky corkscrew curls. "Ingrid?"

"Yes."

Held stroked the lines, smearing the still-wet ink. Stroked from Ingrid to Alarik, and then Alarik to Janez. Stroked back again. Murmured something to himself.

And then *smiled*.

It was the brightest smile Janez had ever seen, and he gaped like a stupid landsman as Held turned it to him. It was transformative. That sombre, ethereal face was suddenly oh-so-human and impossibly beautiful. It lit him up, as if the sun were behind his very skin, and Janez leaned in, reaching up—

He curled his fingers into fists and drew back. No. Good Lord, no. He returned his hands to the table instead, licking his lips nervously.

And jumped, quite violently, when Held's fingers slid into his.

Time stopped.

The dust motes hanging in the air froze in place, tiny sparkles in the dark. Held's skin was dry and cool against his. Fingers filled the spaces between his and tightened. And Janez could barely breathe.

He ought to have pulled away. Ought to have instructed Held on the inappropriate—perfection—of holding his hand in such a manner. Ought to have snuffed out the tension in the room, and his longing to close the space and take advantage of the solitude. To fill the silence with sound other than speech.

He ought to have done a lot of things.

And he did. But—it was the longest time before he could.

Chapter Seventeen

HELD WAS...CONFUSED.

He'd kissed the prince twice. Both times, Janez had gone very still for long moments of pure silence before he'd pulled away.

Yet there was no reluctance in his eyes. No withdrawal. He returned to a bright and easy manner at once, and those little shifts in his stance, those glances, did not abate. And it left Held confused. He was sure, so sure, he wasn't misreading Janez's attraction to him, yet kissing him resulted in nothing.

He'd never kissed someone before—not by choice, anyhow. There'd been mermen, too forward and brusque, who'd seized his hands and kissed without permission. But Held had pushed them away, and that had been that. He'd never reached out first. He'd never done it on purpose.

Was he doing it wrong, then?

It had occurred to him, after that second time in the dark room, that maybe skymen didn't kiss like mermen kissed. But if they didn't, why had Janez responded to the touch? If it meant nothing to touch hands, then why would he react?

Held was left to dine with Doktor, and he churned the problem over in silence as he ate his...whatever it happened to be. Either Janez wasn't interested, and Held was misreading the signs, or Held hadn't kissed him properly, and Janez didn't know what Held was trying to do.

And stuck, alone and without tongue, how could Held convey it?

It would help if he could witness skymen kiss—but they seemed so very reserved, so distant from one another. Perhaps it was simply this regal setting, or perhaps that was their way, but Held struggled to imagine Doktor in a passion and kissing someone. Only Janez seemed to have that fire, and he had reacted so oddly both times...

Held squeezed his fingers more tightly around his fork and resolved to let it be for today, and try again in the morning. Perhaps that was all it was: reservation. After all, he'd only been turned at dawn, and dusk had only just descended. Maybe skymen moved more slowly in these things.

Janez returned not long after dark in new clothes: tighter, stiffer, and more formal. Held watched those powerful legs roam the room as he talked animatedly to Doktor. The fabric was sheer enough to skin that Held could see the muscles move, and the soft weight of his masculinity under the buttons. The itch to undo those buttons—

Held curled his fingers into fists, mortified.

And then Janez turned to him and clutched his elbow, near-lifting him from his chair.

"Komm!" he cried, eyes ablaze.

It must mean come with me, or something of that ilk, for Held was swept from Doktor's rooms and hustled along corridors and passageways, until they burst past those great paintings again. And then ducked into the dark room where he'd been given hope, in the form of a crude diagram and a faint understanding that Ingrid was not Janez's skyling, but that of the man with the hat upon his head. (The relation between Janez and the hat-man still escaped him, but Held cared far less for that.)

But they did not stop at the table—he was dragged past it, to the great windows furthest from the door, and the coverings drawn back. The windows were opened—and sound rushed in.

Music.

The flash of intense hatred was immense. Held curled his lip, his body tensing at the crescendo. He knew nothing of the instruments, nor the piece they played. He'd never heard of music being played in a garden before, nor admired from a balcony above—but it didn't matter. Music meant singing. Music meant he'd be expected to screech and squawk in that shrill, hated voice. Disgust prickled along his skin, rose up under his hair, burned—

And died.

Died when Janez turned to him and clasped him in a hug.

Held stiffened—and slowly, so very slowly, relaxed. Drew up his arms around Janez's neck...and laughed in dizzy delight when Janez began to turn them.

Dancing.

Oh, they were dancing.

It was clumsy and messy. Janez, by the glee on his face and lively energy, liked music. Or at least this music. And his energy was—infectious. Held had no idea how to dance with legs, but he clutched and tried, as much as possible, to follow Janez's haphazard lead. Their feet collided several times; finally, Janez pushed off the hard covers he wore at the ends of his legs, and then there was bare skin and those small, strange little fingerlings, and the energy slowed until Held could copy.

And then—

After that, as they fell into sync, Held found that sky and mer danced much alike. He was twirled, and the fan of his shorter hair was a hypnotic blur when his ribbon came loose. Janez seemed to like it too, as the twirl was performed again and again, both out and reeled back in—under Janez's arm, close and intimate, until Held laughed breathlessly, and that beautiful smile was trained unerringly on his own.

The music was strange. It squeaked and warbled, nothing like the shuddering drums of the palace below. It didn't rattle in the bones and shake in the blood, but rather caressed the skin and kissed the ears with delicate fingers. It felt odd to dance to, something too shallow to its depth and too thin to its energy, yet it invigorated Janez as though he could feel something Held could not.

And that, in turn, bled over into Held's body. The outward twirls ceased, and Janez's hands settled at his back as he taught Held, through laughter and movement alone, some kind of thumping dance that was like a warlike jig between fighting crabs rather than a joyous expression of motion between two men. When Held finally captured the rhythm, he was twirled under Janez's arm again in some odd reward—though for whom, Held did not know—clasped ever closer, and sped in a strange fast walk in a box shape over the soft carpet. So close, that close, Held could smell Janez's very essence. He didn't know what it was the prince smelled of, exactly, but Held could smell it all the same: alluring and heady, something inviting, something intimate by his very knowledge of it. Janez's breath was on his cheek, and the escaped red-gold curls were tickling Held's face.

As his hands kissed Janez's shoulders, tight over the white of his shirt, Held wanted to know how to kiss him so that Janez would understand.

The music stopped.

Applause broke out below—yet Janez didn't release him or turn to the window to join in.

He simply stopped, Held still clutched tight in his arms, and stared.

The entire world was the body pressed to Held's front: the blue eyes boring into his face; the hands firm on his lower back, just above where his frill used to be; a faint pressure at Held's hip, unfamiliar yet somehow warming and pleasant.

Held slid his hands, careful and cautious, to rest on Janez's chest.

He felt a heartbeat, under cloth. Wondered if hair lay there, or if skymen were bald-chested like mermen. Wanted to open the ribbons, open the cloth, and feel for himself. Under the heel of his palm, a gentle bump in the skin, and, in waiting for Janez to move, he absently rubbed at it.

Janez groaned.

Groaned.

A deep and guttural sound, it seemed to emanate from his very ribs, like the reverberating grumble of a deep-sea creature, immense and powerful. His entire body shuddered in a base response. His hips rolled forwards into Held's, and that warm pressure increased.

Something—Janez—was pressing into him.

Held's heart was in his throat. His palms were slick. His body knew this—he did not, but his body did. There was growing heat in his groin. A pressure of his own. His groin was heavy, as though he were swelling. He was shivering—and he wanted more, even as he didn't know what more was. Something would build, he was sure of it, but he knew not why.

With only blind instinct to guide him, he did it again.

A hand dropped lower. Seized Held by the backside. Held whimpered as a wave of intense pleasure rocked through him—his knees weakened, his fingers clutched tight, and he hung on Janez's leg for a moment, helpless—and then it ebbed again, only to return as he was squeezed tighter, and Janez rocked his hips into Held's once more. As his face dropped briefly to Held's neck, and Held felt the scrape of teeth.

"Please," Held whispered. "Please."

He didn't know what he was asking—for more? More of what? The same, or something different? He'd never felt this before. He'd never done this before. Was this—was this—?

The answer broke upon the shores of his brain as the hand clutching at him slid lower still, and he felt the hard grip of a hand between his legs.

This was how men loved.

This was it, wasn't it? That deep groan, the base reaction, the way Janez had moved so fluidly it could only have been an instinct. And the way Held felt him as intensely as though they were one: his breaths, his scent, the very lifeblood in his hands—

The music opened up below. High. Sweet. A world away from the deep roar in Held's ears.

And it disturbed the spell that had descended. It lifted. Broke. Janez pulled away so sharply that the air rushing in to claim his place felt cold. The blue eyes were wild and almost desperate, and he muttered something with haste, far too fast to be caught.

And then he was gone. His shadow flitted away from the windows, and in a moment, Held heard a door open and close again.

He was alone.

The music warbled below, happy and oblivious, and Held leaned his face to the glass to soothe the burning in his skin.

He'd not been wrong. Janez did want him.

A smile broke out across his face, and Held had never loved music so much in all of his life.

Chapter Eighteen

JANEZ ROSE LATE in the morning.

He'd been plagued for the rest of the evening by the memory of Held in his arms, and he hadn't dared leave his rooms. The phantom sensation of that lithe, hard body—the broad shoulders, the firm chest, the sublimely perfect backside—and Held's violent lust upon its capture in Janez's hands.

He'd been foolish to do it. But he'd heard the orchestra from his chambers and wanted to dance so much he'd thrown caution to the wind. He could rarely dance or play the fool with his family, and never in public, so his mind had immediately turned to Held, quiet Held, who couldn't tell anyone the prince's madness.

Janez had never expected it to end as it had.

Good Lord, his head had been turned. He knew lust—knew it very well—but when it came to men, he'd always had more self-control. His little flirtations with desire for men came and went easily. They knew nothing of the art of love and had no interest in learning of it. For other men, Janez had long since found, sex was a careless and brutal coupling, an itch to scratch and nothing more, and no part of the body but the necessary pieces required any attention. He viewed sex as more like dancing than swordplay and had been enchanted by the easy way that Held could turn. His natural grace, his poise and aptitude for learning, followed by the splay of moonlight in his hair when he'd twirled, and the bright smile of unbridled pleasure—

Janez had very nearly kissed him and thought it avoided with the waltz. But then the music had died, and there he'd been: standing alone in the dark, unseen by any, with the thought of *what if* running through his head and an impossibly alluring man pressed against him from head to toe.

Janez couldn't blame his body for its response—it would have responded to even Captain Kühe in such close quarters—but that his brain had followed its lead was less acceptable.

He must not, could not, do this.

The music had saved him, jarring him from that dreamlike state that had come over him. If it hadn't, Janez was certain he'd have brought Held to the floor, opened his trousers, and given him pleasure the likes of which the man had never known. And he'd have been wholly focused on Held, as well. The brilliant pleasure of the dance and the gasp and thrust of lust when Janez had kissed his neck said that Held, spread out upon the floor and drenched in the sweat of pure sexual pleasure, would be more beautiful than anything Janez had ever seen.

But the music had stopped him and spared him the consequence. The risk was too great, and Janez had fled to his rooms.

He'd not cared to visit Rosa, wanting only Held that night, so had sated the need by himself, using his imagination and his own hands. But they were a poor imitation, and the urge had risen twice, thrice more during the night.

He rose late, tired, and despairing of his station. Had he been but a lowly guard, he'd have done it. He'd have drawn Held from the doctor's rooms just before dawn and shown him the exquisite sight of a man of power on his knees, submitting all his rank for another's pleasure and without hope of reward.

But he wasn't a guard. He was a prince. And he was sorely reminded of the fact when he finally left his rooms and the sentry at the entrance to the royal chambers told him King Alarik was shut in the council-room with a messenger from King Sigurd.

"He'll be calling for you soon, Your Highness, I'd imagine."

"I'd imagine so," Janez said.

After last night's mistake—although he could not quite think of it so—Janez wanted nothing less than to hear of his impending marriage. Idiotic though the desire was, he wanted another day to himself and Held. Another day to watch the warmth and wonder in the stranger's eyes. Another day to—

To pretend he could, if he wanted, kiss him. Touch him. Dance with him. In every way possible.

Janez shook himself and smiled at the sentry.

"Unfortunately for the king," he said, "I left earlier this morning to go riding."

The sentry looked dubious. "Did you, Your Highness?"

"I did, indeed. You saw me go."

The sentry coughed. "Ah. Yes, Your Highness. I believe I did, now I come to think of it."

"Good man."

He strode purposefully, taking a servants' route to Doktor Hauser's rooms, and liberated Held from his breakfast—and a strange smell emanating from the little laboratory—with a brisk word and a hand under his arm.

"We must be quick," he murmured. "I'm a wanted man this morning, and I want nothing of it. We're going into the wild for a while, you and I. Have you ever ridden a horse?"

He didn't bother to listen for an answer. They left the palace via the kitchens, and the quick dash across the courtyard to the gate, and the stables just beyond, was the biggest risk of all. But the king apparently hadn't sent for him yet, or word hadn't flown around, for they passed through unencumbered, and Janez hustled Held into the warmth. To add insult to injury, he decided he'd take Alarik's horse.

Alarik, quite unlike his station and dignity demanded, rode no thoroughbred stallion the size of a ship. Instead, his was a black-and-brown mare by the very unkingly name of Molly. He had a special fondness for her, having had her since she was a foal, and swore up and down she'd been named after his wet nurse. Janez had it on good authority that his wet nurse had, in fact, been called Elise, and Molly had been the name of the first girl to ever teach Alarik what his equipment was for.

Molly the mare, however, was more docile than enterprising maids. She snuffled at Janez's hand hopefully, and permitted him to saddle her quite peaceably, nudging at Held's hair in quiet interest. Held, by contrast, looked highly uninterested. Terrified, in fact, and Janez chuckled and decided to retrieve a stool.

"Come on," he urged. "She's perfectly safe."

Held did not agree with him, plainly. Likely the poor man had only ever seen a horse if it was attempting to run him down in the street—officers did tend towards riding right into crowds if late for appointments—and the idea of willingly getting up on one would seem as absurd as the idea of fairies or mermaids being real.

But Janez would not be deterred. If Held liked dancing and the smell of flowers in the garden, then he would enjoy a gentle ride, and Janez knew the perfect quiet glade, stuffed to the brim with wildflowers, and a chattering stream for Molly to drink from.

So. "Come on. Up here."

He dragged Held onto the stool and then—with much cajoling and physical force—wrestled him onto the horse. Held clutched Molly's mane, white-knuckled, and any less amiable a horse would have thrown him at the indignity and stupidity of it all. But Molly only grumbled for an apple and, when provided, urged Janez to command this rider with a gentle shake of her head.

"I know, girl. Don't worry—I'll be in charge, eh?"

He mounted with practised ease, taking the reins and sliding an arm around Held's waist to keep him secure.

"Relax," he said softly, pitching his voice so soothingly that Held did so despite Janez's conviction he didn't know the word.

Good enough.

"Relax," he repeated and twitched his heels.

Molly started happily forward, nosing her way out of the stables without needing guidance. She was the type of horse suited to new riders, and it was just as well—as her gait rolled under them, the more so for the cobbled yard. Held tensed up impossibly, and any other horse would have taken it to mean gallop. Molly harrumphed—voicing mild displeasure at Janez's gentle insistence that they were for the road and not the haystacks against the stable wall—but once beyond the gate, broke into the gentlest of trots.

Held didn't relax until they left the town—not even the view from a horse's height could distract him from his abject terror—but as they broke beyond the city walls and Janez led Molly easily off the road and allowed her to use grass tracks, the smell of open countryside and the quiet (bar disturbed birds) appeared to take their toll.

One hand left the mane and clutched tightly on to Janez's wrist.

"See? This is nice," Janez said.

Held was of a good height to ride with. He was a head shorter than Janez, and it allowed Janez to see past him, yet hold him securely at the same time. As Held adapted to the rhythm of the mare a little more, Janez dared to loosen his grip and began to absently stroke his thumb against the front of Held's waistcoat. Should they go to the glade and stream, or the river itself, where it ran down through the woods? The ride would be rockier, but the forest was secluded, and—

Held's fingers slipped between Janez's and squeezed tight.

Janez's heart hiccuped in his chest—an unpleasant jolt out of sync with the rest of him. For a moment, he did nothing.

And then—to hell with it. He squeezed back. Held relaxed further against him. And Janez knew he was ruined, but there was a large part of him—the younger brother, the second heir, the horse-thief—that didn't care. He did his duty every day of his life. Was he not allowed one lapse? If he were careful, if he were quiet—

He shook his head. No. He knew better. There was no amount of careful that could not be found out. Spies and gossips lurked in every corner. He would not. Should not. This was—this was a break from the drudgery of castle life, and he must not yield to the temptation to take more, not when he would have to end any and all such infidelities. He was engaged, in truth, although no papers were signed and no wife known. But he would be married in a year, and not to this man. So he was, in effect, engaged.

And in any case, he knew nothing of Held's feelings. If the man merely desired him, a physical and carnal sort of want, then all would be well. But if he felt more? Janez didn't know. How cruel would it be to entertain love, only to snuff it out with wedding bells to someone else before the summer had even bloomed?

Yet it was tempting. And Janez was only human. Held's trust in permitting this ride despite his obvious misgivings was alluring. He was a living and breathing temptation against Janez's front.

And so when the paths diverged, he twitched Molly to the left fork, yielding to at least a little temptation.

The woods were dense—the stuff of nightmares to small children. Alarik's taunting him about the place when they were boys was a sour memory. Deep and dark, scary and stark, it was where spare heirs were left for faeries to eat. But to an adult, they were simply cool refuges. They were not, in the grand scheme of things, much of a forest. There were no bears, and rarely wolves. The deer were shy, and the trees too closely packed and low to allow for hunting on horseback anyway. They were far out from the city walls, far enough that without a horse, it would be hours to walk, for little gain. They were private.

In times of war, the aristocracy either fled the coast, or fled to the docks to do their duty and scrape up some glory for their family names. And with winter's grip descending fast, even the children would be indoors now.

Sure enough, as the shadows closed around them, the sheer silence wrapped about their ears like a lover's shawl to reel them in.

Held shifted anxiously as Molly's easy gait changed to a careful and deliberate walk. But then he reached out for the branches hovering close to their faces, and as his pale fingers stroked the bark, a look of rapturous wonder crossed his sharp features.

How could a *tree* possibly be interesting?

A flower of pity unfurled in Janez's chest as Held lost his terror quite absolutely in favour of touching the trees as they passed by. The odd leaf, crisp and colourful, still clung to dark branches, and Held was enchanted by the sound they made as he plucked them free and broke them into soft shards. The man had to be from some dank, dark city, to have never experienced the crunch of leaves in his fingers, or the scrape of branches against his hands. His fascination was absurd, otherworldly even. No man could possibly have lived so long away from the wild.

But then, perhaps he could. Some industrial port by the sea, perhaps. Janez had sailed enough to foreign lands to know them—ugly, brooding towns on river mouths, the sea shiny with oil and shimmering false in the sun. There were southern lands where nothing grew, the air so hot and the soil so dry, and there were western ones, northern ones, where the islands were so small their people crowded the coastlines and created filthy hovels of towns without so much as a bird to be heard, even in the dead of night.

He was a westerner, Janez decided, and it explained his blank incomprehension. Westerners spoke a very different tongue. Perhaps, when they returned, Janez could find him a book or two on the western kingdoms, and he would recognise some town on a map somewhere. Perhaps they could begin to find his home.

And then he would—

Janez shook himself.

Go.

Held had a home, somewhere. Like Janez would have a wife, sometime. This was...passing fancy. Nothing more.

The passing fancy passed from the shadow to the smattering light, filtering through the spaces in the canopy forged by the river. It was but a shallow thing, wide but unimportant, a gravel bed over which little frogs and fishes skittered from time to time. It ran fast, though only up to the knees at its deepest, and Molly walked serenely into the coldness of it and bent her head to drink.

"Easy." Janez laughed when Held leaned back in alarm at the dip of her neck. He slid down and helped Held after him. The water surged around his boots merrily—and Held, to Janez's surprise, lit up. He kicked off his shoes at once—and away they spun, light enough even for this little river to carry—and stripped away the stockings. Bare toes were buried in the riverbed, and the look of rapturous joy—despite how cold the water had to be—was ethereally beautiful.

Janez's breath caught in his chest.

"*Ashara...*" Held murmured. It sounded like a whisper from a whole other universe.

He looked—beautiful.

He shouldn't have. Pale and thin, sharp nosed and too-large eyes, his clothes and hair askew from the ride and the tugging fingers of branches—he looked a mess, waifish and lean, almost feral. He ought to have looked like any other dirty ship's boy, like any other peasant.

But he didn't.

The look of sheer happiness on his face, with his legs submerged to the knees in freezing water, transformed him. He was no peasant, not even a mere man.

He was something from another universe, some other creature in human form, and Janez knew nothing of what he was, what he'd been, or what he'd come to be.

But he wanted—so desperately wanted—to find out.

Chapter Nineteen

THE WATER WAS cool.

Cold, even, but Held enjoyed it so. It surged around his legs and lapped at his skin, familiar and content. It knew him, and he knew it, despite the form. Something of the mer lingered inside him, and the water recognised it, even if there was nothing physical left to know.

But it was not the water that had his attention.

Janez seemed to have no interest in it. He'd retreated to the bank and seated himself on his coat. Parchment lay over his knee, and he appeared to be drawing with small sticks. He ignored Held quite thoroughly.

Yet Held could not ignore him.

The water was cool, but Held was not.

He was no stranger to lust—Meri had described it enough, and indeed, there was that strange, buzzing warmth from Janez's first kiss upon the roof of the world. But the intensity of this, the way he was overly hot despite the chilly air and freezing water, and the physicality of this form's response...

There was something far more urgent than had ever been there before.

His body wanted to do things, even as Held didn't understand what they were or why. It wanted to cross the little river and remove the sticks and paper from Janez's lap. As well as the prince's clothes. It wanted his smell and skin, and it wanted his touch. And it wanted it—

Held's hand crept to the swelling in his groin.

He was...hard.

Mermen had no such external fifth limb as this. It was internal, emerging only in the act of love. He'd supposed—from the first time it had happened—it was merely to void oneself, and skymen had some similar internal organ. But it was stiff, throbbing within its confines, and the feeling was so very different.

Janez was paying no mind, and nobody else was around, so Held unbuttoned the fabric and pushed his hand inside to wrap his fingers around the length.

And jolted.

The touch was sharp and sudden. His hips rocked forward into his hand, and Held barely caught the groan that tried to escape. His legs shivered. His heart raced. And when he squeezed gently, a rush of lust and pleasure so intense it made his very soul shake inside his chest nearly swept him away.

He *wanted.*

And he wanted Janez to do this. He wanted Janez's hand there, and not his own. He wanted those smooth fingers around his flesh. Wanted Janez's mouth against his neck. Body against his own. Wanted that desperate clutch from the darkened room. Wanted—wanted—

Sex.

He knew of it. Knew not how skymen did it, but—he wanted to find out. Wanted to know. Did they twine together like weeds, the way merfolk did? Did they clutch and cling and cry out their joy together? Did they do it at all, or did they do it often? Did men lie with men, and the maids together? Was it a private or a public sort of affair? Did they kiss, and love, or simply twist as one and then come apart again?

He wanted to know how *Janez* had sex. Were his eyes the same shade of blue in the height of passion? Did his hair burn gold or red? Was he a powerful lover, with strength and sobriety, or did he love in a relaxed and contented state, peaceable and pliant?

Would he kiss Held? If Held were to—

Janez glanced up at him—and froze. He stared at Held's wrist, and when Held stroked himself again, Janez placed the paper aside.

And beckoned.

Heart in his mouth, Held crossed the bubbling water until he stood between Janez's legs. Stood shivering as his fingers parted Held's clothes. Shook as a hot mouth pressed to his bare chest, right in the centre over Held's racing heart.

"Oh!"

Janez touched him.

Those fingers kissed his shaft and began to stroke it. Gentle. Soft. Barely there, until they reached the base and squeezed, so gentle and so commanding. Held whimpered. He reached out, blind and uncertain, and clutched at that fine hair. Brought Janez's head to his chest, and shook silently there, mouth pressed to the invisible crown of warmth that Janez wore under the gold. Clung, as his entire being narrowed to the hot touch of those fingers. To the hand resting on the back of his leg, barely under the swell of his rear. To the tightening low in his belly—and lower still—and the heat, the heat, that inescapable *heat*...

As the heat rose to fever pitch, the golden head under his mouth bent.

"Janez!"

Janez's lips sealed about the head of Held's length. Hot. Wet. He sucked until Held threatened to buckle by the sheer force of it, and then—

White.

The world—was—white.

Air.

Held raked it in. Gasping. Found himself softening. Found himself soft, buckled over Janez's frame like water folded over rock. Janez's hands were cupping his rear, secure and hard. Something deep inside Held wanted them to be closer, but he knew not how or what that meant.

And when the colour bled back into the universe, separating out from whiteness into blues and greens and the soft browns of the world above the water, he bent his head against Janez's shoulder to peer down his long form and saw the same hardness echoed in his lap.

Clothed, still.

Held reached. Tugged his clothes apart with determined movements. Janez closed his eyes and pressed his forehead against Held's shoulder, but made no other move. And then his hard flesh sprang free, long and sleek and hairless, and Held touched it in fascination. A pulse hammered inside it. Soft and silken skin, smooth as though wet while it was perfectly dry, but for the very end of it.

Held rubbed his thumb over that damp end, and Janez shuddered. Shivered, as intense as a fit, in Held's grasp.

So Held did it again. And again. And again, until he learned the very writhe and moan of those shivers—and then he slid his hand as Janez had done. Watched the swell and darken of tender flesh with a tired sort of pleasure, a sated joy. This was—this was sex, was it not? This was how skymen did this, yes?

Janez's hand closed about his, and with a sharp jerk of his hips, the prince fell under that same shocking bliss. His eyes went wide and glazed. Held's hand was coated in a thick liquid, burning hot, and when the shaft had softened and sagged from his fingers, he lifted them to taste Janez's pleasure. Bitter. Strange. Yet—alluring. The smell was stark and alien, and he wanted more of it.

Wanted more of—everything.

And of the way Janez stared up at him, mute and mysterious.

Held smoothed his fingers down that golden hair in secret kisses and knew that he was lost, now. Utterly lost.

For he would trade the world for that wide-eyed stare and the firm hand upon his rear—and he only had one more day to keep it.

Chapter Twenty

JANEZ ATTENDED THE war council the following evening.

He dressed in his finest uniform and called his grumbling manservant to fix his hair and face. He went armed, sword and sash slung about his hips pristinely. And he bowed low to both his king and his admiral, the face of a subordinate fixed in place over his own.

For Alarik would not like this.

Yesterday—the river—had been a mistake. Pure and simple. The flushed sight of Held in the grip of carnal pleasure had been too much, *far* too much, and Janez had taken risk in both hands—and mouth—and drunk it down. And now he was lost. Quite utterly lost. He had mixed both his feelings and his body, and now they clung together in a burning passion that was easing, in the quiet moments and in the colour of the sun in Held's near-white hair, into love.

And he was engaged to be married.

Janez knew his duty. To marry. To breed. And, one day, to die with honour and be buried in the family tombs underneath the castle.

But his duty was a cold and miserable one when love danced in dust motes around Held's face. How could he possibly do his duty to his wife when he wanted none but the stranger in Hauser's rooms? How could he feign an interest in some powdered princess when he'd held Held's weight upon his tongue and drunk his pleasure like he was no prince, but a parlour-boy in a harbour-side inn?

How could he be happy?

And Janez had no duty to be happy, no right to have happiness—but he wanted it. He wanted it, deeply and desperately, and why ought he have been shackled to duty when there were others? He wasn't the heir to the throne anymore. He would never be king. He was expendable— the spare heir Alarik had teased him about when they were boys. If he could be placed on the deck of a ship, placed in the path of enemy fire, then surely he could be placed in the path of passion, and his lapses forgiven as any peasant man's would have been?

He sat brooding and silent through discussions of tactic and territory, through the admiral's grumbling about the landsmen in the service and the first minister's simpering excuses that boiled down to the treasury running dangerously dry and there being debts to pay, new enemies to make if they were not paid—

"Winter will ease us," Alarik said. "They will have one last strike at us—one last attempt—and then there will be silence while the ice seals their ports."

"We must strike them then!" the admiral thundered. "Sail north and batter their batteries!"

Janez ignored the argument. Usually, he would have been on it—the benefits of doing so, the risks of running aground on icebergs as big as the ships themselves, the very real danger of exhausting themselves needlessly to be smashed to pieces in the spring, but the chance—the slim and sly chance—of crippling their enemy while they lay helpless.

But he did not. He sat in silence, aware of the curious looks, and said nothing.

"If it could not be done in my father's time, it cannot be done in this one," Alarik said. "Our best hope is the alliance. Who knows? Our spies say they struggle as we do—perhaps the very existence of such an alliance will suffice to silence them and bring about peace."

The admiral harrumphed—a military man from boots to bulbous nose, he thought of peace much as others thought of death and taxes: a terrible, insidious, disgusting thing.

"King Sigurd and his daughters are travelling to the Winter Palace for a ball in their honour. Janez will choose a bride from among them and be married by spring—sooner, if we can persuade King Sigurd to part with his nation's superstitions on winter weddings. And—"

"I cannot."

Janez spoke quietly into the great room, but the sharp silence was as though he had screamed it. The admiral's eyes bulged. The first minister squeaked like a trodden-upon mouse.

And Alarik simply—blinked.

Startled.

"Janez?"

"I cannot marry," Janez said, a little numbly. The phantom sensation of Held's skin against his lips prickled in memory.

"What on earth do you mean?"

"I cannot marry. I—I am in love. With another."

The first minister scoffed. "Love? What does love have to do with marriage?"

"Is your newfound love a lady of standing?"

"No—"

"A servant, then. Take her with you, for all I care," Alarik said. His attention swayed away. "None of the daughters are married as yet—potentially, a permanent alliance may be established if—"

"I cannot."

Janez's voice sounded a little firmer to his own ears, but it must have burst forth too sharply, for Alarik drew himself up, chest pushing outwards. His brows came down. And Janez knew, sure as he knew it was daylight outside the windows, that any chance of his brother listening to him had fled.

For this was no brother. This was a king.

"You are a prince," Alarik said. "Your duty is to your kingdom. Not your heart."

"All men have a right to love."

"Not you."

It seemed to slip out a little too raw, for Alarik winced the moment it escaped. And raw, it stabbed. Truth, yet it stabbed. It pierced Janez's chest cleaner than any sword. Cold and painful.

And his eyes narrowed in anger.

"Father did. As did you. Why must I marry a foreign princess while you lie with a noblewoman?"

He was making it worse, yet he couldn't stop himself. The pain—and the anger beginning to burn from the wound—spurred him on. And that, in turn, fuelled his king's ire, for those stormy blue eyes also narrowed, and the voice was like ice.

"Never. Speak of my wife. In that manner. Again."

Janez clenched his jaw. The room was pink about the edges. His breathing was too hard.

"You proposed this alliance, Janez. Why the sudden change of heart?"

"I was not in love then."

"It was but two weeks hence."

"Things have changed."

"Some whore or servant changes nothing."

"I cannot—"

"Greta changed nothing."

His blood ran cold. Greta. How dare he—*Greta.* His first love. The mother of his *child.* The child he had never seen, never known—did not know, even now, if he had some pretty girl or lanky boy roaming about the world, now near grown and likely discovering the joys of men and women for themselves. He could be a grandfather, for all he knew, and how *dare* Alarik throw Greta in his face like she'd been some common bitch.

"Leave us," Janez whispered.

The admiral shifted uneasily. The first minister looked a little green about the gills.

"Leave us!"

"You are not king here, Janez," came the sharp rebuke, and Janez lifted furious eyes to his bro—his king.

No brother. Not here. Not now.

"You will not wish any, not even your most trusted advisors, to hear what I have to say."

Alarik tensed.

For a long moment, there was nothing but silence. It rang in the room, clearer than any bell. A great oppressive thing, heavy and physical.

Then the chair scraped. The king rose. Crossed to the window. Hands clasped behind his back, he watched the busy hive of activity on the harbour and spoke slowly.

Coldly.

The king of a kingdom at war. He had no family in such a voice.

"Leave us."

This time, there was no hesitation. The admiral bowed out without so much as a word. The first minister, usually so particular, crammed his papers together and scurried after. The silent priest did not linger.

And then the great door closed, and they were alone.

"It is that foreign spy."

Janez knew better than to speak.

"You would betray your kingdom for a foreign spy."

"I betray nothing!"

"We have one chance, this alliance, and—"

"I am not your heir!" Janez exploded. He flew up from the table. The chair toppled, and crashed to the floor. "You have a daughter! A son! If

Sofia's complexion is to be believed, you will have a third before the summer comes! Why must I be the one sacrificed, when I have found love!"

"You have no right to love!"

Alarik's thunderous reply stopped Janez short.

"You have no right," Alarik repeated and finally turned from the window. "You may not be my direct heir, but Sigurd has no sons. Yours may well be future kings. This alliance would last for centuries—so do your damned duty, and—"

"Duty," Janez sneered. "I have done every duty you have ever demanded of me, and now this."

"You will always do every duty I demand of you. I am your king."

"I was your brother, once."

Alarik's jaw visibly tightened. He turned back to the window. His hands, still clasped behind his back, clutched about one another into tight fists and shook faintly.

"Other kings have young sons and would entertain Ingrid for many summers in hopes of a match. Yet more have infant daughters, who would make pretty wives in time for your boy. They know nothing of love. They can grow together with their betrothed and love them. But I— I *have* found it, I *do* know it, and you would—"

"I would have a prince of my kingdom do as he is ordered."

The reply twisted that shard of ice buried in Janez's chest, and he swallowed. Looked down at the table and his shaking hands, pale fists upon it.

"You would have your brother miserable for the rest of his days," Janez whispered. The truth—the pain, the anger, the burden of the second son only released from kingship in adulthood, too late to have enjoyed his youth—bled out like a suppurating wound. "You would make Father proud. Strip Janez of love, wherever he may find it, and condemn him to misery under the guise of a duty you yourself have never followed."

The movement flashed in the dim room. The blow was heavy and hard. The ring—the sigil of their people—slashed into Janez's jaw and left a great, gaping cut.

Slowly, painfully, Janez turned his face from window to his king's face.

And smiled.

It felt brittle. A bubble of blood burst and dripped down his cheek. His collar was damp.

And Alarik's face was stunned. Eyes wide and absurdly young.

"I have no right to love, *Your Majesty*, because the kings of my land forbid it," Janez said. "I have found it—twice—and twice it has been cut out from under me."

Alarik licked his lips. "Jan—"

"I will pick whichever bride can birth a son the earliest," Janez said icily, "and I will do my damned duty until she swells. And when she does, I will don my lieutenant's uniform and return to the sea, and then I will pray—day and night until some god listens—for the storms to drown me and release me."

"Janez!"

A violent hand caught at his shoulder. Janez tore it away.

"If misery is all my duty leaves me, then afford me the mercy of making it brief!" he bellowed. The room was a virulent scarlet. The pain in his chest was a spear that pierced right through. He would bleed ice water onto the stones and dissolve into naught but foam, like the mythological mermaids of old.

He tightened his heart about the cold and sealed it. Pulled his shoulder taut.

And clicked his heels. The prince. The lieutenant. A nameless, faceless man, to die a footnote in history, with no trace of any real life left behind.

"May I take my leave, Your Majesty?"

The words felt thick and foreign, like Held's garbled language. He so rarely used this address, so rarely spoke it—but then this was not his brother, staring at him from the other side of the war room table.

This was his king, and his king ordered him to be bartered for a treaty and a handful of lacklustre ships, with a spitting insult of duty.

Duty! Had Janez not done his duty in nearly drowning in their last skirmish? Had Janez not done his duty in visiting with the princesses in the first place? Had he not done his damned duty whenever it had been asked of him, from the day of his birth to this very instant?

His teeth ground against each another.

And he would do it again now. Because he had no choice.

"May I," he repeated stonily, "take my leave. Your Majesty."

Alarik looked oddly wounded. But then frowned. Jerked his head.

"Go. To the royal chambers."

"House arrest?"

The words escaped before Janez could prevent them. Alarik looked alarmed.

"You are not a prisoner, Janez."

"Am I not." It wasn't a question. And before his brother—his king—could utter a single word, Janez turned on his heel and marched out with all the stiff, brittle grace of a soldier on parade.

So tense that a single weight might snap him in two.

So angry that he wished for it.

Chapter Twenty-One

THE BEACH WAS cold and wreathed in shadows when Held reached it.

Janez had not returned by the time the air had turned its telltale grey and gold, so Held had slipped away with determination in his heart. This would not be the end. It must not. He would entreat with the Witch for more, for longer, for a whole lifetime. He could not leave this life and love behind, not for anything in the world. If she demanded his voice, his bones, his very soul, then Held would give it.

This would not be goodbye, so none was needed.

The sea was very cold, and Held settled up to his neck in the soft tide as the shadows grew longer and the temperature dropped yet further. Tiny sparkles of light began to show in a deep blue—and then it happened.

Pain.

A lancing pain that shot up both legs and drove him into the tide. Salt water filled his mouth. He choked on it and writhed, panicking. Blood. There was blood in the water. Pink and foamy. He lashed out at it and saw the edges of his fingers splitting apart, the skin frayed like fabric. The salt burned. He screamed and suffocated upon the sea. His bones ground together—knuckles drove fingers into one another; his hips wrenched, and his legs collided angrily. The sharp stones on the seabed stripped his skin. His chest hurt, hurt, hurt—and agony burst like fire in his ribs and spine, and gashes tore themselves, like claws from some invisible monster, into the flesh of his neck.

Water.

Oh, sweet water. He gulped at it, breathed it in, and sobbed past the agony in his legs. The salt scoured him; he felt scrubbed raw, fragile, and the terrible fitting of raw and unbridled pain dissolved into pathetic twitches as his very bones dissolved. The water was black with blood— he would die, he would die, surely he would die—and great holes burst open about his waist and chest as skin ballooned and gave birth to brims and breasts that he'd lacked for only three days, yet felt as terrible and alien as though he'd never had them at all.

The scales erupted like pox, great scabs of blood-soaked pain, and he curled in on himself and screamed until the shallows rippled with it. His fingers parted, the webbing thick and lumpy with clots and scars. Yet it was not the pain that tormented his mind as his form returned. It was not the blood or the strange feeling of water instead of air.

It was—

It was *her*.

The soft, supple back, finless and free. The lumpy misshapen chest. The soft arms and round shoulders. The wide hips and gentle belly.

The delicacy.

The *maid*.

He tore at that terrible chest and cried. It looked wrong; it felt wrong. It was not his, not him, not *Held*. This was Calla, and he was not her. He was not; he was not. He was—he—was—

Lost. Imprisoned. Trapped. This body was *wrong*, all of it, from its pretty frill to its soft face. He clutched at his hair—short, shorn, thankfully still so—and wrenched at it as though he could pull the maid away and find the man. He was there—he *was*. Inside somewhere, somewhere—

For the longest time, Held just—cried.

He'd never understood before, but—oh, this was not simply the love of the legend. He'd not been wrong for being a mermaid. He'd missed the sway of his hair, and the drift of the tide, and the strange leg-endings of skyfolk were nothing to be jealous of. But this was about *her* and *him*, and—

He was not her.

Had he ever been? Had all those years been down to this? That loathing of singing, of the high tone of his voice; that displeasure in swimming bare whilst no other seemed to mind; that strange sense of something being wrong when the odd merman had shown interest? That knowledge he was beautiful whilst being convinced he was ugly?

Had that been this?

If their roles were reversed, if the Witch were to change Janez into a merman and bring him down below the sky, would Held still feel so very bad? Yes, he realised. Yes, he would. It wouldn't matter that Janez could kiss him, touch him, be with him—it would be wrong, so very wrong, and it would be all because of her. Because this body was maid, not man. Because it felt like slipping into clothes several cuts too small and being told they were perfect.

Was it possible? For an entire body to be so misplaced? How could it be? He'd been born in it, grown in it; he was his body, and his body was him. Only...

Only the body was her, and Held was him, and that could not be.

It could not, it could not, it could not...

He lay, weak from blood loss and exhaustion, in the dark shallows for the longest time, the thoughts chasing one another like merlings in his mind. And they came back to the same inescapable fact.

He was her.

And he could not stomach the fact.

HE DIDN'T KNOW how many hours had passed before he finally moved.

The tide had turned, and Held had abandoned the shore, diving deep and straight until he hit a great wall of seaweed, tall and deep red in the gloom. There, he tore at the stems and bound them about his loathed chest like a bandage, trapped the bulging chest under layer upon layer until it ached to breathe, but he looked—and felt—a little more like himself.

And a lot less like Calla.

Once bound, he set out northwards.

The Witch had done it once, and she could do it again. She could turn him into a skyman—and if the potion always must be temporary, then perhaps she had another to keep Held a man. To banish Calla, and this terrible, ill-fitting form, and bind him to himself. To separate him from her, enshrine one and dissolve the other.

He would give anything. Anything at all.

And so he swam straight for the Whalelands. She had ordered it, but he'd have gone regardless. The sea was dark and dour, so very unlike the bright brilliance of the world above the sky. He'd missed home, yet it was nothing to the fierce agony of separation. There was no Janez here. There could be no merman even close to his brightness. The Witch had been wrong—the men who walked on water were wonderful creatures, incredible beings, and Held loved one with every fibre of any form he'd ever known.

And so he swam straight and hard, against pain and exhaustion, for the Whalelands.

The season was changing. The sea was cooler than before. He hugged the seabed as the ice-clouds began to pierce the sky. If ice-clouds had come, then the orcas would have too, so Hold slowed and swam carefully as the distance closed.

And then the white towers began to jut from the earth, and Held could have wept.

"Witch!" he called, diving into the courtyard and swirling about the central column. "Witch! I need you! Please! I need your help!"

Silence met him.

"I came back, as you said! And—and it's not enough, I need to go back, I *need* to—"

Silence.

"*Please!*"

A great pain was welling up in his chest again. Desperation. He begged the empty sky and untamed gardens; he pleaded with the columns and the ceilings. Send him back, make him a man again, let him go, please-please-please—

"And why," came the voice—finally, finally, that blessed, terrible voice, "should I help you again?"

Held whirled. She lay atop the central point again, draped as languidly as before.

"I'll do anything," he begged. "Anything—anything!"

"You have nothing I am interested in," she said idly, rolling onto her back. "Begone. You have had your fun."

"I love him!"

A laugh. "How terribly nice. I think you will find that I still have no interest in your little love affairs."

"This—this is wrong, this form, this being, *me*—"

She turned back over, and squinted at him. "This form? It is exactly the same as before."

"Exactly!"

Her eyebrows rose up her pale face.

"Explain."

It was a demand. And Held acquiesced.

"I became a man. Up there. I wasn't a skymaid, I was a skyman."

"Of course," the Witch said. "My husband brewed it. He had no interest in becoming a woman. Of course it turns the drinker into a man."

"Changing back was—was—" Held struggled to find the words. "I'm not this. I'm not her. I'm *him*. It was—every bad thing I've ever felt, every time I've hated something I couldn't even define about myself—it went away when I was a man. I'm *him*. I'm not her, I'm *him*, and I can't—I can't—please don't make me stay like this. *Please*."

The Witch's face was entirely blank.

Slowly, she shook her head.

Held's chest caved in. "Please!" he begged and felt the savage pain rising in his throat. "I can't do this, I can't be this, please, please, there must be something, *something*—"

"Oh, there is something," the Witch said very slowly.

She let go of the plinth. Drifted, oh-so-slowly, to peer into Held's face and touch his shorn hair.

"There is something, indeed," she said. "I could make you a skyman. I could. But are you ready for that?"

"Yes!"

"*Are* you?"

"W-what do you mean?"

"You have not yet learned the truth about what you now are."

"What—what am I?"

"Homeless."

"W-what?"

"If you do this—if you shed this form and take on another in permanence—sky or mer, but man, whichever you choose—then you will lose everything under the sky you have ever held dear."

Her words were cool. Chilling.

And Held caught his breath.

"My home?"

"Your home. Your sisters. Your father. Your clan. Your very flesh and blood will tear you limb from limb and drink your spilled blood."

"W-why?"

"You wish to become the enemy."

"The e-enemy?"

"Humans are the enemy."

"But...but Father said...Father said skymen are—are legends."

"No." The Witch drew herself up. "Did you never wonder, my little mermaid, why I would help you?"

He—yes. Oh, he hadn't wanted to, and certainly hadn't asked, but he'd wondered.

"Why would I care if the great king's daughter found out about humans and fell in love with one? And why would I *help* her?"

"Why?" Held whispered.

"Your father."

"Father?"

"Your father made me a widow."

"He—"

No. No, it couldn't be.

"It was your father who banished my husband to live amongst the humans in the first place, as punishment for bestowing their fishing fleets with luck. Your father who left him to die alone on the land, as vengeance for being their friend. Your father who has forbidden the merfolk to speak of them, to swim to the surface, to know anything about the world above the sea."

"But—but—that's not—that can't be true!"

"Oh, but it is."

"But *why*?"

A thin, cold smile curved the Witch's lips.

"Your father has seen your pretty little clouds fall from the sky before. And the last cloud to fall killed a mermaid. A beautiful mermaid, with hair like the brightest coral."

Mother.

"Go home, Calla. Find out who you were. And then—only then—decide who you *are*."

Chapter Twenty-Two

HELD HAD GOTTEN wind of something and fled.

Janez didn't blame him. He was—glad of it. In a way. After his outburst, Alarik likely would have had the man arrested and thrown into a cell to be tortured for information.

The little room he'd kept in Hauser's quarters was neat and tidy, his meagre things gathered and gone. He'd vanished like a ghost.

Janez knew the signs of someone taken—the chaos, the torn-apart rooms in which they'd stayed, and the sombre silence of the guards. There was none of it. Held had run under his own power, and wherever he'd gone, he'd be safer there. Janez was certain he'd know if Held were held, for after their argument, Alarik would undoubtedly summon him to watch the interrogation.

But he mourned the loss, too.

With Father dead and Mother in the Winter Palace, and now this rift between king and prince, what reason did Janez have to stay? He couldn't bear to enter the royal chambers, for fear of Alarik's anger following him there, or Sofia's chiding. He retreated, rather, to Doktor Hauser's quarters. And then, at first light, he fled the palace entirely for the ships, donning his lieutenant's jacket and saluting his captain properly as the sun came up, weak and sickly over the horizon.

"Good," the captain said with utmost disinterest. "Let us practice the guns."

So Janez spent the day at sea—oh, not far, a mere hour from shore, but at sea all the same. In a world apart from kings and arranged marriages—in a world ruled entirely by the silver epaulette on the captain's shoulder. A world where Janez's duty was to the ship, and whatever emotions he had about whatever persons were irrelevant. Defend the ship or die trying. That was all.

Sometimes, he wished royal duty were as simple.

He wondered bitterly if it wouldn't have been easier if Held had left him lashed to the gun, and the sea had taken him like it had taken Father. He'd long since resigned himself to an arranged marriage, which hadn't seemed so bad when he hadn't been in love. Now—

Now, it was as though he was bound by a different set of rules. As though Father and Alarik—and even the children, much as Janez wouldn't wish his position upon them—could love whom they would and marry if they so desired, and all would be well, but Janez was a tool, rather than a man.

And tools could—would—be discarded.

He steeled himself as the gunnery practice ceased, and the captain stalked critically amongst the men, snapping his displeasure at the slow rate and poor accuracy. He'd give Held a few days to reappear. If he didn't, Janez would retreat to the Winter Palace, meet his bride, marry, and succumb to the inevitable and terrible drudgery and misery of his future.

But he would not return to the summer fortress.

He wasn't so desperate to stay as his brother's compass, if said brother thought so little of him to damn him to a loveless existence. If Alarik cared nothing for him, then Janez would go where people did. Mother loved him, and always had. He would remain with mother until marriage, and then either he would stay and rear his own family there under the shadow of the mountains, or he would go with his new wife to a foreign kingdom, and forge an entirely new life. Whichever one he chose, he would bring Held, too, if he were to be found again.

And Alarik could forge his next alliance alone, using people he cared for more than Janez, perhaps.

When the *Ente* returned to the harbour, therefore, Janez didn't go ashore until nightfall—and when he did, he went to the narrow alley, to Rosa, and found comfort in her plump arms.

"My Karl," she crooned when he'd been calmed and sated. "So very angry tonight, yes?"

"Yes," he agreed placidly, closing his eyes and imagining her fingers combing through his hair to be Held's.

"You have troubles. See this tension, see-see, here." She began to knead his shoulders, and he sighed. "You need no tension. Too young for tension."

"I wish," Janez said sourly and was reprimanded by a bitten ear. He chuckled tiredly, shrugging out of the grip of her teeth, but the massage continued. "I have no right to love, it seems."

"Have right to much love, if you have the gold," she said coyly, and a smile flickered and died upon his face.

"Not your kind of love, Rosa. True love."

"Is true for two gold coins."

He laughed and finally rose from the bed, reaching for his trousers.

"I won't be back."

"No more Karl?"

"No more Karl," he agreed, and sighed. "I have to marry. Whether I want to or not."

"She will love you fine," Rosa predicted with a salacious smile.

"But I won't love her."

"In time, in time..."

"I love another."

She blinked, and then the cheer dipped into something a touch more tender.

"I love another, but duty says I have to marry a stranger."

"Then," Rosa murmured, reaching up to caress him through his breeches. "Perhaps duty is wrong this time, yes? Karl does duty at sea all day and all night—I smell the salt on him. Perhaps on land, Karl has no duty but to himself, yes?"

Oh, how he wished it.

"Yes," he lied anyway and stooped to kiss her one last time.

HE ALMOST MADE it back to Doktor's rooms.

Almost.

He was on the top step when the great doors closed, and his name was called by a voice he fervently did not wish to hear. But he'd made the mistake of pausing, and so was lost.

Alarik would know he'd heard.

"Your Majesty?" he called, not turning.

"Janez, please."

"It is late," Janez insisted, still refusing to move. "I must retire."

"We must speak first."

Janez clenched his fingers on the banister and finally turned. Alarik hadn't risen to meet him. Brothers stared at one another across the entirety of the staircase, suddenly strangers.

"Why the change of heart, brother?"

"What difference would my answer make?" Janez asked.

"I wish to understand—"

"And I gave an explanation that you could. A true one. If you didn't understand in that meeting, then repeating myself now won't help."

"Janez, please, don't be angry with—"

"With the king who orders me to needless misery, or the brother who would see me unloved!"

"That is not true!" Alarik exploded.

"Then tell me where I am wrong!" Janez spat and turned his back anew. The guards shifted uneasily as he burst through the doors, ignoring the command from Alarik to return. They'd come to blows, Janez knew.

Perhaps Alarik knew, too, for he didn't pursue.

Just as Janez thought he could breathe again, not a corridor away, a lantern flared in the gloom, and a soft voice called to him from the darkness. No guard. They stood stern and still, as they did at all hours, but the voice was a woman's. Sofia's. And Janez knew entirely what to expect.

Yet he stopped all the same.

"Where have you been?" Sofia asked, gliding from one of the many drawing rooms to join him in the corridor. The moonlight streaming through the window illuminated her hair, which hung in loose curls about her face. "And where are you going now, so late?"

"To bed," he replied shortly.

"Your rooms are not this way."

"My rooms are unforgivably close to the king's."

She flinched at the title, and her hand clasped lightly at his sleeve. "Janez—"

"If you'll excuse me, Your Highness, it's been a long day."

Her grip tightened.

"No. Janez, please, come to your family."

His jaw clenched. "My family are at the Winter Palace."

She let go then, sharp, and with a small gasp.

"We are your family!"

"The king has made it abundantly clear that you are not."

"He was very upset. He spoke out of turn—"

"He said I have no right to love, Sophie!"

The pet name burst out without thought, and he cursed himself for the slip. Her expression was torn in two, both worried and infuriated, and he turned from her.

"Give Ingrid my morning kiss tomorrow."

"You will deliver it yourself," she said and seized his elbow. "Do not turn from me, Janez!"

He shook her off. The guard at the next set of doors frowned.

"My king follows the thoughts of our father. I am not permitted love. I fall in love, and the object of my affections must be immediately removed from me. Tell me, *Your Highness*, how is that family?"

Her jaw hung loose, and he pressed viciously on.

"I am not so pathetic as to seek home from those who'd wish to see me miserable for all my days. I will do my damned duty, Your Highness, and you can assure him of it, but as long as I am but a tool for the king's—any king's—use, then this is not my home and the people within its walls are not my family," he spat.

"You are not a tool, Janez, you are—"

"A piece to be bartered," he returned. "I didn't learn my lesson from Father. Perhaps I never thought His Majesty to be so cruel as his predecessor, but clearly I was wrong. So I'll go to the Winter Palace, I'll go to *my family* and the poor days I can eke with Mother alone, to remind myself that I haven't been entirely loveless, and then I'll do my damned duty and marry. And the moment the unlucky bride is with child, my duty is done. And then the sea can have me, as she should have done at that battle."

"Janez! Do not encourage death, do not—"

"I encourage nothing," Janez returned and threw off her grasping hand. "I only ask for release. And if my only freedom is in the face of enemy cannon fire, then so be it."

He stormed through the doors, slamming them in the queen's wide-eyed face, and leaned against them for a long moment, simply to breathe.

Tomorrow was Sunday. Church. None would acquiesce to begin travel upon a Sunday.

But the day after—

He would go.

Chapter Twenty-Three

THE NEST ROSE out of the darkness like a beacon, welcoming Held home.

A familiar sight, as were the soft sounds of the clan settling to sleep. They ought to have warmed him, ought to have filled him with contentment, with safety, with the sensation of all being right with the world.

They did not.

They hadn't seen the things he'd done. They'd never seen clouds and the skymen swarming over them. They'd never touched that violently hot skin, or touched that fine, warm hair. They knew nothing.

And they knew nothing because of Father.

It couldn't be true—yet Held had to ask why not.

How had none thought to try to touch the sky before, when it was so possible? How, if the skymen could command the clouds so, had none fallen before? How had Father been so stern and certain, and told him to stop asking questions so soon?

But then—

It couldn't be possible. People would not just forget. Not if—not if—

Mother.

Oh, but it was, wasn't it? Who would tell the tiny merling children of a widowed and grieving king why their mother had died?

Held didn't remember losing Mother. He remembered her song, a soft and gentle thing that had murmured to them in the night and caressed them to sleep with its soothing tones. He remembered the way she'd beaded her hair in tiny shells and stones, and the brilliant colour of it, just like Meri's.

And then he'd been a merm—older, and Mother was gone. He didn't quite remember when she'd died, simply that...she had. He'd been too small, barely three hands long. He'd always assumed she'd gotten sick and died, just as so many had done in a crowded nest like theirs.

The Witch could be lying.

She could be. She hated Father for banishing her husband, but her husband had brewed potions to walk upon the shore. He'd obviously been a powerful sorcerer. What if he had killed Mother? What if—

But why would the Witch hate Father so, and then help Held?

"Calla!"

The shriek went up, jarring Held from his thoughts. For a wild moment, the name seemed to belong to someone else as well, and then a guard had him by the arm, and he was being swept upwards. A crowd. Chattering and repeating his—*her*—name, over and over again, and it sounded alien. Foreign. So unlike the rasping deepness of a dry voice; so unlike the harsh stop-start rumble of the skymen's tongue.

And then Meri screamed and was wrapped around Held's chest in a tight embrace.

"Where did you *go*?" she demanded, her voice shrill and loud and painful in Held's ear. "Where have you been. We were so *worried!*"

Held pushed her off with numb hands, already looking about. Half the nest were gathering. They had paused at the mouth of the palace courtyard.

"I need—I need to speak to Father. Privately. It's urgent."

Meri's face twisted into a puzzled frown. "Privately? Why? Where did you go?"

"It's a *boy*, isn't it?" Balta chirped, eyes wide. "You found a boy! Is it the same boy as before?"

"I—well—yes, but—"

Balta squealed. Meri, by contrast, paled to a sickly mottled green.

"You ran away for a merman? We thought orcas might have seized you! Why would you run away, is he—" She lowered her voice, though the point when they were so surrounded was lost on Held. "—from some other clan?"

"I—well—*sort* of—"

"Calla!"

The name skittered on his ears. It jarred, like Doktor in a temper. He flinched, almost without noticing.

"Father won't be pleased. He'll—"

"Calla."

The deep boom and rumble of Father's voice sank into Held's very bones and shook them, but it was that rare sound from Father: pleased.

The guards scattered before him, and then his arms were about Held like he was a mere merling again, and Father hadn't yet transcended into this cold, angry king.

Like when Mother was still alive.

Held stiffened in the grasp. Did he know? Had he always known about the world above the sky?

"Leave us!"

The nest retreated, with many a backward glance. Father towed Held into the great courtyard by the wrist, before whirling on him in the relative privacy of his sisters and the royal guard alone, and asking—rather than demanding, for once—where he had gone.

"There was a boy!" Balta volunteered, and Held threw her a venomous look.

"Some merman? Is that what's happened to your hair? Well—who was it?"

"I—I can't say…"

Father frowned. "Calla. You are a young mermaid approaching her prime. I have been…expecting this sort of thing to happen. Now, tell me who he was, and we can deal with the matter sensibly. You cannot go wandering off to—"

"It wasn't a merman."

There was a pregnant pause. Held could see Father's mind working, and he cringed back. How to say it? How to—

"A…mermaid, then?"

Balta squeaked. Meri's face pinched tight.

"No, Father."

A breath of relaxation. Then Held opened his mouth, and—

You will be homeless, the Witch whispered in his memory.

—said it.

"A skyman."

Meri closed her eyes.

"A—what?" Father said dumbly.

"There—there was a—I met a skyman. And he's *everything*, Father. He's so—"

"A *what*?"

Held swallowed. The quiet tone was rising. Brewing. A storm was coming, but—how could he not say it? How could he condemn himself, through lies or silence, to never knowing the truth?

To never seeing Janez again?

The very thought sent a shard of sharp pain through his grotesque and misshapen chest, unstopping the words.

"I went to the sky," Held said carefully, "and I—"

"This again." Father's voice dropped.

"It's true."

"It is ridiculous. You can tell me where you've been, or you can keep silent, but I will not tolerate lying."

Held ground his jaw.

"I'm not *lying*."

"There's no such thing as—"

"I walked amongst them, Father!"

It burst from Held's mouth, and Father reeled back. His chest puffed out, so like Doktor in his tempers, and Held wanted to cry all over again. If Father would only listen, only see, then he would understand how very alike they were, how very much he resembled Janez's men. With cleaved fingers and legs, yes, but skymen were simply—simply dry mermen, weren't they?

And Held had been one of them. A skyman. A *man*.

"They're beautiful and clever and brave—they fight these great clouds that spit fire—they have a language—listen, listen, I learned—"

A hand thumped into a column, and the water shuddered.

"Enough!"

Held fell mutinously silent. Balta, wide-eyed at Father's side, looked afraid. Meri wore an expression of tired disappointment, and Held bit his tongue furiously. What did pious Meri know? Held had sought out the truth. Held had seen the Witch. Held had *walked*, even danced, learned a smattering of words of the skymen's tongue, had a whole new name and body for three wonderful, joyous days...

"No more lies."

"They're not lies!" he burst out.

"They are lies, Calla!" Father bellowed. "There is nothing up there. We. Are. Alone."

"Then where did the cloud come from? Who made it sink?" And the bitter look of sorrow on a terribly beautiful face flashed bright in his memory. A half story. "What killed Mother? Where did the Witch's husband go?"

Father's eyes bulged. His mouth gaped soundlessly. The silence that shivered around the throne room was tenuous and trembling.

Too far.

Oh, he'd gone too far.

The entire courtyard held its breath. The royal guard stared openly, their deference abandoned. Balta had fled to a high, safe perch, and peered down with terrified eyes. Meri was white as the men above, her coral-bright hair—Mother's hair, just like Mother's hair—a violent hue in contrast.

Silence.

"A cloud killed Mother, didn't it?" Held whispered.

The question shivered through the water and disappeared. The guards, as one, cringed. Father's eyes widened.

"A cloud killed Mother."

Oh, but it was true. It was so very true.

And Father had—had—

"And you...you moved us away. And you banished the Witch's husband for—for helping skymen. And—"

"Silence."

Father's voice was barely a breath.

"You have been to the Witch."

"Y-yes."

"You have been to Ahtola. To the Whalelands."

"Y-yes, Father. But—"

"Travel north of our borders is treason." His words were ice-cold, and fear curled in Held's stomach, sickly and thick. "Fraternisation with the Witch is treason. She is a dangerous beast, and you have—what? What have you done, Calla?"

What had he done?

He had—

Found the truth. Found another world. Found love.

Found *Held*.

Found himself.

"Everything," Held breathed.

"What have you *done?*"

Father bellowed the final word. The very seaweed in the gardens rumbled. The entire ocean seemed to be watching. Waiting.

"She helped me."

"She helps none."

"She helped *me*. I—I fell in love with a skyman, and she gave me a potion to become one, so I could—"

Father's face twisted in horror. "You *love* one of those disgusting creatures?"

Held seized on it. "Then you admit they're real!"

"They are murderous vermin!" Father exploded. His hand swept out; the clenched fist struck the column again, and great chips of stone were torn free in a mess of blood. Another blow cracked the great support, and then he bore down upon Held, thirty hands of terrible rage. "They have speared and slaughtered thousands of our kind! They turn the sea red and feast upon the bones of whales! They killed your *mother*!"

They had killed her. Oh, seas, the Witch had spoken true. They had killed Mother.

But—

But that was not right. If the cloud had come down and crushed her, as the Witch had said, then the skymen hadn't done that. They'd—they'd killed it, felled it, but—they didn't follow their quarry.

They just threw it down.

It had been an accident, then.

All this, for an *accident*?

"I would see you drowned before I'd let my daughter pledge allegiance to any crab-legged shark! I would see this entire nest bled upon the banks before I'd let those vile beasts have an inch of this kingdom!"

Held reeled.

Drowned?

"You would—you would rather I were dead than love him?"

You will be homeless, the Witch cackled in his mind. *Homeless, homeless, homeless. You cannot have both, my dear little mermaid. You can never have both.*

"Guards!"

"Father!"

His arms were seized, but he didn't struggle, staring in horror at his father. At his beloved father, who had played with them as merlings, who had let them sit in his throne and at his fins during important business, who made time each morning and night to breakfast with them, and wish them good dreams to sleep.

At the raging king before him, gills gaping wide in raging breaths, who would rather his d—son lay dead than loved.

Who had lied to him about the existence of skymen. Who had—and oh, the story was true, wasn't it?—banished the Witch's husband to die alone upon the shore, after a great cloud had fallen from the sky and killed Mother.

"You let her husband die!" Held blurted out and began to writhe against the guards. "You would let *me* die! You—"

"Shut her in the caves until she comes to her senses."

"No! Father, *no!*"

Held screamed, then. Just screamed. And the guards dragged him mercilessly to the cell-caves at the base of the palace, teetering on the very edge of the clan nest. Balta could only stare back, eyes wide and frightened. Meri looked away entirely, shielding her face with her hair. And Father—

Father looked back with such hatred, such violent *hatred*—

The guards thrust Held into the cave, a narrow hole barely large enough for even this small, feminine frame, and one held him down while the others moved the great rock above it.

"No!"

Held fought when he was released. The slap was hard. He tasted blood in his mouth, reeled back—and that was all it took.

The rock scraped into place over the mouth of the hole, blotting out all but a tiny ring of light around its surface, so thin not even his fingers would slide through the gap. And when he beat his hands numb against its pitted surface, it refused to move an inch.

In the blinding darkness, Held screamed until his voice gave out, screamed until the rasp and choke sounded as deep and alien as his voice upon the shore, screamed until surely even the skymen, high above him, could hear.

And then, when he had nothing left to give, he curled his arms about himself and sank to the bottom of the hole, the great crack of pain from tail to temple threatening to split his very soul in two and consume him.

Chapter Twenty-Four

"HAVE YOU EVER been married, Doktor?"

The question came about in the early morning. They were breaking their fast together on the balcony behind the kitchens, overlooking the frosty garden, and Janez interrupted the lecture upon the evils of mushrooms with a question he wasn't sure why he was asking, nor why he'd never asked before. Yet, quite suddenly, he wished to know.

For Hauser, it occurred to Janez, must have had life before Janez did. He'd birthed both king and prince, though he was not yet fifty and looked far younger. His soft tones were from the mountains; his cheap grubbiness about his clothes spoke of a meagre upbringing, rather than any aristocracy, and in all of Janez's years, he'd not once seen the good doctor with a respectable wig upon his scalp.

Who had he been before he became the doctor?

"Yes," Hauser said and returned to his diatribe. "In the villages where I was reared, mushrooms were—"

"And where was that?"

Hauser huffed impatiently. "The borderlands, boy. But another mile and a half, and I'd have been serving another king entirely, and have brought a smarter prince than you into the world."

Janez pulled a face at the mention of it.

"Now, there, mushrooms are rare—the cold, you see—and those that *do* grow—"

"So, where are your wife and family?"

A raw chuckle, almost a croak, escaped the doctor's throat. "Wife and family? I think not."

"But you said you're married."

"I *was* married. No longer."

Janez paused. "I'm sorry."

"I'm not," the doctor said.

"No?"

"No. I needed to pay passage to the capital, to begin my medical studies. Her father was a coachman. He would give no free ride to some upstart student with delusions of grandeur—but to his son-in-law, now, that was a very different matter."

"So you married her for...a ride?"

"For several, if we include every meaning of the word." The doctor chuckled darkly and shook his head. "She was as wild a wench as I was thickheaded. She needed a man to keep her growing belly respectable, and I was once very well thought of—don't laugh so, you'll choke—and fit the bill quite nicely. We wed and moved to the capital. She birthed a girl—supposedly mine, though I've never touched a woman such in my life—and once I had my place in the university and she her little apartment above the river, we parted ways without a word. For all I know, she is still there."

"So—you didn't love her?"

"I barely even liked her."

Janez pushed his bacon about the plate, pondering it.

"Loving a wife is all well and good," Hauser said, "but it is hardly necessary if the marriage is to serve a higher purpose."

"And what higher purpose did yours serve?"

"It allowed me to attend at the university and become a surgeon," he said evenly. "That ring, that signature to falsify a birth certificate, has saved a hundred lives or more by now. And quite likely it paved the way for a better life for the baby. A whore's daughter is no existence, in the city or the country."

"But she will be a doctor's daughter."

"Quite so."

Janez shook his head. "My daughters must be my own."

"Greta proves that loving a woman will be no great hardship for you."

Janez looked up sharply. Hauser simply stared back, unafraid and unashamed, with those great cold eyes.

"I'd have married her, then, if given the chance."

"You would be quite miserable now."

"Probably," Janez allowed. "But then—if never separated, perhaps I'd never have fallen out of love?"

"I doubt that very much," Doktor Hauser said. "You were barely more than a child. And who knows? Perhaps over time, you will come to love her."

"Did you ever love, Doktor?"

The pause was longer, and Janez waited almost with bated breath. Had he? This man who was so single-mindedly devoted to his work? Who could fly into a rage about the mere act of wearing shoes in a sauna room, or dissolve into a passionate diatribe about the godliness of salt-water scrubs upon the skin?

Had he ever torn himself free for long enough to love?

"Yes," Hauser said. "Once."

"Just once?"

"Yes."

"What happened?"

Hauser's lips pursed. "I suppose one would say it was not meant to be."

Janez frowned. It couldn't have been station—a village boy rising to the king's own surgeon was meteoric and spoke of disdain for such things. More likely, it'd been something more personal. More hurtful.

"She...loved someone else?"

"No, no...they were merely uninterested in what any man had to offer."

Janez had played enough at tight discretion to catch the shift apart from 'she,' and blinked in quiet surprise. Good Lord. The way he softened for the women of the castle, from Sofia to the scullery maids, Janez had thought quite the opposite.

Yet—it made sense, did it not? Such a thing was a far more intensely private matter than a love for a woman, and so much rarer to see reciprocated.

"Did you—love...them, enough to marry?"

"No, no, nothing so intense," came the dismissive reply. "I am hardly a romantic, in my field."

Janez swallowed, glancing down.

"Could you marry again, if you didn't love?"

"Me?"

"Yes."

"Yes."

The reply was simple. True. And a lump swelled in Janez's throat.

"I do not want to marry, Doktor."

The truth whispered free. It disappeared into the cold rustle of the trees below them, and the doctor's face twisted in a rare show of sympathy.

"It is your place, Your Highness."

"The rest of my life married to a stranger?"

"She will not be a stranger for the rest of your life."

"You could walk away from your wife. I cannot."

"Oh, but you can. All you need to do is put a child in her belly, and your duty is done. Quite likely after the agony of bearing it to you, she will be as glad to see the back of you as you of her. I feel for her more than I do for you."

"Don't you always?" Janez asked, mock-sourly, and cast his gaze further to the iron-grey sea beyond the walls. "Held ran away. Sometimes, I want to do the same."

"The alliance is needed. Much as we both wish it were not."

Janez's mouth tightened.

"I am not the only way it can be found."

"You would sacrifice your niece or nephew instead?"

It would be cruel of him to put a child in his position, yet—

"Yes."

Because the baby—should he live to his naming day—would be the crown prince for his entire life. And little Ingrid was a princess, destined for such marriages. They would spend their entire lives in that knowledge. They would never know anything else but their destiny.

Janez had not done that. He'd always been the second son, the spare. There'd never been a question of him becoming king, aside from some terrible accident, and Alarik's love match to Sofia had promised babies from the very beginning.

Janez had tasted freedom—despite his father's iron fist, despite Greta. He'd gone to sea. Lost himself in Rosa's arms. Had *Held*.

By all rights, he ought to be left in peace. His naval career would have brought the honour that the family required of him. He needn't father children and create future usurpers of his brother's throne. He could have been a man first, and a prince second.

To have it snatched away by a king who'd married for love, in the great shadow of a dead father who'd done the very same—

And to be matched like *this*, to be the son-in-law to a king who'd wedded a servant girl from some southern kingdom with year-round sun...

It was intolerably unfair, much as it made Janez feel like a sulking child for saying so.

"It's their birthright, not mine."

"If the king would not listen to such then, he will not now," Doktor warned.

"He threatened to have me married by proxy if I refused to go."

"Then if I were you, I would pick the best of the options given to me and attempt to learn to love her."

"That can't be done, Doktor."

"Learn to love? Oh, but it can."

"Not," Janez said, still staring at the flat sea and heavy fog above it, "when one is already in love."

He said no name.

But then, he rather imagined Doktor did not need to hear one.

"YOUR MAJESTY."

Alarik glanced up from his papers at the guard, frowning.

"Captain Kühe to see you."

"Send him in."

Alarik cleared the more sensitive letters from his desk as the captain marched in, and gestured for him to sit, signalling the cup-bearer for wine.

"It's that foreigner, Your Majesty."

"Which foreigner?"

"The one under the prince's protection."

Alarik narrowed his eyes. "What about him?"

"He's gone."

"Gone?"

"Yes, Your Majesty."

"What do you mean, gone?"

"I mean, Your Majesty, I've, ah...I asked one of the servants—very loyal man, very, absolutely trustworthy, sir—"

"Get to the point."

"Yes, Your Majesty. Ah. I was informed earlier today that the foreigner appears to have left."

"Left?"

"His things are gone, and so is he."

"Janez is—"

"With Doktor Hauser, last I heard, Your Majesty."

There was that. Alarik sat back, tugging on his beard a little. So the spy had fled. But Janez remained, apparently unharmed.

"Send someone to check. Quietly. I won't have him know."

"Yes, Your Majesty."

Would the spy return? It would be utterly stupid of him. And if he did, Janez would likely find excuse for that, too.

"If he comes back, or he is seen elsewhere," Alarik said, "then have him followed. Do not intercept him. I want to know what he's looking for."

"Yes, Your Majesty."

"Dismissed."

Alarik stared into the middle distance as the door closed behind the captain. So the spy had moved. Why? What had he learned? Or had he never intended to be in the palace, but elsewhere?

And yet—

It still did not answer Janez's question.

What kind of a spy would save the prince's life?

Chapter Twenty-Five

IT COULD HAVE been a thousand years, or a mere thousand seconds, before the stillness was disturbed.

And when it was, it wasn't light that broke it, but sound.

Beyond the rock of his prison, trumpets were blowing. And it was no ceremonial pomp or celebratory joy.

They were the klaxons of war.

Slowly, Held uncurled this—her, not his, so *this*—bruised and bloodied body from its bed on the slimy stone and pressed broken hands flat against the rock that kept him here. He could hear Father bellowing orders, but not their content. He could hear the trumpets growing louder and more insistent.

Something was coming.

What would happen if the nest were attacked? They'd been attacked before—orcas, other clans, even a whale maddened by sickness once— and they usually abandoned it for a time until the threat passed. Would Father leave him here to starve and die? Or did he intend that regardless, even if they never moved more than a foot from the mouth of Held's grave?

A racking sob rose in his chest, violent and hurt. His own father would kill him. His own father would rather he were dead than have found love.

The trumpets petered out in squeaks and belches. Face pressed to the cold stone, Held felt the water shiver with a great power.

And then a voice.

A voice he *knew*.

He couldn't hear the words—but she was here. The Witch. The Witch had come to their nest. She'd come for—

For what?

For *him*?

The thought rocked him to the very core—yet it was true, for the rock shuddered under his palms, and he'd barely released it before the whispering film of ice crept around its surface. In a matter of moments, it was covered—and then the ice cracked, rent it asunder, and it crumbled to the cave floor like sand.

The light burned.

Beyond it, when Held crept from his prison, squinting, a great shadow towered in the centre of the courtyard, as it had in the Whalelands. A great mermaid in a sea foam dress, that terrible beauty carved from the very marble of her home.

And tangled in the frayed hems of the dress, caught tight like prey in a squid's tentacles, struggled Held's sisters.

His heart stopped.

"No," he whispered. "No, no, let them go, please, let them go!"

The Witch smirked. Her beauty turned ugly all at once, like a macabre statue upon a wall. Like the stone mermaid jutting from the beak of the cloud, eaten alive above the sky.

"There you are, dear," she crooned, as though a mother to a child. "Come here. Come to me."

The courtyard was ringed with guards, spears trained but still, afraid to strike the princesses. Father towered above them, rigid with rage but for the faint tremble of his sword—yet his vast length, his enormous bulk, was nothing compared to the Witch.

She was an immense shadow of power, and it oozed from her like blood, bright from an open wound.

Father was afraid. For his nest? For his daughters? For Held?

The tremble did nothing as Held drifted from the lip of the prison to the Witch's side. And it did nothing when a hand cold as death clasped about Held's throat and choked him, flattening his gills until the very water was cut off, and shook him like a caught cod.

"I give your little mermaid love, and what does her father do? He shuts love in a tomb to die, and calls this pathetic little corner of the seabed the world!"

Her voice boomed and bounced off the great stone pillars and shattered the silence across the bank. The guards tightened. Father did not move.

"I gave your little mermaid truth, and her father calls her a liar."

Silence rang out a second time. The fingers loosened. Held took a great breath—and then they tightened again, suffocatingly so.

"Perhaps it is time the king paid for his arrogance."

"Release my daughters," Father boomed, "and you will not be harmed, Witch."

A great sneer curled her lip.

"Harmed? By—what? Mutant fish? I think not."

The hand vanished. A frond of seaweed, thick and tough as old rope, caught about Held's wrists—and then the water surged. The frond tightened, and he was jerked upwards through the water. Below him, Balta screamed. And then they were being dragged in the Witch's dress, high above the nest.

The seabed fell away. The water brightened and warmed. Below them writhed the guards, tiny dots struggling to keep up. Father's terrible cry of anger echoed after them.

He turned his face towards the light and thought of Janez. Imagined the warmth of his skin. The softness of his hair.

Wanted.

His stomach twisted, and he fought the frond. If he could slip away now, then he could go to the Whalelands and wait for her. He would never escape Father again, not now the Witch had come into their territory and threatened his sisters. He would never—

The terrible drag ceased. For a moment, he floated up as though free. And then the frond was reeled in, and those cold, deathly hands caressed his face like a mother to a young child.

"Who are you, my dear?"

Held stared into that terrible face and knew the truth.

"Held."

"And what is that?"

"A man. A skyman."

"And where are your family?"

Family?

He glanced down at his sisters, who stared back with wide-eyed faces. He looked further, to the blur of his father approaching.

Father had imprisoned him, for love.

Whereas...Doktor had treated his scratches with gentle hands and given him a bed. Janez had danced with him and held him close like lovers. His tongue could command the roll and shudder of words above the sky, and he knew—without ever trying, yet still he knew—that in his own form, he could have walked on water.

He could walk on water. And his family lay above them, waiting for him to do so.

"They're in the sky," he whispered.

That cruel smile twisted her features, yet her voice didn't rise, and her long fingers didn't pinch. The frond fell away until he hung free but for the clasp of her nails about his jaw.

"Open your hands, my dear."

Held did so, and a bottle was slid between them. The Witch leaned close, her hair caressing his face.

"You drink half of it to change back," she said quietly, "but then a man must drink the other. And as long as that man loves you, and only you, then you will live as one of them for the rest of your days. If you cease to be the sun in his world, then you cease to be at all."

Breathless, Held clutched it tight to the deformity of this wrong chest.

"It will turn me back?"

"Yes."

He squeezed it, and the thick liquid inside moved softly against him.

"You will exist but for the love of that man," the Witch said, "and for nothing else. There will *be* nothing else. Do you understand?"

The water surged. She drew her dress upwards—or was it herself, for no tail hung below it—and brought his sisters close. The guards stopped swimming. Father, amongst them, bellowed for their release.

"Do you understand, Held?"

Homeless.

"Yes," he whispered.

"They will try to save you."

"Who?"

"Your sisters. They will try. But they cannot undo this work."

The water felt frozen around him as Held breathed, "I don't want them to."

It was perfectly true.

She smiled.

"If you ask the water for help," she whispered, "then I will hear you. Do you understand?"

No. How could—

"Ask the water for help, and I will hear you."

"Yes," Held breathed.

She smiled once more—and then pushed him away.

He hung in the water before her, an alien form clutching a bottle of pure magic to make it all right. Inside would be himself. His true form. Freedom.

"You fathered three daughters, my liege," the Witch called, her laughing gaze never straying from Held, "but it will be for nothing. You took my husband, my future, from me. And so I will take your daughters, your future, from you. There will be no grandchildren. No royal line. Your kingdom will die with you, and you will be forgotten, as you wished the world to be."

Her smile widened.

And finally, she looked down.

"You fathered three daughters. Now you have but two, and a skyman for a son."

The pause was terrible.

And when Held glanced down—

Oh, what a mistake.

Father's face was wreathed in anger. In shock. He looked quite stunned, as though delivered a great blow to the head—and quite revolted, as though told something foul and evil.

When their eyes locked, he shook his head.

"I have no son," he said, clear as the air above the sky. "There are no skymen here."

And Held's heart broke.

He felt it, as surely as if Father had impaled him upon the sword, and Held's fingers caught at the stopper. Wrenched it free. A coil of oil unfurled upwards—and Held sealed his mouth over the lip, and drank deeply.

And drank *fire*.

He heard the scream—and then his own. His fingers scrabbled uselessly over the bottle, and he barely forced the stopper back on the remaining liquid before his tail snapped clean in two, and the blur of blood obscured his vision. The water swirled around him as he thrashed—and he recalled this pain from the first time, recalled the scouring of salt as his scales floated free, remembered the terrible agony of his gills sealing.

And as they did, he took one great breath—and held it.

Sound bounced about him, as though unable to enter his ears. The Witch threw her arms wide and her head back, and laughed in a scream like an orca before she burst into a thousand black bubbles and vanished entirely. He kicked out—*kicked*, oh, how his legs felt familiar now—at the webbed hand that caught his fin and tore it clean away from his newborn skin. The seaweed about his chest fell loose; his chest burned, ached, *screamed* for air—air—air—

He opened his eyes and struck out.

Writhed. Flailed. The sky glimmered above, too far above, and could come no longer.

Skymen—

Oh.

Skymen could walk on water. But they could not swim.

He could not swim.

Terror seized him, and he writhed in the air. Father's stare found his own. Meri's terrified gaze at his side. Balta, mouth opened in childish horror.

Dark spots were dancing.

He was—

Drowning. As Father wanted him to do.

"Calla!"

He heard Father's voice.

Heard him say, "That is not Calla."

Heard, like an echo coming back from his very soul, "I have no son."

Held blinked, and the world swam before his eyes.

And then—

Someone shouted. Father bellowed an order. And arms crashed about Held's chest, and dragged him upwards into the light. Hair streamed past his face; a tail crashed at his legs with a furious energy.

Air.

Air!

He choked on it and gasped, raking it into burning lungs. The blood streamed from his skin, and he scrabbled blindly at the shoulder under his ribs, at the body holding him aloft in the frozen night.

At—

Balta.

She stared up at him through the water, those wide eyes terrified, yet her arms firm about his waist.

His sister.

Oh, his sister.

He sobbed, hands over his face, and felt the great pain of heartbreak grow worse when she only clutched him tighter and passed the forgotten bottle up through the roof of her world.

And the floor of his own.

Chapter Twenty-Six

A FIST POUNDED upon the door, and Janez sat back from his letters and groaned when the guard announced, "Captain Kühe, Your Highness!" in a pompous manner. Good Lord, what now? Doubtless Alarik had summoned him—well, hang Alarik. Janez wouldn't go, damn it!

"Your Highness." The salute was smart. The words were tart. "That—sailor is back."

"What?"

"The—foreign one. From the ship."

Janez blinked dumbly at him. A foreign sailor had returned from abroad? So what?

"From the harbourmaster's cells, sir."

Oh.

Janez surged to his feet. Held. Damn and blast it—why had the foolish man *returned*? Alarik would have him executed, the mood the damned king was in.

"Where?" he snapped, and Kühe jumped, flushing a deep red.

"He, ah. He'd been in some kind of fight, Your Highness—the night patrol found him on the beach not an hour ago. We, ah, we took him up to Doktor Hauser."

Janez swept out of the study and made straight for the doctor's chambers, without so much as dismissing the captain. If he wanted to stand awkwardly in the halls all night, let him. If Held had returned, then they must leave for the Winter Palace as soon as possible.

Hauser looked wholly unsurprised at Janez's arrival. Held, however, jumped. He looked shell-shocked, much the appearance of a man after a sea battle, and Janez slowed his movements and lowered his voice as he asked after his well-being.

"Pub brawl, I suspect," Hauser said, adding a final stitch to a long gash upon his arm. "He's been fighting. No broken knuckles, but by chance rather than design, I suspect."

"Held? You are well?"

The lamp-like pale eyes fixed on his face—and then the man came up off the bed entirely and flung his arms about Janez's neck. Janez staggered a little under the sudden weight and gripped back instinctively. The hug was desperate, almost violent, and Janez floundered a little, out of depth and unsure of its cause.

"It's all right," he said, a little awkwardly, and glanced at Hauser, who only shrugged.

"I received one as well," he said. "In front of my assistant, too. Bloody impertinence." Despite the grumble, he looked rather pleased.

"I would have paid to see it," Janez muttered and finally pried Held loose only by sitting down. His arm was hugged, and that fair head remained on his shoulder, but the desperate clutch eased, and Held permitted Doktor Hauser to finish treating the wounds passively enough.

"He cannot stay here," Hauser said quietly.

"Alarik?"

"A disappearance like that—he will be convinced the man is a spy. You must leave. Both of you," the doctor said and tightened the dressing over the wound. "The mountain air will be good for the pair of you. Call it doctor's orders."

THEY SET OFF at dawn.

Janez would have preferred to ride alone—he was hardly remarkable-looking, and his tenure as crown prince so short few outside the capital recognised him—but he thought better of it. After all, he'd require the finest clothes for this ball, his own servants who knew his habits, and even his sword. Sigurd was the old-fashioned sort. A man was no man at all if he didn't carry a sword, and Janez rather suspected that, at some point, he'd be invited to a 'friendly' spar, designed to test his mettle as a gentleman.

Perhaps, he reflected glumly, he ought to take Hauser as well. Just in case.

They left as though it were quite normal, and not a rush. In a foul mood at needing to flee from his own home, Janez wanted to seek comfort in Held's hands, lips, body. But he crushed the urge and instead sat in the chilly room, silent and sullen, as a dull-witted manservant dressed him. The only spark came from Held's insistence on doing Janez's hair—he slapped the manservant's wrist, like scolding a child, for attempting to take the brush—and the soft rhythm of the strokes through his curls.

Janez closed his eyes and bitterly did not wish to go.

Held, too, appeared morose and quiet. Perhaps it was shock from the day before, or perhaps he'd caught on to Janez's mood, but the bright eyes were dulled, and his movements restrained. He seemed...needy, and when Janez yielded to temptation and slid an arm about those thin shoulders to hug him, Held burrowed into his side and remained there for a long minute, clutching Janez's waistcoat and clinging.

"It's all right," Janez said, a little pointlessly, and shook him loose. "Come. We'll escape together, shall we?"

But when they descended from his rooms, a plain but large carriage awaited in the courtyard, a mere four guards—two ahead, two behind— to guard it. And the rush hadn't been rushed enough.

"I felt low-key to be best, brother."

Alarik was standing on the great stone steps, clad in his royal cloak, and Janez stared resolutely past him to the assembled entourage. Four guards, two footmen, two servants with the pony and trap, filled with luggage and supplies, and that damnable empty carriage.

It was petty of him. This was duty, not Alarik's fault—yet that thunderous order echoed in Janez's ears. It sounded so terribly like their father's orders, all those years ago. The orders that had quashed the first love affair he'd ever had. The words that had removed his lover and unborn child from the city, perhaps even the kingdom. The command that had finally broken through his happy shell, reminding him he was a prince and figurehead first, and a man a long way second.

The orders that would be repeated, should Alarik's suspicion grow even a fraction more.

Certainly would be repeated, if Alarik were to discover Janez's desires.

So Janez's shoulders tightened, his mouth turned down in a grim expression and no reply. Instead, he turned to Held, told him to come, and strode out for the carriage. He heard his brot—his king's angry mutter over his shoulder but paid it no mind. He would be out of the king's hair the moment the carriage passed through the gates. He would do his duty, be married by the spring, and a father by the following winter. He would secure this alliance.

But nobody, king or not, could order him to like it.

The moment Held joined him in the carriage, Janez swung the little door shut and locked it. It lurched forward, rattling over the cobbles and beyond the great gates. Janez resolutely did not look back.

He was started from his dark thoughts by the light touch of fingers against his as they lurched through the city, and jumped. The light leaking into the carriage was gloomy—there would be rain soon—yet Held's eyes were plainly visible.

"I'm sorry," Janez said, tugging a smile into place on his face. "I am simply...not looking forward to this. Come. Let's have some light, shall we? And improve your language skills a little—perhaps you're secretly a most foul and uncouth sort of person, and I can love you less for it."

He sorely doubted it, but the hope was there, nonetheless.

The rain began as they left the city gates—a driving hammer upon the carriage, thunder growling overhead—and it was the first word Janez decided to teach. Counting came easy, despite the quite laughable pronunciation, and the difference between mine and your. Clothes came less so—again, largely pronunciation, especially about shoes and stockings—but Held seemed oddly fascinated by body parts and would stroke each one after Janez named it.

And he *was* tempted to name others, more, but—

He resisted said urges and looked away from the sight of Held stroking his own fingers as though just discovering he had them. Perhaps he ought to try sentences? Full conversation? Only there was no context—how could he get Held to understand sentences without the context? That was far harder. How on earth did infants learn to talk? Janez was reasonably sure Ekaterina didn't sit with Ingrid for several hours a day reciting 'I am well, how are you?' until something inside Ingrid's head turned it into meaning.

It was difficult, and extremely distracting (with their feet snugly crowded together between their seats on the carriage floor), but the stormy morning passed with simple little lessons, until Held could name a dozen things but not say anything about them.

When the rain eventually stopped, so did the carriage—to rest the poor horses, no doubt, and allow the footmen and guards to empty their water-laden boots—and Janez opted to stretch his legs. The deference beyond the door said it was a good idea: the footmen bowed a little too low, and the guards gave none of their usual bright greetings. The silence was uneasy.

"Forgive me, gentlemen," Janez said loudly as he loped away from the moving prison cell, enjoying the chill of fresh air upon his face. "I am something of a bear so early in the morning. But the day brightens, and so do I. How many miles, Captain?"

The captain—a dark-skinned landsman with an easy countenance—replied that they had made quick progress and would reach their first inn in plenty of time, or press on to the second if the weather held off. Janez left the decision to him and watched Held explore the weeds at the side of the road, plucking a few gaudy red flowers off with careful hands. He returned to the carriage with them, and when the horses had been refreshed at the little stream and Janez had climbed back into his seat, he found Held carefully threading the flower-stems into the hinges of the door.

"Very decorative," Janez said, "though the footmen won't be pleased. They're terribly fussy about that sort of thing."

Held ignored him, and Janez tipped his head back with a smile. Closed his eyes. And dozed, in the gentle rock and sway of the carriage, the thick mud smoothing their passage.

He dreamed, both awake and asleep at once. He was aware of Held's soft murmuring under his breath, caught snatches of a foreign song. But they turned into sirens singing from the rocks, like in the myths, and Janez alone on the *Held*—an abandoned ship with only a lost prince at the wheel, and him driving her to her death, to founder on the rocks while mermaids dragged him down to drown.

He woke with a start, when the water choked his nose and throat, only to blink at the swinging lantern and earn a startled look from Held. The real Held. Not some mermaid on a rock—not a maid at all. Honestly. The mind could do such strange things.

Janez dropped his head back to doze again, and this time, the soft song turned into music at a great ball, with a thousand twirling, swirling ballgowns, the skirts flying out in ballooning circles of colour. But all of the women were faceless, the space between their hair and their chins utterly blank. They spoke nothing to him as they danced with him in turn, and then one would not be removed. Her dress turned white. The ballroom was transformed into a cathedral, the stained-glass windows pouring red down upon the floor, like blood drowning their feet. It stained his boots and crept up her dress. It rose up the walls, ever higher, caressing his skin and sticking to his shirt, yet he could nothing but stand there, repeating marriage vows until he drowned.

The carriage lurched over a rock. Janez opened one eye, breathing wetly, and saw Held, still humming softly and weaving the battered flowers into a chain.

A chain. Oh, a chain.

The dream swept over him again, but now it was no woman standing under a veil in the cathedral, but Held himself, naked as the day he was born but for a necklace of flowers hanging like a noose about his throat. He was quite beautiful, quite erect, and Janez's throat dried at the sight of such uninhibited glory. And then Held spoke in that soft, sweet voice, but only a word: "Mine." He repeated it, over and over, like a tiny wedding vow of his own. And Janez kissed him, alone in this church, kissed him fuller than he would any bride, kissed him until they could have absorbed one another and ceased to exist, kissed him as a long-lost lover, as one determined and destined to live and die by the choice he had made—and Held dissolved into sea foam in his very arms and washed away down the altar steps.

He jerked awake as his dream-self clutched at empty air, and so violently that Held dropped his flower-chain with a sound of surprise and stopped humming.

"I'm all right," Janez murmured, but there was a fine sweat upon his forehead and he was breathing hard. Sirens on rocks, faceless brides, and Held dissolving away into nothingness. And the pain that had lanced through his chest at the last. Janez was no romantic prone to examining his dreams for meaning, but even he could see the message in them.

"You well?" Held asked, sliding across onto the seat next to Janez. He clutched at Janez's fingers, hard and firm.

"I am well," Janez said, both an answer and a correction, and the fingers caressed his own. "I was...dreaming. Just dreaming."

Held's hand dropped to his thigh and stroked it gently. And then that lithe body was leaned up against his side—Janez blinked back the imagination of his dream—and a head came to rest against his neck. A heavy warmth. An intimate comfort.

Janez swallowed and curled his fingers about the hand on his leg.

He had to pull away. He had to cease this. He was travelling to choose a bride; he could not...could not...

He closed his eyes and drifted down into that grand cathedral again. They were dancing at the altar, Held's fine white hair spinning out around his face in a beautiful arc, and he looked so free, so perfect, so joyous...

Chapter Twenty-Seven

HELD PASSED THE first part of the journey with his hand kissing Janez's in the dark, moving room, trying to simply *be.*

Because this was it, now.

Father had left him to drown.

It was Balta who had saved him—silly, sweet little Balta—and Father had left him to drown. Father would have left him imprisoned in that cave until he died of hunger, Held was sure. Father would rather he were dead, than this.

He was alone in the world.

Except for this man. And when they stopped in weak sunlight, Held pressed the bottle into Janez's hand and made him drink it, and this man became the world itself. Janez smiled at him and drank it, pulled a face that said he was not much a fan, and chattered about—possibly the weather, but Held hadn't yet grasped enough of the tongue to know for certain.

He was the world. The beautiful, lonely world.

He was a legend, a skyman far from Held's home, and—

Why did it hurt?

Why did the love that had burned so bright now *hurt*? The broken sensation in Held's chest was as though a bone had healed wrong when he looked at Janez. Still bright, still brilliant...but bearing a cost.

He had lost everything.

Everything.

He didn't know how to feel, or what to do. He wanted to shy away and hide, to wrap himself in the darkness and mourn, but also to cling to Janez and clutch tight the only thing he had left. He wanted to be untouched, and be smothered in it, to override the pain with pleasure.

The bare facts of it were horrifying.

Somehow, the rub of his unwebbed fingers against one another was good.

How could anything be good over what had just happened? How could anything feel right, when his own father had left him to drown? How could Janez's hand about his own be comforting, when Held's very existence now relied upon this man with whom he couldn't even speak?

But she'd told him it would happen.

The Witch had warned him. And when Father had imprisoned him, Held had known that he wouldn't be able to live in both worlds, hadn't he?

He had chosen this one.

What did that mean, that he had *chosen* to lose—

Everything.

He'd thrown everything away. For this body, this man, and nothing more.

And he couldn't quite wrap his mind about what that meant.

WHEN THE LIGHT leaked from the sky, they stopped at a nest. A white construction that jutted from the endless green, it was warm and smelled of food. There was a lot of chatter, and they were all shown into a cavernous room beyond, like the private areas of the palace. Enormous plates loaded with food were brought. A guard with a dark face beamed at Held and told him all the names for the food on them.

And food was dearly welcome. Skymen didn't travel quickly in packs. Much like Fa—much like below, it seemed men of importance like Janez weren't meant to go places unattended, but when grouped together, skymen were terribly slow. Held was faint with hunger by the time he could eat.

The skymen were insular, too. Although the dark guard smiled and spoke slowly to him, the others ignored him. The servants, too, kept to themselves. And none of them would speak to Janez—not that Janez seemed to much mind as he pored over letters. Held let him be, concentrating instead on the dark guard's words, attempting to root his world in something wider and calmer than a single man in the whole universe.

The dark man was named Kapitän, and he spoke with a smoother tone than Janez. The jagged edges of his language were scored off, and Held wondered if skymen didn't all speak the same tongue. It wasn't dissimilar to the way merfolk from beyond the Narrow Mouth spoke when they came to trade—did skymen, too, all speak in different tongues? Did it mean Kapitän came from somewhere else? He also carried a little gold trinket which he opened, showing Held a picture of a beautiful skymaid inside, with a proud nose and similar dark skin, and a drawing of a small skyling, clearly his own. He called them Claudia and Meinsohn, or Held thought he did, and then drove an elbow into Held's ribs, and laughed some joke Held didn't know.

"Eine Frau für meinen Freund!" he called to the maid who brought the cups, and the other guards laughed and cheered.

"Und für mich, Kapitän! Eine Frau!" another called, slapping his thigh. The others began to turn out pockets, and bits of round metal flashed in the light. Held smiled uncertainly, unsure of what was happening.

The maid disappeared—and then another came. Younger, with a prettier face. She was laughing, gathering up the bits of metal, and then she gathered up her skirts and sat in the crowing guard's lap. To Held's surprise, the guard slapped her backside and buried his face against her bosom.

"Held." Janez's voice rose gentle over the chaos. *"Bett, ja?"*

Those words, he knew. Bed. Yes. It was late, and he was tired—and he was determined to brush Janez's hair again in the morning. It was soothing to the pain, Janez had liked it today, and the servants always tied the ribbon too tight. So Held nodded, abandoning his drink and the men to the maids, and took to the stairs.

The little rooms all came off one corridor—Kapitän had the one nearest the stairs, and Held supposed the arrangement was to protect the prince in case of attack. His own was opposite, and nothing more than a little jug of water on a stand and a narrow bed with rumpled blankets. There wasn't even a window. It felt somewhat like a cell, but it would do for the night. He stripped to his underclothes, the chill too great for further, and began to wash his hands and face. Footsteps sounded on the creaky stairs, several pairs, and a door closed farther down the corridor. More shuffled past his room. Another clap of wood to frame.

And then his door opened.

Held jumped as the skymaid slipped inside and shut it behind her. The metal bolt scraped, and she smiled, leaning up against the wood, shoulders pulled in and bosom pushed out.

"Guten Abend," she said.

She was pretty and soft, all curves in a cream dress and dark brown ringlets around her face. Her mouth was painted pink. It smiled, and she ghosted across the little room towards him, stopping not a pace away and swirling to turn her back. He was met by the ribbons holding her dress closed from behind, and then she turned her head to smile over her shoulder, and murmured a question.

Was he—meant to undo it? Undo her dress?

He swallowed, and hastily dried his hands upon his clothes before reaching out and teasing the knot at the nape of her neck free. Her skin was warm and smooth. It burned against his near-numb fingers as he fought with the ribbon, and finally slid it out of its hooks and loops. The dress sagged. She pulled it forward and turned around.

She—wore no underclothes.

Held had seen many a mermaid with nothing to cover their breasts—it was the tradition for those of standing to swim bare—but never a skymaid. In any case, this seemed...different. The room seemed closer. Her breast, when she placed his hand upon it, caused his heart to race. He could feel the soft flutter of her own. And then the dress fell to the floor entirely, and she stood quite naked in front of him.

"Küss mich."

"What?" Held asked.

"Küss mich," she repeated. Her dainty hands pushed him back to the bed. Deftly plucked at the cords on his clothes until his body lay exposed. She caressed his legs and sex until the latter swelled, his crotch heavy and his breathing heavier—and then she repeated her words, soft and sweet, and pressed her lips to his.

Oh.

Oh, the shock of it. A bolt of hunger, and quite unlike the hunger he'd felt before, inflamed him. His hands flew to her back to pull her closer; his mouth opened under her own, and a hot pleasure, a single-minded dedication to the pursuit of it, unfolded in the back of his mind. She was leagues of warm skin and bright life, climbing astride his lap. He touched the swell of her breasts in mute fascination, traced the slender dip of her spine and lower, to the swell of her buttocks. She raised herself onto her knees, tall and proud above him, and pressed his mouth to her breast until he took the soft nub of pinked skin atop it between his teeth and sucked on it. She moaned then, a sweet sound above him, and his very blood jumped at the sound.

And then *desire.*

Pleasure like he'd never known, as she sank down upon his sex with a long, smooth sigh. And then she began to move along it, riding it—him—as though an animal. Her face glowed in ecstasy; her wet, warm grip around him was so intense he was reduced to nothing but this body—sweat between his shoulder blades; a great pressure in his crotch; the silky skin between his teeth and hands; the slide of his body inside hers, buried in silken heat like a wet bloom. His groans, so deep inside his chest they, too, brought the burning to a boil.

A boil.

This—this was—

A bright light seared through his head, erasing all thought. He was a body. Shuddering in hers. Air. Air, rasping in his chest. The shaking of nerves. His heart—his heart, pounding like a drum. In time with his—thrusts. He was thrusting up into the girl. And she cried out in time to him, until the grip became painful, until she buried her face in his throat, until—until—

Her weight pushed him back against the blankets. She smiled at him. Touched her lips to his throat, and his hand to her damp breast. Held heaved a breath and shivered when her lips touched his chest. His stomach. Lower.

She murmured something, and her mouth began to touch him in an entirely different manner. Sealed to his sex, and suckled upon it as he had her breast. The shaking of his nerves intensified—and ebbed again, to a sweeter pleasure, until he was swelling again, and she made a pleased little noise and took it deep into her mouth, much as Janez had in the woods. Held let her, rolling her words about in his mind, and the way her lips had collided with his own.

Küss mich.

Kiss me.

This was how skymen kissed.

Chapter Twenty-Eight

THE FOLLOWING DAY, it was very apparent that the men had introduced Held to the pleasures of women.

Janez had suspected it would happen—the captain had clearly taken a shine at dinner—so he was surprised when, just before dawn broke, Held slipped into his rooms and picked up the brush as though he were a manservant.

"Good morning," Janez said evenly and eyed him for hints of what had happened. He seemed a little flustered, a little wild about the edges, and there were rings under his eyes that suggested he hadn't slept...but otherwise, there was nothing. He could have liked or loathed it, and Janez could not tell.

But it *had* happened. There was a certain air the recently released gave off, in Janez's opinion. They exuded something others could sense, and although he couldn't put his finger on it, Janez knew full well Held had been buried in some pretty girl, and had been so for some considerable time.

Ought that not have made him bitter?

He pondered it as Held brushed his hair and chose a pale green ribbon to tame it with. He could find no bitterness at the thought of Held with a girl—rather, envy. And of the girl. She'd seen, touched, heard, what Janez had not. She'd been permitted to have Held inside her, and he had not. She knew what Held looked like within the grip of passion, and Janez did not.

All right. Perhaps there *was* a little bitterness.

But Janez pushed it back and smiled and thanked him when the ribbon had been fixed to Held's liking. To his mute surprise, Held brushed off his overcoat before opening the door as well as any manservant and trailing after him down the inn stairs.

The guards were still readying themselves; the footmen looked impatient.

"We ought to have been gone with the dawn, Your Highness, but them guards was up too late whoring," one of them grumbled. The other struck him sharply and told him to mind his manners.

"They will suffer accordingly," Janez said, enjoying their paling faces. "I've ridden enough horses after too much wine and too many women to know it's an uneasy combination." He stretched his face up into the sun—it was pleasant, a little cool, but dry. "I think we shall sit and watch the world go by today. Held?"

Held nodded at the sound of his name, and soon two servants had been relegated to the trap, and prince and pauper were seated behind the carriage driver. Janez had another overcoat brought for Held and a blanket for both their legs. He laughed when Held grabbed his arm as the carriage lurched forwards and began to roll, the horses impatient after so long harnessed and halted.

"It's better here," Janez said. "Better than being stuffed in that box all day."

And better it was—they had passed from the plains and flat forests that ran down to the sea, and the mountains were rising up ahead. It would be another day before they found the narrow pass and followed it to the gates of the Winter Palace, but the sky was clear and the mountains sharp in the distance. The winter snows had struck low already; the peaks towered ahead, jagged teeth on the horizon, and grew with every hour. Janez yearned to be there.

He'd spent his earliest years at the Winter Palace, had learned to walk in the shadows of those mountains. At fifteen and fresh-faced, he'd been presented to the aristocratic world under their brooding masses. He'd hunted wolves on their slopes and seen the great thunder of avalanches in the dark winters. Whenever he'd gone to the sea, to the summer fortress and its busyness, he'd admired most the waves with white-tipped peaks and great troughs below.

The sight of those mountains, even at this distance, was soothing.

They meant, however, that the road grew rockier and harsher. The carriage wheels grumbled and crunched; the horses were dissatisfied, and their voicing of discomfort appeared to make Held more nervous. And Janez knew full well these horses were not as kindly towards nerves as Molly.

"Captain!" he called again. "I must pause us for just a moment. It is getting a touch too cold—I must step back into the carriage."

He waved off the demand for a fire to be made and warming pan prepared—the lantern would do, the wind was mostly at fault, he insisted—and soon had them shut into the carriage once more, windows drawn up against the cold and any peeking intrusion. And gave into quiet temptation. He drew the blankets around both their shoulders and pulled Held near.

Held—clutched.

They had touched before—that dance, those little brushes and clasps of hands, the river—but Held had never gripped so hard before, and Janez wondered if it were simply the cold, or some lesson from the night before. He almost burrowed into Janez's arms, his hands flat against Janez's back...and then they were teasing at the hem of his shirt, the cool smoothness of palms against his skin.

He took a breath. His ribs struggled to allow it.

How—how could such a simple touch—

He swallowed and fought not to react. Oh, his body did—and perfectly inappropriately, too—but the blankets allowed no outward sign of it. Held's face pressed against his neck, his lips touching Janez's pulse, and he must have felt it racing, but he made no murmur. And Janez made no movement. This was only...for warmth. Nothing more.

He lied to himself, and he knew it very well.

"NO WHORES TONIGHT, Captain."

Janez said it in a low, private tone as he stepped down from the carriage. The night had rushed in; the mountains towered dark above them now. The sky was a pure black, and there was a smell in the air that Janez remembered from being only two feet high and still in skirts.

There could be snow tonight.

"We will reach the palace tomorrow," he continued, "and I want your men to be at their finest. Not their most delicate."

The captain coughed awkwardly but relaxed when Janez offered a small smile.

"Certainly, Your Highness."

This inn was larger, grander, and able to cater more easily to travelling dignitaries. Janez was afforded a suite of rooms, with great bolts upon the doors and a roaring fireplace. He retired at once, leaving the men to their meals, and read by candlelight until the maid came up with the meal. He ate sparingly, distracted by what morning—or rather, afternoon—would bring.

The first and simplest was Mother. He dearly missed her, and he'd brought letters from Sofia and Ingrid—and, in theory, the baby, although of course a baby couldn't write, and Ingrid's imagination didn't extend to grasp that babies didn't, as a rule, like tobogganing down palace stairs on homemade sleds. It would be a warm panacea to his unease, to sit with Mother and speak of family, like she was no widowed queen and he no prince, but simply a woman entering old age and an as-yet unbound son.

But the second was, of course, the ball. It was a mere few days hence. A great gathering of lords and ladies to welcome King Sigurd and his daughters. If it were merely a ball to find a wife, any wife, with no insistence upon success, Janez might have been quite enamoured with the idea. But to examine three girls, as though chattel, with a view to siring sons? The poor grace of it stung, and he couldn't imagine his bride-to-be was entirely thrilled at the idea either.

Still, he would make the effort. He wouldn't be so dispirited upon meeting them—no, he would be charming, polite, good-humoured, and try to make the best of a bad situation. Who knew, perhaps it would be tolerably fine. All that was ultimately needed, in the end, was enough compatibility to rub along together nicely. He'd be at sea much of his life, and she with her duties to her people. Love was not required. Casting his mind to the hands against his back in the carriage, he thought it just as well.

Determined, he undressed to his underclothes and cracked open a window to allow the music from the inn below to creep up into his suite. He drew the curtains for privacy, and then lifted his arms and imagined a lady between them. He hadn't waltzed in any dignified sort of manner for nearly two years, and it wouldn't do to forget the steps or tread on the princess's toes.

"My lady," he entreated the phantom at his front and stepped forward.

To a drunken fiddle, the prince danced alone. And with every soft increase in skill and speed, his heart cracked just a little more.

Chapter Twenty-Nine

HELD COULDN'T SWEEP the girl from his mind.

Or rather, the way she'd touched her mouth to his. The reverence in her movements. The strangeness of the contact, and the little word she'd whispered before doing so. Held didn't understand, exactly, but—he did, too. It hadn't been unlike the reaching out of a kiss. That was how skymen kissed, wasn't it?

If so, then Janez had never kissed him at all. And Held's heart clenched at the thought of it. He'd clasped his hand—more than once—but never, if Held had understood the girl, *kissed* him. They'd laughed, touched, danced, even pleasured one another—and not kissed.

How was Held to keep, or even have, this man if they never kissed?

He threw back the blankets and slid from the bed. The passageway was empty, lit by warm lanterns. He padded silently along to Janez's rooms and hesitated at the door. A warm glow showed through the cracks, and he knocked hesitantly, wondering—for the first time, armed with new knowledge—if Janez was even alone. The guards had had maids the night before, too. Who was to say Janez had gone without?

A voice called. Janez's voice. Held recognised the welcome and slipped in, snapping the door shut behind him.

"Held!"

Janez's voice was pleased. The name sounded warm and wanted. He was standing in the middle of the room in loose white clothes, clearly not dressed for company but for the gleaming shoes on his feet. He gestured at them, saying something, and then lifted his arms and began turning about the room as though dancing with some invisible partner.

He looked—quite mad, actually.

But also quite beautiful, with his hair askew, ribbon-free and falling in gentle curls about his shoulders, and the loose flow of the clothes both hiding and revealing his thin frame and easy grace. The look of concentration, and the raised hands, open and empty, begging to be kissed.

Touched. Not kissed. Not to the skymen.

Held stepped forward as Janez turned back to him, and slid his palms into those empty spaces.

The touch was raw heat and rough skin. It was as blinding and breaking as that first, on the roof of Held's world and the floor of Janez's. He shivered at the very presumption, yet wanted nothing more than to slide his fingers between those long, white digits, and feel the oh-so-foreign pulse of a heart, a heart that beat so much faster than any he'd ever known, pound against his own as though they were one.

Janez's broad smile dipped into something softer, gentler, and he curled his fingers about the back of one hand, and dropped the other. As before, his arm came around Held's waist, yet...tighter. Firmer. They were pulled closer until he had no natural option but to run his freed hand up the loose sleeve and settle it on Janez's shoulder, as though it was by Held's design and not this skyman's that they remained clasped tight like lovers.

He gripped the rough cloth under his fingers, and Janez's smile widened.

And when he began to lead, it was not the wild, laughing dance of the first time. It was slow, little more than an idle circle. All along his body, from knee to chest, Held could feel another's. Janez's leg, just barely between his own, a chest breathing in tandem with his, even the faintest wash of air against his cheek. And when he looked from their clasped hands to that handsome face, those impossibly blue eyes were focused on Held, and Held alone.

And there was something there.

There was. He was sure of it. Something in the focus. Something in the way they moved, but Janez's entire face was still. Something in the almost intimate embrace—

The girl's words spilled, and Held only prayed they were correct.

"Küss mich."

The dance stopped.

He hardly dared to breathe. Had he said it right? Had it meant what he'd thought? Had it—

Held's thoughts stopped when Janez's hand slid from his fingers and brushed down the side of his face.

Everything stopped.

That light touch. The backs of his nails. Cool and light. The endless blue of his eyes.

The hand at Held's waist fisted in the fabric there, and Held licked his lips. The blue flickered down.

Held whispered it again.

"Küss mich."

The hand turned on his face. A palm touched his jaw. A thumb slid under his chin and pushed. Held rose up onto his toes automatically, the hand at his back steadying and firm. Pulling. And—

Oh.

He whimpered, and the room slipped away under his eyelids. In the dark, there was only this. Only the soft heat of lips against his own. Something inside him—deep, primal, *alien*—surged. He arched up into the body before him. Felt the hand slip aside and cup the back of his neck. And for a moment, he merely hung there, gripped somehow tight and somehow barely held, with nothing but those lips on his and some indescribable, fierce possessiveness burning him from the inside out. This man—this man—

This was how the skymen kissed.

And it was no gentle guidance or soft attachment. It was something deeper. Something rawer. Delicate and dangerous. Of course this was how, this simple press that screamed in a thousand tongues at once. These creatures controlled the clouds and walked on water. Of course they didn't simply wind their hands together, but stopped all, stopped everything, halted their very existences for—

For *this.*

As cool air whispered between them, as Janez pulled back, Held kept holding on. He followed, grasping for hair and skin, and found that sweet mouth again. And this time, it opened. It kissed not sweetly now, but hungrily; it consumed, and the hands at his back and nape dug as though pulling him into Janez's very self, very *soul*—

"Nein," Held breathed when Janez broke the kiss again. *"Nein."*

He wanted to ask for more. Wanted to know how skymen loved. Wanted to know if they kissed in other ways, and learn every variety of kiss they knew. But the language escaped him; the words were never there. This body held the desire, but none of the details.

How could he—how would he—

He touched. The shirt was half-open, and Held pulled at the ribbons until it came apart entirely. His fingers trembled against the heat. The skin here, from sleek neck to the shadowed lines at the tops of the trousers, was sea smooth, and Held trailed the backs of his nails in a mimicry of Janez's earlier motion.

And watched in fascination and fierce hunger as a shiver followed him.

"Held..."

The voice was deep. Grave. Some warning reverberated there, yet the hand at his back had drifted a little lower. And Held didn't know why, or what it would do lower, but something intense and urgent, from head to toe, wanted to know.

So he pressed closer and pushed his hand higher. His lips sought Janez's neck and rested there, at the perfect height. He could feel a thundering heartbeat under his mouth and kissed it, as his fingers found the darker skin and gentle peak of a nipple and circled it, curious.

The body supporting his arched—a powerful undulation, like the shiver of an earthquake through the sea. And then Held gasped into a hungry sky-kiss. His lower body was held fast to Janez's, one hand high, just where his leg ended in a swell of pure sensation, and the other still clasped between hand and hip. Held felt every inch of Janez's body. He could feel raw heat, the crush of their clothes between them, and the sharp bite of teeth against his lower lip when he touched that soft darkness again.

He wanted closer. He wanted everything, and if he didn't know how everything could be between men, then this body did. It craved touch and bare skin. It yearned for heat. He gave in as he pushed the shirt open wider and pulled at the cords. In a moment, the hands at his legs and back were turning him—them—in another dizzy dance, faster than before, and then he fell, the deep softness of the bed yielding under him.

In the midst of the blankets, he was alone for a mere moment.

And Janez did what still came clumsily to Held. In swift movements, the clothes were flung to the floor. He stepped right out of the shoes, as though they had never been. And then he stood, bare as a royal of the deep, a tall form of divine beauty, gold and white in the low lamplight.

Not for long.

Held leaned in to touch, but was crowded back down to the blankets as Janez crawled over him, entirely naked, and pressed those dizzying lips to wherever they could reach. And Held dismissed his adoration of men's hands. It was a man's mouth that held true power. He gasped when it kissed and whimpered when the bite at his shoulder turned hunger into heat. The kisses along his chest as his shirt was unlaced and spread open were skittering claws of feeling all along his skin, and then that mouth traced lower still, ever lower, until he lay bare and all the new words escaped him. Until he could do nothing at all, nothing but feel.

But then, as the burning seemed to mount to a fever, dangerous and destructive, and elusive thoughts skidded after one another in a tangle—*yes*, and *more*, and *please*, and *Janez-Janez-Janez*—the kisses stopped.

Just—stopped.

He was tugged, under the arm. Pulled. He wriggled from his trousers and sat naked against the pillows, dizzy with abandoned hunger yet drawn by curiosity as Janez—bare shoulders speckled with sweat, hair a mess—rose from the bed like a god from the ocean, and padded barefoot across the carpet. Perfection was wrought in every line, and when he bent to retrieve a small dish from the side, something oddly primal stirred in Held's blood. He wished to take those hips in hand and—

And what?

He knew it, but he didn't. It whispered in the darkness in the back of his head, somewhere he couldn't yet see, tantalising but out of reach.

Still, when Janez returned with the dish and began to touch wet, slippery fingers to Held's flesh, stroking and rubbing in some deep, sensual massage, Held wondered if perhaps, perhaps—

"Küss mich?"

Janez laughed softly and kissed him. Their mouths were askew. The affection was somehow dimmed yet more beautiful for its slip. And when a heavy leg was thrown over Held's, another kiss came. Firmer. More purposeful.

Then Held was pushed back and made to watch.

Made to watch a god, a skyman, on his knees in front of mere merfolk, stretch up in a powerful arch. He rolled his hips in idle thrusts, like a gentle tide, the flesh jutting from him like islands from the sky. His hands worked at his body, and Held could not be parted so long from such beauty. He reached, touching hands and lips to shadows and smoothness. He tasted salt and the sea, sweat and sky, and he felt the groan deep in Janez's very bones. Only to be pushed back again, and his mouth—no, his entire head—caught in rough hands and soft lips. A great weight bore down, and Held gasped as his very skin was enveloped in tight heat. As Janez straddled him and sat, as though upon a chair, and if Held had burned before—

Now, *now*, he dissolved.

He scrabbled for purchase on slick skin, crying helplessly in the storm as he was caught within. Janez rose and fell like a cloud upon the waves—head buried in Held's neck, lips and teeth caught against his skin—and Held was trapped, pinioned beneath and within this myth, this legend. The softness of the bed rocked like the sea in a storm; Held swayed, cradled between that blanket-sea and brilliant sky, and clawed for skin and hair. Found mouth. Grasped it in his own and cried there the indescribable, incredible, so utterly unfathomable *rapture*—

He broke. Came apart. Shattered, under and inside that immense divinity. Burst into the sea foam that would be the end of him, of all his kind when their days ran out.

And—

Breathed.

His skin was slick.

Teeth caressed his earlobe. Soft. Gentle. Turning the flesh and tugging, as the kisses had below. As the air returned, Held nudged his face against that alongside his, grasping blindly for hands and heat.

"Küss mich," he whispered again, his voice soft and slurring.

A laugh.

And then a swipe of lips against his cheek, his nose—his mouth.

Held closed his eyes, tangled fingers numb from the deluge of pure feeling into soft curls, and surrendered.

He knew but a handful of words, yet had found, against all odds, the very ones he needed.

Chapter Thirty

JANEZ WAS USUALLY a prompt and early riser.

But, although he woke early—so early the curtains were not so much as lightened by the dawn, and the inn sat still and silent around them, brooding under its mountains in peaceable slumber—he wasn't inclined to move.

For movement meant separation.

And how absurdly romantic it was, some post-coital bliss, no doubt, but Janez very much did not want to separate. Held was sleeping, his hair askew across the pillow, and when Janez pushed a hand across smooth skin under the blankets, he discovered perfect warmth and a desire so strong, he felt drunk with it.

He wanted no ball.

In fact, he wanted no life at all. For the doors to be bricked up, and to die here, drinking this ecstasy.

His lips touched the long column of Held's neck, and the body between his hands stirred with a murmur. A hand stroked through his hair, gathering it into a clump, and then Janez was being pressed backwards into the mattress as a lithe form arranged itself all along his body, knees sliding between his own, chests and mouths meeting in the dark. Janez stroked both hands down smooth spine and the soft swell below, and held on tight. As though he could fuse them. As though if he only held on, the evening would never come.

As though the world outside could wait.

They took their pleasure lazily, in idle kisses and soft touches, and it was coincidental—at least on Janez's part—rather than the purpose of the matter. He didn't want what he had last night; he wanted, rather, to simply touch. To love, rather than to make it. Blood went where it would. Bodies reacted as they could. Yet it was not the point. The point was to kiss that soft mouth and drag fingers through fine hair. The point was to memorise the skin under his palms and learn the way Held whimpered when fingers closed about his sex. And eventually, when the whimpers grew too desperate, to laugh in delight and submit peaceably when Held captured his exploring hands by the wrists, planted them aside, and subjected his body to an attack by teeth and mouth—the lazy pleasure brewed into a biting climax, together, messy, in the tangle of an inn's old blankets.

When it was over, to then return to the point of the matter. To draw the man-in-command close and nest in this too-hot mess, nose to cheek, breaths intermingled. Held's heart beat faintly against his own, and Janez could feel his smile and contentment. Could hear—

The captain barking orders in the yard below the windows.

Janez sighed and let go. Rose. Held sprawled in the bed a little longer, wild hair and stained skin dangerously alluring as Janez leaned in to explore it with his fingers. But when he raked both hands through his own hair and reached for the brush, in an attempt to tame the curls, a sharpness crept back into that pale gaze.

And Held moved. Lunged, almost. Snatched the brush and smacked Janez on the knuckles with it. Hard.

"Ow!" he yelped and then laughed as he was shoved into a chair and his head attacked. The bird's nest began to resemble hair again, and Janez submitted to being washed, groomed, and dressed as though Held were his manservant, not his—

Lover.

The word uncurled like a flower in his mind, and Janez grimaced. He'd yielded. Oh, but he shouldn't have yielded.

Yet when he rose from the chair to tie his trousers, and have the great overcoat slid into place—the gentleman in the mirror returning, not the wild-haired, wild-eyed cad who had risen from the bed—Janez couldn't stick firm to the regret. It slid away. He turned on Held in a moment, cupping that narrow face in both hands, and kissed him with all the hunger of a starving man.

And there he spoke the truth.

"I love you," he breathed, and Held stared back at him, uncomprehending. "I am promised, yet I love you."

It was the most honest he'd ever been. And it hurt.

Held clutched at his elbows and stretched up. The kiss was soft and sweet—and then the captain shouted in the yard, damning his men with a cock-pox, and Janez broke it with a soft laugh.

"Dress," he said, pushing gently. "Dress!"

Held scowled, fiercely angry for a split second, and then his expression smoothed and he slipped out. Janez listened to the drum of his feet going into another room before turning back to the mirror to pull his collar a little more firmly in place. There was a smile on his face, and he forced it away.

He had yielded.

And he failed to even regret the failure.

THE WINTER PALACE was, in theory, a royal retreat during the winter months. Overshadowed by the mountains, cupped from behind by a vast lake, and supplied by the great river that washed ever northwards to the sea, it was a shelter from the iceberg-spotted sea and raging storms.

In reality, its grandeur and luxury had served as a diplomatic tool for centuries. An ancient castle in stupendous style, it was simultaneously more welcoming and more imposing than its shoreline summer counterpart.

The other departure from theory was, of course, its nature as a retreat. It wasn't. It was more home than the summer fortress, and his father's death had driven his mother from the sea entirely. Now, the queen dowager lived permanently by the mountains, the good air helping her humours and the silence, rather than the terrible drum of the sea that had slain her husband, soothing her grief-ridden mind.

His mother—much like his sister-in-law—had been an aristocratic lady before her marriage, rather than a foreign princess. It hadn't been an arranged match, but one of love. She'd dearly loved Janez's father, and they'd courted at a time of peace, when the king had been freer to marry those of good standing rather than those strictly of royal standing.

Janez was jealous of his father's freedom in that regard, but the rules of peace and the rules of war were different things, and he banished the bitterness from his mind as the great doors to the palace opened. He was welcomed into the great dining hall by a red-faced captain bellowing his name and title, and saluting in such an exaggerated fashion that he knocked his very hat off.

Janez ignored him, marching straight to his mother's chair where he dropped to one knee and kissed the rings adorning her fingers.

"Your Highness," he said gravely, lowering his eyes to the floor. "I am honoured by your kind reception."

"And I by your attendance, Prince Janez. Please, sit."

He sat in demure silence while she ordered more food and wine to the table before dismissing the guards and servants entirely.

Finally alone, the formality broke, and they giggled together like children sharing in secrets.

"That captain is such a pompous arse, I thought he would give himself a stroke and pass clean away if we were to greet each other properly. Come here, and give your old mother a kiss."

"Hardly old, Mother," Janez protested but reached to kiss her cheek all the same.

Neither he nor Alarik much resembled their mother. She was darker-skinned, with dark hair she kept tightly coiled to prevent it frizzing in the damp. She'd been tall and regal (too-thin and perhaps hard-looking) when queen, but age and grief had softened those physical edges and rendered her quite fat. It suited her better, despite the cause. Yet her beauty glowed in spite of the terrible loss that had chased her here. She'd always been a *happy* woman, perfectly suited to the role of benevolent queen and mother of future kings. Janez's childhood—so often regimented by duty and service, by strict tutors and stern swordmasters—was peppered with memories of Mother's stories by the fire in place of any maid or governess, and on her insistence upon cradling them through illness and injury, despite the distance most aristocratic mothers kept from their broods. Indeed, his very earliest memory was Mother singing as she brushed his hair for bed. Of how she'd rest him, all of three years old, against her breast and soothed him to sleep with that rhythmic brushing and her soft melody.

Father had been distant. His brother had always been someone to navigate, thanks to his destiny as king. But Mother—oh, Mother had always been quite simple. She loved him, and Janez her, and all else was of no concern.

So he didn't speak of balls and princesses, of Sigurd and empty shipyards, or even of his despair of marriage and his failure the night before and this very morning. Instead, he sat back in his seat and said, "Ingrid is taking after me, Mother."

"After you?" Mother laughed. "In that she is running her poor father ragged, or in that she has learned how to charm the entire palace guard to treason?"

"Both."

"What is the latest?"

"She managed to persuade them to dress her in a guardsman's uniform and teach her the first strikes of sword fighting. Alarik caught her challenging a kitchen cat to a duel."

"I can't imagine he was thrilled."

"Neither was the cat."

"Did he scold?"

"Spluttered, rather. I didn't know if he was going to laugh, or lock her in the dungeons for a tearaway."

He updated her with trivial stories as they broke bread—of Ingrid's adventuring, of the baby's hair slowly turning a rusty blond, of Sofia glowing suspiciously of late—and so was taken quite by surprise when Mother sat back, wine glass in hand, and said, "So tell me of this friend."

"Friend?"

"Rumour travels faster than you do, Janez. I hear of a foreigner who dragged you from the water and has scarcely left your side since."

Janez laughed and lied, as was his strength. "Mother. He is quite simple. I feel sorry for him. That is all."

"You feel sorry for cats, Janez, so you hand them to the cooks to keep the mice at bay."

"He cannot speak the language. He would be subject to much suspicion and abuse, what with the current war."

"And you are certain he is not of the enemy?"

"I am."

"Still," she said. "I know you, Janez. This is not kindness for some simpleton. You are fond of him."

His hackles rose slightly.

"I'm fond of a great many people."

"But of him, most of all."

"Not at all," Janez replied. "If it's company you speak of, I'm most fond of a port-girl with particular charms."

"Oh, I'm sure. And a particular price, no doubt."

Janez lifted his glass in silent acknowledgement, and Mother smiled.

"All the same," she said. "I would advise that you—get this out of your system, perhaps. By the spring, you are likely to be married. You will certainly be betrothed. And your wife will deserve your devotion."

"And she will have it," he said woodenly.

"You have met them? Sigurd's daughters?"

"Never."

"Hm. I have met the father—he came to our own wedding, all those years ago. He is pompous, but pleasant enough. He is likely, I would imagine, to value his daughters' happiness."

"As he ought."

"And I value my son's," Mother said. "Janez. Tell me. Did you offer to do this, or has Alarik commanded it?"

Both.

Still, was it? Was it truly both, when Alarik had only ordered what Janez had already agreed to do? And when he had agreed to it, there had been no reason not to. No reason to suppose he would fall in love with anyone but the woman he was supposed to.

"I would not see you miserable," Mother said softly.

"I would not see us defeated in war," he replied, just as low. "I have no choice, Mother."

She reached out and squeezed his hand. But she said nothing, and he knew himself to be correct.

"They arrive tomorrow," she murmured. "Celebrations will be the following day. Find some happiness, my darling. Carry it with you into the ballroom. One of them may well be the very thing you need."

No, he wished to say. *The very thing I need is in a servant's quarters and cannot say the word for flowers correctly.*

"Maybe, Mother," he said instead and wished it could be true.

Chapter Thirty-One

HELD HAD THOUGHT the palace by the sea to be grand.

The palace by the mountains was grander.

It was much like Ahtola—great white towers jutting from the mountainside, capped by dark roofs. There were five of them, with covered bridges between them, and a courtyard encircled at the base by great white walls, punctured only by the gates that had allowed them access. Even the very image of it caused a twinge of pain to erupt anew in his chest—but its life, its vitality, was not like the Whalelands, and so Held was soothed again.

Now, he stood in one of those towers, peering from the narrow window at some dark creature circling below and screeching in a cracked, croaking caw, and wondering what it could possibly be.

The room was small and close, like that first inn, but it had this window, and the floor was thickly covered in furs. He'd lain amongst them, admiring their softness for the longest time before the cawing creature had caught his attention.

It seemed as though he was on the very top of the world—was *this* the sky, to skymen?—but the great mountain stretched ever onwards above him, until Held felt dizzy just trying to see the top. Maybe there was no top. Maybe the world went on forever, and his pe—merfolk had it wrong all along. They were on the bottom of the world. The skymen in the middle. And maybe something else, even more incredible, above the blue.

He was disturbed from his thoughts when a knock rapped at the door, and it cracked open. Janez. Looking grand in his most regal attire, so stiff and formal and utterly perfect—and so out of place in this little servant's room. Held beamed and dragged him across to the window to point down at the creature.

"What is it?" he asked.

"Ein Vogel."

"Virgil," Held attempted but earned no laugh. Instead, he was pressed to the stone and glass by a great weight, intense yet gentle, and arms like ropes circled his middle. "Janez?" he asked softly, reaching behind himself awkwardly to catch at the curls buried against his spine and stroke them.

The grip tightened. And then the fingers spread wide on his belly. One hand was pushed higher, under the shirt, to cover one side of his chest. The other pushed lower, into cloth and undercloth, to cup his sex in its hot palm. Held groaned as his body was stirred into life and sighed when he felt Janez's rouse as well. Gripped so tightly he could barely move, he clutched instead at the stone walls that bracketed the window, bracing himself there, and shifted his legs a little further apart when he felt that warm, welcome weight against his thigh. Rocked into the maddening, wonderful rasp of Janez's rough palm against his swollen flesh. Chased that high, that pleasure, and reached it when Janez's teeth sank into his neck, and he was seized there like a possession.

Like he belonged.

He sank into the afterglow, and they went to the floor together. Janez's hands still roamed, his hardness unyielding, and Held twisted over to kiss him, quite drunk with happiness, and work open Janez's clothes until he found it. Hard flesh, hot and wanting. He pushed further, opening loops and buttons until they all gave way, and freed the man from the prince's attire. He kissed the crown of that need—to a choked moan from his victim—and then kissed higher. Bit at the little places he was learning, on belly and chest. Spread himself over this skyman's form, catching that need between their bodies, and absorbing the urgent roll of pleasure that rocked up Janez's body. Held caught at it, caught at him, and they moved together as though tangled together in a calm sea. For all Janez had been urgent, Held wished for calm, for time to see the beauty escalate into divinity when Janez reached his peak. When he did, it was exquisite. Unfathomable. Still so utterly beautiful and utterly alien—the sweat at his temples, the rasp of air in his chest, the blank stare of the blue abyss...and then Held's heart broke as the bliss dissolved. The fair brow creased. Janez covered his face with one hand and let out a wrenching sound of pure agony.

Held let go as if he'd been burned—but it wasn't pain, or at least not something physical, for Janez clutched him, seizing him tight once more and taking another reeling gasp from Held's shoulder.

"Don't be sad," Held begged, utterly at a loss of how to convey it. He dragged the furs around them, clutched fistfuls of hair and cloth, begged his body to show what he couldn't say. "I'm here. You can't be sad if I'm here. You just can't."

It wasn't allowed, or it ought not have been. How could Janez—handsome, wonderful, kind, generous Janez, who owned Held's very existence and held it like a delicate treasure in the palm of his hand, who could snuff him out with so much as a whisper of love to another—how could someone that utterly central to another's world possibly be sad?

It took a while for the grip to ease, but when it did, Janez's eyes were red-rimmed. He rose clumsily, but rather than leave, he sank to the edge of the bed and sat with head in hands. His posture was of such pure misery that Held dropped to the floor between those long legs, resting his hands on Janez's thighs, and peered up hopefully into a lost and empty gaze.

"Tell me," he whispered, and Janez frowned faintly—then gestured at the desk and asked for parchment. It was one of Held's many new words, and he rose to fetch it. A single sheet, old and dusty, had been left in the desk. The inkwell was near dry, the liquid clotted and thick, but Janez appeared to have no need to write eloquent prose.

Instead, he drew a king.

A crown and a round head, a scratchy little beard, and lines for limbs. He drew a queen, with the crown and a huge round skirt. He drew himself, with a tiny crown and tail of hair, and then he drew the lines—above for himself and the king, and below for the king and the queen.

Held watched curiously, waited patiently, for little Ingrid to appear, but she did not. Instead, Janez touched each figure and said its name, waiting until Held nodded to continue. And then he touched the line between king and queen and whispered, *"Verheiratet."*

Held frowned in confusion.

"Verheiratet," Janez repeated softly and then pointed to his picture. Circled the empty space to its left with his finger. *"Unverheiratet."*

He repeated them again several times until Held thought he, perhaps, saw it. The line was this...'very-tat,' or whatever it was Janez had said. The king and queen had this 'very-tat.' And Janez did not.

Oh.

Oh.

Ingrid had come from the line. From the very-tat. And the king and queen—

Married! Janez was saying they were married, and he was not.

But then Held frowned. Why was this a source of sadness? Or needing explanation? He had—well, he'd assumed Janez wasn't married. Ever since Ingrid had transpired to be his niece, not his daughter, Held had assumed Janez had no wife, no princess.

And then Janez drew a maid. A big skirt. A little crown shaded in another colour—a queen, maybe. But not like his brother was king?

And a line. From Janez to the new queen.

"Ich muss heiraten."

The words. Three of them, by the way he sounded them out. I. The next one Held didn't know. And one so similar to—to—

He touched the new line, still wet.

"Du. Verheiratet?"

Janez nodded.

The look of pain on his face was so intense that Held felt his very ribs caving in. There was no air in the room. No. No! Janez could not—must not—*married*? He would be married? He would—he would have a wife, and—and children, and he would—oh, he would love her, love them, how could he not, and—

Held seized the parchment from him and tore it in two. "No!" he shouted, and then, *"Nein!"* The grief poured out in a burning rush. His vision blurred, and hot salt water rained down his face. He struck out and caught Janez across the cheek; the prince flew up, catching him firmly and crushed them together in a hug so fierce it could never be broken—

And Held broke.

Broke apart, right there, and howled. Screamed grief, agony, pain, death, fear, *hatred* into Janez's shirt. Yet he knew, he *knew* by the look of such agony, by their shattered coupling, by the way his hair was wet where Janez had pressed his face, that Janez didn't want this. He didn't want this. The king—the king—that vile, angry, suspicious king had done this. He had done this—

Held worked his arms free from Janez's hold, put them around his chest and clung tight.

To—death.

Janez would marry. He would love her, because that was what husbands did, love their wives. He would love her, this princess with the shaded crown. There would be no more kisses, sky or mer. No more love, either shining in his eyes or pressed into Held's skin from his hands. And Held—

Held would die. Would burst into sea foam, and die.

Janez was whispering, *"Ich liebe dich,"* over and over into Held's hair. Held knew not what it meant, but it didn't matter.

Janez was going to get married.

And Held was going to die.

Chapter Thirty-Two

THE BALL CAME too soon.

A thousand years would have been too soon, but two meagre days—

It was torture.

Janez kept to his rooms as much as possible, under the guise of allowing their esteemed guests time to settle in and enjoy Mother's company, and without the need to put on airs and graces for diplomatic negotiations. In reality...

In reality, it was as though his heart was breaking. Held looked much the same. His violent reaction to the truth had been crushing. After, he had seized Janez by the hair and kissed him, kissed him so fiercely it ought to have branded them both in bruises, and refused to be parted for the night. So the following day, Janez stayed in his rooms with Held always within arm's reach, and yet— They did not touch.

Part of Janez wanted to take and be taken until there was no life left in him, no energy to think and mourn this loss. Another part of him was so sunken in depression that he could do little. Held, for his part, seemed to mourn. He brushed Janez's hair every hour, until ribbons carpeted the floor, and then would undo his work by combing his fingers through the curls, holding them out straight and releasing them in a hypnotic, repetitive study. The sun sank, and rose again. As it dipped towards the mountain peaks yet again, Janez knew he must move. But it felt like drowning.

Mother sent a veritable army of servants as the sky deepened to a rusty copper, and although Held guarded Janez's hair jealously, the others were grudgingly permitted to wash and dress the man, until— until he was no man at all, but a prince on display. The shirtsleeves billowed; the stockings suffocated his legs. The boots had been polished until they seemed to emit more light than the sun itself, and his collar was so starched Janez sourly thought he could have shaved upon it. And the shave itself, by God! Any closer, and it would have removed skin and bone. He was puffed and powdered to within an inch of his life until a feminine man, forged in grace and elegance and wealth, eyed him back from the looking glass with a cold and calculating countenance.

It was not himself, and Janez sighed.

"I suppose we ought to get this over with," he murmured.

He wanted very much to kiss Held goodbye, as though he was going off to war. But servants gossiped, so he contented himself with gripping his hand tightly before letting go and sweeping out of his chambers, looking for all the world like he were perfectly eager to meet his future bride.

The ball was in its infancy, lords and ladies only just starting to mingle and exchange news and rumours. Hushes followed him through the great hall as he made his way to Mother, nodding and smiling to those whom decorum insisted he must. When he reached her, he bowed deeply in a public show of respect that overrode his private wish for affection.

"Your Highness," he said gravely. "My compliments on such a fine showing."

"Prince Janez." Mother's voice was the same cool formality of public, but her eyes showed sympathy, and the upturn of her mouth was entirely false. She could read him—had always been able to do so. "I trust you are well?"

They exchanged pleasantries, and Janez sucked down several glasses of rich wine. His side felt cold without Held pinned to it as he had been these last two days. The perfumes and powders lurking about his person felt dirty.

He cursed himself. That ship's gun should have drowned him.

The trumpets at the ballroom doors blared, and Janez hastily wiped the grim thoughts from his mind as he turned to watch with a small smile and a respectful air. The great wooden doors swung open, and the announcer boomed the news—His Majesty King Sigurd had graced them with his presence. When the crowd parted, Janez would get his first glimpse of the woman he was to marry.

King Sigurd was an old man—the pure whiteness of his beard, and the great volume of his gut, testified to that—but his wife, a pretty little queen on his arm, was younger by a full thirty years or more. They made a perfectly mismatched couple, the great white bear and the lithe dark lady, yet their smiles and the easy rest of her hand upon his arm seemed so genuine that Janez envied them at once and fought to keep it from his face. Behind them trailed three young ladies, fans aloft, and Janez at once set about watching them.

"My dear Queen," Sigurd boomed in a voice that could have shaken icebergs from the land and unleashed them upon the sea. "A splendid show, quite splendid. And ah, Prince Janez. A pleasure to meet you at long last, Your Highness."

He extended a hand, quite unlike the custom of Janez's people, and Janez smiled through having his fingers crushed.

"And you, King Sigurd. I trust your travel was easy. I must defer all praise for the show to my mother, I'm afraid, and extend my apologies for my absence the last few days. Your Highness," he added, bowing to kiss Queen Elena's gloved hand.

"Kept busy with the war effort, no doubt!" King Sigurd boomed. The easy chuckle that rolled out of him caused the crowd to close, and a gentle hubbub to strike up around them. The orchestra began to play lightly. "My ambassadors tell me you are a naval man."

"I am."

"Excellent. Can't be abiding these shy fellows who never leave their libraries," Sigurd rumbled. Janez murmured an agreement. "Please, pass my compliments to your brother."

"Of course. He extends his own to you and looks forward to your company at the Summer Palace when the weather eases."

Rumbles of wouldn't that be nice followed, under a thin veil of bartering— Sigurd would only do such a thing, Janez knew quite well, if an engagement was reached out of tonight.

"May I introduce my daughters," Sigurd continued, and for all his turgid obesity, love of warfare, and affection for perhaps inappropriately young brides, his chest swelled with a perfectly genuine affection. He beamed like a jolly baker when he swept his arm aside and beckoned the three young ladies to his side. "Brigitte, Alessandra, and Carolina."

Janez bowed, already studying. They curtsied, doing quite the same.

In physical appearance, they were much alike. Short, curvaceous, much taken from their mother in their curled hair and dark skin. They seemed as polished as he felt—but Sigurd was famously soft on his offspring, and it wasn't difficult to see past the fans and perfectly fixed smiles to the women beneath.

The oldest, Brigitte, was utterly disinterested, perhaps to the point of having another in the wings that her father knew nothing about. She stared back at Janez with a frown over a closed fan, a challenge in that stormy gaze. She promised a fight if he tried to take her hand; she promised anger and misery on both sides, and perhaps even the will and power to ensure no alliance would be found there. Janez dismissed her mentally at once—she either was repulsed by his presence, or infatuated by another's, and he'd no desire to tie himself to one who actively didn't want him.

Next stood Alessandra, perhaps the prettiest by a slim margin—and Janez knew that look the moment it caught his eye. She bit her lip and smiled. Dropping her eyes, she curtsied so low that her dress threatened to slip entirely. She, too, shut her fan, yet dragged it through the circle of finger and thumb in a manner entirely provocative. Had Janez been the same man, cut loose and emotionally free as the wind—as he'd been when he'd offered himself as the tool through which to gain Sigurd's help—he'd have ended the matter then and there, and flirted back with abandon. But she wanted something thrilling. She was excited by the entire affair—either she wanted a man for the night or a man for every night hence. Either way, Janez knew it spelled danger. She'd either want others, too, and rumour would spread like wildfire in mere months, or she'd want him alone, and place Held in harm's way to secure him.

But Carolina, the youngest, was no absolution. She regarded him shyly, barely meeting his eyes and withdrawing her hand from his kiss as soon as was permissible, and then hid behind her open fan. She couldn't have been more than a few years younger than he, yet she shrank like a little child still believing boys to be mucky creatures best avoided. Like her sisters, she was a very beautiful woman, catching the eye of all the men in the room—yet, unlike them, she appeared to wish to sink through the floor and vanish entirely.

Janez mentally sighed. He'd let her be. The choice, it seemed, was clear.

Alessandra helped it along, too. After only a minute or two more of conversation, she passed off her fan to her older sister and dropped a hint so clear it was almost indecent.

"A princess does like to dance—would you indulge me, Janez?"

The bold use of his name caused Janez to automatically agree, unsure of what to make of her. A hopeless romantic, or the excitement and danger of a loaded gun? He set his glass aside, took her delicate hand in his own, and indulged.

She was a fine dancer, energetic and graceful, and very beautiful when a fine flush rose from her breast, darkening her skin even further. He led her through three dances before releasing her waist, only to find her fingers tightening on his other hand, and her eyes glancing towards the great doors to the ballroom.

"I have always wanted to see the gardens," she said. "Father says the Winter Palace is famed for its gardens."

It was famed for the great glass greenhouses within them, not for their beauty, but Janez bowed and offered his arm.

"My lady may get cold," he warned. "The gardens run down to the lakes by the mountains, and are cool after sunset."

"I'm sure another dance would warm me," came the sunny reply, and he led her down the stone steps without a murmur, again not sure of her motive. Oh, skin-to-skin, he was sure. But in what manner?

As the lights fell away, she turned upon him in the shadows of the fountains and kissed him boldly upon the mouth. Her hands were tiny at his waist, her body firmly against the front of his in a manner not at all that of a princess, or some demure innocent. She kissed with intent. Not a year ago, he'd have met it with his own eagerness.

Not a year ago, he'd have thanked his lucky stars to be palmed off to such a vivacious bride.

But this was not last year. Gently, he took her by the shoulders and held her at a little length.

"You do not want me, Your Highness?"

"I would not dream of—"

"I would dream," she interrupted and bit her lip. "I am no stranger to what men like, and you are far more handsome than I dared to hope. I would keep you satisfied."

He frowned.

"I am not a beast to be tamed."

"Not ever?" she asked. "Brigitte is so sour, and Carolina is a little girl and wants nothing of marriage and sex."

He'd never before heard a highborn woman say the word and blinked in mute surprise. The only feminine voice he could recall uttering it was Rosa, and even she would breathe for him to love her. Oh, men had asked for sex, men spoke far more crudely, but it sounded almost foreign from Alessandra's pretty lips.

"Think on it?" she murmured, pressing back against him. Her hand cupped him, and he felt himself stir almost automatically. "I have the Anderssen rooms. If you were to come to me tonight, I would welcome you. All of you. Alliance and marriage, or none, should you wish neither."

And then she was gone, slipping back up the path to the palace, leaving Janez standing dumbfounded in the gardens.

He had to be honest with himself—if not for Held, he might have been tempted. If he'd been untethered by the emotion that clutched at his chest whenever those pale eyes lifted to his own, he might have followed her. Might have strayed to the wrong room tonight and asked for her hand in the morning in the manner more befitting both their stations.

But Held's whisper, that soft urge to kiss him, had infected Janez's skin and soul, making him uneasy at the touch of Alessandra's lips upon his own.

How was he supposed to marry her—or indeed any of them—and sire children and potentially a new dynasty for Sigurd's kingdom, if the very touch of her lips and hand upon him left him cold?

Her words sparked in the back of his mind, and he turned to head back into the light. Carolina. She'd referred to her as a child, uninterested in such things. But the princess was twenty-five if she was a day, and quite beyond the first bloom of womanhood. How uninterested was uninterested, Janez wondered, and he decided to seek her out.

She was easy to find by her unease—Janez caught her hiding behind her fan again, an admiral's son loudly inviting her to dine with him at his father's estate in the spring. Janez slipped smoothly to her side with a fresh glass of wine and a polite smile. Over the heads of some dancing lords and ladies, he could see Sigurd watching as Mother murmured to him with a business-like fervour.

They awaited a decision and wished to see him make it.

But the chilly look Carolina threw him said that she utterly disagreed.

"My lady looks a little flushed," Janez said. "Would you care to take some air?"

She glanced between him and the drunken son and pursed her lips.

"Very kind," she said, lifting her hand. It hung loose in his own, and she slid it free the moment they left the ballroom, setting her glass aside. "I advise directing your attentions to my sisters, Prince Janez. I would protest a match until the very end."

"Why so?"

She frowned, lifting her fan a little higher.

"I need give no reason," she replied, a little sharply.

"Need, no, but I would prefer one." He glanced about. "Would you join me, my lady? I would but speak with you privately."

"Speak?" she echoed, the scepticism stark.

"Yes, my lady. Simply speak."

"I am not some servant girl that you can—"

"I have absolutely no designs upon you," he said. "I am no more pleased by the prospect of marriage than I suspect you are, but I also suspect you and I could help one another."

She seemed to waver at that, glancing up and down the hall.

"It would be indecent."

"There are many guards in the gardens. There'd be no rumour if we stayed within the reach of the palace lights."

"You will certainly not be leading me into some dark corner."

"No. Alessandra, perhaps."

It slipped out before he could stop it—and quite suddenly, Carolina giggled. The sound and smile vanished as quickly as they'd come, yet he'd heard them all the same. Ah. So a humour beat beneath the breast, did it?

"All right," she said and slipped her gloved fingers back over the hand he'd lifted for her to take. "The fountains, then? I have a soft spot for water."

"You like the sea?"

"Greatly. Though I know nothing of naval warfare. Father says you are a lieutenant?"

"Yes. When the war is over, doubtless Alarik will make me a captain. It is the tradition."

They discussed ranks—she knew their names, though not their importance—and the beauty of the sea crashing at the straits to the north, where their corner of the world spilled out into the great oceans of the east, over which Sigurd's forces held dominion. When they reached the fountains, she sat with her skirts gathered under her and said, "There is no point to you and I."

"Is there not?"

"No. I will not marry any man."

"You are religious, my lady?"

"Not at all," she parried, still holding the fan like a shield between them. "I have no interest in marriage, or love, or children. I only want my books for company, and that is all."

Janez blinked at her, quite at a loss. "That sounds lonely," he said.

Carolina snorted.

"Of course it does—to a man." She said it scornfully. Janez fought the urge to roll his eyes. She sounded just like Sofia when Alarik had done something idiotic. "Is it so unbelievable that one can exist without losing her head—and her freedom—in exchange for a silly promise and being forgotten once she's old and can no longer bear children?"

The bitterness was tart and angry, and Janez shrugged a little.

"As unbelievable as a man forced to marry a stranger, rather than the one he loves," he said quietly.

She paused, then: "You love another?"

"Yes."

"Marry her."

"I cannot."

"You are a man, you can do whatever—"

"I cannot," he repeated. "I am a prince, not a man. You are condemned to a loveless marriage and motherhood. I am condemned to be bred just the same, and then die for my country on a ship in a foreign sea. I am not allowed love any more than you are."

"But you want it."

"Yes."

"You *have* it."

"Yes," he repeated, safe in that knowledge. He did. And he could not let it be known to Alarik, not now his brother had proven to be just like their father.

"I take it," Carolina said quietly, "that she is some...servant girl, or the like, that she is unsuitable to marry?"

"The like," Janez admitted.

The fan came down slowly. Her gloved hand groped over his and squeezed his thumb.

"I am sorry. It's a silly rule. My mother was no noblewoman, but Father loves her greatly, and she him. And she's just as clever as other queens."

"More so—I daren't say it within her hearing, but my mother may be wise and wonderful, yet she is no scholar."

They giggled guiltily together, and then Carolina patted his hand and withdrew her own.

"In the end, though, we would be required to—to have a child."

"Yes."

"Then—no."

"You would not?"

"Absolutely not," she said, but the fan didn't rise to hide her. "I am sorry."

Then she rose from the fountain, rearranged her skirts, and flowed back up to the palace steps, leaving Janez by the trickling water to think.

He had two options.

One wanted him, and spelled danger and misery.

The other did not, but would be as wise and wonderful a choice as anyone could want.

Chapter Thirty-Three

HELD LAY AWAKE much of the night, expecting any moment to shatter into sea foam and die.

He dared not leave the prince's chambers, to see Janez falling in love with another. He didn't want to see the end of the world—he wanted, when it came, for death to take him by surprise.

But oh, Held didn't want to die.

He'd only just found this beautiful world. He'd only just shirked that terrible wrongness, and the coffin of his soul that his former form had been. He'd barely wound his mind about the terrible loss of his home, that awful truth of their supposed love for him. To have meagre moments above the sky with Janez, and now—now—

The music taunted him, far away and foreboding. The lights dancing across the darkness were like an enemy on the approach. As the hours drew out, longer and longer, and the morning never came, Held settled in Janez's bed. Drawing the curtains around this nest of comfort and familiarity, he buried himself in the pillows to catch Janez's scent, and die here if he could not do so in his lover's arms.

And there he lay, wide awake and waiting.

Waiting.

Simply *waiting*.

After a time, the music faded away below. The palace quieted at long last. And—

Boots sounded outside the doors.

Held knew the sound of him and threw back the curtains as Janez stumbled into the room. The door crashed shut too heavily. Held flung himself from the bed and into Janez's arms. Janez made a surprised sound—he tasted of wine, and his hands were clumsy at Held's back. But Held didn't care for any of it.

He breathed. Janez had returned. So Held had another chance, another day, to keep him. To not let Janez marry that maid, that princess, and fall in love with his new wife. He took hold of the opportunity with determination. Tearing at Janez's clothes, he pulled with mouth and body. They collapsed down into the bed as one. He took Janez with desperate aggression, until they curled together in an exhausted, sweat-soaked mess, and Janez's fingers combing through Held's hair calmed the violence.

Dizzy, Held clung. Jealousy had burned out of him in the heat of it. Here, he focused on Janez's heartbeat under his ear. Counted his breaths.

Held closed his eyes and wanted to cry.

Instead—

When he woke, the bed curtains were still open, and watery light was streaming through the windows. The palace was silent. A great creature was circling in the grey outside. Janez was serenely asleep beneath him, head turned towards Held's, curls tangled across the pillows in a great, golden mess.

He was beautiful.

And Held's. If only for the night, he'd been entirely Held's. He'd not yet been seduced by the princess he was supposed to marry. If Held could only stop the marriage, only stop it from happening—

He found himself sifting his hands through the curls, gently parting them and smoothing out the knots. As the mess began to resemble hair again, Janez stirred and more colour appeared in the cracks of his eyelids. He moved, rolled, and buried Held in body and bed, and they came together again, in a slow and tender hour that passed as slowly as the tide from the shore.

And after—

After, Held took Janez's face in both hands and kissed him, kissed him hard and deep and demanding, and said, "I love you," over and over again until Janez gave up trying to understand or speak over Held's tongue, and simply submitted to the sound.

Held would not lose this.

Not ever.

HELD SLIPPED FREE in the night.

He'd seen the river from the window, winding away from the palace like a great eel, and though his form was no longer of the sea, some part of his soul must still have been. He missed the water, the clutch of her comfort, and it called to him like home. Faced with losing his love and his life, Held so desperately yearned for home.

He waited until there was no light but the cold disc of white in the sky—until Janez slept so deeply that he didn't stir even for Held's touch upon his curls—and then he slipped free. He flitted through the palace like a ghost, the water singing to his very mind. Though he didn't know the way, he somehow found the gardens, and then the meadow, and then the shallow bank of a great yawning channel.

It flowed, slow and sedate, nothing like the chattering stream he'd seen in the woods, but water was water, and Held was—had been—one of its people. Father may not have wanted him; the nest may have been repulsed by him; but they were not, had never been, the entire world under the waves.

If only he'd known that then.

Its bite was icy upon his bared legs, but Held sank to the thigh and sighed in contentment at the familiar touch. The sudden weightlessness of his body was a strange relief. The curl of life and air—*his* air, not theirs—about his skin was soothing. A caress, like a lover. And a hard slap, too, like a scolding mother. His chest ached in homesickness, that ever-present pain of being ripped out of his own world.

Oh, he'd known—the Witch had said—he couldn't come back. But the surface was not a death knell to the merfolk. He should have liked them to visit him. He should have liked a great many things.

Any day now, he would burst into sea foam.

The sudden weight of it—his impending death, home forever being out of reach, the possibility of Janez no longer loving him—bore down upon his shoulders with a great, physical weight, and Held bowed under the pressure with a choked cry. He was going to die. Oh, he was going to die. He was not some love-struck child. Losing Janez would destroy him—but he'd have *lived*. He'd have lived half of a life, yes, but he'd not have literally burst and died upon that moment, upon the moment of Janez's affections turning for another.

He would *die* for this princess and her damned crown.

She would kill him.

Even Janez would kill him—much as Held didn't believe for a moment that he intended or knew he would do it. It was the prince's fickle emotion that would condemn Held.

"Help me," Held whispered to the river.

He touched his fingers to its flat surface. They rippled softly.

"I do not wish to die. Help me keep him. *Help me.*"

The ripples expanded outwards. And—glowed.

Held caught his breath as a circle of bright blue light, cold and pale, formed on the surface of the water, shimmering, and then sank. It began to flow downriver—or maybe swim, for it travelled faster than the water kissing Held's legs—and long after it was out of sight, Held stared after it in silent astonishment.

Skymen could not do that, could they?

He'd never seen Janez do it, or the skyling that had drowned before him. If they could, why had Janez not begged for help? Why had the skyling not cried out? They'd not known Held was there to save them, after all. And Held hadn't done it at the little stream, that day Janez had touched him for the first time as a lover.

What had it been?

Was it—

Witchcraft?

Chapter Thirty-Four

WOULD-BE GROOM AND would-be bride breakfasted apart.

And late—Janez didn't rise until the sun was high above the mountaintops, and the foul aftertaste of smoky wine did little to improve his mood. Perhaps Mother felt the same, or perhaps she merely anticipated it, for when he dressed and descended, she met him to break bread alone.

"I take it," she said, "that by your tempers last night, you found no easy answer?"

Janez paused over the meats and sighed. "It depends how selfish I wish to be," he admitted, and Mother frowned.

"How is that?"

"The most sensible choice for my purposes is Carolina. But the best for the women in question is Alessandra."

Mother propped her chin on her hand and smiled at him. "Do explain."

"Why the look, Mother?"

"Because you rather remind me of someone at this moment."

He frowned; she merely smiled again and gestured for him to explain himself.

"Very well. Alessandra was very forward with me...and made her attraction known. She would be happy to be wed, I feel, and an...enthusiastic wife. But I fear she wouldn't be satisfied by my unwillingness and would turn to other men. And you know what follows."

Scandal. She didn't say it, but she nodded all the same.

"With Carolina, there is no such concern—but also no such attraction. Men repulse her, as does her duty to bear children. She would be far more sensible for me, but quite miserable."

Mother nodded.

"But in the end, Janez, you are the man in this marriage. It is your choice."

Janez shifted uncomfortably. "It shouldn't be."

"No, but that is the way of the world."

"I wouldn't condemn either to misery."

"They will be quite used to the idea, as are you." That, Janez thought, was patently false. Used to an idea didn't mean acceptance of it. "We women are excellent at making good of a bad thing. And if you are kind and loyal to whomever you chose, I doubt she would mind very much."

Janez thought of Carolina's fan, and her disgusted expression, and thought Mother was not completely right about that.

"Alessandra would be happier," he said. But she, too, came with a price. Janez had always preferred the company of women with Alessandra's lust for life and love, but the wider world was less patient. If she were prone to affairs, Janez's heart cared not—so would he be, for this entire union, and to a man, no less—but rumour was a dangerous thing. If she were known to be unfaithful, then any children would be rumoured to be bastards. It would endanger the very lineage that Alarik and Sigurd wanted from this alliance. It would jeopardise the very point of the thing. If he were forced to marry, why marry a woman who would potentially risk the very thing the marriage sought to gain?

But then—

The ugly little word crept up in the back of his mind. In the end, he had to get his wife pregnant.

And to get Carolina pregnant, he would have to rape her.

A shudder rocked out from his shoulders, and Janez pursed his lips in disgust. No. There would be no such—such violence, such abomination, in his bed. Marriage bed or otherwise.

"The choice is clear," he said as he pushed back from the table. "Excuse me, Mother. I believe I must speak with King Sigurd."

THE KING AND his family had been granted the entirety of the south wing—the warmest place in the palace, and the most beautifully crafted. Even as a child, Janez had been forbidden to play games in the south wing, and he felt an appropriate sense of gravity weigh upon him as he was announced and shown into the great drawing room where Sigurd awaited him.

And, to Janez's surprise, awaited him alone.

"I trust all is well with your wife and daughters, Your Majesty?"

"Come now, Prince Janez, you haven't come here to make idle chat about women," Sigurd guffawed. But then his gaze sharpened, and he waved Janez to sit. "Or have you?"

"Idle, no. About women, yes."

The gaze sharpened further.

"You have taken a shine to one of my girls, then?"

Janez raised his eyebrows. "They are all perfectly engaging—"

"I watched you with them all, Your Highness. You spoke not a word to Brigitte."

Janez allowed himself a small smile as he sat. "I...felt that the good lady might break my nose if I tried."

Thankfully, Sigurd chuckled again.

"Ah, yes. She is a fine woman. Would make a fine queen, if she could learn a queen's place."

Janez chose to ignore that remark.

"You quite turned Alessandra's head. And young Carolina, for that matter. I've never seen the girl so enchanted by another being. Between you and I, young Janez—" The king leaned in close. "—her indifference has been quite the problem. If you *were* to... Well, dowries can be negotiated."

Janez fought to keep the frown off his face. He'd supposed Sigurd to be a proud and protective father, but perhaps he'd been wrong. Was the man honestly offering a higher dowry if Janez would take his problem child from his hands?

Janez sat back. Let the cool rush of warfare, of diplomacy, roll over his soul, and cool his own sense of injustice. If the king wished to negotiate, then so be it.

"Indeed, I would have thought an indifference to be a virtue," he said. "Rumours follow flirts, Your Majesty. I'd like to think any rumours about my future wife entirely false, and not be forced to entertain them myself."

Sigurd raised a snowy eyebrow.

"Carolina is no such woman," he said stiffly.

"Her sister, however..."

The wide mouth thinned.

"Alessandra is—"

He stopped.

"Yes," Janez said calmly. "Alessandra is. A very beautiful and charming young lady, most utterly engaging, yet...I rather get the impression that she is very engaging with a great many men."

"I assure you, sir, that her virtue remains!"

"I make no slight upon her virtue," Janez said, although he plainly did. He'd never been cupped like that by any virtuous soul—man or woman. "However, it cannot be denied that such a pretty and vivacious woman is like a candle to the moths that are men."

Sigurd harrumphed. The shrewd look was back, and the men weighed each other up in a brief silence.

And then, finally, Sigurd said, "She is young. Foolish. She harbours romantic ideas."

She harboured more than that. But Janez sensed there'd be trouble if he mentioned her offer to him the night before, and demurred.

"And if she should harbour more earthly ideas? A wife of indifference would be preferable to a wife covered in rumour." Frowning, Sigurd opened his mouth, and Janez delivered the killing blow.

"How are we to trust that my sons are my own?"

Silence.

And there lay the risk of it. For both of them. Janez cared little—he'd be a king in name only, should his wife become Sigurd's heir, but Sigurd's investment in this alliance was, of course, a male heir. A grandson to inherit his crown.

And if that grandson were even supposed to be from another man's loins...

"However," Janez relented, "she is perfectly charming company. If, perhaps, you were to exchange Carolina's heightened incentive for Alessandra's..."

"You play a hard bargain, Janez."

The use of his name made Janez smile. A deal had been struck, then, even if Sigurd wanted to save face and not admit it.

"I admit, you're not what I supposed. The last I heard of you was a thin, meagre sort of man playing at war and whores. Certainly time has crafted a general, not a mere soldier."

Time, or Father's harsh lessons. Janez allowed a thin smile.

Sigurd seemed to read his mind. "Children are what their fathers make of them. I would not have any of my daughters married off to some fool, or birthing an idiot's sons."

Janez inclined his head.

"Tell me, why not my eldest?"

"I have no designs upon your throne, Your Majesty. I do this for my country, not myself. If in my duty, I can obtain a good name for my sons and a pleasant wife with whom to spend my days, then I consider it a fine enough duty to have," Janez lied. "And Alessandra made for pleasant company—an excellent dance partner."

Sigurd hummed.

Then lifted a silver bell from the table at his elbow and rang for a servant. One of his own appeared, clad in the northern greens, and bowed deeply when told to summon the Princess Alessandra.

She came so quickly it was apparent the girls had been listening at the door, and her face was bursting to smile around its polite facade. Sigurd said, "Prince Janez has petitioned me for your hand in marriage, my dear," and the beam escaped.

"Really, Father?" she gushed, and then composed herself before turning that wide smile upon Janez. It dimmed a little, into something older, slyer, more flirtatious, and her tone dropped accordingly. "I am flattered, Your Highness."

Janez rose and bowed to kiss her hand. She didn't let go of his once he did—instead, she slid her fingers about his elbow and tucked herself against his side as though they were already lovers.

"Now, then," Sigurd said, the old king receding to show the father behind. "I believe an announcement is in order?"

Janez smiled, playing the part, and led his—fiancée, so it seemed, from the drawing room to meet with Mother once more.

And his chest constricted under his waistcoat, tight as if his ribs had been cracked.

Held would not like it. Hell, *Janez* would not like it. But he could make Alessandra happy, and grant her children without the violence and hate it would require with Carolina, while they both did their duty.

If she strayed, so be it. He wouldn't demand her faithfulness, only her discretion.

Janez would have to hope it would be enough.

Chapter Thirty-Five

HELD WAS WOKEN in the night by Janez's hand upon his shoulder and a soft voice in his ear.

"Komm," Janez murmured—come, one in Held's collection of sky words—and then he put a finger to Held's lips and added, *"Still jetzt,"* in a whisper.

Held scowled, kissed the offending finger, and threw back the blankets. Janez was already dressed in heavy winter clothes, and Held felt oddly offended. Even that thick, soft hair had been brushed and tied back. The moment Held had pulled on his own clothes and greatcoat, he shoved Janez down into a chair and took the ribbon out. He'd done it wrong anyway.

"Held—"

Held rapped Janez's knuckles when he attempted to take the brush, and began to rearrange his hair. What, did he think his *wife* was going to do this?

Janez submitted quietly enough, and Held dared hope the offence had been understood, for when a new ribbon was in place, Janez turned on him, taking his face in both hands, and kissed him firmly upon the mouth.

Then he said, *"Komm,"* again and headed for the door.

It was dark and cold, the air icy, yet the palace was busy in a hushed, frenetic sort of way. Servants rushed about with lamps; as Held was led into the great courtyard, he saw one of the four-legged beasts snorting and shifting in the ropes a skyling had wound about its face and neck. The skyling glanced at Held and called out, only for Janez to bark an order.

"Er kann nicht reiten," he shouted and swung himself upon the seat that had been tied to the animal's back. "Held! *Komm.*"

The skyling heaved, Janez pulled, and then Held was seated, too, behind Janez and so terribly far from the ground. He clutched about

Janez's chest and greatcoat with both hands, petrified, and the beast shifted uneasily below them.

"*Was?*" Held asked tentatively in Janez's tongue, pointing at the animal. It was so much bigger than the one from their trip to the river, and Held couldn't imagine it was the same sort of thing. If the previous one had been a fish, this was a shark.

"*Ein Pferd,*" Janez said.

Ironford? Was that the animal's name, or its type? Or—

The thought was cut off when it reared. Held yelped, burying his face between Janez's shoulders, and then—oh, then, it galloped. Galloped! It set off at a full run across the courtyard, and Held clung in terror, with Janez the only thing to keep him from falling. Ironford thundered out of the courtyard and through the great gates—and they were swallowed by darkness. All Held knew was this terrible cold, the surge of Ironford beneath him like an angry sea, and the rough rasp of Janez's greatcoat about his face.

And yet—

The longer the terrible charge continued, the more Held's body was forced to relax. The more he caught Janez's rhythm urging the beast onwards, the less it felt he were was about to fall.

Slowly, he turned his face to the side and peered at the darkness flashing past.

To find that it was not as dark as he'd thought. The great white eye was open above the mountains, perfectly round and sending silvery light pouring over the land. And that land was gleaming a bluish-white in the gloom. When Held dared to look down, Ironford's legs were churning up white foam from the ground. He grew sick from the height again and looked up to Janez's hair for distraction, white flecks clung to the dark ribbon and were turning to water amongst the red.

One floated down out of the air and kissed Held upon the cheek.

Cold.

He flinched at its icy touch and rubbed it away hastily on Janez's coat. It felt like a soft iceberg, and Held didn't like it. Why were they out on Ironford in the middle of the night with this foam all around them? They could have been in bed. They *ought* to have been in bed.

But they just kept going, and the foam kept falling. The echoes of other beasts and the occasional shout from other skymen said they led a charge—but where was the enemy? Why were they charging? And in the dark, too.

But over the thunder of the beasts, and too afraid to loosen his grip, Held couldn't have voiced the questions or understood the answers. So he clung on and waited, trusting. He might have dozed a little. As the sky began to lighten, and a chilly air rushed at them, he even managed to burrow his fingers into the front of Janez's coat and earned himself a quiet laugh.

The sky was a bright sword-grey when they stopped at a little inn on the road, but it wasn't for long. New beasts were waiting, a servant blue-faced in the cold holding their ropes. Held, to his quiet disgust, was heaved up behind Kapitän, and Janez only laughed at his imploring face.

There was an advantage, though—Kapitän rode an even larger beast that kept an easy pace with Janez's new white creature. Now, Held could enjoy the view of Janez's hair streaming out behind him, and the bright flush of cold high in his cheeks. He looked oddly delicate, gentle and refined, and Held was struck with a fierce urge to bite and break him.

He *did* doze on that second stretch, missing the mountains as they fell away, until he blinked a second time and found the air had gone dark once more. Dwelling lights peered out of the gloom, yet they didn't stop. Some of the other riders had fallen behind, exhausted, but Kapitän and Janez pressed on. Held's body ached. His eyes were blurry. His hands were frozen, and his backside numb. Yet they rode on and on and on, and never stopped.

IT WAS THE sound of the sea that woke him. There was salt in the air, and the animal's gait changed, and Held was awake all at once, clinging to Kapitän in a flash of terror.

A warm laugh and a single word—*"Vorsichtig"*—was his reply, and then the darkness parted to warm lights down on the harbour front, and the cry and call of skymen in the clouds.

They had come back.

And the harbour was heaving.

Men ran about every which way. The clouds had been lashed to the stone walkways, and skymen swarmed them with crates and the great, grey beasts that had tried to drown Janez. Despite the night, lamps glowed all about the place like anglerfish.

And Janez leapt right amongst the fray.

He simply jumped down from the beast and waded into the crowd, barking orders. Kapitän lingered only long enough to help Held down before he, too, walked into the chaos, his loud voice booming above the hubbub.

Held stood lost amongst the noise, and stared.

They were preparing to steer the clouds again, he decided. One had drifted free, hanging low in the water, and a hundred men or more were climbing its great white tops. Why? Where were they going? And why had Janez ridden with such urgency to join them?

Janez.

Held looked wildly about and then followed the flash of red-gold along the stone arm that jutted out into the sea. He hung back, uncertain, as Janez engaged a man in a blue coat in a vicious argument, which was quickly broken by the arrival of a great fat man in a large hat. Was Held supposed to follow Janez aboard the cloud? Or was Janez staying ashore? He was to be married—why would he be allowed to take a cloud to sea if he was to be married?

Colour caught Held's eye.

He twisted about to stare, and a line of bright blue—like the river, and like that strange plea in the mountains—slithered away around the corner at the very end of the walkway.

There was a low wall, beyond which lay jagged rocks and rotting seaweed, dusted white by the icy foam drifting down from the steel-grey air. Held leaned over the stone, and watched the blue line dive away into the deep. The water swelled. Something stirred.

There was something down there.

Held glanced over his shoulder. The men were busy. None looked his way. They wouldn't miss him for the moment.

He clambered over the wall and scrambled down the rocks to the water's edge. They were slippery with seawater and ice, but they weren't what made him stumble.

It was the moment the water swelled a second time, and bodies broke the surface.

Twenty-two hands in length, with great pale eyes and fashionably bare chests. Hair the bright, brilliant colour of coral.

Mermaids.

Chapter Thirty-Six

THE RAVEN HAD come in the night. Their spies had spoken. The enemy fleet had sailed and was intent on one final battle, one last attempt at taking the kingdom before winter froze the war.

It had been a miracle that the pass hadn't already been closed—as it was, they'd left at once and still struggled through heavy snowfall. He ought to have left Held sleeping, safe in the Winter Palace with Mother, but—

But a part of Janez had selfishly wanted Held with him, should—should this be the end.

This was war. And Held had saved him once before from a death at sea. Perhaps he would do so again. Perhaps death would be an adequate solution.

Janez brutally cut the thought as they finally entered the city boundaries. It wasn't the time. As the harbour's mayhem closed about him, the weight of his station rolled down his back and dissipated, and his rank sat close about his shoulders like a cloak.

He was a lieutenant.

And his ship prepared for war.

He swung down from the horse and waded in, heading straight for the *Vogel*. She'd been stripped for repairs after their last engagement but now floated near-ready, her hull low in the water from the weight of her guns. The crew were hauling her powder barrels aboard, and Janez made for her ropes to get aboard and join them.

"Your Highness!"

The rusty scratch of Lieutenant Bauer's voice was an unpleasant noise, like the scrape of a knife upon a plate. Janez winced and stepped back.

"Your Highness, you ought to be at the palace."

An entire day and most of the night riding, and now this insolent little—

Janez paused. Breathed out and said, "I am the lieutenant of a ship about to launch, Bauer. I ought to be here."

"The king gave orders—"

"Unless the captain himself releases me from my duty to this ship," Janez said stiffly, "any hearsay about the king does not move me."

Bauer's eyes bulged. "Hearsay!"

"Yes, Bauer, hearsay. Unless you have a royal seal?"

"How dare you, sir!" came the raspy indignation, his eyes bulging like a squashed frog's. Janez fixed him with an utterly cold look.

"You forget yourself, Bauer."

The bulging bulged further still—and then the deep rumble of the captain's voice came between them, followed by his form.

"You both forget yourselves."

The reprimand was swift, simple, and striking. Bauer coloured. Janez cooled. How easy rank made it to forget a slight, instead of station. How simple, to yield to the captain's authority—yet how that, too, won Janez the argument, when the captain ordered Bauer aboard and Janez to the harbourmaster to muster any hands that could be spared.

"Five sick from the whorehouses, and two more rotting in the gaols for rape. Perhaps a touch of royal blood can open the master's fist when it comes to his landsmen."

Janez privately doubted it, as he was ill remembered there for releasing their foreign prisoner. But an order meant that the captain either hadn't heard of any such command from the king, or had chosen to ignore it.

So Janez inclined his head and hurried away.

Pressing was Janez's most loathed duty in the navy. A wooden crate of angry, stupid fellows with no wish to be there cried out for trouble, and in any case, Janez could privately admit he was something of a romantic when it came to the liberty of men. He would have liked at his side only those who wished to sail with him.

But then the pragmatist—the administrator, the diplomat, the heir apparent for that brief period between the death of his father and the birth of his nephew—made himself known once more. This was war. The allure of adventure and prize money was snuffed out in such times. Zeal for king and country fuelled many, to be sure, but in such bitter conflicts, with the protective cloak of winter almost about them, there was only so much that zeal could do. And Janez was not so well known by sight as to fuel a little more.

Still, he collared a handful of men from the builders' yard, and a fishing boat returning at quite the inopportune moment delivered them up to the ship without much fuss. They swore and grumbled, of course, but seemed to know that if he didn't press them, another ship would.

And so Janez came aboard to report to the first lieutenant these new hands, and felt the roll of a deck under his feet for the first time since that fateful day a blessed stranger had dragged him from the water. Oh, but it felt like home.

It was comforting, that gentle sway, even muted as it was by the moorings. Janez had been ranked since he was thirteen years old, a princeling of a midshipman, and much as he feared what each straying from a safe harbour might mean, there was a part of him that would always find home upon the sea.

How fitting, then, that his love had arisen from it.

The first lieutenant looked harried and pursed his lips in disapproval at Janez's report. "It's not enough," he said. "We need two dozen more, at least. The enemy could be with us at any time, but we barely have the men to—"

And then, of course, it happened.

Dawn was barely breaking to the east, and under the first slivers of grey morning light, the first cry from a lookout on a sister ship arose.

"Sails!"

The harbour froze as one, barely breathing.

"Sails!" came the cry again. "Sails on the horizon!"

An explosion of noise. Of movement. Of activity, driven now by the desperation of hours, not days. They were almost here. The crews flocked to their ships with their last things. The ropes slithered and snaked away from their mooring posts. The anchor chains squealed, and sails were unfurled and began to swell.

And Janez's heart clutched tight in his chest.

Held.

Where the devil was Held?

Chapter Thirty-Seven

"BALTA," HELD WHISPERED. "Meri."

They stared back at him with great, sad eyes, their skin a mottled green in the icy shallows, and Held thought, out of nowhere, that they seemed so very strange. Had he been so, in that form?

Balta opened her mouth, but a harsh gurgle emerged, and she ducked her head beneath the sea again, ghostly pale and out of focus.

And then—clearly shouting, yet barely audible to Held—she said, "Calla?"

The name sounded as though it belonged to another, as though they spoke of someone from long ago, entirely apart from Held.

It sounded—

Oh, but it sounded as foreign as Janez's tongue. And so much less pleasant to behold.

"It's Held now," he said in their own speech, the hard edges of the name jarring and difficult in such a flowing language.

"Halda," Balta attempted. Then: "Held."

Garbled and odd, it was his name all the same, and Held couldn't help smiling and reaching for her. His sisters had come. His family.

But—no. Not. Because he was no longer Father's child, and they were.

"Why are you here?"

"The Witch. She—we went to her. To save you."

"*Save* me?" Held flared up at once. "There is nothing to save me from but Father! He would have seen me drown! He would have—"

"They killed Mother. You cannot blame him for his shock. He—"

"Janez didn't. And neither did I. But Father would have killed me."

Meri spoke up, sharp as ever. "They are barbaric. Cruel. They kill, and—"

"And so do we," Held retorted. "I'm not a little mermaid anymore, Meri! We drive the dying from our nests, and we have wars, too, and— and Father killed the Witch's husband. And skymen are the same! They have—they are flawed, but they are beautiful, too, as we are, and I am one of them now. I'm one of them!"

"You asked for help."

Balta's imploring words struck home. Held paused, the anger cooling.

And that terrible pain returning. They'd come back to Janez's home, not run away. So, Janez was still to be married. And Held—

"If he falls in love with someone else, I'll turn to sea foam, and die," Held whispered. "And he's getting married."

Meri's eyes dropped. Balta's widened.

"He'll love her if he marries her."

Of course he would. Janez was so passionate and bright, so devoted and intent, that if he married, he would lavish attention and devotion upon his new bride until he fell in love with her. He'd be enraptured in no time. And Held would—

"We went to the Witch," Balta said and held up a package wrapped in seaweed. Bright blue water trickled from it, the same iridescent, magical colour at the ripple that had rolled away from Held's fingertips. "We've been waiting days. She said if you called for help, it would guide you here."

"What is it?" Held asked. "How can it stop—"

He opened it and paused. Inside lay a knife. Deadly sharp, perhaps a hand-length at the blade, and the hilt that same violent, violet-blue.

"We traded our motherhood for it," Balta whispered. "If you use it as she said, you'll be turned back and can come home."

The two halves of her words caught in Held's mind. They had traded their motherhood? Their fertility? So they would never have merlings, never continue Father's line, and the nest would dissolve and be destroyed by the inevitable infighting for power that would follow Father's death?

That, Held realised with a shock, was the Witch's revenge. All of Father's children—one of the sky, two struck barren—would never produce merlings. Heirs. His line was ended. That was what the Witch had meant by his sisters' sacrifice. She had known they would bargain for him, and this was the only thing they had that the Witch wanted. She had known all along.

But then, why offer Held a way back?

Unless—

Unless the Witch knew he would not take it.

And thus the second half sunk in. Go back, and not die? He ought to have seized the chance. Ought to have severed his life's dependence upon a skyman's—any skyman's—love. Ought to have agreed eagerly, and ask what he needed to do.

But—go back? To that form, to that terrible entrapment? To lose this body, its angles and lines, and regain the curves and sweeps that had tormented him? For his voice to rise into the heavens again and be too terrible to use, and for the great frills about his waist to touch his arms and remind him of being her again, all of the time, until the end of his days?

To compound the agony that would be losing Janez with the torment of becoming Calla once more?

"How—how would this save me? How could this possibly save me?"

He didn't mean to hear an answer, yet one came regardless.

"If you strike this skyman in the heart," Balta said, "and allow his blood to touch your feet, then you will be turned back, and you can come home."

Strike—

Kill him? Kill *Janez*?

Held recoiled, dropping the knife onto the rocks. "No!" The word rang out, and he stared in horror at them. "No!" He couldn't. He *wouldn't*. Who would kill their lover, for losing them? How would *this* prevent it? It was no saviour. It was no solution.

"If you don't, you will die!" Meri proclaimed, and Held turned on her in an instant.

"I would have drowned below if not for Balta!" he raged. "Father would have had me drown! So would you! Why would I—"

And the wrenching pain at his father's look of disgust was consumed in a fire of anger. Pure, unadulterated anger.

Why would he go back to those who had rejected him? Why would he welcome reconciliation with those who had stood by as he suffocated? Why return now that he knew the truth of their love and its conditions and its falsehoods?

When here, above the sky, he had Janez?

Even if he were destined to lose him again—along with his life—had Held not found a truer love here? They could barely speak to one another, yet Janez laughed with him, loved with him, had been so unfailingly kind and patient, and had adored him, even if this princess was to end Held's world.

The anger sealed the wound into a savage scar, and Held rose, stepping back from Balta's grasping hands.

"I would rather die in the sky, with one who has truly loved me, than drown in the deep under the weight of those who do not."

A great cry rose—both from Balta and from beyond the harbour wall—and Held made his choice.

He turned his back upon the sea and walked back into the sky.

Chapter Thirty-Eight

"HELD!"

Ah!

A flash of white-blond hair caught Janez's eye. Held was scrambling over the harbour wall and running full pelt towards the ship. Janez leaned down from the railing as Held clambered up the webbing, seized the collar of his coat when it came into reach, and hauled him up and onto the deck.

"Stay close," he said. As the ship lurched free of her moorings, a little of the melancholy eased. The enemy lay on the horizon. His captain had the command. And his kingdom was falling away behind him. But if he died here, at least Held was with him.

The *Vogel* was a bloated ship, lethal at close range but a slow sailor. She lurched free of the dock with clumsy determination, startling a yelp from Held which made Janez laugh. He then found the man a short sword and pressed the hilt into his hand.

"Stay here," he ordered, dragging him to a hollow by the foot of the quarterdeck stairs. "Here." He repeated it until Held echoed him, and then turned and left for the gunners.

In truth, *Vogel's* slowness would help protect her. Her sister ships flocked together ahead, to meet the sails creeping over the horizon. *Vogel* would be a little later to the action, despite the skilled rush of her crew and the great roll of the guns being brought to their stations, far earlier than their need. She was a heavy gunner and would fare well if the enemy were already too occupied to rake her upon her approach.

And approach they did. Creeping ever closer over a vast sea.

As they passed out of the harbour's shelter and into open water, the enemy grew larger upon the horizon, blurred by the oddly gentle snowfall obscuring the air. Janez squared his shoulders and scraped together his courage.

They would meet.

Then, one would yield. And die.

THE FIRST SHOT came some two hours after they had sailed. The king's ships had come together again, forming a great line between their home and their aggressors. The enemy had echoed the action, their iceberg banners now visible and clear to the naked eye—yet still too far. Naval warfare was a close thing, acted out in bloody clashes and bursts of action separated by thousand-yard threats and endless waiting.

Until the whites of their eyes could be seen, the *Vogel* would be ineffective.

But the first shot rang out all the same.

A distant boom, a puff of smoke, and a great splash some two hundred yards before them. The sound of drums ghosted after it. The hustle of men aboard the enemy ships gathered together, and the men upon Janez's own snarled like dogs.

A warning.

And the first ships—their sisters, shouting in their tongue above all others—kissed.

It was an explosion of action and noise. Smoke billowed from decks. Shrill screams followed every crack and boom of the great guns. A sail was torn asunder; a mast buckled dangerously. A dark shape—flailing, a man—fell from a railing, and was lost. Great splinters burst like seed heads from hulls.

And the *Vogel* inched nearer, ever nearer.

Yet Janez saw the panic in the faces of the men as the first ships began to engage, and the *Vogel* began to turn to starboard. He saw their uncertainty. He saw their hesitance that could swiftly turn shy, and he drew his sword.

A great fleet, indeed, but they had defeated greater. A warning of death, to be sure, but they had all been warned before. And what, in the end, was death? Merely to sleep. To have peace from the world at last, where no enemy could be found.

The coolness of courage settled upon his soul, and he raised the sword aloft.

"For the king!"

The men took up the cry and echoed with one great voice.

And then they saw the whites of the enemy's eyes.

"At the ready!" the captain boomed.

The man rallied.

Janez took a breath.

And—

Another man's whites. Another. And another. The *Vogel's* great sweep to her starboard brought her into line with a ship under an iceberg flag, and the captain roared the order.

"Fire!"

The explosion was deafening. The guns bellowed, one after another after another down the line. Their battle partner was raked, and raked them in return. Their sisters answered—and then the men rolled the guns back in and fired anew.

It was hot and smoky work. The acrid stench coated the air. By the fourth round, the enemy could not be seen but for the flashes of lights about her decks as she fired. Blind, they battled. Deafened, they fought on. Senseless and stupid, they warred by muscle memory and sheer luck alone, praying for their respective gods to save them.

Yet they had fought enough that the men knew the enemy's strengths and weaknesses. Their foe fired with great accuracy—for every flash, great splinters burst from their masts and railings. For every boom, great holes were torn in their sails. The deck was slippery with blood under Janez's boots. But she had no great engineers, and her ships were weak-hulled. The men aimed their returning fire low, concentrating on sinking her rather than slaughter. They would not defeat her by strength of numbers, but by the strength of the sea. She would be felled through her belly, and only there.

They survived if they sank her, and all her vile sisters, and only then.

It seemed an age and a mere moment. Janez slipped amongst the guns, issuing orders, replacing lost boys where he could, dragging the wounded below where they might stand hope. It was a lifetime, and a second. His shoulder was torn open by a splinter the length of his arm. A lucky escape brought a fourteen-pounder ball within inches of his face, its heat melting a clump of his hair like butter in the sun.

He breathed death and fire and carried on. He slipped in other men's lives and continued. He heard them fall and die about him, and pressed through. Cheered with the gunners when their enemy was finally breached and began to take water. Bellowed with the officers to bring the ship about, and renew their efforts on her sisters.

Here was no prince. Merely a man, desperately clinging to his own survival.

There was no arranged marriage. No miserable future. No war in the home—only this war, in his heart and lungs and head. He could fight his best, and die all the same.

Nothing stood in his way, but fate.

And then—

It came so suddenly that for a moment, he simply wondered.

Wondered why the men were dragging him to the deck, and shouting over one another at his side. Wondered why Held had left the spot he'd ordered him to occupy, and was clutching at his hand and arm. Wondered why he could hear that musical language that Held spoke as his birth-tongue, with no stuttering attempts to make Janez understand.

Janez wondered.

He'd heard the great boom of a gun, and the deck had rocked beneath his feet, but what was the matter? This was a ship in the midst of a battle. Had they not all felt it so?

Someone—someone was crying his name.

And then he felt the bite of rope about his knee, tight and hard, and looked down.

Oh.

His smoke-stained breeches and a bloody belt of rope. And nothing below.

Simply—nothing.

"I see," Janez murmured, and then the sea herself rolled in. She bellowed in his ears and rocked under his shoulders, hard as wood yet so kind and soothing. He could feel nothing. Why could he feel nothing?

He could hear—

Mermaids.

He could hear mermaids calling his name from very far away.

And Janez opened his mouth to answer, and drowned.

Chapter Thirty-Nine

HELD SAW IT.

Like the world slowed, he saw the great ball, black and terrible, parting the smoke and fog before it.

He saw the impact, and the snap of white bone burst forth from Janez's leg, tearing through cloth in a spray of red and tiny pink splinters as if nothing had ever been there to stop it.

He saw the entire lower leg come away, like a scale. Easy. Insignificant.

And he saw Janez—stop.

"No!"

Held reached him before he even fell, and when he did, it was a terrible and stuttering thing. His skin was smeared in black and red. His body shook in the hands of the men who helped him.

And the blood—the blood—

Held lashed out with the sword, slashing rope from one of the grey beasts, and abandoned the weapon to cinch the rope tight about the shattered remains of leg. Blood. Bleeding was—bleeding was bad. He didn't have to have been a skyman all his life to know it. He hauled at the rope to close the blood from the gaping wound, and prayed to all the oceans that it would work.

A leg.

A *leg*.

Dear seas, he'd lost a *leg*.

"You will not leave me, you will not die— Janez, *listen* to me!"

Held was vaguely aware he was shouting. Yet Janez only stared down at the wound, muttered something inaudible, and—

Died.

He—

No.

He collapsed, fainted, passed out and was swept away—but he did not, could not, die.

He *couldn't.*

HELD WOULD NOT leave.

The battle was over. A deathly hush coated the ship. The other skymen had wrapped Janez in great blankets and kept repeating a word—*tot, tot*—but Held wouldn't let them move him further. He clutched at the body and snarled at any who tried to remove him; once, he lashed out with Janez's dagger, and then the persistence ceased. They looked at him with great pity, and Held knew their thoughts. They thought the prince to be dead already, but he knew the truth.

He *knew* it.

He could sense no movement within Janez's chest, and the air buffeting the cloud rendered him unable to feel if Janez breathed—but Held knew that he yet lived. For Held lived. And had the Witch not been clear? If Janez ceased to love him, then Held would turn to sea foam and die.

And dead men, sky or otherwise, didn't love.

So he defended the body fiercely, not wanting them to tip it over the side as they had with all the other corpses, sewn up in their hammocks like bread in bags. And, when left alone, he rubbed warmth into Janez's exposed head and hair. His curls were matted with blood. His face bore great cuts that would surely scar, and his ear had been torn away on the left side. The blankets, wound tight about his body, left no illusions as to the state of his limbs.

Could skymen live without a leg?

A merman who lost his tail would certainly die as the loss of the fins rendered them unable to swim. And mer society was cold and cruel. A merman would have been abandoned to die, for Janez's wounds. Even driven out of vulnerable nests, so they didn't attract predators.

Held wouldn't allow it to happen to Janez. If the skymen drove him out, then Held would go with him. He still had one leg. Maybe skymen could walk with one leg. And if Janez couldn't walk, then Held would walk the places he needed to go. Perhaps he could learn to carry him. Or maybe that great animal that had carried them to the water, and had pulled the carriage, could carry Janez about all the time instead?

Whatever happened, Janez would live. And Held would protect him if the skymen turned on him.

They did not. Indeed, as darkness fell and the cloud quieted, they seemed to ignore Held and his charge—but for the man with the robes who came and muttered in rhythms, sprinkling sweet-smelling oil on Janez's forehead. He came and went every hour or so, and dabbed Held's hands with the oil too, and spoke...not *to* him, exactly, but Held had the odd sensation it was *about* him. As though the man in the robes was speaking to some invisible being about the two of them.

It was dawn before the soft rush and swell of the wood under Held's feet began to shudder, and the men began to swarm about the cloud again, to corral their reluctant beast to obedience. Held paid them no mind, concentrating instead on unpicking the matted blood from Janez's hair. His skin was a terrible grey, greyer than the cloth they'd wound him in, and the rope that Held had seized tight about the mangled limb was a knot of black, hard blood.

"This is why you are a myth," Held whispered to him fervently, as he heard the telltale scrape of stone, and the cloud shuddered in agony. "Any merman would have died. But you are legend. Legends don't die."

They did, of course, but Held had utter faith. If Janez hadn't died the moment that great ball had torn his leg away, then he wouldn't die now. Held would insist upon it.

He flashed the knife again when the men came, but they bore a flat board, and moved gently and softly as they pulled back the blankets, lifted Janez upon it, and bound him by the waist. One of them kept repeating words Janez had taught him what seemed like an age ago—the words for well and good. And they murmured Janez's title, too, almost in reverence.

Held trusted them—but not quite enough to release Janez's blankets. He trailed alongside the board as it was lifted upon hefty shoulders, and borne to the walkway. He followed it down to the stone harbour side and knelt with it upon the flagstones as the men called for someone.

"Tot," said a man with little round wires seated upon his nose after kneeling and taking Janez's wrist. *"Tot,"* he repeated and shook his head.

The cry went up. *"Tot, tot, der Prinz ist tot."* Unease rippled through the crowd; the men took their hats off, and a boy was cuffed about the head to do the same.

Held frowned. What did they mean? They'd said it aboard the cloud, too—was this their word for death? Did they mean—did that wire-wearing man mean—?

"Nein!" he insisted loudly, and took back Janez's hand, clutching it fiercely between his own. *"Nein!"* How to—how to— "Not *tot!*" he attempted, but his word for not and theirs didn't work well together, and the mutterings and confused looks said they didn't understand.

Janez wasn't dead. He *wasn't*. He *couldn't* be—

Clattering sounded upon the stones, and beasts broke through the men who parted before them. The red-faced man who had put Held in the stinking room when he'd first come to the land swung down from the animal, and the colour drained entirely from his face.

"Nein," he murmured and then seemed to shake himself, barking orders to two of the men. He gestured at the castle, high upon the cliff side. The board was lifted again; Held stood with it, gripping Janez's wrist hard in his hand. He was not dead. Held would not allow them to dispose of him like a corpse.

The board was carried upon the shoulders of four men, who wound after the beasts back up the hill. The entire town seemed to gawp—maids hung out of windows; men in doorways removed their hats, and everywhere that dreadful word whispered. *"Tot, tot, tot."*

And then, in the shadow of the great gates, there was another clatter. A familiar one, though Held had only heard it once before. A gait that he knew.

The bright-coloured animal with the sweet disposition came careening from the open gates, bearing a single rider.

Janez's brother.

Alarik.

Held had seen very little of him, and not at all since they'd gone away from the sea. He looked much like Father: he wore a great cloak over his shoulders, and from under a bright yellow hat, his hair streamed that same glorious golden-red as Janez's. He looked splendid. Important. Regal.

And his face was wreathed in open-mouthed horror.

He brought the beast up short. It reared under him with a cry, but his eyes remained fixed upon the board.

Upon the body.

Upon *Janez*.

"Nein," he breathed.

The red-faced man from the stinking room spoke, but Alarik entirely ignored him. He nearly fell from the beast. The board was lowered to the ground, slowly and reverently, and for a brief second, Alarik hovered over it, hands hung in the air and open, as though he was quite uncertain what to do.

And his face—

It cracked down the middle. His mouth sagged. His eyes gleamed. Lines broke out across his forehead and cheeks. Then the sound, the *sound.*

The king of this world above the sky made a shriek like a man dying and fell upon the body in a fit of anguish. He rocked like a mother with a dying child, clutching the broken head to his breast in much the same way. And Held didn't speak the tongue, yet knew with utter certainty that Alarik spoke no words.

Simply—screamed.

The blood stained his fine shirt and great cloak; the splash of death and destruction against him looked almost absurd. The wailing of a grief-stricken child beneath the gold ought to have been ridiculous. It wasn't.

The men crowded about, as if to shield the king from view with their own bodies. Held clutched tightly at the wrist in his grasp and fought for the word. Surely, Janez had told him the word for not. Surely, he had learned it somewhere, at some time, *surely—*

A creak of a voice, sharp and belligerent, broke through the ring of would-be guards, followed by its owner. Doktor crashed to the stone by the body, a great flatfish with bulging eyes, cold despite the sight and sound before him.

"Hör auf mit dem Geheule!" he snapped and forced Janez's body down a little in Alarik's arms. The king would not let go, but Doktor barked, *"Ruhe!"* and a deathly quiet fell as that shorn head pressed down into the blood-spattered cloth above Janez's chest.

And paused.

Then he whispered, *"Er lebt noch."*

Raised his head.

"Er lebt!" Doktor shouted, and a great cry rippled through the crowd. A mimicry as the word rang out again and again. Doktor rose to his feet— that shabby, funny-looking little skyman—and in that instant, the king was servant and Doktor was king.

Held squeezed the hand still clamped between his own and committed the words to memory.

Er lebt meant alive.

Chapter Forty

THE SUN HAD long since set by the time Doktor Hauser snuffed out the bright lanterns above the bed and drew the sheets up over the prince's broken body.

"You can go," he told his assistant, a dumb but keenly intelligent young man by the unfortunate name of Fleischer. "I will keep watch during the night. Return in the morning, with plenty of fresh water to be boiled."

Fleischer nodded and scuttled out. Brilliant and uncouth, he didn't bother to change his blood-soaked clothes before he left. A faint, weary smile crossed Doktor Hauser's face. That boy would make a fine surgeon in time.

Once the room was dulled to a gentler candlelight, Hauser stripped to the waist and went to work scrubbing the blood from his arms. Messy business, amputations. The left leg had been ripped away below the knee. The knee itself had been a shattered pulp of splintered bone and flesh. He had taken as little as he dared, and only time would tell if it had been enough. But Janez breathed.

Feebly, yes. His pulse hammered like a rabbit and jumped in a new rhythm quite inhuman. But he breathed. It beat. He lived.

For tonight.

Karl Hauser had never been a sentimental man. It didn't do in his profession. Men died every day. Most men who met with cannon fire didn't live long enough to meet the good doctor. Had Janez stood but a little lower to the ground, he too would have been dashed away, like a mouse before a lion.

He was lucky to breathe. And if he should die before the dawn—well, it wouldn't be on Karl Hauser's conscience.

Yet...he would regret it.

Blameless, yes, but he would regret it all the same. Like most surgeons, Hauser was ignorant of decorum and politic and said the wrong thing many a time, both accidentally and on purpose. His first meeting with Janez had been many summers ago, when the boy-prince had jumped from rocks into the sea and misjudged the depth.

"When you grow a tail and become a merman, then—only then—can you jump into the bay and not be considered a simpleton," the doctor had said, whilst setting the broken bone as painfully as possible, to teach the wildling a lesson.

The little wildling had howled, as predicted. But the following morning, he'd hobbled down on his new crutches, all smiles and sunshine, and asked 'Herr Doktor' if he wouldn't teach him the proper way to jump into the harbour so as not to break the other ankle.

(He had not.)

Blood scrubbed away, Hauser donned a fresh linen shirt and discarded the ruined apron. He then filled a cup with strong mead and sleeping powder and presented it to Held. The little foreigner had barely moved an inch from the bedside since bringing Janez in—although he'd gone green and been valiantly sick when they'd sawn the knee off. Now, he merely blinked sleepily and took the offered vessel.

"Drink."

That word, Janez had taught him. The cup tilted. The mead sank down.

"You may sleep here tonight," Hauser said, knowing full well it was pointless. Mindless chatter, however, might comfort them both. He brought a blanket. Held tucked it around himself and then turned those great pale eyes back to the body in the bed.

"Dead?"

The word was quite unexpected. Where had he learned that particular one?

"No," Hauser said gently.

"No dead."

"Not dead."

"Not dead," Held echoed and lapsed into silence once more.

Hauser was no fool. Simple, he'd told Janez back then, and the king a few days later, but it was clearly false. Held was no simpleton. Simply foreign. From where, Hauser doubted they would ever know—doubted, by the way Janez had looked at him, that Janez even cared to know now. But that gaze was intelligent. That rope he'd heaved around the mess of leg had undoubtedly saved Janez's life. Hauser got the impression that young Held had much invested in saving that particular life.

Sighing, he rolled his neck. The powder would take effect in half an hour or so, and then he would move the boy to a pallet and get some rest himself. If the prince chose to die during the night, there was nothing anyone could do now.

A commotion at the door made him frown—more wounded, no doubt, if the physics and herbalists in the harbour had finally admitted they were no doctors. But the frown turned to a scowl when the door was cracked open and an anxious face squashed between cap and chinstrap squinted at him through the gloom.

"The, ah, His Majesty, ah—"

"God Himself is wiser than to disturb a surgeon at his work, sir," Doktor Hauser said sternly.

The squashed face turned a sickly green. "But—but the *King*, sir—"

"A spine, my dear man, I'm sure you have one." And when the sentry could only make a strangled noise of distress, he harrumphed, "Fine!" and shoved him back into the hall. Stepping after, the doctor shut the door quite firmly behind him, a wooden barrier between his patient and his lord, and stood before the king in his open shirt and bloodied breeches.

A king who had aged a thousand years.

In any other mood, even Doktor Hauser would have yielded to the bloodshot eyes that met his own. The king seemed three hundred, not thirty-three. His hands grasped stiff and arthritic at Hauser's shoulders, and his mouth fumbled for words in a haggard face. His clothes were still smeared with rusty stains where he had cradled the broken body to his chest. His fingers were still the same claws they'd been on the torn overcoat.

Yet Hauser's mouth tightened.

"I will send word in the morning," he said.

"He lives. He *lives*."

"For the moment."

Something flared in those familiar blue eyes. Something jagged and infected, oozing pain and pus like a diseased wound.

"Doktor—please—my *brother*—"

"I would suggest turning your attention to more serious matters, Your Majesty." Beside him, Hauser could feel the sentry cringing. "The alliance will be broken. Even if he lasts the night, His Highness will be siring no sons. There is far too much damage—"

"Hang the damned alliance!" Alarik exploded. His hands bit into Hauser's shoulders making them ache. "Damn the war and damn the bloody lineage! My brother—my *blood*—I must see him. I must!"

"You must not," Hauser returned, but he yielded a fraction. Perhaps Alarik's priorities weren't so badly skewed. "He still breathes. I will keep watch in the night."

Alarik was shaking his head before the doctor had finished speaking.

"I must see him. I will keep watch."

An eyebrow crawled up the doctor's forehead.

"Are you a doctor?"

"I—"

"Or perhaps a surgeon?"

"Well, I—"

"Forgive me, Your Majesty, but perhaps you have learned the arts of both science and medicine whilst I have been amputating a man's leg?"

"Doktor."

The whisper was fractured. The break was clean and clear, breaking the word in two, visible to the naked eye.

Hauser paused.

The king was no king. He was a man, wearing his brother's blood, stinking of gunpowder and gore.

"I will have no kings in my rooms," Hauser said slowly, "but I may permit a patient's family."

Alarik's eyes closed.

"Go and wash. Thoroughly. Cold water and soap. Yes, Alarik, soap! Then, dress again in only white linen—roll the sleeves up, and wash your hands again once you have finished. Then I will permit you to sit with him. But you are no king in these rooms. I outrank, my assistant outranks you—hell, Alarik, the very jars outrank you. One moment of disobedience, one second of risking my patient, and I will not hesitate to barricade that door against you."

Alarik simply nodded.

"Of course, Doktor."

"And that includes, Alarik, if the patient does not want you there."

Blue blazed as his eyes flew open.

And then it dimmed.

"Yes, Doktor."

And then, as quickly as he had come, he was gone.

HELD WAS A bundle of tired limbs and barely open eyes in the chair by the time the knock sounded on the door. A pale gaze flickered up, and Hauser put a finger to his lips before rising.

The sentries had been doubled. And the king stood before him, scrubbed pink, and dressed in heavy linen underclothes, the sleeves rolled to the elbow.

"Quiet," Hauser said sharply and allowed him inside.

Every other time the king had cause to enter these rooms he'd been full of commentary—a mixture of horror, disgust, and awe at the jars and their collections, at the sawdust on the floor, at the lanterns swinging from the ceiling to aid surgeries when the sun could not be found.

Tonight, he stepped in—and immediately forgot all but the man in the bed.

His face—quivered.

His entire being seemed to collapse, as though the string that held him up had been cut. With a low moan, he stumbled across the room and caught himself on the instrument stand. His hands shook. His back trembled. A hand reached out and then recoiled, and the next moan was broken by a sob.

And, very faintly, two words.

"My brother."

Hauser watched in silence as a broken man—no king, no leader, just a mourning man—shivered by the bed. The words were repeated once more and then shivered out of existence again.

The next was simply—*sorry*.

An apology to fall on deaf ears. An apology far too late. And too vague. For what did the king, the man, the brother, apologise? Their icy rift? The reckless order? The ball that had torn away the leg and perhaps yet the life?

Or for anything, everything, that would seep into his brother's soul and bring him back from the brink?

Wordlessly, Hauser pushed a stool to the side of the bed and guided Alarik to sit. For a moment, he did. And then after another moment, he pushed himself back up and touched his lips so gently to Janez's forehead that he didn't so much as mark the sweat that beaded there.

"I am here," the doctor heard, in a whisper softer than the gentle drop from a sleeping man to death itself.

And then the king's gaze flickered up and met pale, foreign eyes that stared soundlessly from the other chair. The words changed.

"We are here. We are here, brother."

Chapter Forty-One

THE NIGHT WAS long.

Held's eyes itched, and his brain burned to sleep, but he found he could not. He could barely move from the chair, extending one hand onto the bedspread to tuck his fingers into Janez's and feel the weak pulse of life under hot skin. He could go no further.

Alarik stayed also, but his watch was wide awake. He'd come in a blind panic, eyes streaming and voice hoarse, but they'd dried during the endless vigil, and his voice was a continual murmur, a comfort, a balm in the dark. Held knew not the words, nor the message, but he knew the intention.

For some hours, the candles burned down, and Janez simply breathed. But when the hourly chimes struck three in the harbour below, he stirred, muscle rippling under Held's arm, and the king's level tone changed.

"Ich bin hier," he said, leaning forward and resting a hand on Janez's forehead. *"Ich bin hier, mein Bruder."*

A shimmer of light showed, and Alarik called for Doktor as Janez's eyes opened. They roamed. His breathing grew louder—a wet rasp not unlike the choking breath he'd taken in Held's arms upon the roof the world, the very day they'd learned of each other's existence.

"Doktor!" Alarik called again, and Janez started. His hand rose from the bed; Held caught it, forcing himself up in the chair to clasp the hot fingers between his own.

"Held."

His name was a rough rasp, and Held squeezed the fingers tight.

"I'm here," he said. But of course, Janez would not understand—or even hear, it seemed, for his eyes skated to the ceiling, dull and wide, and he murmured his brother's name in another hoarse croak.

"Ich bin hier, Janez," Alarik murmured, the refrain familiar now to Held. *"Ich bin hier."*

Doktor came, carrying a lantern and dressed in heavy night robes. He spoke quietly, palming Janez's face and neck, and then he was gone again. Janez barely seemed to register his presence, and fear swelled in Held's gut. He was sick. His skin had been hot, those nights together in his rooms, but it had been slick. Now, under Held's fingers, it was rough and dry like beach sand.

He was very, very sick.

"Wir sind hier, Janez," Alarik murmured, his eyes flicking up once to Held before he leaned over the prince's face and pressed his lips to that bruised forehead. The kiss was tender.

Janez's reaction was not. His arm came up, elbow catching Alarik under the chin. He fought, a great cry rising in his throat—and then Doktor was tearing back into the room. The noise stuttered; the body in the bed thrashed, throat gurgling, and Doktor forced a strap between teeth and frothing lips.

He fitted.

Held had seen this in mermen infected with great parasites—before the death. He'd seen the savage clawed form of their hands, and the vomit and bile spilling from their lips. Janez thrashed much the same— the blankets curled around him, and his limbs scrabbled where he lay, too senseless to find his aggressors, too maddened by the great heat under his skin to free himself.

And then, as suddenly as it had begun, it ceased.

He slackened, like the wind dying from a cloud, and his head rocked free of the strap.

"Janez!"

"Kannst du mich hören?"

Their urgent enquiries went unanswered. Held crept from the chair onto the bed and clutched up one hand to his chest. Had he—no, no, he could not have—

Doktor palmed his neck again. Held stroked the slack wrist in his grip and found that weak pulse again, jumping in erratic beats.

"Wasser."

Doktor's command was sharp. To Held's shock, Alarik turned from the bed and hurried into the dark room beyond them, more servant than king in that moment.

"Is he going to die?" Held whispered and then swallowed. No, no. They would not understand. *"Tot?"*

"Nicht tot," came the flat reply, and Doktor began to loosen Janez's clothing. He stripped back the sheets, and Held seized upon the idea. Janez was hot. And the heat made the illness worse, much like with his own kind. If he were cool...

He helped expose Janez's flushed skin, until only his sex and the bandaged wounds remained concealed. When the king returned, it was with a great basin of water and ragged cloths. Doktor packed them, drenched and cold, against Janez's neck and armpits, even against his sex and bloody stump, and then he took Held's hand and forcibly wrapped the fingers around a dripping rag before lowering it to his chest and wiping the water off there.

Held seized upon it. Keep him cool. He shook Doktor's hand off and repeated the motion himself, wetting chest and neck until the rag was rubbed dry, and then returning it to the bowl and beginning again. Around him, Doktor and Alarik talked in low tones. Held caught *tot* several times, but refused to hear its context. Janez would not die. He could not die. Not now—not after everything Held had lost, every hope Held had pinned onto him—not when Held's very existence now centred on this man—

No, he would not die. Held would not permit it.

Time stretched out there, in the gloomy light of the sickroom. Twice more, Janez opened his eyes, and called for both Held and Alarik; twice more, he seemed unaware of their replies. He didn't fit again, but he shouted, even screamed, and for long minutes, in one of these spells, Alarik clutched his face in both hands, their foreheads pressed together, and begged alongside him.

"Wir sind hier, mein Bruder," he said, over and over, the refrain falling on deaf ears. *"Wir sind hier."*

Janez would only clutch his arm, look right into his face, and ask for Alarik. And the look of pain on Alarik's face was so sharp, so jagged...

He was a broken, damp-faced brother, sitting clutching Janez's arms and whispering fervent prayers as Janez slipped under the fever again and lay quiet. Lay dying.

Held shook off the thought. He would not lose Janez. He would not lose the man he loved quite literally more than his own life. "He will not die," Held told himself firmly and started over again with the cloths. If the fever would break, then Janez would live.

If.

It burned hot and bright, oblivious to Held's work and Alarik's murmurs. Doktor came again when the chimes sounded five times and forced some mixture down Janez's throat. And truly forced: Janez did not stir. He lay silent and still, his skin aflame, and Alarik, too, had lapsed into silence. He simply clasped one hand between his own, lips resting upon the knuckles, and stared with red-rimmed, dry eyes at the body between them.

The bells chimed six.

The bells chimed seven.

The bells chimed eight, nine, ten—

A guard came and was sent away. Doktor's assistant came and went, slipping in and out of the rooms without so much as a glance at the little vigil. Another potion was forced into the unresponsive prince, and the bells chimed eleven.

Perhaps Held slept. Perhaps he didn't. Alarik, he sensed, did not. The king sat perfectly still, almost meditating, fixed perfectly in position.

A chime rang out in the city below—and the skin under Held's rag shivered.

He paused, glancing up at the still face. A shadow seemed to pass over it, so very fine and indistinct, and for a split second, panic seized Held's heart. No. *No*, no, he could not—he could not—!

The chest rose again, and the movement shimmered.

Water.

Held abandoned the rag and touched his dry hand to Janez's forehead. It came away damp.

He was—cooling.

Cooler. Breathing, but cooler. His skin was slick. No longer the parched texture of sand, but the soft slickness it had been the last time he'd flushed so deeply.

"Doktor!"

Alarik's voice rang out and broke in the middle. The shiver came again, and the lax head rolled. Blue eyes, the pupils mere spots of darkness in that churning sea of every blue that Held had ever known, sought out the sound.

"Held?"

Held stroked his forehead and kissed it. He hardly dared...oh, he wanted, but he hardly dared...

The eyes skated past him. Searching. His name was repeated again, very softly, and Held crooned on some deep-seated instinct.

"I am here," he said, safe in his own tongue. "I am with you. And I love you now even more than before, you know, because you have asked for me above any other."

Janez would never understand the words. Alarik, by his dumb look, clearly did not either. But the roving gaze ceased, and fingers lifted clumsily. Held caught them, kissing them in his own manner, and repeated himself gently until the urgency faded from that beloved face.

Doktor came. Janez seemed unaware of him, or of Alarik, but Held kept murmuring to him, even began to sing one of Mother's old songs, and he remained calm.

And soon, he slept.

Not the shuddering sleep of a fitting man, nor the cut-string placidity of a dying one. But merely—slept. As he had that night in the Winter Palace. As he would any other night, in any other place.

He slept, and Held kissed Janez's fingers with his own and knew the worst had passed.

Chapter Forty-Two

JANEZ WAS QUITE insensible.

It was not surprising. He was terribly weak, the infection terribly strong, and Hauser was forced to remove further dying flesh on the second day and cauterise it more savagely than before. Insensible was perhaps best.

It was causing the king great distress, however. Janez would look right through him, and beg for his brother, his mother—even the father who had had little relationship with his younger son. He would ask for Held, also, but Held must have made a habit of speaking in his own tongue around the prince, for he would murmur or sing to him softly in some other speech, and Janez would quiet again, tame and trusting. He never seemed to know that the voice came from the same man mopping at his forehead with cold rags or holding his hand, but he seemed to know that it meant Held was at least nearby.

And Hauser was not stupid.

Wives sat and sang such to dying husbands. Dying husbands calmed at such attentions. That fixed gaze from the very first day had been of no simpleton or spy, but of a suitor. If, of course, it was possible to regard washed-up sailors with no name or home as suitors for princes.

Alarik seemed either unaware, or uncaring. He had to be driven out of the sickroom to attend to business, but returned with the darkness of each evening without fail, and slept each night in the chair by the bed. Held gave it up entirely and curled on the coverlet next to Janez, his voice the only thing, some nights, that could penetrate the shock and enable Janez to sleep properly.

And sleep he did.

He had to be forcibly roused to drink and would slip under again within moments. Even when Hauser stopped administering anything for the pain, Janez slept through it, body too weak and shattered to begin to process what had happened. As the third day rolled over them, the fever died entirely, and he had to be buried in blankets to stop the cold entering what remained and destroying him. If pneumonia set in now, Hauser was sure it would kill him.

On the fourth day, Hauser had him removed back to his personal rooms—for the king's sake, if nobody else's. If he was going to die—and it was as yet all too likely—then he ought to pass in the comfort of his own bed, in Hauser's opinion. And the king would be able to rejoin his family, only a handful of rooms away, and be comforted in turn by wife and children.

And if Alarik didn't receive such soon, he'd become a patient in his own right.

Hauser didn't presume—never had—to interfere in the king's business. Not for Alarik, not for his father before him. But a king had to be composed and involved in his kingdom. A kingdom at war, even more so. This lurking in the sickroom to attend to a dying brother was not the privilege of a king, and Hauser knew what really lurked at the core of it.

Had they not fought, Janez would likely not have donned uniform and gone to sea.

Had they not fought, he'd likely have never been there in the path of cannon fire.

Had they not fought, he would likely have been standing on the royal balcony alongside his king and brother, watching the ragged ships come in.

But the prince had donned the coat of a lieutenant of his own accord and boarded the ships with no forceful hand at his back.

Hauser had little personal patience for sentiments such as guilt or remorse, but his lack of patience didn't equate to a lack of understanding. For all his reputation as a hard, hot-tempered king, Alarik was no cold-hearted bastard of a man. It would suit him better to be so, carrying the weight of a kingdom on his shoulders, but it was not the case, and those were the facts. He blamed himself, Hauser knew, and a king could not afford to carry guilt—however misplaced—that would distract him from his duties.

And should Janez actually die, Hauser knew that part of the king would die also.

And should he not?

The leg would never grow back. The naval career was snuffed out. Likely, the alliance also. What woman would want a husband so hideously scarred? What kingdom would accept an alliance duty-bound to die along with its participants at the end of their lives, with no permanent join between houses? Allegiance outlived men. Enemy nations would continue to be long after the deaths of every man who had caused the original offence.

And while, yes, Hauser had told the lie to prevent the marriage that Janez hadn't wanted, told a lie to protect two people from lifelong misery, he had no illusions that a solution must be found. Would the king now place his son in Janez's place? Or his daughter? Betroth a tiny child to another infant, in some faraway land? He had always resisted the idea, violently at times, yet Hauser suspected he'd left the king with no choice now.

One misery exchanged for another. And so went the life of man.

And so, when Hauser had Janez moved, he didn't inform the king beforehand, and waited for him to attend—as he invariably did—after the afternoon council had been satisfied. He occupied himself with an experiment in the meantime, and lost himself in the effect of boiling mice in vinegar—dead mice, he wasn't some sadist—only to be pulled from it when he heard the strangled cry from the next room, and the door was flung open.

"Doktor! He is—"

"Quite well, quite comfortable, and do not hurl about so," Hauser said crossly, snuffing out the flame under his pans. "I have had him moved to his rooms."

"He still needs you. He must be moved back imm—"

"When you cease to regard medicine and science as witchcraft and divine intervention, Your Majesty, then perhaps I will permit you to issue instruction to me regarding the care of my patients. But until then, may I suggest you keep praying to thin air, while I save lives," Hauser interrupted heatedly. "The prince may yet live, may yet die, but that is up to him and luck now, not confinement in these rooms. And it will do you better to sleep in your bed, with your wife, and not in that infernal little chair."

"Until he comes to his senses, I will sit up with him."

"Do not be ridiculous," Hauser said sharply. "He is unaware of your presence, and made no worse for the lack of it. You have a kingdom to run, Alarik. I find it difficult to believe the situation has not endangered this engagement that has been thrust upon him. Is his bride-to-be aware of the duties he can no longer perform?"

Alarik's jaw worked.

"That is a no, then. And the war? I take it the battle was won, going by the lack of northerners with icebergs on their chests rampaging about the place?"

"You would do well to remember your place."

"And you yours, Your Majesty."

Alarik's lips thinned. "I have not had the time—"

"You have had plenty of time. Your guilt is blinding you to the further damage that may be caused by this."

"My kingdom is second to my brother's life!"

"Is it?"

The question brought the king up short, and Hauser softened. Marginally.

"You may love your brother very much," he said, a little more kindly, "but your kingdom is, and must be, your primary concern. It has always been before. If your brother's life were of such utmost importance, he would never have been permitted to join the navy, stand on a ship, or be married off like an instrument of diplomacy. You would have shielded him from it all—"

"He would have loathed me for it."

"But you would have done it anyway. You have always balanced your love for your family against the needs of your people, as any king must, and at this moment, your people need you more than he does."

Alarik was shaking his head. "You do not understand, Doktor—"

"I understand that you carry blame for the injury."

Alarik paused. His eyes were too bright.

"The enemy is at fault. Do not let them take the upper hand now."

The royal jaw hardened, and the king drew himself up.

"You will issue orders to the guards, to Held, to your assistant. And they are your orders, too. If Janez—if—"

"If the shadow comes for him," Hauser promised, "you will be sent for the moment I am aware of it."

The king nodded jerkily.

"He sleeps in his rooms. Keep the curtains closed against the light, it will only disturb him."

"Held is with him?"

"Of course. He is not alone."

Alarik opened his mouth to speak again—and then seemed to decide against it. He turned on his heel and marched out, no doubt to the prince's rooms, and then—one hoped—to his own.

Hauser relit his burners and offered up a meagre prayer to a god he'd never truly believed in.

If Janez were to die, let him die tonight. If not—release him from the grip of disease, and ease two men's suffering, not one.

Chapter Forty-Three

ON THE NINTH day, Doktor opened the windows.

The breeze was cold and refreshing, and Janez was quick to stir to its caressing fingers. His voice still murmured and crackled like the drum of crab claws on the sand—but his eyes brightened at the light streaming through the glass, as they'd not done since that terrible moment upon the cloud. A hand lifted. Grasping. He began to rise.

"Doktor?" Held asked uncertainly, clutching that wayward hand. It was cooler than the past few days, and the returning grip a little firmer. But should he rise? Janez seemed to think so—he made that huffing sound of exasperation that Held had come to associate with disapproval of Doktor and his diktats.

But Doktor had no diktats. He smiled and slipped under Janez's other arm to pull him up against the pillows. They conversed in low tones. Held heard the words for windows and chairs, and then Doktor was looking at him.

"Hier," he said, and Held grasped under Janez's armpit. Between them, they lifted him from the bed, and carried him to the plush red chair, bathed in morning sun.

He felt so—

Light. So utterly frail and fragile between them. He felt more mer than sky. There was none of the great, warm strength that had borne down on Held in the secret spaces of beds. There was none of that easy might, that hot power, that sheer energy, that had both captivated him and swept him away, like an all-consuming and irresistible tide. Something had been lost—something taken—and Held clutched at Janez's arm even after that broken body finally relaxed into the soft frame.

But then Janez opened his eyes and smiled.

Bathed in bright light, clear and alert for the first time in days, the blue was all the colours of home rolled into one. His hair burned, the red and gold a great wash all mixed together, like sand rolling down a collapsed bank, speckling and dancing in the deep. There were lines—deep lines, hollows, shadows of pain where the smile failed just yet to reach—yet Held's heart squeezed tight inside his chest regardless.

The feeling spilled out. "I love you," he said, in some feeble attempt to smooth the pain away and find the missing pieces—but it was lost on him. And Held knew of no other way to make him understand.

When Doktor brought the basin, though, and unwound the cloth from the bloody stump that was all that remained of the shattered leg, an idea occurred. A distraction, perhaps, and some way to comfort. The water jug on the side was still full, and Janez had looked so happy and hedonistic the last time...

That red-gold hair was greasy to the touch. Janez started, only for Doktor to tut and still him. And then Janez simply closed his eyes, and Held watched the lines and shadows ease a little as he patiently combed the water through that curly hair—again and again, over and over, until the colour gleamed brighter than before, and the damp slide of the locks through Held's fingers felt like it had that very first time they'd touched.

And when it did, Held exchanged comb for brush, and brushed all the water away again, in long and lingering strokes, until the hair fell wispy and free, that soft sensation still so impossible to understand kissing his fingers where it lay. Janez's hands were curled in his lap, twitching with Doktor's attendance, but his hair kissed Held's fingers in silent apology.

And then Janez spoke.

Whatever he said, it made Doktor pause. Answer yes, in a slow sort of way.

And then smile. He patted Janez's knee and completed the new wrapping with deft movements before rising and crossing to the great doors. Not the door to the room, no, but the doors in the walls. Clothes flew from the recesses beyond: simple whites, the warmer garments of the Winter Palace, those that had been so gentle against Held's cheek yet so rough when he'd bunched them in his fists as they'd come together in that laughing, joyous crash.

His heart swelled just to see them, and Doktor laid them out on the bed until they formed a bodiless skyman, stretched out and ready.

"Held."

He gestured. Held went, puzzled, but understanding dawned when Doktor held out the undershirt, and pointed to Janez.

The items were simple, and Janez was content to let Held dress him. There were no teasing plucks, no kisses. But he smiled when Held dared to brush back a loose curl, and asked for a ribbon when it only returned.

"In a moment," Held said and smiled when Janez tried—and failed—to mimic the sound.

The loose undershirt was of a heavy, warm fabric, but the sleeves were loose like the shirt from the ball. The sleeveless undercoat hugged his battered torso, its deep blue colour allowing Held to pretend he'd merely imagined the vivid painting of injury around Doktor's work on that now-wasted chest. He worked thin gloves patiently over the scored hands, and then Doktor came about to help lift Janez again, and allow the trousers to be exchanged for a fresh, crisp pair more designed for company.

Held paused.

The leg gaped empty. And there were two of each of the remaining items on the bed: shoes, and stockings. Janez was staring out of the window with a fierce sort of determination, as though he didn't wish to look down. Doktor had retreated to his instruments, cleaning them a little too keenly. There was a sudden weight in the air. A silence, of a sort, despite the crash of the tides outside and the cries of skymen battering their tools upon a cloud. Held recognised the expression on Janez's face. Not from sight, but from memory—of how muscles felt to make such an expression. He remembered it from contorting his own mouth into such an unhappy sneer of hopeless, helpless *hunger*.

Janez was hurting. And not from the leg, but from somewhere inside.

Held fisted his hands around the stockings.

He would make it stop hurting.

Why should Janez hurt? His touch could infect the very mind and sweep away all sense to make one senseless, yet do so with sensation itself. His tongue spoke nonsense, yet his body spoke all languages that had ever existed. He could be understood, yet never said a word Held could comprehend. He transcended language, rules, even the entire world—and he hurt, when he was shy only of divinity itself.

There was no need for Janez to hurt.

It had to stop. Now.

Held found pins in the brush collection. He dropped clumsily to his knees at Janez's foot, and rolled the spare cloth like a kelp wrap. He stuck it with the pins in much the same manner, until the fabric was snug against the bottom of the stump: hiding and protecting Doktor's handiwork, yet returning the welcoming fit of the cloth and the way it accentuated Janez's body, only more beautiful when it was bared. The remaining foot was lifted—and the tiny nails kissed softly with his thumbs before anybody could notice—and the stocking whisked up, the shoe buckled into place. Now, the only thing out of place was the soft fall of hair the colour of a clear sky as the light rose in the morning.

The ribbon had to be blue.

Held still didn't grasp the significance of ribbon colours. Janez had insisted on the white one at the Winter Palace, but this one would be blue. He found it hidden amongst its fellows in the brush box and took his time smoothing every curl and strand into its hold, easing out the loops until they fell identically.

Doktor had slipped from the room. Held took the moment to press his nose against the softness and inhale.

A hand came up to grip his arm and squeeze lightly. The soft rasp of cloth between them was unpleasant, and Held hoped for healing soon. Kisses helped hurt, did they not? If he could only kiss them, perhaps they would be better.

The door opened just as Janez let go, and Doktor returned with a long stick, held out ahead of himself as though presenting a sword. He tossed it in the air, twirled it once, and presented it to Janez, a white handle first, as though offering it.

Janez stared.

Then slowly reached. With his left hand, not his right. And took it.

Placed it down, black tip to the carpet, and leaned forward. His fingers curled around the whiteness and began to shake.

And then he stopped.

Face downturned, his entire body leaning forward to press the stick into the floor, Janez simply stopped. His whole arm was shaking, and shoulders too. A curl freed itself from the ribbon and fell forward over shadowed eyes.

Doktor frowned.

"Jeder einfache Mann kann das, und du bist ein Prinz."

His voice was a low, grumbled croak. It whispered between them, like a tiny secret, and rustled in the air like wind.

"Das ist dein Werk!"

Anger.

Janez bellowed his reply. The sudden shock of noise from so long in a quiet horror made Held jump. Doktor flinched back also—and then his face closed. He spat something back, louder and harsher than before, and turned on his heel. He slammed out of the room, speckles of whiteness shuddering free from the ceiling as the door hit home, and Janez made an explosive noise that Held knew without doubt to be a curse. His hand upon the stick had never stopped shaking.

Slowly, Held stepped around the chair and dared to kiss the other hand. He lifted it and pressed his lips to the cloth-covered knuckles as he'd seen Janez do at the Winter Palace. He watched, too, as Janez had. Watched that handsome, pained face as Janez closed his eyes—and when that churning blue was obscured, Held pulled.

Pulled on the hand in his grasp. And pulled hard.

Janez looked up at him, red ringing the blue, and something so terribly painful was written in the lines around his mouth. He made a cracked sound, no word at all. And Held pulled again.

He didn't know what Janez had said to make Doktor fetch the clothes. But the undercoat and shoe meant that Janez had to go somewhere. And wherever it was, whatever for, he must go. Skymen belonged in the sky, not in dark rooms. They belonged corralling clouds and dancing in the sun and burning everything they touched with their brilliance and madness.

Janez belonged there.

Not here. Not with red-rimmed eyes and a shivering lip, with vile painted colours upon his skin and quaking from the simple act of holding a stick.

So Held pulled—and Janez rose up out of the chair.

For a moment, he staggered. Held caught at him, and as Janez steadied, the stick a crude replacement for his leg, Held slid his arms further and clasped that now-frail chest to his shoulders.

And held on.

Janez's face dropped against Held's neck, and the chest between Held's hands heaved for a brief moment. Then stilled. Until ever so faintly, Held felt a hand grip the back of his neck and *squeeze*. Held...held.

They were still as statues, unmoving in the midst of this great upheaval. Held would hold on forever, right here, if it would only restore the smile. If it would relight the eyes, catch the hands that had pulled him from his prison. He'd have done anything. Any deal the Witch cared to name, any price she demanded him to pay, and he'd have paid it.

The grip fell away. Janez straightened. When Held let go, that handsome face was wet, and Held used his sleeve to dry it, unsure of the source. That mustered a small smile before Janez looked down at his remaining foot and the black stick, and leaned.

The stick creaked, bearing his weight, and in a jerky hop, he stepped forward.

Stopped. Breathed. Shifted the stick a little along the carpet. And stepped forward again.

The agony on his face, the thin tension in his hands, the harsh gasps in his throat—Held could even see the jump of his heart, punching in his neck with a furious violence. He wanted to stop it. But that angry determination was the man who rode on clouds. The skyman who had fallen through the roof of the world. So Held let it continue, too and always, as some proof that the fire had taken a leg and nothing more.

It had cost—Janez dropped to the end of the bed and sat there with a reeling gasp—but not all. Held stepped close, grasped the soft hair between his hands, and pressed his lips to the warm, invisible crown Janez seemed to wear there, a band of gentle heat hidden under gold.

A hand clasped the back of Held's thigh, high and intimate, and he was stuck fast to Janez's side. There, with Janez's head cradled in his arms, heavy and secure against his chest—there, it was as though Held could keep this particular skyman all for himself, right there. Could this simple touch hold him—hold them—together, away from fire and water?

He turned his head to rest his cheek upon Janez's hair and caught blue eyes in the looking glass.

Blue eyes that were distant. That topped a tight expression. A man staring at the empty space where his leg had once been. And—though Janez knew it not—in the arms of someone who loved him.

"I am not supposed to love or care for any being with legs—mythical or not," Held told him. "Yet I do." A flicker of a confused smile crossed those pale features. "I know you cannot understand me, but...I love you. So much so that I would cease to be without you. This is...nothing. You remain, as do I. This means nothing."

Janez was shaking his head, with that faintly bemused expression, yet Held must have conveyed *something*—emotion, if not meaning—for Janez rapped the stick once against the floor and struggled to stand.

And gently pulled away.

The skyman stood in the looking glass, tall and proud, handsome in his sleeves and silken hair. The shoe and stick matched in their gleaming blackness—the deep blue of the ribbon and the undercoat set his eyes ablaze.

They shimmered.

The water spilled over. His lip shook, and with a choked sound, Janez lowered his face into his hand to hide. Another strangled cry escaped his heaving chest. Held's heart twitched at the show of pure misery. He stepped forward, between man and mirror, kissed his hand, and then drew it down to press his lips to the closed lids over streaming eyes. Pressed comfort and love there, pressed whatever it was that had spellbound him the first time Janez had touched his mouth. He wiped away the salt water with his lips—men were made of the sea, but lived in the sky. He knew that now. And when the storm calmed, he touched their mouths so faintly together they barely touched at all.

"You are a skyman," he breathed there, a secret he would have given the world to be able to say so Janez understood it, "and no less for this."

Janez's eyes remained closed. His hand came to rest against the back of Held's neck. Their foreheads rested upon one another.

And they breathed. Together. Held watching, Janez—waiting, perhaps. The sounds of hammers in the harbour drifted endlessly through the open windows, yet it was as though time moved around them, not through them, and left them as statues, forever intertwined. They had turned to stone and ceased.

"*Ich liebe dich,*" Janez croaked. Thick and throaty. His face was dry again, his skin pale yet too warm under Held's thumb where it grazed a shadow of the sickness that still lingered.

Held mustered a word. One of the few he knew, and the only one he'd learned for himself. The one that Janez kept saying to him. The word that Alarik had wept in the sickroom.

"*Mein.*"

Blue eyes flashed. Shoulders straightened. The chest expanded in a breath...and when that sharp gaze shifted higher, staring over Held's head to the looking glass, there was a hardness there. A brightness.

"*Du bist mein,*" Janez murmured, and the smile was a little firmer than before.

"Mein," Held echoed. On a whim, he pressed his lips to the rasp of rough hair along Janez's jaw—and then time restarted.

He could hear boots.

Held stepped back just as the door opened, and Doktor entered, carrying fresh blankets.

He eyed them and stopped.

Janez took another breath and tore his eyes from the looking glass. He turned, the stick twisting in the carpet a little, and smiled at Doktor. It was thin and full of pain, but there was a determination behind it, like eyes under a mask.

"Doktor," he said. *"Gehen wir sie überraschen."*

Doktor smiled warmly—the authenticity somehow strange on his cold, angular face—and waved at the door.

Fingers tightened on the stick. A breath pushed at the undercoat.

And then—one lurching, hopping step at a time—the man walked back into the sky.

Chapter Forty-Four

"WE NEED A solution, Your Majesty."

Alarik longed for the days—and luxuries—of mad kings and cruel lords. In such days, without the wolf at his door, he would have had this damned councillor's head on a pike, simply for the whining annoyance.

"I am *aware*," he said heavily, the groaning emphasis a warning.

A warning not plain enough, it seemed, for such an idiot man. For he chirruped, "Without King Sigurd's assistance—"

"I know perfectly well what we face without his assistance!" Alarik thundered.

An uneasy silence fell, and Alarik leaned back in his chair, massaging his temples. He sorely did not want to be here. If not for the good doctor's banishment—and Sofia supporting it all the way, bless her soul—he'd have been sequestered in his brother's chambers with that odd little foreigner, watching for—

His gut rolled, and he pushed the thought away. No, no. Janez had lived thus far. And if he should be broken and rendered into a childish thing in need of constant care, then so be it. He was the brother of the king. If he needed care, he would have it, and the very best.

But none at all if his kingdom was defeated. He rallied his thoughts and sighed.

"Councillor Baumgartner, you may take your leave."

Thoughts would be easier without this twittering idiot.

"Your Majesty—"

"Your leave, Councillor."

That, at last, seemed sufficiently dangerous. The councillor gathered up his books and retreated, bowing all the way, and only when the guards closed the great doors behind him did Alarik lean forward again.

"Although impertinent, Your Majesty, he makes a point," the first minister said. "We must secure that alliance—or find another."

"And we shall, but it will not be with Janez," Alarik said icily. "He has paid enough of a price. More than enough."

"Perhaps the young princess, Your Majesty? If we look north, rather than west—King Olaf has been recently blessed with a son, and has no love for our enemy."

"What can we offer above all others? There are plenty of princesses of Ingrid's age, and with greater purpose to Olaf. They trade, too, like us."

"Defence," came the swift reply. "They have the material, but not the skill or treasury for naval . We have the opposite. And our enemy is their own—long have their shore villages been subject to raids and pillages."

Alarik frowned at the maps spread out on the council-room table. "You propose a joint navy, of a sort?"

"Potentially, Your Majesty."

It was grossly ambitious…but it could work. Olaf held the straits; he controlled access to the great oceans of the west, on which Sigurd's men preyed. Olaf had never been an enemy—or much of a friend, it had to be conceded—but a formal alliance…

And he had but one son. If Ingrid were to wed the boy when they were both of age, then she would be the mother of a king in her turn.

"Send an entreaty to Olaf," Alarik commanded. "Make no disguise of our intention, he is not a man to fall prey to flattery. And—"

A guard slipped from the room when the great knock sounded upon the door, and Alarik bit back a curse.

"If that is that wretched—"

The door opened.

Alarik's temper was snuffed out like a pinched candle flame. *Janez.* Dear Janez. Standing, grey-faced, his weight supported by a mere stick, his trouser rolled and pinned to obscure the missing leg, the existence of which was made all the more obvious by the great, gaping space below it, and the single shoe. He was dressed in his habitual garments—shirt and waistcoat, loose breeches—rather than the uniform he was meant to wear to such occasions.

Oh, but hang the occasion! He stood. He lived. And although he looked dreadful, there was a mask in place. Not his brother, but his second heir. No sibling, but a sailor and a diplomat. Still, Alarik couldn't bring himself to address him as such.

"Brother," he murmured.

"My apologies, Your Majesty, for my lateness."

Alarik shook himself.

"It is nothing. Sit. Boy, fetch more wine."

The councillors gave greetings and wishes for well-being. A cupbearer brought a glass of wine, which was drained in an instant and immediately replaced. Janez's hand shook upon the table, and his hair was darkened at the temples—but after the second cup, he relaxed back into his chair a little and waved those trembling fingers.

"Please, do not let me interrupt official business."

Alarik cleared his throat. Very well. If Janez insisted on the meeting being concluded, then he would conclude it, and as swiftly as possible.

"We are discussing a potential alliance with Olaf, to expand our naval capability."

It was apparent within moments of the ensuing discussion that Janez was there by sheer force of will, and that alone. He was usually one to speak up with great knowledge of naval matters and the potential for the improvement of the service. But now, he sat passively and quietly while the admiral trumpeted about questions of supremacy in a shared force, and said nothing when the minister of the treasury decided that a joint merchant service to protect trade ships would be an excellent plan, but a joint fighting force too costly.

Alarik cast a glance at that grey, absent face, and decided against further matters.

"This is all irrelevant if Olaf is not willing to join with us," he said. "Send the word, and we will open our arms and tables to negotiations for Ingrid. Doubtless she would like the opportunity to go abroad once in a while, and visit other lands, and be the better lady for it."

Rumblings of hesitant agreements.

"You may take your leave, gentlemen. We will resume in the morning."

Only when the last of his advisors had left them, and the servant had been despatched to fetch Doktor Hauser, did Alarik permit himself to shed crown and kingdom, and look not at his second heir, but at his younger brother.

The younger brother who had fought with him so bitterly, who had thrown such angered words of his unhappiness and sense of personal injustice at his lot in life, and then had nearly died on the filthy deck of a lowly sloop for the country and family that had so used him.

The younger brother whose face was pallid, the hair at his ears damp, and whose fingers shivered faintly upon the table.

"While I cannot express how glad I am to see you up," Alarik said, "I also cannot shake the idea that you ought not to be."

A very faint smile crossed that grey face, but the head was shaken.

"I wished to see my family."

"Your family would have come to you."

"As though I were dying?"

Alarik flinched.

"I have no wish to do so," Janez said, "and I felt as though I was suffocating. I needed to move."

Doktor Hauser slipped into the room without a word. That foreigner, Held, trailed in his wake but hung back as the doctor exchanged his patient's wine for something else, pale and foaming.

"I wish to eat with family," Janez said weakly to him.

"You shall. This will ease the pain, but will not induce a sleep."

Alarik thought Janez looked so stretched thin and exhausted that if the pain were removed, he would be bound to sleep. But he said nothing as the cup was lifted in a quivering grip, and Janez drank the dubious liquid down.

"Doktor," Alarik said uncertainly. "Are you quite sure—"

The cup slammed down.

"I am not a damned child!" Janez's eyes flashed fire. "Do not speak around me like I am some dumb—"

Held slipped from the shadows. Wrapping his fingers around Janez's wrist, he slid his other hand under the cup and urged it upwards once more. To Alarik's surprise, Janez—far from backhanding the impudence—yielded and drank. And when the cup was empty, Held removed it entirely and retreated behind the doctor like he was merely a servant doing a duty.

But Alarik knew of few servants who would shield their masters from cannon fire, or remain up with them for nights on end through fever-dreams.

He cleared his throat. "I believe Ingrid would delight in seeing her beloved uncle, no?"

She would. And by Janez's response—to grasp for his cane, and mutter about the royal chambers—Alarik knew that something other than enemy fire had struck him.

"Doktor. Leave us a moment. Take Held, too. We shall come shortly."

When the door closed, Alarik rose. He took the seat beside Janez and clasped his wrist, a narrow band of too-warm skin between glove and sleeve.

And said, "The first night after—after, I sat up with you in the doctor's chambers, so sure you were to die. Do not give me hope now, only to endanger yourself by pushing too hard, too soon."

Janez stared blindly at the table. Licked his lips. Breathed, "I could hear you."

"Me?"

"You said you were there. But when I reached, you weren't. Nobody came."

Alarik's chest tightened. Those muttered pleas, the weakly clutching hands. They echoed in his ears and grasped at him with phantom fingers. He felt guilty, even as he knew he had no reason.

"You looked right into my face," he said, fighting to keep his voice even, "and you begged to know where I was. You knew no one, Janez. I was there, I promise you. The only ones who were not were Mother, as the pass has not yet reopened, and the children. Ingrid has been begging to see you. Sofia came. I came. *We were there.*"

Janez's eyes reached his own at last. They were wide and desperate. He looked almost like a child again, and it struck Alarik deep in his gut.

He reached out and clasped the back of Janez's neck, bringing their foreheads gently together.

"You were never alone," he breathed and felt shaky fingers curl into the crook of his elbow. "Never."

When he leaned back, Janez's eyes had closed. He was far too pale, trembling visibly, and his hair was dark with sweat all about his face. He was still sick. Still weak. But the grip of his hand said there was more damage in refusing him than in permitting the exertion.

"Come," Alarik said softly. "Ingrid has pined for her favourite. The guards can bring a litter, if—"

"I will walk."

"Janez—"

"I will not appear weakened to spies and strangers. Not in time of war."

Alarik somewhat thought that war had little to do with it but held his tongue. He offered an arm and helped him to his fe—foot.

It was a slow and painful process up to the royal chambers. The awkward hop was clearly agonising, and Janez refused all assistance beyond the council-room door. By the time they reached the private wing, even his voice had failed; he could only grunt his thanks to the guard who opened the doors.

"Uncle!"

Ingrid's cry was shrill. A blur of yellow and blue shot from the bay window, and before Alarik or Doktor Hauser could step between them, the child was upon her beloved uncle. The crash to the carpet sounded painful, yet Janez didn't cry out.

Rather, he clutched her close, and buried his face in her yellow curls. Her thrilled chatter—including, of course, a scolding for bringing no gift from his visit to Grandmama—masked any noise he might have made there, but his shoulders shook, and in a moment more, she implored him not to cry.

The door closed behind Hauser and Held, and Alarik threw his kingdom to the wind. He knelt, something he hadn't done since he was a boy, and wrapped arms about his brother and daughter. Skirts rustled, and his wife joined the huddle—until they could consume Janez in the warmth and welcome he'd been so bitterly unaware of in the grips of that terrible fever.

The enemy had taken nothing.

And Alarik would be damned if they were to try again.

Chapter Forty-Five

HEALING CAME SLOWLY.

Held could see the pain that Janez would not paint upon his face. When the chamber doors closed behind Doktor and the last of his potions in the evening, Janez would collapse into the pillows like the very life had been drained from him to leave an empty shell.

Yet once there, he would rage. He cried, more than once, with hands clasped over face as Held brushed his hair. He threw things in outbursts of anger and shouted until Doktor returned, summoned by white-faced, anxious guards. Or he would lie passive and silent under Held's help and then dismiss him with a single word and turn into his pillows.

In his servants' quarters, only the adjoining room, Held could hear him cry regardless.

And for a little time, Held could do nothing. Janez was in too much pain for Held to lie with him and soothe the passions. The potions made him sick, and still the fever came and went so he could not abide touch. Other times, he simply didn't seem to want it and would shy away.

But as the dark nights slowly shortened, and the white foam upon the land melted away, the shadows of physical pain began to ebb from that pale face, and the terrible wasting thinness of his body was arrested by the continual offerings from the kitchen.

There was another pain, too.

He used the cane religiously outside of the rooms, even in front of little Ingrid and that tiny, mewling skyling that seemed to have no name, but the moment the doors were closed, Janez seemed to want no part of it. He would fist his hand into the bed sheets that lay hollow where they'd once been full and refuse to move again for the rest of the night, no matter Held's persuasions.

The stump was the injury.

But the wound, Held feared, ran deeper.

Held knew little of such things. Merfolk could not lose fins and live: they were rendered unable to swim and cast out by nests that couldn't afford any weakness attracting predators. An orca pack could destroy a nest in a matter of hours and only steered clear for fear of their meals fighting back too hard. A nest of merfolk unable to escape was nothing short of begging for the packs to come.

The nearest Held could imagine below was the loss of an arm, but he'd never seen it. The sea attracted teeth for blood, and to have an arm torn free the way Janez's leg had been would ensure death, either by the bleeding alone, or by being hunted down.

Here, Janez lived. And would continue to live.

And yet—

Held had the strangest of impressions that Janez believed it to be half of a life, and the others around him believed it to be a blessed one.

They certainly lavished attention that Held hadn't witnessed the last time they'd been here. But for all that Janez seemed to genuinely enjoy the company during the daylight, it seemed to make the nights darker still. Always, always, he would look at Held with those wide eyes, every shade the ocean had ever been, and turn away.

There was something there, Held was sure.

Something perhaps Janez didn't mean to say—or didn't know how to—was in that gaze every evening, and Held ached to know it, and to smudge it away. But he couldn't. The fitful nights of pain could only be interrupted by Doktor or his servant coming with smoking potions to help Janez sleep. It meant Held could do little. He waited, busying himself by brushing that shining hair each morning and evening until it flowed like water. Each time, he would finish with a kiss against the crown of warmth about Janez's temple, the invisible sign of the king of Held's new world. And he waited. When the potions ceased, and the nights could be tolerated without tears or clenched teeth, Held vowed he would fix it. He would heal the other wounds, whatever they were and wherever Janez carried them, head or heart.

He had lived. Held would ensure he did not regret the choice.

The first bloomings were beginning to poke through the ground, the first night that Doktor didn't come. Held lay awake much of it, awaiting that knock upon Janez's door and the light ghosting through the chamber like an anglerfish on the prowl, but it never came, and morning saw Janez exhausted, yet unchanged.

And so the following night, Held came to help him undress, and to brush his hair—and then set the brush aside when the curls had been defeated as best they could be and kissed that invisible crown.

He rested his lips there and stayed.

After a moment, Janez's hand came up to clasp at his elbow, and he said Held's name questioningly. Held sighed and kissed the high forehead, and a sharp cheekbone, and then the mouth that dared to question him.

Janez would not question.

For Held knew the thought that had been burning, in the way Janez stiffened and his grip tightened to the point of pain and desperation.

He had believed—

Oh, but a prince could be a fool, too.

"How could you believe," Held whispered against his mouth, kissing and silencing him again when the habitual protest of incomprehension arose, "that this would change me? Change us? You are—"

He was more beautiful than ever. For he'd brushed the fins of death and come away. Scarred and scathed, but he'd come away regardless. Come back.

And in his madness, when he had burned so in Doktor's rooms, he'd called for Held and quieted for his song.

"You are mine," Held murmured and struggled for the words. Janez must understand this. *"Du—du bist...mein."*

Janez's face—changed.

That devastating blue deepened, an ocean shelf collapsing to the unfathomable depths of the open water. The lines about his eyes eased, and new ones about his mouth formed. The expression seemed to break in the middle and relax at the edges, and Held kissed it away fiercely, as though he could catch the sorrow upon his tongue and keep it from ever escaping again.

Janez simply caught at the back of his neck, his lips yielding to Held's, but Held had no intentions of some goodnight kiss and peeled back the bed sheets to slide into their warmth. His fingers caught blind and familiar against the ties and ribbons of Janez's nightclothes, and soon he found the smoothness of still-pink scars, healing and raw, and the strong thump of a heart that had not yielded, never yielded, to what the cruelty of the world had wanted.

Held dropped his mouth to kiss the heartbeat. It beat for the both of them.

"Nein," he breathed when Janez's hands stroked down his spine. Held caught them both, narrow wrists encircled entirely by his fingers, and thrust them deep under the pillows. Finally, a little laugh escaped Janez's lips, and quite suddenly, he submitted. Held's heart clenched tight at that.

The body unclothed, and its owner peaceable, Held could take his time. And he did. Each new scar—face and neck, and the great score over the shoulder that had bloodied the king's arms—was mapped with lips and teeth, kissed and tugged until the skin about it flushed. And Janez sighed with a gentle, breathy sound of pleasure, all traces of pain gone from his countenance, as though Held had pulled it all away. He tugged the pain from tired muscle and bone, leaving soft marks upon rib and hip. He kissed pleasure into belly and lower still, and pushed his hands, spread wide, underneath to hold Janez entirely within his command and steer him through the quiet ecstasy better than any skyman had ever driven any cloud.

"Held—"

His name was the last breath Janez took before the pleasure washed over him, and Held kissed all evidence of it away before rising up that heaving, flushed body to bite at his lower lip until it bruised and swelled between his teeth.

"I love you," he told it, and Janez made a faint noise. *"Ich—ich—"*

"Ich liebe dich."

Janez said it soft and clear, and staring with those suddenly dark eyes right into Held's face. It was the same expression as those hot nights in Doktor's rooms—but for the fact that Janez looked right at him and saw him. Truly saw him, saw perhaps more than Held had ever been able to reveal. And his fingers traced the side of Held's face, and—

Oh, but Janez had given him the words. So many, many times.

"Ich liebe dich," Held echoed, and the smile that washed across Janez's face was little short of breathtaking.

"Du liebst mich?"

It seemed to be an involuntary question, for Janez at once made a face and murmured something else, but Held knew the words either side, and the middle sounded so very much the same—

"Ja."

That look.

And a shiver in Janez's fingers.

Oh, but he had questioned it. He hadn't known, or not believed.

"I love you," Held repeated and kissed that fine mouth. Janez's hand caught at the back of his head, capturing him. Drank his air. His *soul*. The other tugged at the strings of his shirt, and Held shrugged out of it blindly and clumsily.

The first had been quiet and serene. The second was quite different. Frenzied—like the end of their dance in the darkened room; like the night Janez had told him of the marriage. But—less saddened. There was something brighter, something fiercer, in the way Janez touched him. In the way their hearts beat as one. In the way that battered yet unbroken body arched beneath him as Held took it, and the clutch of Janez's hands so deep they left bruises.

And after—

And after, shaken apart and his soul showing through the cracks in his skin, Held slid sideways into the messy nest of a bed. He pulled Janez close until he breathed through the once-more chaotic curls, and Janez's mouth was resting against his neck, close and intimate and entirely, completely perfect.

"Ich liebe dich," Janez whispered there, and Held tightened his grip for a moment.

For it was true.

And Held had been quite, quite wrong.

There was nothing—no cloud, no princess, no king—that could take that from him.

Chapter Forty-Six

THE DOCTOR HAD lied for him.

It had escaped Janez's notice for some time—none but family would speak of such a delicate matter to the prince, of course—but as Alarik began to make noises about Ingrid's schooling, about the need for her to learn other tongues and perhaps take a tour of their neighbouring kingdoms to meet other lordlings her own age, Janez realised.

He'd become somehow exempt from marriage.

And when he enquired as to the alliance with Sigurd, in only the second council meeting he was able to attend after mastering that damnable cane, the room went tellingly quiet.

"The Princess Alessandra feels...feels it is no longer in both of your interests," was all Alarik would say on the matter in public. Later, hovering at Janez's elbow as he struggled to his feet—no, foot—he added, "A lady wants children, Janez. And now that you cannot give them to her...well..."

Janez, wisely, said nothing.

The relief at the doctor's lie was sharp and palpable, and he breathed easy for the first time in months, quite irrespective of his wounds. The kingdom believed him to be impotent, or castrated, or something along those lines. They believed him incapable of siring children. And perhaps, had Janez been a prouder man, he'd have found the stain upon his manhood insulting— But then, such men were not in the habit of enjoying the kind of sex that Janez did.

So he remained quietly relieved and said nothing to reveal the falsehood. Although he did smuggle the doctor a supremely large bottle of port from the war room for his stores.

"For going beyond the requirements of the service," was all he would say, and Doktor simply eyed him like a cautious lizard and chuckled.

"In which case, you're quite welcome, Your Highness."

And so Janez was largely left to heal alone—or rather, alone in the dutiful sense of the term. Alarik dogmatically insisted he remain in the royal chambers as much as possible; Sofia, for once entirely in tune with her husband, pressed Ingrid and the baby on him as much as possible, to guilt him into staying. Ingrid was delighted with the situation and, in truth, Janez found her joy infectious. Sitting upon the great rug in the nursery, his hair plaited like a girl's and Ekaterina scolding them both for their inability—despite the decades between them and the differences of their sexes—to concentrate on her lessons for more than a moment at a time, Janez felt—

Calmer.

At peace.

Loved.

He felt quite loved, in the bosom of his family by day and, much more literally, the bosom of his lover by night. Held seemed to enjoy the darkness. He kept distant and dutiful by daylight but at night crept into Janez's rooms without fail and would strip away the clothes and sheets between them as though entirely offended by their presence.

The wounds would never heal. Janez mourned the great thunder of the sea, and the roar of the world under the deck of his tiny wooden worlds. But with Held's lips upon his hair, murmuring words from another land, Janez felt as though the cannon perhaps hadn't snuffed out all there had ever been about his life.

He felt happy, despite the pain.

And he felt free, despite the cane.

Which was why he was surprised, on the first day of spring, when a messenger arrived in a breathless rush, holding out a scrap of paper with a note upon it, and said the King demanded his presence.

"Demanded? Are you sure?"

"Demanded, Your Highness. He's—a panic—there's ships—approaching—"

Janez rocked to his foot, nearly falling as he groped for the cane. Ships! What the devil was Alarik summoning *him* for? Launch their own, for God's sake!

But the answer came quickly and clearly—or rather, clearly that Alarik hadn't lost his mind—when Janez burst onto the royal balcony with his spyglass and, training it upon the horizon, saw a fleet nestled outside their harbour flying not the terrible ice sigils of their enemy, but a great brown bear upon a golden field.

King Sigurd's sigil.

"Why the devil is he here?" Janez asked the messenger, who simply shrugged, still fighting to catch his breath.

"I don't know, Your Highness. I just—got sent—by—"

"All right, all right. Where am I to go?"

"The council room."

Janez took his time, in spite of the messenger's urgency. It wouldn't do to appear breathless and shaking with the pain in front of Sigurd. The man was of the old world, Father's world. He prized soldiers of war. The lack of a leg would not phase him—would even impress him—but fainting away like a virgin on her wedding night would earn Janez contempt.

And so, when he limped heavily into the war council, he was the picture of a war-bred man: heavily scarred, perfectly dressed, and the cane loud and firm upon the floor.

But it faltered all the same when Carolina rose from her father's side.

"My dear Prince," she said, that ever-present fan dropping entirely to the table. "I am so pleased to find you well. Please, sit—you must still be in great pain."

"It is not so bad," Janez answered automatically, even as his eyes narrowed and his mind scoured the situation before him. Sigurd and Alarik sat close together, a map spread between them. Sigurd was regarding Janez with a calculating eye, none of the proud and affable father that had attended the ball not two months since. And Carolina— this, too, was not the same woman that had held her fan like a shield between them and turned Janez away so firmly.

"If you are quite able, walk with me a little, then?" she entreated. "We came in from the great courtyard, and the flowers are in bloom. I should like to pick a few."

"Carolina," Sigurd rumbled.

"The gardens, Papa!" she scolded, turning on him like Sofia upon her husband in a matrimonial clash. "What must you think of him—of me!— that going to the gardens with all those guards could be considered indecent, I do not know!"

Sigurd subsided with a grunt and finally nodded. Carolina dismissed him like a queen already, turning back to Janez and abandoning her fan on the council table.

"I would offer my arm, my lady, but as you can see..."

"Then the other. One arm is as good as another," she said, daintily slipping her fingers into his other elbow. Janez hadn't the balance yet to crook it, and her grip tightened a fraction as he limped. She followed like a warm ghost, from the council room and out through the great hall to the warm, sunlit courtyard.

Only there, in the company of the little fountains below the steps and a cluster of birds chattering away in the rainbows cast by the water, did Carolina drop the facade, as they stopped to sit on the little wall that overlooked the rose paths.

"I have told Father that I love you."

Her voice dropped. The sunny disposition, the pampered princess, was gone. *This* was the fan-for-a-shield woman from the ball. And Janez found he far preferred her, for the frankness.

"Why?"

"The ambassador said that you are—unable."

Janez raised an eyebrow. "To what, exactly? I can walk, after a fashion. I have my wits about me. I—"

She cast a glance about and leaned in a little. "To lie with a woman."

"Ah."

"To—sire children."

Janez said nothing.

"Alessandra said she couldn't possibly marry a man who couldn't make her a mother—which is ridiculous, she *means* a man who cannot make love to her—"

So that tart sharpness ran in the family, did it? Janez smirked.

"—and Father quite agreed. He has his lineage to think of, after all. But *I* thought...well...we get along, do we not?"

So that was the game.

"I think we do, or certainly can."

"I did find you pleasant company. I just—I cannot, Janez. I cannot lie with someone. The very idea..." She shivered, despite the warmth, and Janez eyed her.

"So you wish—what? Your father would not allow you to marry a eunuch."

"My father will do what his daughters entreat him to do. If I proclaim love, he would let me marry for it. You are still a prince. You would still wed our kingdom to yours, if only for our lifetimes. And I *do* have sisters. I am not his only hope for grandchildren—not even his best."

Janez hummed.

"This could be our solution, Janez."

Her hand gripped his, separated by their respective gloves. It was true. This alliance was needed, desperately, for the defence of Alarik's realm. And she was indeed a clever and interesting woman. Her love of the sea, her affection for her books—she could be both a dutiful wife to the wider world, and genuinely good company within their own, private one.

And Janez would be her protection, he realised. By binding herself to a man the world thought impotent—that *she* thought impotent—Carolina would be released from the duties of sex and pregnancy, both of which seemed to appal her. And he, in turn, would be free to have Held with no jealousy or reproach from a jilted bride. She would likely even welcome the distraction.

But it would be a lie.

He lowered his voice.

"You wish to marry me, because if you do, you need never be subjected to that which disgusts you."

Her answer was perfectly simple.

"Yes."

"It—frees you, in a way."

"Yes."

He said nothing. Her grip tightened in his.

"I would be a wife," she said, "and childless by *virtue*—by your devotion to your country. I would be wed to a war hero, and nobody would be blamed but the enemy for our lack of issue."

He licked his lips.

"I cannot let you believe the lie, if that is why you are here."

"The—lie?"

Her hand withdrew.

"My surgeon lied," Janez whispered. "He knew—he knew the only reason I would be forced to marry you or your sisters would be to sire children. To be bred. So he lied."

"You *are* capable, then?"

"Perfectly so."

Her lips pursed. "Why does the idea of children repel you?"

"It doesn't," Janez replied honestly. "I have had at least one before. But I am already in love. I love—utterly. And the notion of lying with another, of fathering children into a marriage that doesn't want them—where *nobody* wants them..."

Father's disdainful expression flashed in the back of his mind, and Janez flinched.

"I was the spare son," he said quietly, "and I know how it feels to have one's father despise you. I will not be that father, Carolina."

She paused.

Her hands twisted in her lap, and she whispered, "Father loves us very much—but I can see it in his eyes. He wishes at least one of us were a boy."

A silence swept between them. She seemed to be thinking. Janez, oddly, felt as though he'd little to lose. A princess—however bold—was not about to march before two kings and announce the state of his manhood. And if she left again, without her plan in place, what of it? Janez was, to the world, unwanted once more.

Except to Held. Who was, Janez supposed, a world unto himself.

"Do you wish to lie with me, Janez?"

The question was very soft. Very quiet.

Janez's reply was the same. "No."

"Would you?"

"If I did not love another, perhaps. But I do."

"Will you always?"

Janez brought his gaze up to hers. She looked—afraid, almost. Afraid of his reply. Afraid of his *lie*.

"Yes."

A simple truth. And true it was. He knew it. Held was under his skin, coiled about his heart like a serpent, and Janez would never be free of him.

And never try to be.

Her gloved fingers slipped once more over his.

"You may never touch me as a man would his wife," she whispered, close and intimate but for the words, "and I will never submit to you."

Janez laughed.

"Carolina," he said, perfectly frankly, "this is rather more than I think you wish to know, but it bears saying—in such affairs, it is *me* who submits."

She laughed, too, then. A flash of brilliance lit up those dark eyes, and her smile beamed white from that face Janez had thought beautiful, but was wrong about entirely. It was ethereal, not mere beauty. It was divinity in the physical, and quite perfect. Yet naught but warm affection beat in his chest, his body and mind already possessed by another.

"I fear I must ask for one kiss on our wedding day, to keep suspicion at bay."

"All right. I will permit that one thing," she said and patted his wrist. "And you are a fine dancer. If you find the art again, I reserve the right to own place as the lady you lead upon the floor."

"Done."

A bird shot past overhead, and Carolina rustled to her feet.

"Shall we, then?" she asked, extending a hand to help him rise. "Father will need some persuading."

"Alarik, too, perhaps. He has become overprotective."

"And when we have informed them of our supposed love," Carolina continued peaceably, hand tucked once more against his elbow as they passed back into the coolness of the great hall, "would you show me the library? I have heard many things about the library here..."

"Of course," Janez said. "And when the summer comes, I will show you the ships. Perhaps I will commandeer one last sloop and show you the way the sea kisses a stern at ten knots."

He kept the smile upon his face as he entered the council room once more and spoke of their supposed love.

Perhaps princes could, in fact, have a happy ending.

Epilogue

THEY RETURNED TO the royal chambers together.

Held watched peaceably as Janez kissed Carolina's hand, and the great doors closed behind them. And then they parted, mere friends, and Carolina bestowed a smile upon Held before taking her abandoned book from the dresser and vanishing into her adjoining rooms.

That door closed, too, and Janez turned once more—as he always did, in the end—to Held.

Held smiled.

The marriage ceremony had been a grand and lavish affair, and Held had stood through it as a mere manservant, nursing the secret closed in his breast. The kiss at the great stone plinth had been brief, and jealousy had sparked, but then it had been over.

Janez was married now.

"Liebst du sie?" Held asked coyly, as he undid the cloth at Janez's throat. It dropped away; he kissed the skin beneath it and released the button of his collar.

"Nein."

The reply was soft and simple, as it had been for the last hundred nights in a row, and Held kissed past each button as he removed undercoat and shirt. He worked determinedly and carefully, yet dropped the clothes to the floor like rags. And only when the prince had been stripped away, and the skyman stood naked before him, did Held speak again.

"Du liebst mich?"

Janez smiled.

"Ja."

Held kissed him.

It was not like the hungry and desperate kisses of the Winter Palace. It was not like the shy and uncertain thing of the Summer ones.

It was simply—theirs.

They came together like smoke curling into the sky. They twisted about one another as though they relearned these forms anew every night. And so as the palace celebrations fell finally silent beneath them, it was Held who made love to the groom on his wedding night, while the bride slept alone in an adjoining room.

Lover. And wife.

Two people. Two beings. Never to be one. Holding this tiny world between them in perfect, absolute balance. A triangle of defence against anything the world—any world—had to offer.

And when Held's form was sated, when the twist of their bodies demanded peace instead of pleasure, and he stroked the curly hair of the head resting upon his chest, he knew the map for the rest of his existence.

This place. Right here. Wherever that bed may be, Held would be bound to this skyman, this legend turned to flesh, until the end of his days. He'd lost everything he'd ever known, become a myth and learned to walk on water, left an entire world beneath the waves, bound his very existence to another, for this.

"Do you love her?" he whispered, in his own tongue. The only conversation he'd ever taught to Janez, in a language best forgotten now.

"No," came the soft reply, mangled about a skyman's throat.

"Do you love me?"

A smile against his neck. A hand that curled into the skin about his hip.

"Yes."

And Held knew he would live forever.

Glossary of German Words

Bett, ja? - Bed, yes?
Bitte - Please
Blumen - Flowers

Das ist dein Werk! - This is your work!
Du bist mein. - You are mine.
Du liebst mich? - You love me?
Du. Verheiratet? - You. Married?

Eine Blume - A flower
Eine Frau für meinen Freund! - A woman for my friend!
Ein Pferd - A horse
Ein Vogel - A bird
Er kann nicht reiten. - He cannot ride.
Er lebt! - He lives!
Er lebt noch. - He is still alive.

Fisch - Fish

Geh nicht - Don't go
Gehen wir sie überraschen. - Let's go surprise them.
Guten Abend - Good evening
Guten Morgen, Biene. - Good morning, bee.

Hier - Here
Hier drüben - Over here
Hilfe - Help
Hör auf mit dem Geheule! - Stop it with the wailing/crying/whining.

Ich bin hier. - I am here.
Ich bin hier, Janez. Ich bin hier. - I am here, Janez. I am here.

Ich bin hier, mein Bruder. - I'm here, my brother.
Ich liebe dich. - I love you.
Ich muss heiraten. - I have to get married.
Ich verdanke Ihnen mein Leben. - I owe you my life.

Ja - Yes
Jeder einfache Mann kann das, und du bist ein Prinz. - Every simple man can do that, and you are a prince.

Kannst du mich hören? - Can you hear me?
Komm - Come
Kommt - Come
Küss mich - Kiss me

Liebst du sie? - You love her?

Mein - Mine

Nein - No
Nicht tot - Not dead

Onki - Uncle/endearment

Pilz - Mushrooms

Ruhe - Quiet

Salat - Salad
Sie verstehen kein Wort von dem, was ich sage, oder? - You don't understand a word of what I'm saying, do you?
Speck - Bacon
Still jetzt - Quiet now

Tot - Dead
Tot, tot, der Prinz ist tot. - Dead, dead, the prince is dead.

Und für mich, Kapitän! Eine Frau! - And me, captain! A woman!
Unverheiratet - Unmarried

Verheiratet - Married
Vorsichtig - Careful now

Was? - What?
Wasser - Water
Wir sind hier, Janez. - We're here, Janez.
Wir sind hier, mein Bruder. - We're here, my brother.

Zwei Blumen - Two flowers

About the Author

Matthew J. Metzger is an ace, trans author posing as a functional human being in the wilds of Yorkshire, England. Although mainly a writer of contemporary, working-class romance, he also strays into fantasy when the mood strikes. Whatever the genre, the focus is inevitably on queer characters and their relationships, be they familial, platonic, sexual, or romantic.

When not crunching numbers at his day job, or writing books by night, Matthew can be found tweeting from the gym, being used as a pillow by his cat, or trying to keep his website in some semblance of order.

Email: mattmetzger@hotmail.co.uk

Facebook: www.facebook.com/mattjmetzger

Twitter: www.twitter.com/MatthewJMetzger

Website: www.matthewjmetzger.com

Other books by this author

Big Man (coming April 2018)

Coming Soon from Matthew J. Metzger

Big Man

Excerpt

THIS WAS HOW everything started—on a Friday afternoon, at the very end of school, three days into the summer term and in the middle of an unreasonable, unseasonable heatwave. It had been a Friday like any other until Tom Fallowfield stuck his boot in.

Literally.

It went a bit like this, to Max's admittedly patchy memory of the entire incident.

At three thirty-one, the bell rang, and he was dismissed out of his maths class. Friday was a notorious day for people being bored and at a loose end, so Max had—as was his habit—hurried off to his locker to try to get out of school before anyone caught up to him.

At three thirty-six, Max reached his locker. His fingers fumbled with the lock in a hurry, the metal loose in his grip because it was so ridiculously hot. Sweat was dampening the hair at his temples.

At three thirty-eight, his fingers slipped on the waxy cover of his geography textbook and sent the whole pile tumbling to the floor.

And at three thirty-eight-and-a-half, a dirty Adidas trainer pressed down on said textbook just as Max reached for it.

That was kind of when Max knew he was a bit fucked.

"All right, Fatso?"

He didn't have to look up. The trainer narrowed it down to one of two people who would stomp on the textbook he was trying to pick up, and the deep, drawling voice—like some villain out of a film—narrowed it down to one. Jazz Coles. And Jazz Coles was bad news.

Max swallowed convulsively and gathered the rest of his things to his chest protectively. He staggered back to his feet and turned to shove them all back in his locker. His hands were shaking. There was sweat breaking out on the backs of his thighs and under his arms, pooling in the joints and fleshy bits.

"Oi. You gone deaf, Fatso? All that grease clogged your ears?"

"M'just in a hurry, Jazz," he mumbled.

"You what?"

"I said, I'm just in a hurry," he said a bit louder and squashed his other books into the locker haphazardly. The corridor was slowly emptying, and the emptier it got, the faster his heart was beating.

"You're fucking rude, you are. You ought to look at someone when he's talking to you. You want Tom to teach you some manners? Tom's good with manners."

"Sorry," Max mumbled, turning hastily before the threat could be carried out. The metal of his locker bit uncomfortably into his back, pressing grooves into his fat, and he could feel his shirt beginning to stick to him. "I'm in a rush, that's all."

All three of them were there. Jazz Coles, Aidan Hooper, and Tom Fallowfield. Fallowfield was in Max's year, the other two the year above. They went to some football club or something together—Max wasn't sure. All he knew was that Jazz was the clever one, with the orders and the insults, while Aidan was the sidekick who screeched like a hyena and kept them supplied in fags and weed on a regular basis from his older brother's grow, and Tom...

Tom was the dangerous one. When the insults stopped, Tom started. And nobody wanted Tom to start anything.

"Not got time to talk to us, then?" Jazz drawled. "Why's that? You busy?"

"I—yes. Yes, just busy, that's all, busy weekend..."

"Busy doing what? Got a new girlfriend?"

Tom snorted. Aidan cackled and said, "Eurgh, Jazz, man, I'll bring up my lunch."

"Imagine that sweaty sack of lard slithering and grunting on some poor girl. You'd crush her, wouldn't you, Farrier?"

Max's face heated up, and his hair stuck to his scalp. He could faintly smell his own underarms, and the metal glueing shirt to back was beginning to heat up too, at Jazz's cool, slow delivery.

"Fatso Farrier, the flat-fucker. 'Cause that's what she'd be once you were done. Best stick to boys, yeah? Let your boyfriend fuck you, then nobody'll suffocate."

"I don't have a girlfriend. Or a boyfriend."

"Would you like one?"

"I—no, I, uh—"

"Just as well," Jazz continued blithely. "Nobody has a drowning in folds fetish. So if it's not a girlfriend or a boyfriend with some sick kinks, why're you too busy to talk to us?"

The corridor was empty. Max started to panic.

"Answer me, Farrier!"

"I—just—plans, you know, plans..."

"What plans? Sale on at Greggs?" Jazz asked. "New bakery opened up? Or is Mummy taking pity on her lonely little wobblebottom, and baked you a chocolate cake?"

Aidan gave a whooping cackle, and Jazz kicked the forgotten geography book towards Max. It skittered across the dusty floor, hitting Max's shoe with a dull thump.

"Best not leave that here," Jazz said. Hands in his pockets, pale face regarding him through narrowed blue eyes, he looked calculating—and Max couldn't figure out what he was calculating. "Oi! Fatso! Pick it up, then."

"Thank you," Max mumbled, hoping it would buy him a bit of a reprieve from...whatever Jazz was planning, and stooped to pick it up. His fingers scrabbled uselessly on the plastic cover, wet with anxiety.

"Thank you?" Jazz echoed. "Very polite, Fatso, might want to make it sound fucking sincere next time."

"Here, Jazz, fancy a game?"

That deep rumble was the only warning that Max got before Tom's boot—because of course Tom, totally mad, sadistic Tom Fallowfield, wore boots to school on a regular basis—connected with the side of his head.

Hard.

Max would have liked to say that pain exploded in his head, that he saw visions of God or heard the heavenly choir, that it was like dropping into a Tim Burton movie.

Actually, he just heard a massive bang.

And then he woke up in the back of an ambulance, and knew he was in deep shit.

That was how it started.

www.ingramcontent.com/pod-product-compliance
Lightning Source LLC
Chambersburg PA
CBHW030611170726
48283CB00002B/559